THE BOOK
of
SALADIN

V

By the same author

THE BOOK
of
SALADIN

◆

Tariq Ali

VERSO

London • New York

First published by Verso 1998
© Tariq Ali 1998
Paperback edition published by Verso 1999
© Tariq Ali
Reprinted 2008 (twice), 2010
All rights reserved

The moral rights of the author have been asserted

Verso
UK: 6 Meard Street, London W1F 0EG
USA: 20 Jay Street, Brooklyn, NY 11201
www.versobooks.com

Verso is the imprint of New Left Books

ISBN-13: 978-1-85984-231-7

British Library Cataloguing in Publication Data
A catalogue record for this book is available from the British Library

Library of Congress Cataloging-in-Publication Data
Ali, Tariq.
    The book of Saladin / Tariq Ali.
        p.   cm.
ISBN 1-85984-634-6 (cloth) 1-85984-231-3 (pages)
1. Saladin, Sultan of Egypt and Syria, 1137–1193 – Fiction.
2. Jerusalem – History – Latin Kingdom, 1099–1244 – Fiction
3. Islamic Empire – History – 750–1258 – Fiction. I. Title.
PR6051.L44B66 1998
823'.914–dc21   98–44080
                                                            CIP

Typeset in Fournier by M Rules
Printed By Worldcolor Fairfield

For

Robin Blackburn

Contents

DAMASCUS

JERUSALEM

LETTERS TO IBN MAYMUN

The Near East in the late twelfth century

BYZANTINE EMPIRE

Black Sea

Constantinople

Caucasus Mts

GEORGIA
GREATER
ARMENIA

Trebizond

L. Sevan   AZERBAIJAN

Khilat   • Dvin

Caspian Sea

Lake Aral

KHWARIZM

Bukhara
•
Samarkand
•

SELJUK SULTANATE
OF RUM

• Iconium

• Amid

L. Van

KHURASAN

LESSER ARMENIA

Antioch

Aleppo

Hisn Kaifa
Mosul
•

Euphrates
Tigris

TERRITORIES OF
SELJUK ATABEGS

PERSIA

Cyprus

Mediterranean
— Sea —

Alexandria

Tripoli
Beirut
Acre
Jaffa
Ascalon
Damietta

• Baalbek

• Damascus

Takrit

Baghdad
•

Hamadan
•

Isfahan
•

KHUZISTAN

• Kirman

Jerusalem

Koran

ABASSID
CALIPHATE

IRAQ

Basra
•

Cairo
Fustat

Bilbeis
Sinai

Shaubak

Aila

Syrian
Desert

Persian Gulf

INDIA

FATIMID
CALIPHATE

Ashmunein
•

NEJD

OMAN

Assiut
•

EGYPT

R. Nile

Aswan
•

Red Sea

Yambu
•

AL HEDIAZ

• Medina

NUBIA

Jiddah
•

Aidhab
•

Mecca
•

AL-YAMAN

SUDAN

Aden

ETHIOPIA

▨ Frankish territory

0   500   1000 km

Explanatory note

Any fictional reconstruction of the life of a historical figure poses a problem for the writer. Should actual historical evidence be disregarded in the interests of a good story? I think not. In fact the more one explores the imagined inner life of the characters, the more important it becomes to remain loyal to historical facts and events, even in the case of the Crusades, where Christian and Muslim chroniclers often provided different interpretations of what actually happened.

The fall of Jerusalem to the First Crusade in 1099 stunned the world of Islam, which was at the peak of its achievements. Damascus, Cairo and Baghdad were large cities with a combined population of over two million – advanced urban civilisation at a time when the citizens of London and Paris numbered less than fifty thousand in each case. The Caliph in Baghdad was shaken by the ease with which the barbarian tide had overwhelmed the armies of Islam. It was to be a long occupation.

Salah al-Din (Saladin to Western ears) was the Kurdish warrior who regained Jerusalem in 1187. The principal male characters of this story are based on historical personages. They include Salah al-Din himself, his brothers, father, uncle and nephews. Ibn Maymun is the great Jewish physician-philosopher, Maimonides. The narrator and Shadhi are my creations, for whom I accept full responsibility.

The women – Jamila, Halima and all the others – have all been imagined. Women are a subject on which medieval history is usually silent. Salah al-Din, we are told, had sixteen sons, but nothing has been written about their sisters or mothers.

The Caliph was the spiritual and temporal ruler during the early days of Islam. He was elected by acclamation by the early Companions of the Prophet. Factional disputes within Islam led to rival claims, and the birth of the Shiite tendency split the political heirs of Mohammed. The Sunni Muslims acknowledged the Caliph in Baghdad, but civil war and Shiite successes led to the establishment of a Fatimid Caliph in Cairo, while the Sunni faction displaced by the Abbasids reached its zenith by establishing a Caliphate in Cordoba in Muslim Spain.

Salah al-Din's victory in Egypt led to the dissolution of the Fatimid dynasty and brought the entire Arab region under the nominal sovereignty of the Caliph of Baghdad. Salah al-Din was appointed Sultan (King) of Syria and Egypt and became the most powerful leader of the medieval Arab world. The Caliphate in Baghdad was finally destroyed by Mongol armies in 1258, and ceased to exist until its revival in Ottoman Turkey.

Tariq Ali
June 1998

Glossary

Andalus	Islamic Spain
atabeg	high dignitary
banj	hashish
chogan	polo
dar al-hikma	public library
Dimask	Damascus
Franj	Franks or Crusaders from the West
ghazi	Islamic warrior
hadith	sayings of the Prophet Mohammed; the body of traditions about his life
hammam	baths
hashishin	assassins; members of the Shiite sect of that name
Ifriqiya	Africa
Isa	Jesus
Ka'aba	the sacred stone in Mecca
Kadi	a Muslim judge with extraordinary powers to preserve law and order in a city

al-Kuds	Arab name for Jerusalem
khamriyya	Bacchic ode to the joys of wine
khutba	the Friday sermon in the mosque
labineh	yoghurt or yoghurt-based drink
maidan	flat land for a playing field or a parade ground
mamluk	slave
Misr	Egypt
mi'ẓar	a large sheet-like wrap worn both as a mantle and by pre-Islamic Arabs as a long loin cloth
Musa	Moses
mushrif	a controller of finances
qalima	the word of Allah
Rumi	Roman
saqalabi	a white slave
Sham	Syria
tamr	date wine
Yunani	Greek

CAIRO

ONE

On the recommendation of Ibn Maymun, I become the Sultan's trusted scribe

I have not thought of our old home for many years. It is a long time now since the fire. My house, my wife, my daughter, my two-year-old grandson — all trapped inside like caged animals. If fate had not willed otherwise, I too would have been reduced to ashes. How often have I wished that I could have been there to share the agony.

These are painful memories. I keep them submerged. Yet today, as I begin to write this story, the image of that domed room where everything once began is strong in me again. The caves of our memory are extraordinary. Things that are long forgotten remain hidden in dark corners, suddenly to emerge into the light. I can see everything now. It comes to my mind clearly, as if time itself had stopped still.

It was a cold night of the Cairo winter, in the year 1181 according to the Christian calendar. The mewing of cats was the only noise from the street outside. Rabbi Musa ibn Maymun, an old friend of our family as well as its self-appointed physician, had arrived at my house on his way back from attending to the Kadi al-Fadil, who had been indisposed for several days.

We had finished eating and were sipping our mint tea in silence, surrounded by thick, multi-coloured woollen rugs, strewn with cushions covered in silk and satin. A large round brazier, filled with charcoal, glowed in the centre of the room, giving off gentle waves of heat. Reclining on the floor, we could see the reflection of the fire in the dome above, making it appear as if the night sky itself were alight.

I was reflecting on our earlier conversation. My friend had revealed an angry and bitter side, which had both surprised and reassured me. Our saint was human just like anyone else. The mask was intended for outsiders. We had been discussing the circumstances which had compelled Ibn Maymun to flee Andalus and to start on his long fifteen-year journey from Cordoba to Cairo. Ten of those years had been spent in the Maghrebian city of Fez. There the whole family had been obliged to pretend that they were followers of the Prophet of Islam. Ibn Maymun was angered at the memory. It was the deception that annoyed him. Dissembling went against his instincts.

I had never heard him talk in this fashion before. I noticed the transformation that came over him. His eyes were gleaming as he spoke, his hand clenched into a fist. I wondered whether it was this experience that had aroused his worries about religion, especially about a religion in power, a faith imposed at the point of a sword. I broke the silence.

"Is a world without religion possible, Ibn Maymun? The ancients had many gods. They used their worship of one to fight the supporters of the other. Now we have one god and, of necessity, we must fight over him. So everything has become a war of interpretation. How does your philosophy explain this phenomenon?"

The question amused him, but before he could reply we heard a loud knocking on the door, and his smile disappeared.

"Are you expecting someone?"

I shook my head. He leaned forward to warm his hands at the brazier. We had both wrapped ourselves in woollen blankets, but still we felt the cold. I knew instinctively that the late knock on the door was for my friend.

"Only the retainer of a powerful man knocks in that fashion," sighed Ibn Maymun. "Perhaps the Kadi has taken a turn for the worse, and I will have to see to him."

My servant, Ahmad, walked into the room carrying a torch that trembled in his hands. He was followed by a man of medium height, with undistinguished features and light red hair. He was wrapped in a blanket, and walked with a slight limp in his right leg. I saw a sudden flash of fear cross Ibn Maymun's face as he stood and bowed before the visitor. I had not seen this man before. It was certainly not the Kadi, who was known to me.

I, too, rose and bowed. My visitor smiled on realising that he was a stranger to me.

"I am sorry to intrude at such an hour. The Kadi informed me that Ibn Maymun was present in our town, and spending the night in your illustrious house. I am in the house of Isaac ibn Yakub am I not?"

I nodded.

"I hope," said the stranger with a slight bow, "that you will forgive me for arriving without warning. It is not often that I have the chance of meeting two great scholars on the same day. My thoughts were floating undecided between the merits of an early night or a conversation with Ibn Maymun. I decided that your words might have a more beneficial effect than sleep. And here I am."

"Any friend of Ibn Maymun is welcome here. Please be seated. Can we offer you a bowl of soup?"

"I think it will be good for your constitution, Commander of the Brave," said Ibn Maymun in a soft voice.

I realised I was in the presence of the Sultan. This was Yusuf Salah-ud-Din in person. In my house. I fell to my knees and touched his feet.

"Forgive me for not recognising Your Majesty. Your slave begs forgiveness."

He laughed and pulled me up on my feet.

"I do not care much for slaves. They are too prone to rebellion. But I would be grateful for some soup."

Later, after he had eaten the soup, he questioned me on the origins of the earthenware bowls in which it was served.

"Are these not made from the red clay of Armenia?"

I nodded in surprise.

"My grandmother had some very similar to these. She only brought them out for weddings and funerals. She used to tell me that they were from her village in the Armenian mountains."

Later that night, the Sultan explained to Ibn Maymun that he needed to engage a trustworthy scribe. He wished to have someone to whom he could dictate his memoirs. His own secretary was too engaged in intrigues of various sorts. He could not be fully trusted. He was quite capable of distorting the meaning of words to suit his own future needs.

"You know well my friend," said the Sultan, looking directly into the eyes of Ibn Maymun, "that there are times when our lives are in danger every minute of the day. We are surrounded by the enemy. We have no time to think of anything but survival. Only when peace prevails can one afford the luxury of being left alone with one's own thoughts."

"Like now?" said Ibn Maymun.

"Like now," murmured the Sultan. "I need someone I can trust, and a person who will not flinch from revealing the truth after I have turned to dust."

"I know the type of person Your Highness needs," said Ibn Maymun, "but your request poses a problem. You are never in one city for too long. Either the scribe must travel with you, or we will have to find another one in Damascus."

The Sultan smiled.

"Why not? And a third city beckons. I hope to be visiting al-Kuds soon. So perhaps we will need three scribes. For each of the three cities. Since I am the author, I will make sure not to repeat myself."

My friend and I gasped in amazement. We could hardly conceal our excitement, and this appeared to please my exalted guest. Jerusalem – al-Kuds to the Islamic world – was an occupied city. The Franj had become self-satisfied and arrogant. The Sultan had just announced, and in my house, that he intended to dislodge the enemy.

For over three score years we, who had always lived in this region, and the Franj, who came across the water, had been at each other's throats. Jerusalem had fallen to them in 1099. The old city had been shattered and ruined, its streets washed in Jewish and Muslim blood. Here the clash between the barbarians and our world had been more brutal than in the coastal towns. Every Jew and Muslim had been killed. Congregations in mosque and synagogue had risen in horror as news of this atrocity spread through the land. They had cursed the barbarians from the West, and pledged to revenge this ignoble deed. Perhaps the time had now come. Perhaps the quiet confidence of this man was justified. My heart quickened its pace.

"My friend, Ibn Yakub, whose home Your Excellency has privileged this night, is one of the most reliable scholars of our community. I could think of none better than him to be your scribe. He will not breathe a word of it to anyone."

The Sultan looked at me for a long time.

"Are you willing?"

"I am at your service, Commander of the Loyal. With one condition."

"Speak."

"I have read many books about the kings of old. The ruler is usually portrayed as god or devil, depending on whether the account is written by a courtier or an enemy. Books of this sort have no value. When truth and untruth lie embracing each other in the same bed it is difficult to tell them apart. I must have Your Excellency's permission to ask questions which might help me to clarify the meaning of a particular episode in your life. It may not be necessary, but we all know the cares which rest on your shoulders and I . . ."

He interrupted me with a laugh.

"You can ask me whatever you wish. I grant you that privilege. But I may not always reply. That is my privilege."

I bowed.

"Since you will come to the palace regularly, we cannot keep your appointment secret, but I value discretion and accuracy. There are those in my circle, including our much-loved Kadi, al-Fadil, who will envy you. After all, our al-Fadil is a gifted writer and much admired. He could certainly write what I dictate, but his language is too ornate, too precious for my taste. He clothes the subject in so many fancy words that it is sometimes difficult to perceive his meaning. He is a word-juggler, a magician who is the master of disguise.

"I want you to take down what I say as exactly as you can, without embellishments of any sort. Come to the palace tomorrow and we will make an early start. Now if you will excuse me for a few moments, I wish to consult Ibn Maymun on a personal matter."

I left the room.

An hour later, as I went to inquire whether they were ready for another bowl of chicken broth, I heard the loud and clear tones of my friend.

"I have often told your Kadi that the emotions of our soul, what we feel inside ourselves, produce very major changes in our health. All those emotions that cause Your Highness upset should be smoothed out. Their cause should be uncovered and treated. Have you told me everything?"

There was no reply. A few minutes later, the Sultan left my house. He was never to return. His retainers would arrive at regular intervals with gifts for my family, and sheep or goats to celebrate the Muslim festival of al-Fitr, that commemorates the sacrifice of Abraham.

From that night till the day he left for Jerusalem, I saw the Sultan every single day. Sometimes he would not let me return home, and I was assigned my own quarters in his palace. For the next eight months, my life was taken over by the Sultan Yusuf Salah-ud-Din ibn Ayyub.

TWO

I meet Shadhi and the Sultan begins to dictate his memoirs

Ibn Maymun had warned me that the Sultan was an early riser. He woke before dawn, made his ablutions, and consumed a cup of warm water before riding to the Mukattam Hills on the outskirts of the city. Here the citadel was being built. The Sultan, a keen student of architecture, would often overrule the chief builder. He alone knew that the reason for the new structure was not to defend Cairo against the Franj, but to defend the Sultan against popular insurrection.

The city was known for its turbulence. It had grown fast, and attracted vagabonds and malcontents of every sort. For that reason, Cairo frightened its rulers.

Here, too, the Sultan tested his own skills and those of his steed. Sometimes he would take Afdal, his oldest son, with him. Afdal was but twelve years old, and this was his first extended stay in Cairo. The Sultan would use the time to train the boy in the arts and the politics of war. Dynasties, after all, are made or lost on the battlefield. Saladin had been taught this by his father Ayyub and his uncle Shirkuh.

When the Sultan returned that morning, I was waiting for him. I touched my forehead in silent greeting.

"You have arrived at exactly the right moment, Ibn Yakub," he said, leaping off his horse. He was flushed and sweaty, with his eyes were shining like those of a child. Happiness and satisfaction were written on his face.

"This augurs well for our work, my friend. I will take a bath and join you for breakfast in the library. We can have an hour alone before the Kadi arrives. Shadhi will show you the way."

An old Kurdish warrior in his nineties, his beard as white as the mountain snow, took me by the elbow, guiding me gently in the direction of the library. On the way he talked about himself. He had been a retainer with the Sultan's father long before Yusuf was born, and long before Ayyub and his brother Shirkuh had moved down to the plains of Mesopotamia.

"It was I, Shadhi, who taught your Sultan how to ride and wield a sword when he was not yet eight years old. It was I, Shadhi, who . . ."

In more normal circumstances, I would have listened intently to the old man, and questioned him in great detail, but that day my thoughts were elsewhere. It was my first visit to the palace, and it would be foolish to deny that I was in a state of great excitement. Suddenly my star had risen. I was about to become a confidant of the most powerful ruler of our world.

I was being taken to the most celebrated private library of our city. The books on philosophy alone numbered over a thousand. Everything was here from Aristotle to Ibn Rushd, from astronomy to geometry. It was here that Ibn Maymun came when he wanted to consult the medical formularies of al-Kindi, Sahlan ibn Kaysan, and Abul Fadl Daud. And, of course, the master himself, al-Razi, the greatest of them all. It was here that Ibn Maymun wanted his own books and manuscripts to be kept after his death.

Entering the library, I was entranced by its magnitude and soon lost in lofty thoughts. These volumes, so exquisitely bound, were the repository of centuries of learning and study. Here was a special section containing books unobtainable elsewhere, works denounced as heretical. Such books, to put it another way, as might help to unlock closed minds. They were only available in the reading rooms of the Dar al-hikma if the reader was prepared to offer the librarian an extremely generous gift. Even then, not everything was possible.

Abul Hassan al-Bakri's *Sirat al-Bakri*, for instance, had vanished from the shops and the public libraries. A preacher at al-Azhar had denounced the book, a biography of the Prophet of Islam, as a total fabrication. He had informed the faithful at Friday prayers that al-Bakri was roasting in hell because of his blasphemy.

Here now in front of me lay the offending book. My hands had trembled slightly as I removed it from the shelf and began to read its opening lines. It seemed orthodox enough to me. I was so absorbed that I noticed neither the recumbent form of Shadhi prostrate on a prayer rug in the direction of Mecca, nor the unannounced arrival of the Sultan. He interrupted my private reverie.

"To dream and to know is better than to pray and be ignorant. Do you agree, Ibn Yakub?"

"Forgive me, Your Excellency, I was . . ."

He signalled that we be seated. Breakfast was being served. The Sultan was preoccupied. I had suddenly become nervous. We ate in silence.

"What is your method of work?"

I was taken by surprise.

"I'm not sure I grasp your meaning, Commander of the Brave."

He laughed.

"Come now, my friend. Ibn Maymun has told me that you are a scholar of history. He spoke highly of your attempt to compile a history of your own people. Is my question so difficult to answer?"

"I follow the method of the great Tabari. I write in a strictly chronological fashion. I ascertain the veracity of every important fact by speaking to those whose knowledge was gained directly. When I obtain several different versions of a fact, from several narrators, I usually communicate all of these to the reader."

The Sultan burst out laughing.

"You contradict yourself. How can there be more than one account of a single fact? Surely there can be only one fact. One correct account and several false versions."

"Your Majesty is talking about facts. I am talking about history."

He smiled.

"Should we begin?"

I nodded and collected my writing implements.

"Should we start at the beginning?"

"I suppose so," he muttered, "since you are so wedded to chronology. I mean it would be better to start with my first sight of Cairo, would it not?"

"The beginning, O Sultan. The beginning. Your beginning. Your first memories."

I was lucky. I was not the eldest son. For that reason not much was expected from me. I was left to myself a great deal, and enjoyed much freedom. My appearance and demeanour did not pose a threat to anyone. I was a very ordinary boy. You see me now as a Sultan, surrounded by all the symbols of power. You are impressed and, possibly, even a bit frightened. You worry that if you exceed certain proprieties your head might roll in the dust. This fear is normal. It is the effect which power has on the Sultan's subjects. But this same power can transform even the most diminutive personality into a figure of large proportions. Look at me. If you had known me when I was a boy and Shahan Shah was my oldest brother you would never have imagined that I could be the Sultan of Misr, and you would have been right. Fate and history conspired to make me what I am today.

The only person who saw something in me was my paternal grandmother. When I was nine or ten years old, she saw me and a group of my friends trying to kill a snake. As boys we would compete with each other in these foolish things. We would try and grab a snake by its tail and then swing it, before crushing its head on a stone or, as the braver ones among us did, stamping on its head with our feet.

My grandmother, having observed this scene carefully, shouted at me.

"Yusuf! Yusuf ibn Ayyub! Come here at once!"

The other boys ran away, and I walked slowly towards her, expecting a blow around my ears. My grandmother had a legendary temper and, so Shadhi had once told me, she had struck my father across the face when he was a grown man. No one dared to ask the cause of such a public display. My father had left the room and, so they say, mother and son did not speak to each other for a year. In the end, it was my father who apologised.

To my amazement, she hugged me and kissed me in turn on both my eyes.

"You are fearless, boy, but be careful. Some snakes can strike back, even when you have them by the tail."

I remember laughing with relief. She then told me of a dream she had experienced before I was born.

"You were still inside your mother's belly. I think you kicked a great deal. Your mother used to complain sometimes that she felt she was going to give birth to a colt. One night I dreamt that a large man-swallowing snake was crawling towards your mother, who was lying uncovered in the sun. Your mother opened her eyes and began to sweat. She wanted to move, but could not lift her body. Slowly the snake crawled towards her. Then suddenly, like the door of a magical cave, her belly opened. An infant walked out, sword in hand, and, with one mighty blow, decapitated the serpent. Then he looked at his mother and walked back into her stomach. You will be a great warrior, my son. It is written in your stars and Allah himself will be your guide."

My father and uncle laughed at my grandmother and her foolish dreams, but even at that time this interpretation undoubtedly had a positive effect on me. She was the first person to take me seriously.

Her words must have had some effect. After this incident, I noticed that Asad al-Din Shirkuh, my uncle, was beginning to watch me carefully. He took a personal interest in my training as a horseman and sword-fighter. It was he who taught me everything I know of horses. You are aware, are you not, Ibn Yakub, that I know the complete genealogies of all the great horses in our armies? You look surprised. We will talk about horses another day.

If I shut my eyes and think of my earliest memories, the first image that fills my mind is the ruins of the old Greek temples at Baalbek. Their size made one tremble in admiration and awe. The gates leading into the courtyard were still intact. They were truly built for the gods. My father, as representative of the great Sultan Zengi of Mosul, was in charge of the fortress and its defence against the Sultan's rivals. This was the town where I grew up. The ancients named it Heliopolis, and worshipped Zeus there, and Hermes and Aphrodite.

As children, we used to divide into different groups at the feet of their statues, and hide from each other. There is nothing like a ruin to excite the imagination of a child. There was magic in those old stones. I used to daydream about the old days. Till then the world of the ancients had been a complete puzzle. The worship of idols was the worst heresy for us, something that had been removed from the world by Allah and our Prophet. Yet these temples, and the images of Aphrodite and Hermes in particular, were very pleasing.

We used to think how exciting it would have been if we had lived in those times. We often fought over the gods. I was a partisan of Aphrodite, my older brother, Turan Shah, loved Hermes. As for Zeus, all that remained of his statue was the legs, and they were not very attractive. I think the rest of him had been used to build the fortress in which we now lived.

Shadhi, worried at the corrupting effect of these remnants from the past, would try and scare us away from the ruins. The gods could transform humans into statues or other objects without their losing their minds. He would invent tales of how djinns and demons, and other ungodly creatures, would gather at these sites whenever there was a full moon. All they discussed was how to grab and eat children. Hundreds and thousands of children have been eaten here by the djinns over the centuries, he would tell us in his deep voice. Then, seeing the fright on our faces, he would qualify what he had said. Nothing would harm us, since we were under the protection of Allah and the Prophet.

Shadhi's stories only added to the attraction. We would ask him about the three gods, and some of the scholars in the library would talk openly of the ancients and of their beliefs. Their gods and goddesses were like humans. They fought and loved, and shared other human emotions. What distinguished them from us was that they did not die. They lived for ever and ever in their own heaven, a place very different from our paradise.

"Are they still in their own heaven now?" I remember asking my grandmother one night.

She was enraged.

"Who has been filling your head with all this nonsense? Your father will have their tongues removed. They were never anything else but statues, foolish boy. People in those times were very stupid. They worshipped idols. In our part of the world it was our own Prophet, may he rest in peace, who finally destroyed the statues and their influence."

Everything we were told increased our fascination with these things. Nothing could keep us away from them. One night, when the moon was full, the older children, led by my brother, decided to visit the sanctuary of Aphrodite. They were planning to leave me behind, but I heard them whispering and threatened to tell our grandmother. My brother kicked me hard, but realised the danger of not including me.

It was cold that night. Even though we had wrapped ourselves in blankets, my teeth were trembling and the tip of my nose was numb. I think there were six or seven of us. Slowly we crept out of the fortress. We were all frightened, and I remember the complaints when I was compelled to stop twice to water the roots of an old tree. We became more confident as we approached Aphrodite. We had heard nothing except the owls and the barking dogs. No djinns had appeared.

Yet just as we entered the moonlit temple courtyard, we heard strange noises. I nearly died, and clung tightly to Turan Shah. Even he was scared. Slowly we crept towards the noises. There stretched out before us was the bare backside of Shadhi as he heaved forwards and backwards, his black hair waving in the wind. He was copulating like a donkey, and once we realised it was him we could not restrain ourselves. Our laughter swept through the empty yard, striking Shadhi like a dagger. He turned and began to scream abuse at us. We ran. The next day my brother confronted him.

"The djinn had a very familiar arse last night, did it not Shadhi?"

Salah-ud-Din paused and laughed at the memory. As luck would have it, Shadhi entered the library at that moment with a message. Before he could speak, the Sultan's laughter reached a higher pitch. The bewildered retainer looked at us in turn, and it was with great difficulty that I managed to control my features, though I too was inwardly bursting with laughter.

Shadhi, by way of explanation, was told of the story that had just been recounted. His face went red, and he spoke angrily to Salah al-Din in the Kurdish dialect, and stormed out of the room.

The Sultan laughed again.

"He has threatened revenge. He will tell you tales from my youth in Damascus, which he is sure I have forgotten."

Our first session was over.

We left the library, the Sultan indicating with a gesture that I should follow him. The corridors and rooms we passed through were furnished in an endless variety of silks and brocades, with mirrors edged in silver and gold. Eunuchs guarded each sanctuary. I had never seen such luxury.

The Sultan left me little time to wonder. He walked quickly, his robe streaming in the wind created by his rapid movements. We entered the audience chamber. Outside stood a Nubian guard, a scimitar by his side. He bowed as we entered. The Sultan sat on a raised platform, covered in purple silks and surrounded by cushions covered in satin and gold brocade.

The Kadi had already arrived at the palace for his daily report and consultations. He was summoned to the chamber. As he entered and bowed, I made as if to leave. To my surprise, the Sultan asked me to remain seated. He wanted me to observe and write down everything of note.

I had often seen the Kadi al-Fadil in the streets of the city, preceded and followed by his guards and retainers, symbols of power and authority. The face of the state. This was the man who presided over the Diwan al-insha, the chancellery of the state, the man who ensured the regular and smooth functioning of Misr. He had served the Fatimid Caliphs and their ministers with the same zeal he now devoted to the man who had overthrown them. He embodied the continuity of the institutions of Misr. The Sultan trusted him as a counsellor and friend, and the Kadi never flinched from offering unwelcome advice. It was also he who drew up official and personal letters, after the Sultan had provided the outlines of what he wished to say.

The Sultan introduced me as his very special and private scribe. I rose and bowed low before the Kadi. He smiled.

"Ibn Maymun has talked much of you, Ibn Yakub. He respects your learning and your skills. That is enough for me."

I bowed my head in gratitude. Ibn Maymun had warned me that if the Kadi had become possessive of the Sultan, and resented my presence, he could have me removed from this world without much difficulty.

"And my approval, al-Fadil?" inquired the Sultan. "Does that mean nothing at all? I accept that I am not a great thinker or a poet like you, nor am I a philosopher and physician like our good friend, Ibn Maymun. But surely you will admit I am a good judge of men. It was I who picked Ibn Yakub."

"Your Excellency mocks this humble servant," replied the Kadi in a slightly bored fashion, as if to say that he was not in the mood for playing games today.

After a few preliminary skirmishes, in which he refused to be further provoked by his master, the Kadi sketched out the main events of the preceding week. This was a routine report on the most trivial aspects of running the state, but it was difficult not to be bewitched by his mastery of the language. Every word was carefully chosen, every sentence finely tuned, and the conclusion rewarded with a couplet. This man was truly impressive. The entire report took up an hour, and not once had the Kadi had occasion to consult a single piece of paper. What a feat of memory!

The Sultan was used to the Kadi's delivery, and had appeared to shut his eyes for long spells during his chancellor's exquisite discourse.

"Now I come to an important matter on which I need your decision, Sire. It involves the murder of one of your officers by another."

The Sultan was wide awake.

"Why was I not informed earlier?"

"The incident of which I speak only happened two days ago. I spent the whole of yesterday in establishing the truth. Now I can report the whole story to you."

"I'm listening, al-Fadil."

The Kadi began to speak.

THREE

A case of uncontrollable passions: the story of Halima and the judgement of the Sultan

Messud al-Din, as you will recall, was one of Your Grace's bravest officers. He had fought by your side on many an occasion. Two days ago, he was dispatched by a much younger man, Kamil ibn Zafar, one of the most gifted swordsmen, I am told, in our city. The news was brought to me by Halima, herself the cause of the conflict between the two men. She is now hiding under my protection till the matter is resolved. If the Sultan were to see her, he would understand why Messud lies dead and why Kamil is prepared to suffer a similar fate. She is beautiful.

Halima was an orphan. There was no rosy childhood for her. It was as if she knew the transgressions that were destined to flow from her. She stepped into adult life and startled it with her beauty, her intelligence, her audacity. She became a serving woman in the household of Kamil ibn Zafar, where she worked for his wife and looked after his children.

Kamil could have done what he wanted with her. He could have used her body when overcome by desire, he could have installed her in his house as an official concubine. But he loved her. She was not the one to demand that he should marry her. The pressure came from him, and the marriage duly took place.

Halima insisted on behaving as if nothing had changed. She refused to stay at home the whole day. She would serve Kamil at home, and then remain in the room while his male friends were present. She told me that although Kamil was a kind and considerate man, she did not feel the passion for him that he felt for her. Her explanation of the marriage was that it was only through such a link that he felt she would be his property for life. Yes, Sire, that is the word she used. Property.

Messud had first seen Halima at the house of his friend, Kamil, who had opened out his heart to him. Kamil told Messud of his love for Halima, and how he could not live without her. The two men spoke of her a great deal, and Messud came to learn of her most appealing qualities.

On the occasions when Messud called to enjoy a drink with his friend, and Kamil was absent, he would accept a small glass of tea from Halima. She would speak to him as an equal, and regale him with the latest stories and jokes from the bazaar, often at the expense of your Kadi, O merciful Sultan. And sometimes the darts were aimed at the Caliph in Baghdad and at your own good self.

Kamil's mother and his oldest wife were shocked by Halima's behaviour. They complained bitterly, but Kamil was unmoved.

"Messud is like my own brother," he told them. "I serve under him in the glorious army of Yusuf Salah al-Din. His family is at home in Damascus. My house is his house. Treat him as you would someone who is part of our family. Halima understands my feelings better than you. If Messud displeases you, then keep out of his way. I do not wish to impose him on you."

The subject was never raised again. Messud became a regular visitor.

It was Halima who made the first move. Nothing is more attractive than forbidden fruit. One evening, when Kamil and the rest of the family were at the funeral of his first wife's father, Halima found herself alone. The servants and armed retainers had accompanied their master to the burial. Messud, unsuspecting

Messud, unaware of the death in the family, arrived to eat with his friend. He found the beautiful Halima greeting him in the empty courtyard. As the setting sun shone on her light red hair, she must have reminded him of a fairy princess from the Caucasus.

She did not give me an exact account of how our noble warrior Messud ended the afternoon by resting his satisfied body on hers, his head pressed gently on her peach-like breasts. I know Your Grace appreciates every detail, but my modest imagination is incapable of satisfying you today. Their passion for each other became like a slow-working poison.

As the months passed, Messud would look for opportunities to send Kamil on special missions. He would be drafted to Fustat, or to supervise the construction of the new citadel, or to train young soldiers in the art of sword-fighting, or sent on any other mission that occurred to Messud's twisted and obsessed mind.

Halima told me that they had found a trysting place, not far from the Mahmudiya quarter where she lived. Unbeknown to her, Kamil's mother had started having her followed by a loyal servant, until the lovers' routine had become well-established. One day she sent a messenger to fetch her son. She pretended that death itself was knocking on her door. Kamil, sick with worry, rushed home and was relieved to see his mother well. But the look on her face told him everything. She did not speak a word, merely nodding to the twelve-year-old servant-spy and indicating to her son to follow him. Kamil was about to leave his sword behind, but she told him he might soon have some use for it.

The boy walked at a brisk pace. Kamil followed him in a daze. He knew his mother disliked Halima. He knew that wherever he was going, there he would find her. But he was hardly prepared for what he saw when he entered the room. Messud and Halima, lying naked on the floor, were drowning each other in bliss.

Kamil screamed. It was an awful scream. Anger, betrayal, jealousy were all wrapped up in that scream. Messud covered himself and got up on his feet, his face disfigured by guilt. He did not put up a fight. He knew what was his due, and he waited patiently for his punishment. Kamil ran his sword through his friend's heart.

Halima did not scream. She grabbed her cloak and left the room. She did not see her lover's spurting blood send her husband into a frenzy. But the boy observed everything. He saw his master punish the dead body of his friend. He saw him cut off the offending organ. Then, his anger spent, Kamil sat down and wept. He talked to his dead friend. He pleaded to be told why Messud had regarded Halima's body as more important than their friendship.

"If you had asked me," he shouted at the body, "I would have given her to you."

At this point in the Kadi's story, the Sultan interrupted him.

"Enough, al-Fadil. We have heard all that we need to know. It is a wretched business. One of my finest horsemen lies dead. Killed, not by the Franj, but by his best friend. My day had started so well with Ibn Yakub, but now you have ruined it with this painful story. There is no solution to this problem. The solution lay within the problem. Is that not the case?"

The Kadi smiled sadly.

"At one level, of course, you are correct. Yet looked at from the point of view of the state, this is a serious offence, a question of discipline. Kamil has killed a superior officer. If he were to remain unpunished, news would spread. It would demoralise the soldiers, especially the Syrians who loved Messud. I think punishment is necessary. He should not have taken the law into his own hands. Justice in Your Highness' realm is my responsibility and mine alone. Only you can override my decision. What do you suggest in this case?"

"Your choice, al-Fadil."

"I demand Kamil's head."

"No!" screamed the Sultan. "Flog him if you must, but nothing more. The offence was caused by a fit of uncontrollable passion. Even you, my friend, would have found it difficult to exercise restraint in such circumstances."

"As the Sultan desires."

The Kadi remained seated. He knew instinctively, from long years of service to his Sultan, that Salah al-Din had not yet finished with this story. For a few minutes, none of us spoke.

"Tell me, al-Fadil," said the familiar voice, "what has become of the wench?"

"I thought you might like to question her yourself, and I took the liberty of bringing her to the palace. She should be stoned to death for adultery. The Sultan must decide the sentence. It would be a popular decision. The talk in the bazaar is that she is possessed by the devil."

"I am intrigued. What kind of animal is she? As you leave, have her sent to me."

The Kadi bowed and, without the tiniest acknowledgement of my presence, he left the room.

"What as yet I cannot understand, Ibn Yakub," said the Sultan, "is why al-Fadil brought this case to me. Perhaps it was because he could not risk executing a Misrian officer without my approval. Perhaps. I suppose that's the reason. But one must never underestimate al-Fadil. He is a sly camel. I'm sure there was a hidden motive."

At this point a retainer entered, and announced that Halima was outside the door. The Sultan nodded, and she was ushered before him. She fell on her knees and bowed, touching his feet with her forehead.

"Enough of this," said the Sultan in the harsh voice of a ruler sitting in judgement. "Sit down in front of us."

As she sat up, I saw her face for the first time. It was as if a lamp had lit the room. This was no ordinary beauty. Despite her sadness, her tearful eyes were shining and intelligent. This one would not go willingly to the executioner. She would fight. Resistance was written on her face.

As I turned to the Sultan, pen poised and waiting for him to speak, I could see that he too was bewitched by the sight of this young woman. She must have been twenty years old, at the most.

Salah al-Din's eyes betrayed a softness I had not seen before, but I had not been with him before in the presence of a woman. He was staring at her with an intensity which would have frightened anyone else, but Halima looked straight into his eyes. It was the Sultan who finally averted his gaze. She had won the first contest.

"I am waiting," he finally said. "Tell me why I should not hand you over to the Kadi, who will have you stoned to death for your crime."

"If love is a crime," she began in a self-pitying tone, "then, Commander of the Merciful, I deserve to die."

"Not love, wretched woman, but adultery. Betraying your husband before God."

At this her eyes blazed. The sadness had evaporated and she began to speak. Her voice changed too. She spoke with confidence and with no trace of humility. She had entirely regained her self-possession, and spoke to the Sultan in a confident voice as though addressing an equal.

"I could not understand how small this world can be for two people. When Messud was not with me, the memory of him became a torment. I care not whether I live or die, and I will submit to the Kadi's punishment. He can have me stoned to death, but I will not beg for mercy or shout my repentance to the vultures. I am sad, but I am not sorry. The short spell of happiness was more than I had thought possible in this life."

The Sultan asked if she had any relatives. She shook her head. He then requested Halima to tell her story.

I was two years old when I was sold to the family of Kamil ibn Zafar. They said I was an orphan, found abandoned miles away by Kurdish traders. They had taken pity on me, but the term of their pity was limited to only a couple of years. Kamil ibn Zafar's mother could not conceive again. Her husband, they told me at the time, was dead. She lived in her father's house, and this kind old man bought her a child from the streets. I was part of the seasonal trade. That is all I know of my past.

Kamil was ten or eleven years old at the time. He was kind and loving even then, and always attentive to my needs. He treated me as though I was his real sister. His mother's attitude was different. She could never decide whether to bring me up as a daughter or as a slave girl. As I grew older, she became clearer as to my functions in the house. I still ate with the family, which annoyed the other servants, but I was trained to become her serving woman. It was not such a bad life, though I often felt lonely. The other serving women never fully trusted me.

Every day an old man came to the house to teach us the wisdom of the Koran, and to recount the deeds of the Prophet and his Companions. Soon Kamil had stopped attending these lessons. He would go riding with his friends, and shooting arrows at the mark. One day the teacher of holy texts grabbed my hand, and put it between his legs. I screamed. Kamil's mother rushed into the room.

The teacher, muttering the name of Allah, told her that I was indecent and licentious. In his presence she slapped my face twice, and apologised to him. When Kamil came home, I told him the truth. He was angry with his mother, and the teacher was never allowed near our house again. I think that she was nervous of Kamil's affection for me, and she soon found him a wife. She chose her sister's daughter, Zenobia, who was two years older than me.

After Kamil's wedding, I was made to attend to the needs of his young wife. I liked her. We had known each other since I had first entered the household, and we often shared each other's secrets. When Zenobia bore Kamil a son, I was as delighted as all of them. I looked after the child a great deal, and I grew to love it as if it were my own. I envied Zenobia, who Allah had blessed with unlimited amounts of milk.

Everything was fine – even Kamil's mother had become friendly again – until that fateful day when Kamil took me aside and told me that he loved me, and not just as a brother. Allah is my witness, I was wholly surprised. At first I was scared. But Kamil persisted. He wanted me. For a very long time, I resisted. I felt much affection for him, but no passion. Not so much as a trace.

I know not what would have happened, or even how it would have ended, had Kamil's mother not attempted to marry me off to the son of the water-carrier. He was a rough type, and did not appeal to me. Yet marriage, as Your Grace knows, is never a free choice for women. If my mistress had decided my fate, I would have married the water-carrier's boy.

Kamil was upset by the news. He declared that it would never happen, and immediately asked me to become his wife. His mother was shocked. His wife declared that she was humiliated by his choice, taking her servant as a second wife. Both women stopped speaking to me for many months.

Imagine my situation. There was no one to talk to about the problems of my life. In bed at night, I used to weep, yearning for the mother I never knew. I considered the choices confronting me quite coldly. The thought of the water-carrier's son made me feel ill. I would rather have died or run away than bear his touch. Kamil, who had always been kind and loving to me, was the only possible alternative. I agreed to become his wife.

Kamil was overjoyed. I was satisfied and not unhappy, even though Zenobia hated me, and Kamil's mother treated me as if I were dirt from the street. Her own past hung over her like a cloud. She could never forget that Kamil's father had deserted her for another, while she was heavy with their child. He had left Cairo one night, never to return. I am told he has a family in Baghdad, where he trades in precious stones. His name was never mentioned, though Kamil used to think of him a great deal. What I have recounted is his mother's side of the story.

In the kitchen, there was another version which is common knowledge. I was told it only after the servants were convinced that I would not carry tales to the mistress. For the truth is that Kamil's father ran away from our city when he discovered, on returning from a long voyage abroad, that his wife had coupled with a local merchant. The child in her belly did not belong to him. Kamil confirmed this to me after we were married. His mother knew that I had been told, and the very thought filled with her hatred. What would have happened to all of us Allah alone knows.

Then Messud, with eyes like almonds and lips as sweet as honey, entered my life. He told me tales of Damascus, and how he had fought by the side of Sultan Yusuf Salah al-Din ibn Ayyub. I could not resist him. I did not wish to resist him. What I felt for him was something I had never experienced before.

That is my story, O great Sultan. I know that you will live without misfortune, you will win great victories, you will rule over us, you will pass judgement, and you will make sure your sons are brought up as you wish them to be. Your success has put you where you are. This benighted, blind and homeless creature puts her trust in you. Allah's will must be done.

While Halima had been talking, Salah al-Din had drunk in every word, observed every gesture, and noticed every flash of the eyes. She had the look of a wild, but cornered, cat. Now he inspected her with the steady, emotionless gaze of a Kadi, as though his face were made of stone. The intensity of the Sultan's gaze unnerved the girl. This time, it was she who averted her eyes.

He smiled and clapped his hands. The ever-faithful Shadhi entered the chamber, and the Sultan spoke to him in the Kurdish dialect, which I could not understand. The sound struck some deep chord in Halima. Hearing them talk in their tongue startled her, and she listened carefully.

"Go with him," the Sultan told her. "He will make sure you remain safe, far away from the Kadi's stones."

She kissed his feet, and Shadhi took her by the elbow and guided her out of the chamber.

"Speak frankly, Ibn Yakub. Your religion shares many of our prescriptions. In my place, would you have allowed such a beautiful creation to be stoned to death outside the Bab-el-Barkiya?"

I shook my head.

"I would not, Your Highness, but many of the more orthodox within my religion would share the view of the great Kadi."

"Surely you understand, my good scribe, that al-Fadil did not really want her to be killed. That is what all this business is about. He wanted me to take the decision. That is all. Had he wished, he could have dealt with the whole matter himself — and then informed me when it was too late to intervene. By asking me to listen to her story, he knew that he was not consigning her to the cruel uncertainties of enigmatic fate. He knows me well. He would have been sure I would keep her alive. If the truth be told, I think our Kadi, too, fell under Halima's spell. I think she will be safe in the harem.

"Now, it has been a tiring day. You will break some bread with me, I trust?"

FOUR

A eunuch kills the great Sultan Zengi and the fortunes of Salah al-Din's family take a turn; Shadhi's story

The following morning, I arrived at the palace at the agreed time and was taken to the library by Shadhi. The Sultan himself did not appear. I busied myself with volumes hitherto unknown to me.

At noon I was told by a messenger, with Shadhi trailing behind him, that matters of state were occupying the Sultan and that he had no time that day.

I was about to leave when Shadhi winked at me. I was wary of this stooped old man, who was still vain enough to dye his white beard with henna and whose well-oiled bald head glistened dangerously in the sun. My face must have registered confusion.

"Matters of state?"

The old man laughed, a rasping, loud, vulgar, sceptical laugh, as if to answer his own question.

"I think the Defender of the Weak is not inspecting the citadel as he should be at this hour. Instead, he is exploring the cracks and crevices of the girl with red hair."

I was slightly shocked, not even sure myself whether I was disturbed more by the words that Shadhi had spoken or by the message they conveyed. Could it be true? The Sultan's speed on horseback was legendary, and I wondered whether this same impatience had characterised his movements in the bedchamber. And Halima? Had she yielded willingly, without a struggle or, at the very least, a verbal plea for patience? Was it a seduction, or a violation?

The report was probably accurate. I was desperate for more information, but I refrained from comment, not wishing to encourage Shadhi further. This irritated him. He was trying to develop a familiarity with me by sharing a secret, and he took my lack of response as a snub.

I hurriedly took my leave of him and returned home.

To my surprise, when I returned the next morning, I found the Sultan waiting for me in the library. He smiled at my entrance, but wanted to begin immediately, wasting no time in pleasantries. In my mind's eye, I thought I caught a brief glimpse of Halima, before the Sultan's familiar tones forced me to concentrate my attention on his words. My hand began to move on the paper, pushed as if by a force much greater than me.

Spring always came to Baalbek like a traveller with stories to tell. At night the sky was like a quilt sewn with stars. During the day it was an intense blue, as the sun smiled on everything. We used to lie in the grass and inhale the fragrance of the almond blossom. As the weather grew warmer, and summer approached, we would compete with each other to see who would dive first into the small freshwater lake, endlessly supplied by several little streams. The lake itself was hidden by a clump of trees, and we always treated its location as our little secret, though everyone in Baalbek knew of its existence.

One day, while we were swimming, we saw Shadhi racing towards us. He could run in those days, though not as well as in his youth. My grandmother used to talk of how Shadhi could run from one mountain village to another, over distances of more than twenty miles. He would leave after the morning prayer and return in time to serve breakfast to my grandfather. That was a long time ago, in Dvin, before our family moved to Takrit.

Shadhi told us to get out of the water and run as fast as we could to the citadel. Our father had summoned us. He swore at us, threatening vile punishments if we did not obey his instruction immediately. His face was taut with worry. On this occasion, we believed him.

When my older brother, Turan Shah, inquired as to the reason for such haste, Shadhi glared, telling him that it was for our father to inform us of the calamity that had befallen our faith. Genuinely alarmed, we ran as fast as we could. I remember Turan Shah muttering something about the Franj. If they were at the gates, he would fight, even if he had to steal a sword.

As we approached the citadel, we heard the familiar sound of wailing women. I remember clutching Turan Shah's hand, and looking at him nervously. Shadhi had noticed this and correctly interpreted my anxiety.

As he lifted me onto his shoulders, he whispered soothing words in my ear.

"Your father is alive and well. In a few minutes you will see him."

It was not our father but the great Sultan Zengi who had died. The Defender of the Faith had been murdered by a drunken eunuch while he slept in his tent by the Euphrates.

He was fully engaged in the Holy War against the Franj. My father had been put in command of Baalbek by Sultan Zengi, and now he was worried that we might have to pack our tents and move again.

It was Zengi who had defeated the Franj and, after a month's siege, taken the city of al-Ruha, which they called Edessa. The city had become a jewel set in the dagger of our faith, as we looked with longing towards al-Kuds and the mosque of Caliph Omar.

I still remember the words of the poet, often sung in Baalbek by both soldiers and slaves. We used to join them, and I think if I begin to sing, the words will come back:

He rides in a wave of horsemen,
They flow o'er the earth like a flood,
His spears talk to the enemy
Like tongues encrusted in blood.
He's merciful and forgiving
But not in the heat of the fight,
For in the battle's fire and rage
The only law is might.

My father had enjoyed warm relations with Sultan Zengi and was genuinely upset by the manner and cause of his death. Years later, Shadhi told me the real story.

Zengi was fond of wine. On the night of his death, he had consumed an entire flask of wine. While still in his cups he had sent for a young soldier who had caught his eye during the siege. The Sultan used the young man to assuage his lust.

Yaruktash, the eunuch who killed Zengi, had loved the boy. He could not bear the thought of his sculpted body being defiled by an old man in a hurry. In a fit of jealousy he followed the boy, and observed what took place. He brought wine to the guards outside the tent, making them drowsy. While they slept, he crept in and stabbed his master to death, joined by the young soldier whose body was still warm from Zengi's embrace. It was a crime of passion.

The scribes who write history pretend that the eunuch and his friends had stolen Zengi's wine. Fearful of being discovered, they had killed their ruler in a drunken frenzy. But this version doesn't make sense. Shadhi told me the truth. He must have heard it from my father or my uncle. Little escaped the notice of those two men.

At the time I knew little or nothing of this. Nor was I especially interested in the affairs of that other world inhabited by adults. Once again, I benefited from not being the eldest son. That was the privilege reserved for Shahan Shah. He was obliged to sit next to my father during Friday prayers, and when other matters were being discussed. He was being trained in the arts of rulership. Turan Shah and I would sometimes find it difficult not to laugh when Shahan Shah began to adopt my father's way of speaking.

The occupation of our coastal cities, and even of al-Kuds, which the Franj call the Kingdom of Jerusalem, had become, for me, one of the simple facts of life. Sometimes I would hear my father and my uncle Shirkuh talk of the past, often when the children were present. They would be speaking to each other, but we were the real audience. It was their way of making sure we understood the scale of what had taken place in our lands.

They would talk of how the barbarians had first arrived, and of how they ate human flesh and did not bathe. Always they told sad stories of the fate of al-Kuds. The barbarians had decided to kill all the Believers. All of your people, Ibn Yakub, as I'm sure you know better than I, were collected in the Temple of Suleiman. The exits were blocked, and the Franj set the holy sanctuary on fire. They wished to wipe out the past and to rewrite the future of al-Kuds, which once belonged to all of us, the People of the Book.

The only story that really moved me as a child was that of al-Kuds. The cruelty of the barbarians was like a poison that makes men mute. Al-Kuds was never absent from our world of make-believe. We used to climb on our horses and pretend we were riding to drive the Franj out of al-Kuds, an event which usually meant driving Shadhi out of the kitchen. Yet the real day is not so far away, Ibn Yakub. Our people will soon return to al-Kuds. The cities of Tyre and Acre, of Antioch and Tripoli, will once again belong to us.

That the Franj must be defeated was obvious, but how could we emerge victorious when the camp of the Believers was so bitterly divided? For a start, there were two Caliphs: one in Baghdad who ruled only in name, and another in Cairo, who was weak. The collapse of the Caliphate had led to little kingdoms springing up everywhere. My father told us on the day Zengi died that unless we were united the Franj would never be defeated. He spoke as a general, but his words were also true in a greater, spiritual sense. The animosities within our own side ran deep. We were fiercer in fighting our rivals than in resisting the Franj. Those words have always stayed with me.

"And your father?" I asked the Sultan. "You have not yet spoken of him. What kind of a man was he?"

My father Ayyub was a good-natured man. He was a cautious and trusting person. When trying to explain something to us, he would ask in his soft voice: "Is it simple? Is it clear? Does everyone understand?"

In a more tranquil world he might have been content in charge of a large library or as the man responsible for the regular functioning of the public baths of Cairo. You smile, Ibn Yakub. You think I underestimate the qualities of my father. Not in the least. All I am saying is that we are all creatures of our fate, and our lives are determined by the times in which we exist. Our biographies are determined by circumstance.

Take Ibn Maymun, for instance. If his family had not been compelled to leave Andalus, he might have been the Vizir of Granada. If al-Kuds had not been occupied, you might be living there and not in Cairo.

Take our Prophet himself. It was fortunate, was it not, that he received the Revelation at a time when two great empires were beginning to decay. Within thirty years of his death, the Believers, with the guidance of Allah, had succeeded beyond our wildest dreams. If we did not succeed in civilising the lands of the Franj, the fault is ours alone. It was human error that prevented us from educating and circumcising the Franj. The Prophet knew that reliance on Allah alone would never be enough. Did he not once remark: "Trust in Allah, but tie your camel first"?

My father, you must understand, never liked to travel. He was a man of sedentary habits, unlike my grandfather, who, by the way, was also called Shadhi, and my uncle Shirkuh. These two were never satisfied in one place. My enemies often refer to our family as adventurers and upstarts. Even the Prophet, may he rest in eternal peace, was called an upstart, so that does not upset me. As for being adventurers, I think that is true. The only way to move forward in this world is through adventure. If you sit still in one place, you get burnt by the sun and you die. Yet I know that my father would have liked to have stayed in Dvin, in Armenia.

The news of Zengi's murder was not just a personal blow. It meant turmoil and trouble. Zengi's two sons lost little time in asserting their rule in Mosul and Aleppo. My father had little confidence in their capacities. He was proved wrong, of course, but who was to know at the time that the dour and puritanical Nur al-Din would rise to such heights?

My father's fears were soon to be vindicated. Within weeks, the armies of the ruler of Damascus were at the gates of Baalbek. Resistance, my father knew, was futile. He felt that there was no reason to spill the blood of the Believers. He negotiated a peaceful surrender, and the people were grateful.

Years later, when my father and I were riding together outside Damascus, the edge of the sky turned suddenly red-gold. He noticed this first and we drew in our reins, paying silent homage, for what seemed a long time, to the inimitable beauty of nature. As we began to ride home, none of us spoke. We were still awed by that sky which had changed again as the first stars began to appear. Just as we reached the Bab Shark, my father spoke in his soft voice.

"We often forget that even a necessary war is seen as a calamity by most people. They always suffer much more than us. Always. Never forget that, my son. Engage in battle only when there is no other way."

Why is it that we forget certain crucial facts, and have to work hard to recall them, yet other events remain clear in our minds? I still remember that day. It is fresh in my mind. My oldest brother, Shahan Shah, had died suddenly some years before, and my father had not fully recovered from the blow. He was still distraught. For some reason, relations between him and Turan Shah had never been close. My brother, who I loved, was far too undisciplined and headstrong a personality to appeal to my father. One day I heard my mother shouting at him: "Turan Shah, is it not enough that you leave a bitter taste in your father without annoying me as well. You are nothing but pain and trouble. Did you hear me . . ." So many stones had been thrown at him that he was no longer frightened of them, and he would laugh at our mother.

Since Turan Shah was excluded from the list, I was the next in line for my father's attentions.

I was sixteen years of age and had been presented with a hunting hawk and a fine steed from Kufa. I think it was the first time that my father had taken me seriously. He treated me as an equal. We discussed many problems. He talked about his fears and worries, about the future, about a time when he would no longer be there to guide me.

The very thought of his mortality sent a chill through my body, and I began to tremble. I wanted to embrace him and kiss his cheeks, to weep on his shoulder, to shout "I don't want you ever to die", but I contained myself. There is a sacred boundary between father and son which cannot be crossed by emotion. Lips stay silent. The heart remains helpless.

I became aware of all this some years after we left Baalbek. My father had not surrendered the citadel without conditions. He was rewarded with a fief of eight villages near Damascus, a large sum of money, and a house in the heart of the old city. Once again, we were on the move. I was sad to leave the old temples and the streams. I had grown to love Baalbek. Life was happy and sheltered. To this day it brings a smile to my lips.

But it was Damascus that made me a man.

To my relief, the Sultan had stopped speaking and I could rest my weary hand. He noticed my plight and shouted for his attendant. Instructions were given. I was to be bathed and oiled. My hands were to be massaged till each finger had lost its tiredness. After that, I was to be provided with a meal, and permitted to rest till he returned. He wanted an evening session that day. He was due to ride through the city to inspect the building of the new citadel, his citadel, and he was being dressed for the occasion.

Just before I left his presence, I was amazed to see the entrance of a transformed Halima. This was not the tear-stained, sad-eyed creature whose tale we had heard in silence a few days earlier. She walked in with a confidence that took me aback. It answered the question that had been troubling me. She had not been violated. He had been seduced.

Now Halima wanted to visit the citadel with him. Her audacity astonished Salah al-Din. He refused. She persisted, threatening to disguise herself as a soldier and ride out after him. His eyes suddenly hardened, and his face became stern. He spoke in a harsh voice, warning her not to leave the palace without his permission. Outside these protected walls, her life was in danger. Kamil had been whipped in public only yesterday, but the crowd, which included many women, had demanded the stoning of Halima. The news that she had obtained refuge in the palace had not been well received.

Halima still had a defiant look in her eye, but the Sultan's will prevailed. He suggested, as a conciliatory gesture, that she might perhaps take her midday meal with me. She gave me a slightly contemptuous look, and left the room.

"Sometimes," muttered the Sultan in a weary voice, "I think I'm a better judge of horses than of men. Halima is more troublesome than a filly. If she deigns to eat with you this afternoon, Ibn Yakub, I am sure that you will offer her sage advice."

Halima did not honour me with her company that day. I was greatly disappointed. Shadhi's arrival, just as I was about to start eating, did not improve my humour. I was not in the mood to listen to the tales of old men, but courtesy dictated that I share my meal with him, and one thing led to another. He was soon boasting of his own exploits. His singular prowess as a rider featured in every episode.

Prior to this meeting, I had never spent much time with him, nor had I taken him particularly seriously. Yet now as I watched him, while he spoke, I saw something in his mannerisms which struck me as familiar. They alerted me to the real reason why he was treated with such respect by servant and master alike. He lifted his right hand, and raised his eyebrow just like Salah al-Din.

I let the thought pass. It was not such a surprising observation. Shadhi had probably spent more time with the Sultan than anyone else, and the young boy had picked up some of the characteristics of the retainer. Yet as the old man carried on talking, the thought returned to me. This time, I interrupted him.

"Respected uncle, I have a question for you. You talk much of your past exploits and adventures, and your stories are of great value in helping me to understand the Sultan. Yet I would like to know something about you. Who was your father? And your mother? I ask not out of curiosity alone, but . . ."

He interrupted me fiercely.

"Impertinent Jew! I have killed men for less!"

My face must have paled slightly, because he immediately burst out laughing.

I can't believe you are frightened of an old man like me. Since what you are writing will not be published till we are all dead and gone, I will answer your question. My mother was a poor woman in Dvin, the only daughter of a woodcutter who delivered wood to many big houses in the area. Her mother had died giving birth to her, and her father never married again. That is a rare enough event in these times, but was unheard of when my grandfather was young, over a hundred years ago. He was as big as a giant, and his ability with the axe was known in all the nearby villages. He could fell a tree faster than anyone else in that part of the world.

He had become close friends with a young cook in the house of Shadhi ibn Marwan, the Sultan's grandfather, and decided that this was the man for his fifteen-year-old daughter. They were married. My mother became part of Ibn Marwan's household. I have not yet told you, scribe, that my mother was as renowned for her beauty as my grandfather for his strength. What had to happen, happened. The master caught sight of her and bent her to his will. She did not resist. I am the result. When I was born, the Sultan's late father, Ayyub, and his uncle Shirkuh were already over ten years old. Their mother was a ferocious lady. When she heard the news, she insisted that the cook and my mother – I was still in her stomach – should be given some money and sent to a neighbouring village.

Shadhi ibn Marwan gave in to her. When I was born, my mother named me Shadhi, to annoy everyone. There my story would have ended, were it not for the fact that, when I was seven years old, my mother's husband died. He had been a good father to me and treated me no differently from his own son, who was a year younger than me.

I have no idea how the news reached Ibn Marwan. All I know is that one day, with his retinue in attendance, he rode into our village and spoke to my mother in private. Allah alone knows what they said to each other. I was too busy admiring the horses and the beautifully coloured saddles.

At the end of their conversation, my mother called me in and hugged me in a tight embrace. She kissed both my eyes while trying to keep the tears out of her own. She told me that, from now on, I was to work in the house of Shadhi ibn Marwan, and to obey him blindly.

I was very upset, and I wept for many months. I missed her greatly. I would go and see her once or twice a year, and she would feed me my favourite cakes, made of maize and sweetened with mountain honey.

It was only when we were leaving Dvin, and moving southwards to Takrit, that I found out about my real father. I had gone to say farewell to my mother. I knew we would never see each other again. She had my brother and his wife and their children, and I knew they loved her and would look after her, but I was still overcome by sadness. As we parted she kissed me on the forehead, and told me everything. I cannot recall how I felt at the time. Long, long ago. I was both pleased and angry.

*

Shadhi's story had confirmed my suspicions, and I was desperate to question him further. Before we could speak, the Sultan had entered, with his two sons by his side. They were introduced to me, but it was obvious that they had come in search of Shadhi. His eyes had lit up on seeing the boys. As he took them away, the Sultan whispered: "Did she?" in my ear. I shook my head, and he burst out laughing.

FIVE

Ibn Maymun's wisdom and his prescriptions

One evening, after two long and exhausting days with the Sultan, I returned home to find Rachel, my wife, in deep conversation with Ibn Maymun. She was registering a set of complaints against me with our great teacher, knowing how much influence and respect he commanded in our household. As I entered the room, I heard her tell him how the amount of time I was spending in the palace was affecting my way of thinking, my character, and my attitude to "less privileged mortals". Most important of all, I was being charged with the neglect of my duties to her and to our family.

"I think this is a case for the Kadi," replied Ibn Maymun, stroking his beard thoughtfully. "Should I transmit your reproach to him, and demand that he punishes Ibn Yakub?"

My laughter annoyed Rachel, and she left the room, her face as hard as the stale bread she had been compelled to serve our unexpected guest. Ibn Maymun was tired. His duties to the Kadi were heavy, given that he lived in Fustat, some two miles distant from the Kadi's palace. He visited him early in the morning, on every day, attending to his needs as well as his children's, and those of the inmates of the harem.

Thus he spent most of the day in Cairo, returning home late every afternoon. Waiting for him was a unique combination of people: Jews and Gentiles; noblemen and peasants; friends and enemies; and young children and their grandfathers. These were his patients. The price of success was that Ibn Maymun was much in demand. The number of his patients increased by the day and, true physician that he was, he could never turn anyone away.

Sometimes, when desperately in need of rest, he would spend the night at our house in the Juderia, a short walk from the palace. Here, he told me, he could enjoy total peace and recover his energy. I apologised to him for Rachel's outburst.

"Be careful, Ibn Yakub. Your wife is a good woman, but her inner strength and her love for you is slowly ebbing away. She will not tolerate your absences for ever. You seem to spend most of your time at the Sultan's palace. Why not tell the Sultan that you need to be with your family on the Sabbath?"

I sighed. I too was feeling weary and worn out that evening.

"I understand you, my friend, but was it not you who recommended me to Salah al-Din? There are times, I admit, when I feel like a prisoner. Yet I would be telling you an untruth if I claimed to be unhappy. The fact is, I like this Sultan. I would like to be riding by his side as we approach the Kingdom of Jerusalem, and I would like to be present when the city falls to our armies, when Jerusalem becomes al-Kuds again, and when we can pray once more in the precincts of the Temple. We buried the sun in Jerusalem. We will meet there again. It would be worth my whole life to see that day. A bright new age is drawing near to our sacred city. I have faith in Salah al-Din. In his own quiet way, after much thought, he will retake Jerusalem."

The sage nodded his head.

"I understand you only too well, but Rachel's needs are no less important than your desire to be part of history. Find a balance. Happiness is like good health. You only miss it when it disappears."

Ibn Maymun retired to bed after our short exchange.

Alone, I reflected on his advice. How best could I preserve a balance between my work and my family? Rachel wanted me to return home to resume my work on the history of our people. That, for her, was far more important than becoming a court scribe.

She did not understand that Ibn Maymun had deliberately turned me away from my own work. He was concerned that my researches would alienate the Rabbis. Fearful of our fragile status in this world, he did not want me to provoke a dispute with our great religious scholars, whose understanding of our past was limited to the scriptures. Ibn Maymun agreed with me that the movement of our people westwards had begun long before the Fall of the Temple or the siege of Masada. We had discussed the subject many times.

As I went out into the courtyard to relieve myself, I was startled by the brightness of the starlit sky. I stood and stared at the stars for a long time. I saw them take different shapes and, heaven help me, I could have sworn that I saw Halima's simple beauty reflected in one glowing cluster. I had become fascinated by Halima. She refused to leave my thoughts. Why had she not shared a meal with me today when Salah al-Din had encouraged her to do so? And why had he encouraged her? Did he regard me as a eunuch? Was she sharing his bed tonight, or had he already drunk his fill and moved on to another oasis?

It was already late, but all these questions continued to torment me as I made my way to our bedchamber. Rachel was awake, but she was still angry. I spoke to her in a tender voice, but she refused to answer my questions. Nor did she submit to my desires. Sleep eluded us both that night. We lay in silence, waiting for the day to break.

Ibn Maymun always began the day by sipping a large cup of warm water. Whenever he stayed with me, I was compelled to observe the same ritual. It cleansed our insides, he insisted, and prepared the body for the shock of the new day. Ibn Maymun's prescriptions were essentially preventative. The secret of his medical success lay in the importance he attached to what we ate – and how much. Eight large cups of water during the winter months, and double that amount during the summer, was essential to good health.

On these matters he was very stern. Debate was discouraged. It was easier to argue with him on the relative merits and demerits of our religion. That did not bother him at all, but he insisted on the sanctity of his medical prescriptions. I could never understand the reason for his firmness. Perhaps it had to do with the fact that he earned his living as a physician. If word had spread that he was unsure of the efficacy of his own treatments, his patients might have taken their custom elsewhere. Yet perhaps not. Patients came to him because they knew his cures were successful.

Now he was busy preparing an ointment for the Kadi. The room began to smell of onions and garlic. To these, he was adding mustard, wormwood, arsenic, crushed bitter almonds and vinegar. I felt sick and rushed immediately to open the door to the courtyard, to let in some fresh air. He smiled.

"Is the Kadi ailing?" I asked him. "Or are you preparing to poison him? The smell alone would send me to an early grave."

"He is not ill, but he is very upset."

"Why?"

"He is beginning to lose his hair. He does not wish to grow completely bald. He may be older than us, but he is still a vain man. Perhaps he has his eye on a young wench."

"If his eye fell on a young girl, she would be offered to him on a tray made of gold. His lack of hair would play no part at all. Leaving all that aside, what good will your stinking concoction do?"

"This ointment will strengthen and thicken the hair that still remains. Who knows, it might even make it grow again."

"Why is the great al-Fadil so concerned? Surely the loss of hair is a sign of great maturity. Not far from where we sit, in days gone by, the ancient priests and kings used to shave their heads to demonstrate their power."

"True. But the Prophet of Islam had a fine crop of hair. He did not like the thought of it turning grey. He insisted on dying it, with a mixture of red anemone and oil of myrtle; or so their traditions tell them."

I was about to challenge this assertion, but the look on his face made it clear that he was not prepared to answer any more questions on the medical treatment he was preparing to rejuvenate our Kadi.

Instead he began to talk of the Kadi's skills as an administrator, his sense of justice, his ability to challenge even the Sultan's decisions and, above everything else, the quality of the advice he offered his ruler.

As we left my house to walk towards the palace, Ibn Maymun took me completely by surprise.

"Answer me truthfully, Ibn Yakub. Has your heart abandoned Rachel?"

I shook my head in vigorous denial. Yet my heart had begun to beat a little bit faster, as if to rebut me. My mind was confused, and I could not speak. He continued to interrogate me.

"Are you sure that the warm, luxuriant braids of a new addition to the Sultan's household have not bewitched you?"

I shook my head again. How could he possibly know about Halima? I had kept my thoughts to myself. I wasn't even sure of my own feelings. How in heaven's name had Ibn Maymun reached this conclusion? For a moment I was too shaken to speak. When I regained my composure, I asked him to explain himself. At first, he shrugged his shoulders and did not reply. I insisted.

"In the course of my work, I have had the opportunity of listening to the problems of many households. What Rachel tells me is not new. It is an old story. She asked me to pray for her. I declined. I told her that to know and to sleep is better than to pray and be ignorant."

"Neither of us slept last night. My conscience is clean. My soul is free of guilt."

"And your heart?"

"It dreams. You understand that well. Is not a world without dreams worse than hell?"

"Talk to her, Ibn Yakub. Talk to Rachel. Share your dreams. Destiny has never permitted our people the taste of too much honey."

We parted.

SIX

Salah al-Din's boyhood memories of Damascus; Shadhi's account of the Sultan's first taste of carnal knowledge

I was told to follow the attendant to the Sultan's bedchamber. He was resting, but sat up on my arrival, leaning against cushions of every shape and description. He gave me a weak smile. His chest was heavy. His throat was sore. I offered to return when he was feeling better, but he shook his head vigorously, insisting that the day must not be wasted.

"Life is short, Ibn Yakub. In times of war Allah can withdraw any of his *ghazis* from this world."

I watched in silence as the attendants prepared his medicine. Ginger had been boiled in water, till the mixture went dark. Salah al-Din sniffed the concoction and turned his face away. The second attendant sweetened the ginger-water with generous amounts of honey. This time the patient scowled, but sipped the mixture slowly. He signalled for the jug to be left behind. The attendants bowed and retired. Even as they left, Shadhi entered the room and felt the Sultan's forehead.

"No fever. Good. Make sure you drink the last drop. A word for you, Ibn Yakub. Limit your presence. He should rest his tongue today."

He left without waiting for the Sultan's response, which was a curse and a smile. He spoke in a hoarse whisper.

I am missing the old city today. Whenever I feel unwell, I am reminded of my tiny room in Damascus. We used to live in a house, not far from the citadel in the western part of the city. As I was lying in bed one day, possessed by a fever which seemed to have been inspired by Satan himself, Shadhi entered my room – just as he did a few moments ago – and felt my forehead. Then he whispered in my ear: "Ibn Ayyub, recover your strength. Recover your strength."

It was his special way of informing me that our family had suffered a loss. I was not in a fit state to understand his message, and I remember having bad dreams that night. By the next morning, the fever had run its course. That same day my father entered my room, to tell me that my grandmother had passed away. I wept loudly and my wrenching sobs must have moved him. It was the only time in my life that my father held me in his arms, and stroked my head with tenderness.

He spoke soothing words. Allah, in his infinite mercy, he told me, had permitted her a long life. She had left this world without regrets. Her last words to her son concerned me. She had, according to my father, scolded him for paying too little attention to me and my future. As he told me all this, he was gently feeling this amulet which you can see resting on my chest.

It was first hung around this neck by my grandmother. Every year she would remove it and lengthen the string, muttering invocations to some unknown gods – I never heard her calling Allah in these special prayers – to make me strong. It is my lucky charm. I cherish it because of her, but it has also become a part of me. Before I join each and every battle, I hold it in my fist and rub it gently across my heart before praying silently to Allah for our success.

It was in Damascus that I became a man. For the first few months I used to yearn for the freedom of Baalbek. Damascus was a city full of dangers. Not a day went by when we did not receive news of someone important or someone close to someone important being assassinated.

My father's instincts had, as usual, served him well. The atabeg of Damascus had placed him in charge of the citadel. My father was responsible for the defence of the town. His sudden rise to power had made him enemies. The local notables, many of whom claimed descent from the first Believers in Allah and his Prophet, were openly hostile and regarded all of us with contempt. For them my father and my uncle Shirkuh were nothing but Kurdish adventurers, clever opportunists who sold their services and their souls to the highest bidder. It is difficult to deny that their disdain concealed an element of truth.

At the time of our arrival, Damascus was governed by the atabeg Muin al-Din Unur. It was he who, tiring of the growing factionalism amongst his commanders, had asked my father to reorganise the defences of the city. Unur was an enemy of the Sultan Zengi and his son, Nur al-Din. My uncle Shirkuh was a military commander working directly under Nur al-Din. If I had been a Turcoman loyal to Unur and his master, Abak, I, too, would have been more than a little nervous. After all, it was hardly a secret that ours was a close-knit clan. My father and his brother, far from being enemies, were as close to each other as the handle to the sword. Unur, however, trusted my father. On his deathbed, or so we were told, he advised the Sultan Abak to retain my father's services.

Abak was not totally convinced. He was a weak man, much given to wine and women, and easily swayed by unscrupulous advisers. Though in this case, I must confess, their worries were not without foundation. If Nur al-Din attacked Damascus, would my father take up arms against an army led by his brother Shirkuh? This was the question that bothered them day and night.

My father was adept at wearing a mask. He was a great courtier, in the sense that he listened attentively and said very little. When Abak apprised him of what was being said, my father smiled and told him: "Perhaps they are right to suspect my loyalty. You are the sole judge. To this day I have never spoken an untruth. If my presence worries you, I will leave with my family tomorrow. Just speak the command."

The supreme ruler of Damascus chose to retain my father's services. It was a mistake that cost him his throne, but it united the Believers and brought closer the day when we would reclaim our lands from the Franj.

I know what you're thinking, Ibn Yakub. You're wondering what would have happened if we had been expelled from Damascus. I have little doubt that the end result would have been the same, but only after the spilling of much blood. My father's actions were not solely determined by the needs of his family. Those wars in which Believer fought against Believer were truly repugnant to him.

The effect of all these rivalries was to limit our freedom. We were not permitted to ride alone. We were barred from exploring the city after dark. We were warned never to enter the wine-cellars. My father threatened to flog us in public if we violated this last injunction.

It was the forced company which drove me to playing *chogan*. Given that my brother al-Adil and I had several guards, we decided to make use of them. Every day we would ride out of the Bab-al-Djabiya at sunrise. First the soldiers would perform their duty and teach us the art of swordsmanship. Then, after a short rest and some refreshments, we were shown how to fight on horseback. At the end of our training session, we entertained ourselves by teaching the soldiers how to play *chogan*.

It is a strange fact, is it not, Ibn Yakub, that the more one exerts oneself, the less tired one gets? After riding for two hours, I could easily ride the whole day. Yet on days when it was not possible to leave the house, I felt listless and exhausted, just like today. My physicians praise Allah and tell me that it is all to do with how the blood flows through the body, but do they really know?

The Sultan fell silent. Assuming that he was deep in thought, I made some small corrections to the text, but when, quill poised, I looked up at him to resume our work, his eye was firmly closed. He was fast asleep.

I have not previously drawn attention to the fact that Salah al-Din ibn Ayyub was possessed of only one working eye. He had not yet told me of how he lost the other, and Ibn Maymun had warned me that this was an extremely touchy subject. Under no circumstances should I raise it myself. Being a disciplined scribe, I had cast all curiosity out of my mind. To tell the truth, I had become used to his infirmity, and rarely gave it much thought. Yet seeing him like this, fast asleep, with his bad eye wide open, created the impression that he was half-awake, an All-Seeing Sultan.

It gave me a strange sensation. I wanted to know how and when he had lost his eye. Was it a childhood accident? If so, who had been responsible? How did it affect his bearing in war? My mind was flooded by questions.

How long I would have sat there, gazing on the sleeping Sultan, I do not know. A gentle tap on my shoulder alerted me to the presence of the ubiquitous Shadhi. He placed a finger on his lip to demand silence, and indicated that I follow him out of the chamber.

As we sat in the courtyard, enjoying the winter sun, dipping bread in *labineh* and munching radishes and onions, I asked Shadhi about the eye. He smiled, but did not reply. I persisted.

"Salah al-Din will tell you himself. It is the one subject we never discuss."

"Why not?"

No reply was forthcoming from the old man. Instead he wiped the yoghurt off his drooping moustache and belched. Perhaps, I thought to myself, he is in a bad mood. Something has upset him. But I was wrong. It was only the forbidden subject of the missing eye that had silenced him.

He asked me whether Ayyub and his family had reached Dimask in the chronicles I was transcribing. I nodded.

"Then," he said with a lascivious smile, "the Sultan has told you of his youthful escapades?"

"Not yet."

"Not yet, not yet!" he mimicked me and roared with laughter. "He will never tell you. The memory of great men is always faulty. They forget their past so easily, but fortunately for you, my good scribe, Shadhi is still alive. Let us first eat some lamb, and then I will tell you tales of Damascus which our great Sultan will never remember again."

After we had finished our meal, the old man began to speak.

"I won't bore you with stories of our first visits to the Umayyad mosque, where the great Caliphs preached the Friday sermon and where long ago the congregation trembled in silent rage as Muawiya held up the bloodstained shirt of the murdered Caliph Uthman. I will leave all that to the Sultan."

Shadhi laughed loudly, as if what he had just told me was an almighty joke. He was given to laughing a great deal at his own remarks, something to which I was now accustomed, yet it never failed to irritate me. Outwardly I smiled and nodded politely, to neutralise the intense gaze to which I was subjected following such outbursts. After drinking another cup of buttermilk, and noisily wiping the residue off his lips and moustache, he began again to tell his story.

"It was a hot summer afternoon. Everybody was resting. Your Sultan was fourteen years of age, perhaps not quite fourteen. Taking advantage of the hot weather, he defied his father's instructions and went to the stables. He found his favourite horse, mounted it bare-backed, and left the city all on his own. It was foolish of him to imagine that he could leave the gates without being recognised. Dangerous, too, since his father had enemies in the city. But who can restrain the wildness of youth?

"The guards stationed at the gate were intrigued. They knew that the children of Ayyub were not usually seen out on their own. One of them rushed to the house and reported his departure immediately. Ayyub was woken up and informed of what had taken place. Curiously, he appeared pleased rather than angered by his son's disobedience. I saw him smile.

"He asked me to ride after Salah al-Din, but without any trace of panic. My instructions were to follow him, to observe where he went, but to keep a careful distance. In other words I was to be a spy. Naturally, I did as I was asked.

"It was not difficult to pick up his trail. Just outside the Bab al-Djabiya, as you will see when the Sultan takes you with him, there is a very large maidan, bisected by a river. When you stand on the ramparts of the citadel, the light of the setting sun can play strange tricks with your eyes. The *maidan* becomes a giant green carpet made from the finest silks. It was here that Salah al-Din and his brothers played *chogan*. It was here that they raced horses and learnt to wield the sword and the bow and arrow. The river is surrounded by a large grove of poplar trees.

"In the distance I could see him galloping ahead, his head uncovered and without any protection. I saw him rein in his horse and dismount. I did the same and tied my horse to a tree. Then I walked towards the boy, making sure he did not see me. Soon I had found a suitable position behind some bushes, and there I could observe him quite clearly without being seen in return. You're getting impatient with this old fool, Ibn Yakub, but I'm almost there.

"Salah al-Din had taken off his clothes and jumped into the river. He was swimming first with the flow and then against it. I laughed to myself. What a strange boy. Why had he not told us that all he wanted was a swim? Some guards would have come and kept watch till he had finished. End of story.

"I was about to walk to the bank and hail him, when suddenly I saw a woman who must also have been watching him walk towards where he had left his clothes. She picked them up and folded them. Then she sat and waited for him to finish. He swam to the shore and said something to her. I couldn't hear the words since, on glimpsing the woman, I had once again taken my distance. She was laughing and shaking her head. He was insisting. Suddenly she jumped up, discarded her clothes and jumped in with him.

"She was a mature woman, Ibn Yakub, at least twice the age of the boy. The rest you can imagine. When they had finished their swim, they dried them-selves in the sun, and then that sorceress mounted our boy and taught him what it was like to be a man. Allah be praised, Ibn Yakub, but they were shameless. There underneath the clear blue sky, under the gaze of Allah in his heaven, they were behaving like animals.

"I waited patiently, making a mental note of everything as I had been ordered to do by the master. She left first. She just seemed to disappear. He lay there for a few moments and then dressed himself. At this stage, as you can imagine, I was tempted to declare my presence. This would have been my revenge for that episode in Baalbek, but I had my orders. I rode back to the city, not waiting for young Salah al-Din to regain his composure. Back at the house, I reassured his father that all was well.

"Ayyub, may he rest in peace, wanted to know everything. Happily, I was in a position to supply him with each and every detail. I have given you a very short version, O learned scribe, but at that time it was all fresh in my mind.

"Ayyub, to my great surprise, clapped his hands and exploded with laughter. Perhaps he was relieved that it was a wench, rather than one of his soldiers or a young mare! His severe face returned as he threatened me with a terrible fate if even a word of what had transpired ever found its way to Salah al-Din.

"It was difficult for me to remain silent. I had always felt close to the boy and, in different circumstances, this tongue of mine would have defied the instructions. But there was something in Ayyub's tone that warned me against disregarding his injunction. Despite the strong temptation, I obeyed him."

"You mean," I asked, "that to this day the Sultan is unaware of what happened? Can this be possible?"

Shadhi grinned, and picked his nose.

"I waited for the right moment. I told him on his wedding night. He was in a cheerful mood, and he laughed, but I should have known him better. A month later, when I thought he had forgotten the whole business, he asked me for an explanation. His face was stern. I told him. He expressed surprise that neither of his parents had ever raised the matter with him. I shrugged my shoulders. That was hardly my responsibility."

SEVEN

The Spring Festival in Cairo; an erotic shadow-play in the Turcoman quarter

Weeks passed. It was no longer winter, yet the spring had not yet begun. I had still received no word from Halima, and the intoxication was beginning to lose its effect. On Ibn Maymun's advice, I had stopped tormenting my own heart by yearning for her. I had not seen him now for many days. At home, Rachel had recovered her good spirits. Our lives had adjusted to a new routine.

In the palace, the Sultan was busy with his most trusted family members, discussing his strategy for liberating al-Kuds. This was the only time I was denied entrance to his council chamber. The deliberations in which he was engaged were not intended for ordinary ears. These were truly confidential talks. An indiscretion or a thoughtless boast, the Sultan always used to say, could cost our side an entire army and set back our cause for decades. Yet it would be dishonest of me to pretend that I was not upset. I thought of myself as someone in the total trust of his ruler. The Sultan must have noticed this, for he tried to soothe my hurt pride.

"Ibn Yakub, what you are writing is known to me, the Kadi and three other people. If I were to permit you to attend our military council, everyone would know who you are and this would be dangerous. One of my brothers or nephews might think that you hold the secret to my succession. They might torture or kill you, and then forge documents claiming whatever they wish people to believe. Do you understand?"

I nodded and bowed my head, acknowledging the truth in the words he had spoken.

The Cairenes greeted the early morning mists of spring as they had done for hundreds of years. The city was taken over by its people. All were equal on that first day of spring. In the schools and colleges, the students either stayed away, in preparation for the late-afternoon festivities, or came and kidnapped their teachers, holding them prisoner till a ransom was paid. The money was spent on food and wine, freely distributed to the poor throughout the day.

I had avoided the streets for the last few years, in fact, ever since some revellers had thrown Rachel into a fountain, the better to see her breasts through her soaked clothes. Her objections had been mild compared to mine, but this year I was determined to spend the whole day in the company of the common people. Who would be the object of their humour this year? For the last three years they had targeted the Kadi al-Fadil, laughing at his poetry, mocking his pomposity, and cruelly mimicking his courtroom manners.

Ibn Maymun, who never missed a festival, admitted that the mock trial of a donkey, accused of pissing on a preacher, had made him laugh aloud. The student acting the part of the Kadi had heard the arguments, questioned the donkey and then pronounced his judgement. The donkey was to be publicly humiliated. His penis was to be sliced into five portions, arranged on a platter, and served to the preacher it had insulted. Furthermore the donkey was to be forced to bray in public, at least five times every day. When asked whether he accepted the verdict, the donkey emitted a loud fart.

"Their thoughts and actions are by no means lofty," Ibn Maymun had told me on that occasion, "but only a deaf and blind person could deny that they are hugely popular."

Rachel and I went to where the big procession was due to assemble. This year the youths were all wearing thin beards as they laughed and joked on the streets. Snake-charmers and jugglers were competing for attention with acrobats and contortionists and conjurors. There were spellbound children everywhere, their innocent laughter bringing a smile of joy to the face of even the most cynical adult.

We bought leopard masks and had barely managed to cover our faces when we were surrounded by other masked leopards of all sizes. We began to exchange greetings, when one of them suddenly extended his arms and began to feel Rachel's breasts. She slapped the offending hands, and the masked offender ran away.

Who would be elected the Emir of the Spring Festival? It was Rachel who first noticed the candidates for the "Emir". A young man climbed a wall of shoulders and began to introduce the choices. As each one was paraded, the crowd made its preference clear. The transvestite attired as a dancing girl, with exaggerated make-up and water-melons masquerading as breasts, was declared the Emir by loud acclaim. He was led to the ceremonial mule, painted red, yellow and purple for the occasion, with green encircling its posterior.

The Emir of the festival, holding a fan in one hand, mounted the animal, and the whole crowd, including Rachel and myself, began to sing and dance. The Emir fanned himself in an exaggerated fashion, anticipating the summer to come. Four naked men, their private parts covered by a *mi'zar*, and their bodies smeared all over with a white fluid, suddenly emerged from the heart of the crowd. They were loudly cheered.

Two of them carried bits of ice and jugs of cold water and drenched the Emir. The other two rushed up and fed him a bowl of warm soup. They put a blanket round his shoulders to drive away the cold.

The ceremony over, the four naked men took their places in front of the ceremonial mule and began to fart, each attempting to better the performance of the one who preceded him. There was total silence as we strained our ears to capture the rough music of these gifted farters. Such musical farting was a much-appreciated accomplishment on these occasions, and the final crescendo, performed in unison, won much applause and laughter. Their performance proved strangely infectious, and those of less advanced years attempted to mimic the masters of the art for the rest of the afternoon. Mercifully their success was limited, and we did not have to pray to Allah to send us a breeze from heaven to cleanse the air.

At last the procession began to move. Its pace was slow, deliberately slow. It gave the participants time and opportunity to purchase and consume small flasks of wine from wayside vendors. We were winding our way to the large square outside the Sultan's palace. Would he appear and greet the crowd? This was the first time he had been physically present in Cairo during the Festival.

In previous years the Kadi al-Fadil had made a token appearance, to be greeted by a display of a thousand phalluses. The Kadi had quickly retreated, and refused to address the common people. This year, with the Sultan in the city, the Kadi was taking no risks. He could not afford to let the Festival degenerate into an orgy. His inspectors had appeared on the streets the previous night, accompanied by the criers, shouting out a warning: all obscene displays would be severely punished. The response of the people was equally severe. A transvestite had been picked to be the Emir.

When we reached the square outside the palace, the noise had subsided. It was as if everyone simultaneously had felt the Sultan's presence. He was seated on his horse, surrounded by his personal bodyguards. As our Emir approached, Salah al-Din rode forward to meet him. Words were exchanged between them, but only the transvestite heard them. A hundred different versions were circulating later that afternoon. The Sultan was seen to smile. Then he rode back into the palace.

The revelry would continue late into the night, but many of us, exhausted and hungry, began to make our way home as the sun began to set. Rachel and I had removed our masks. We were buying some wine to take home when a face I thought I recognised approached, bent over my ear and whispered.

"Ibn Yakub, if you want to see some real fun tonight, go to the Turcoman quarter, just behind al-Azhar. Don't go to the Bab al-Zuweyla this year. The shadow-plays will be something unusual."

Before I could reply, the man had disappeared. Why was his face so familiar? Where had I seen him before? My inability to place him began to irritate me. Then, while we were eating our evening meal, I remembered who he was, and the memory made me gasp. He was one of the eunuchs, Ilmas by name, who worked in the harem. I had seen him, on occasion, talking to Shadhi and whispering in the Sultan's ear. He must be a spy sent to observe the shadow-players, and to report on each of their performances. He had spoken to me conspiratorially, but was his whispered message in reality an order from the Sultan? Usually the players performed just outside the Bab al-Zuweyla. Was the eunuch Ilmas trying to keep me away from something? I gave up and decided to follow his advice.

The festivities were approaching a natural climax as I walked back through the maze of lamplit streets to the Bab al-Zuweyla. Reassured by the fact that nothing unusual was taking place there, I walked on till I had reached the Turcoman quarter. The square was lit by lamps, and people were drinking and eating as they discussed the events of the day.

Salah al-Din, according to the gossips in this quarter, had complimented the "Emir" on his eye make-up, and asked whether he and his friends would come and celebrate the impending liberation of al-Kuds. At this critical point, our transvestite leader had evidently lost his tongue and simply nodded like a child in the presence of a magician.

The odour of hashish, not at all unpleasant, wafted by me at several points. At a distance I could see a large gauze cloth, behind which the shadows of the musicians and the actors could be seen preparing for the first of the evening's performances.

The play began at midnight. It was the story of a beautiful girl, surprised with her lover by an angry husband. The anguished crowd sighed with sympathy as the lover was slain and the woman dragged away by her husband.

During the interval, the fate of the woman was the only subject of discussion. Angry debates shook the square. Should the husband have killed her as well? Why had he killed the lover when it was his wife's fault in the first place? Why kill anyone? Love was sublime and no laws, Allah be praised, could prevent the attraction of one person for another.

As the evening progressed, I realised that what we were watching was no ordinary tale. I seemed to know all these characters – or was my imagination at work, seeing parallels where there were none? The emotional tension in the square indicated that I was not the only one to have noticed a degree of coincidence.

The second part of the performance removed all my doubts. The husband was sentenced to a public flogging at the Bab al-Zuweyla, and the errant wife was sent to a lame preacher, blind in one eye. The preacher, instead of offering her spiritual sustenance, soon seduced her, and at this point the curtain began violently shaking. A shadow-copulation began, with a cucumber symbolising the preacher's penis and a gourd his victim's vagina.

On most occasions, when these plays reach their bawdy climax the audience joins in with unrestrained laughter and slow claps, but not tonight. With entry effected, the musicians began to hum a dirge. This union, they were telling us, was not a joyous one.

The atmosphere during the second interval was more restrained. People spoke in whispers. Misfortunes like this were common in the town, but it was obvious to everyone that the half-blind preacher was a barely disguised version of the Sultan. That was why Ilmas, the eunuch, had wanted me to come here tonight. Was this Halima's revenge? I felt a hand on my shoulder, and turned to confront the grinning visage of Ilmas.

"How did our great scholar find the play?"

"Who wrote it, Ilmas? Who?"

"Can't you guess?"

I shook my head.

"I think," he whispered, "the authorship will be obvious before the performance concludes."

There was something in the way he spoke that sent a chill through my body. Instinctively I felt that I should leave at this point, and not stay till the end. I was curious to see how it would end, but I was also fearful.

The Sultan trusted me. If he found out that I had been present at this occasion, but had not provided him with a detailed account, he might question my loyalty. If I stayed till the end, I would have to tell the Sultan. If I left now, it would be proof enough that I had a low regard for the play and did not believe it merited any special report.

I nodded a farewell to Ilmas, who could not conceal his surprise, and began to walk away.

EIGHT

The story of the sheikh who, in order to keep his lover at home with him, forces his sister into marriage with the man, and the disastrous consequences for all three

"You had better proceed immediately to the audience chamber, Ibn Yakub. The Sultan has been waiting for you and he is not in good spirits this morning."

Shadhi's tone worried me, but from his eyes I learnt nothing. Perhaps it was my now waning guilt at having attended the shadow-play. I had misinterpreted his voice.

The Sultan was indeed looking stern, but he was not alone. The Kadi al-Fadil was seated in front of him. Both men smiled as I entered the chamber. That, at least, was reassuring. I bowed and took my place, just below the Sultan's throne.

"Peace be upon you, Ibn Yakub," said the Sultan. "I'm glad you did not stay for the final act of the performance in the Turcoman quarter last night. Al-Fadil and I were admiring your good taste and judgement."

The Kadi aimed his stern gaze straight at me. I did not avert my eyes. He smiled with his lips, but his eyes remained hard.

"The eunuch who betrayed the Sultan's trust was executed early this morning.

If you take a walk this evening you will see how his head decorates the Bab al-Zuweyla."

I nodded my head in appreciation. Should I ask them why the foolish Ilmas had decided on the course which had led to his beheading, or was it better to remain silent? Curiosity triumphed. I looked at al-Fadil.

"Why did the eunuch Ilmas decide . . .?"

"The answer lies in the play. He was in love with the red-haired temptress. She had rebuffed him several times. The only way to possess her was in his imagination."

"Enough!" said Salah al-Din with a frown. "We have more important matters to discuss. Begin, al-Fadil, and prepare to write, scribe."

The Kadi raised his glass of lukewarm mint tea to his lips, draining it in a single gulp as if he needed extra strength. Al-Fadil was not a well man. Ibn Maymun had told me that his diet was unhealthy. His weight was too heavy for a man his size, and he suffered from swollen knees. Today, as he spoke, he paused frequently to regain his breath.

"A few days ago, a young woman, not yet twenty, was handed over to one of my inspectors by her husband's father, and charged with adultery. The young woman admitted that she had a lover, but she insisted that the reason she had found one was because her husband refused to consummate their marriage. According to our laws, that is no justification for adultery. Hence I had no option but to sentence both the girl and her lover to be stoned to death.

"She is the younger sister of Sayed al-Bukhari, one of our most respected and venerable sheikhs. It is a story, Commander of the Valiant, that fills my heart with sadness. The final decision rests with you. The sheikh al-Bukhari awaits your decision. I took the liberty of bringing him with me. It is best that you hear the story from his lips rather than mine. His words will carry greater weight if spoken by him. What is the Sultan's pleasure?"

Salah al-Din remained silent. He was thinking. What could he be thinking? Probably making up his mind whether this affair was best handled by the Kadi, so that it was al-Fadil who took the blame for what might not be a popular decision.

"Send for al-Bukhari. We will hear his case."

A few minutes later, a tall, well-built man, too proud to dye his white hair, was brought to the chamber. He fell on his knees and touched the Sultan's feet with his head.

"I am sorry we meet in these conditions, al-Bukhari," said the Sultan, in a remarkably soft voice. "I remember well your presence at our evening discussions several years ago. I valued what you said then, and it is for that reason that I have agreed to hear your story myself. Explain to me why your sister should not be punished, as our merciful Kadi has decreed."

The sheikh looked at his ruler gratefully. A sad smile appeared on his face as he began his story.

"If anyone should be punished, O merciful Sultan, it is not my unfortunate sister, but me.

"I alone am to blame for the terrible misfortune that has befallen her.

"Some five years ago, a mysterious visitor entered the crowded room where I used to provide my interpretation and commentaries on the *hadith* that were written down by my great forebear. May Allah forgive me, for I had no idea that I was about to dishonour my ancestor.

"The new arrival attracted the attention of all those who were present. He was a young man with striking features. His sparkling grey eyes illuminated his pale face. His hair was the colour of wheat. A silent question appeared on the faces of the Believers. Who was he?

"He had come to Cairo as a child, on a trading vessel from the land of the Franj. His father, a merchant from Genoa, had died suddenly. The sailors on the ship refused to accept any responsibility. It was bad luck to sail with an orphan. The superstitions of these people were primitive. The boy, who was seven or eight years at the time, was adopted by a merchant in the street of sword-sellers. This man's first wife, who was childless, lavished great care on the boy and he grew up, Allah be praised, as one of the sons of the family. Naturally he had to be circumcised, and his new family obtained the services of Your Excellency's own barber, Abu Daniyal, to perform the rites.

"They called him Jibril, which pleased him greatly since it was the original version of the name that he had been given on birth – Gabriel. Once he spoke our language, his adoptive mother often talked to him of his real mother and his sisters, whom he missed greatly. They promised him that when he grew up they would ensure his return to Genoa. The education he received was so refined that soon it became difficult to say that he had ever been anything else but one of us.

"He grew up to be an extremely intelligent logician, much attracted to the writings of our friends in Andalus. It was his interest in logic that caused his friends to send him to my lectures. They thought I might cure him of his addiction to heresy. Indeed I might have done, but for the fact that he was a very beautiful young man. His sudden arrival had unsettled me.

"He would arrive twice a week and sit at my feet, drinking in every word I uttered with his shining, attentive, but always questioning eyes. Was it just my imagination, or did I, on occasion, catch a glimpse of torment in those grey eyes?

"At the end of my talk, while others asked polite questions to help me elaborate on certain points, this young Jibril would question me in such a way that to even reply to him would have demolished the architecture of my thought.

"One day, they all came late to my class. When they arrived, I was stunned. They were intoxicated, and Jibril was completely naked. His colleagues were laughing, but he did not seem to understand that he was the cause of their mirth. When I asked him to explain himself, he replied that they had all tried to sharpen their memories by drinking a strong dose of a fermented infusion of cashew-nuts. The others, he continued, had lost control of their wits. He alone had remained sane. I covered him with a sheet and put him to bed.

"I cannot lie to the Sultan or his great Kadi. I must confess that I was bewitched by the demeanour of this young man. When he was present, I spoke as if he was the only one in the room.

"I was in the grip of the old disease brought to our world by the idol-worshipping Yunanis and the accursed Rumis. Jibril, through no fault of his own, became the fountain of all my misery. His absences gave me the most unbearable headaches. I would fall on my knees and pray: 'Ya Allah, why are you punishing your slave in this cruel fashion?'

"One day he came when I was alone in the house. My face must have expressed all the emotions that my heart was trying to repress. He reacted well, and declared his feelings for me. May Allah forgive me, but we became lovers. The flowering of his passion aroused me in such a way that I was transported to the sixth heaven. We had tasted the forbidden fruits. Our conscience had become a fathomless abyss. Nothing else mattered any longer.

"I see from the face of our venerable Kadi that my frankness is only arousing feelings of disgust. I will not continue in this vein much longer.

"I am what I am, but I am still one of you. Please try and understand.

"Soon I could not bear to be without him. I began to think of how I could live with Jibril forever. The idea came to me one day when I saw him talking to my sister. She is a beautiful girl, and it was clear to me that her feelings for Jibril were no different to mine. Why should he not marry her? Then he could live in our house quite openly, without fear of cruel tongues. To tell you the truth, I would not have even objected to sharing him with my sister.

"Jibril accepted the plan. The wedding took place. He moved in to our house, but from the very first week it was obvious that my sister was unhappy. Jibril gave her cold comfort. He felt no attraction for women. Not even a tiny spark. Therein lay the real cause of this tragedy. My sister took a lover. Jibril and I enjoyed much happiness.

"We lived just for ourselves. Our selfishness, instead of receding, grew by the hour. Nothing seemed to affect us. The khamsin would blow sand in our hair. Our throats would become parched. Stars would chase each other in the night sky. My sister would sit quietly, gazing patiently at the window, waiting for the next message from her lover. Autumn came and went, followed by a rainy winter. We never felt the night cold. The barking of stray dogs never disturbed our peace. He knew how to love and he taught me the virtues of submissive tenderness.

"It was only when the merciful Kadi, may Allah give him inner strength, sent for me one morning that my heart was seriously troubled. The rest you know.

"I place my head at your feet, Commander of the Merciful. Do with it what-soever you wish, and I will accept whatever punishment you decree, but, in the name of Allah, I plead with you to spare my sister further humiliation. She has suffered enough for my sins."

The Sultan stared at the ground in silence. He had appeared to be moved by the intensity of the love described by the sheikh. The Kadi and I looked at each other. How would he decide this particular case? Would he ask to see Jibril and keep him as an attendant at the palace?

"One thing is clear to me, Sayed al-Bukhari. Your sister deserves no punish-ment. Al-Fadil will make sure that she is freed today. The Kadi will also make sure that the man she loves will marry her in the sight of Allah and with his blessing. As for you and Jibril, this is a more difficult decision. As a scholar, per-haps you could give me some help. Is there anything in the *hadith* that could help me decide your case? I have studied most of the *hadith* myself, and I cannot think of any precedents in this regard.

"While you give my request further thought, and consult other scholars, I think the time has come for Jibril's family to honour their pledge to him and send him on a journey to his place of birth. Let him meet his sisters. And let it be a long absence. Is my meaning clear?"

Our bearded scholar had come to the palace determined to save his sister from the stone-throwers. He had come fully expecting to sacrifice his own head and possibly even that of his young lover. As he realised that the Sultan had, in effect, pardoned him, tears of gratitude slid down his cheeks like a torrent, drenching his beard. He bent down and kissed Salah al-Din's feet.

After the departure of the bearded scholar, a man much relieved, none of us spoke. It was time for the midday repast and I rose to take my leave. To my surprise, the Sultan asked me to stay and eat with him and al-Fadil.

We walked out of the cool semi-darkness of the audience chamber into a blinding sun and a gust of hot wind, harbingers of the miseries that lay ahead. The Cairo summer was not far away.

We entered the eating room to be greeted by Afdal, the oldest son of the Sultan. He rushed forward to embrace his father, before bowing to the Kadi and me. Salah al-Din put on a stern face.

"Why did you not go riding today?"

"I was fast asleep. The others left without me."

"That is not the story I heard. I was told that when Shadhi and Othman came to arouse you, all they got was a shower of abuse. True or false?"

Afdal started laughing.

"True and false. Othman tried to wake me up by pouring cold water on my head, while Shadhi stood behind him and bared his gums. In these circumstances, Abu, it was difficult for me either to restrain my tongue or to go riding with them."

The alert eyes of the twelve-year-old were sparkling with mischief. Afdal looked straight at his father to determine the reaction. Salah al-Din smiled and stroked the boy's head.

"This evening you will ride with me to the citadel."

"When will it be finished, Abu?"

"When I am dead and, Allah permitting, you sit in my place. You will celebrate its completion. Do you understand?"

Afdal's face clouded. He clutched his father's hand and nodded. The Sultan hugged and gently guided him out of the room.

The food laid on the floor before us could by no means be described as a feast.

The Sultan's austere tastes were highly praised by the people, since the contrasts with the Caliphs in Baghdad or his predecessors in Cairo could not have been more pronounced. This admiration was not universally shared. The Sultan's household and his brother al-Adil in particular, mocked his simplicity and often declined to eat with him. He ate only one full meal a day, and that was in the evening.

We were served some wheat bread to dip in a modest bean stew, a plate full of fresh cucumbers, onions, garlic and ginger, and nothing else. The Kadi suffered from chronic indigestion and, on Ibn Maymun's instructions, was not permitted to eat beans. These, as is well known, only served to exacerbate his problem. While the Sultan and I ate the stew with relish, the Kadi broke some bread, nibbled a cucumber, and drank a glass of tamarind juice.

As we ate, it became obvious that the Kadi was somewhat displeased. The Sultan asked him if it was the lack of variety in the food which upset him.

"The Sultan knows that I am under the medical instructions of Ibn Maymun. He has prescribed a very strict diet and obliges me to reduce the amount of food I eat. No, it is not the food that worries me, but Your Highness's excessive generosity."

The Kadi was unhappy with the pardoning of Sayed al-Bukhari. He felt it established an unfortunate precedent. The Sultan heard his complaint in silence. The table was cleared and a large bowl of fruit was placed before us. The Sultan had still not replied, and none of us spoke. The Kadi felt the weight of the silence. He bowed and took his leave. The minute he had left the room, Salah al-Din roared with laughter.

"I have come to know all his tricks. He's not worried about al-Bukhari. In fact he is pleased with our decision. Did you know, Ibn Yakub, that al-Fadil often attended al-Bukhari's lectures? He was close to him. But if people complain that the sheikh was let off too lightly, the Kadi will sigh, agree with his interlocutors, and tell them that the problem is our Sultan. There are times when he is too soft-hearted. He will also insist that the next case is dealt with severely so that our authority is reaffirmed.

"Now tell me something, Ibn Yakub, and speak the truth. Was the food we have just consumed sufficient or would you have preferred, as is your wont, to compete with Shadhi as to which of you can bite more meat off a leg of lamb? Speak the truth!"

I decided to lie.

"It was more than sufficient, Commander of the Generous. It was a meal which could have been prepared by Ibn Maymun himself. The only function of food, in his eyes, is to keep us healthy in mind and body. When he stays with us, my wife never serves meat."

Salah al-Din smiled.

NINE

The young Salah al-Din is abandoned by his mistress for an older man and gets drunk in the tavern; his uncle Shirkuh decides to divert him by taking him on a short mission to conquer Egypt; Salah al-Din becomes the Vizir at the court of the Fatimid Caliph

I did not want to leave Damascus. Can you believe that, Ibn Yakub? I had grown to love the city. Despite my father's injunctions to the contrary I had explored every quarter and every street, usually on my own, but sometimes with my brother. We used to pay a few street-pedlars to sell us their clothes. This simple disguise was our armour against most would-be assassins. In this fashion I wandered the city at will.

On a summer's night I have seen the full moon light up the dome of the Umayyad mosque. I have watched bare-footed labourers carrying bricks on planks, precariously perched on their heads. They might have been building a five-storied house for some merchant or other. I loved throwing stones in those ancient ditches outside the old walls of Damascus. And I have seen women with translucent eyes, the colour of sea-water, bought and sold for bagfuls of dinars in the market-place. I am attached to Cairo, but make no mistake, Damascus is the heart of our world. Its fears and worries have become mine.

Till now, Baalbek had been my favourite home, but it was displaced, and you know precisely why, don't you, my good scribe? Shadhi told you of my first love. You look embarrassed. It was better left to him than me. My own memory is now hazy. What I remember well is the day she left me, not because of the parting, but because something much more important than our puny lives was taking place outside the city walls.

She was a woman some ten years older than me, possibly more. She gave me great pleasure and taught me how to enjoy a woman's body. One day we had arranged to meet just after sunrise, but when I rode to the glade by the river she was not there. I waited and waited. Still no sign of her. I was about to leave when she arrived, out of breath and with a puffy face. She had been crying. I realised that this idyll, too, had come to an end. She kissed my cheeks and then my eyes. She had found a man closer to her own age and, by contrast, I must have seemed a bit dull.

Naturally, I was upset, but what could I do to ease my pain? I could not discuss the matter with anyone because, in the dream-world that I inhabited at that age, I thought nobody else knew. It was our secret.

So I rode back to Damascus in a jealous rage, weeping tears of anger and of sadness. So preoccupied was I that I did not notice anything. I went home and changed, and dragged my brother out of bed. We went to the only tavern in the city which opened before the midday meal. It was run by Armenians in the Christian quarter. Not only did they ask no questions, they also served some of the best wine in Damascus. This was not brought by traders from the lands of the Franj, but made from Taif grapes, grown in the mountain vineyards in the highlands just above Mecca. It is said that the wine of Taif is so potent that it can transform dwarves into giants.

When Adil and I arrived, the tavern was virtually empty. A few eunuchs who had come to recover after a hard night somewhere in the city were too intoxicated to bother about us.

We began to drink the wine which is forbidden by our Holy Book. Adil could see that I was upset, but dared not ask the reason. He stole occasional glances at me, and would press my arm to comfort me. He knew. It was instinct, just as I knew that he went to male brothels and had set his heart on a young flute-player. He may not have known the exact reason for my sadness, but he could tell I was nursing a wounded heart.

Slowly the wine took its effect. The serving-woman carrying the flasks began to change shape in front of my eyes. Was it a gazelle? I became blind to the world outside. Soon we were singing impromptu songs about women who betrayed their lovers, about the lover's revenge and the kadi's displeasure. Food was placed before us and we ate without knowing what it was that we were eating. Then we sang some more, and this time the eunuchs joined us. I cannot recall now how long we were there, but I can remember Shadhi, my guardian angel Shadhi, shaking me firmly by the arm to wake me up. If I shut my eyes I can still see his worried face, and hear his voice whispering: "Yusuf Salah al-Din. Yusuf Salah al-Din. Time to come home."

The thought still makes me shiver with shame. You know why, Ibn Yakub? That was the day that our great Sultan of Aleppo, Nur al-Din, the oldest son of the slain warrior, Zengi, was outside the gates of Damascus. He wanted to take the city, and at his side was my uncle Shirkuh. Inside, commanding the armies of his enemies, the rulers of Damascus, was my father Ayyub.

My uncle had sent a secret messenger two weeks prior to that day to alert my father. Both men knew they would never fight against each other. My father's main concern, as always, was to avoid bloodshed. He negotiated a settlement acceptable to the ruler of Damascus. No blood stained our streets that day. Nur al-Din took the city unopposed. All this took place while I was in my cups, feeling sorry for myself.

I arrived in time to see Shirkuh hugging my father on the ramparts of the citadel. At first I thought it was an apparition, but then my uncle lifted me off the ground. He hugged me with such force that my stomach turned and the Taif wine let me down badly. I vomited at his feet. All I can remember is the horrified look on my father's face, and Shadhi's roar of laughter.

Nur al-Din was the first ruler who had a plan for uniting the Believers and driving out the Franj. He believed that until there was one Caliph as the fount of all authority, the Franj would always play on our weaknesses and rivalries. Nur al-Din could not have been more unlike his illustrious father, Zengi. Where Zengi allowed his instincts to determine his strategy, his son took advice from his commanders and emirs. He examined every detail, weighed every option, and closely studied the special maps prepared for him, before ever reaching a decision. Unlike his father, he never permitted even a drop of wine to taint his lips.

Nur al-Din was determined to conquer their Kingdom of Jerusalem. In order to achieve this aim he needed a powerful and reliable Misr, whose ruler was strong enough to resist Franj attempts to take Cairo. Misr was possessed of great wealth and weak rulers. A beautiful bride waiting for a husband.

I remember the Sultan often asking my uncle Shirkuh: "Any news from Misr?" and Shirkuh would shake his head with a strange expression on his face. "Do not expect any good news from there, My Lord. Their Caliph, the pretender al-Adid, is addicted to *banj* and brothels, and surrounded by mothers and grandmothers who scheme and plot each minute of the day. It is the vizir who rules, and his successor is usually his assassin."

One day there was news from Misr. It was the summer of 1163 and there was excitement in the palace. It was announced that Shawar, the most recently deposed vizir, had escaped with his life and arrived in Damascus. A few days later, a more official messenger arrived from Cairo, carrying a letter from Dirgham, the new vizir. He brought with him a large ivory box inlaid with gems, containing some of the most flawless diamonds to be viewed in our city.

Nur al-Din smiled and handed the box to his secretary, with instructions that it should be placed in the great treasury of the state. The accompanying letter offered other inducements, and pleaded with the Sultan of Damascus to abandon Shawar. Nur al-Din called my father and uncle to his council chamber.

"I think we shall take Misr. Can you imagine the state of a country whose rulers plead with us to back them and not a deposed vizir? They will make similar offers to the Franj. It is imperative that we reach Cairo and Alexandria before the enemy. Shirkuh, you will lead our soldiers with the bravery of a mountain lion.

"Treat Shawar as one would a juicy date on a long march through the desert. Once his usefulness is over, spit him out as you would the seed. Do not delay. He has promised us a third of the grain revenues of Cairo. Hold him to his word."

Shirkuh insisted on taking me with him. I was reluctant. It was not that I disliked the thought of combat. The fact was that I had grown accustomed to meeting a group of friends on most evenings, and we would think heretical thoughts, and recite and discuss poetry. On some nights I would go to a secret assignment near the public baths, to exchange glances and sometimes a little more with a young woman whom I was not permitted to marry.

I was slightly upset at the eagerness with which my father agreed to his brother's request. I had no time for farewells. Shadhi was sent to keep an eye on me. Within three days of the decision being made, we were on our way to Cairo. The combination of Ayyub and Shirkuh was formidable. The "mountain lion" was indomitable, impulsive, incautious and injudicious. My father was crafty, but careful. He was a brilliant organiser of supplies. It was thanks to him that the sword-makers and the tent-makers had been alerted to Shirkuh's needs. He made sure that they had the raw material to provide our expedition with everything needed.

Thus began the journey which finally ended in this palace. If, at that time, a friend had joked that I would one day end up as the Sultan, my uncle and Shadhi would have laughed all the way to Misr.

We are never fully in command of our own biographies, Ibn Yakub. Allah pushes us in a certain direction, the courage and skill of our commanders can change the course of a battle, but ultimately a great deal depends on fate. To a large extent it is who lives and who survives on the battlefield, or on the track to where the fight will take place, that determines our future. I learnt this elementary fact during my first campaign.

We rode for twenty-five days, following the paths of the old wadi to Akaba Eyla on the Red Sea. This was to be our longest stop before the march to Cairo.

It is not easy, Ibn Yakub, to march with over nine thousand men, and the same number of horses and camels, from Damascus to Cairo, avoiding marauding detachments of Franj. We could have defeated them, but it would have been a distraction that would have delayed our mission.

Our Bedouin guides knew all the routes through the desert; there were twenty-five of them attached to our army. They needed neither maps nor stars in the sky to guide them. They knew the location of every oasis and even the tiniest watering holes did not escape their notice. Without this knowledge, it would have been impossible to refill our goatskins. All soldiers rightly fear thirst more than the enemy. It is tedious now to recall or describe every detail, but it is during such marches that good commanders discover many truths about the men who will fight under them. The men even learn to detect the moods of their horses.

Shadhi it was who taught me how to look after horses. To this day he can tell when a horse gets dizzy, and sees the world whirling in strange circles before his dimmed eyes. Imagine if that happened in the heart of a battle! Why, the rider would become even more disoriented than the horse. It was the same Shadhi who taught me how to draw sweet and frothing milk in abundance from the firm teats of a mare.

During the night we would light a fire and sing songs to keep our spirits high. Like most of the men, I slept in a tent, but I envied the Bedouin guides and the soldiers under their influence, who covered themselves in blankets, lay on the sand, drank date wine from flasks made of camel hide, and told each other stories about the desert before the victories of our Prophet. They went to sleep with the starlight shining on their foreheads.

We had been on the march for fifteen days before we reached our target. The partisans of the Cairene vizir, Dirgham, were waiting for us at Tell Bastat, half a day's march from Bilbais. My good uncle Shirkuh was always reluctant to lose the life of any of his men without good reason. He suggested to Shawar that since this was primarily a Misrian question, it should be Shawar and his followers – as the claimant – who should give battle. He, Shirkuh, would intervene only if it became necessary. Shawar won. The Caliph in Cairo abandoned Dirgham. Shawar entered the city through the Bab al-Zuweyla and was reinstalled as vizir. Only then did what Nur al-Din had shrewdly suspected begin to come true.

Once in power, Shawar grew nervous of our presence. He would have been better advised to fulfil his side of the bargain. This would have made it difficult for Nur al-Din not to recall us to Damascus. Instead, foolish and vain as a peacock, Shawar thought he could form an alliance with the Franj to defeat us. He sent a message to King Amalric of Jerusalem, a man who had previously been engaged in numerous intrigues with the ill-fated Dirgham. At the same time, he constructed a veritable pyramid of excuses to demonstrate why our forces should not enter Cairo. Shirkuh, compelled to kick his heels at Fustat, was livid.

His instinct was to defy military logic, to raid the city, and to capture Shawar. But the logistics of such an operation were daunting, and our casualties would be high. His emirs resisted the adventure. In desperation he looked at me.

"What do you think, Salah al-Din?" he asked me.

I was torn between family loyalty and good sense. I thought hard and finally came down against him. To my surprise, he was not angry at all. If anything, he was impressed with my reasoning. Even as we were talking, a messenger brought news that a Frankish force under the command of Amalric was heading towards Bilbais.

Like Nur al-Din, the Frankish King had understood that if he did not take Misr we would, and that would be the end of his Kingdom of Jerusalem. Of all our sultans and emirs the Franj feared no one as much as they did Nur al-Din. They were not wrong. He was single-minded in his resolve to drive the Franj out of our lands. The passion that raged in his heart almost made you feel that he regarded the occupation as a personal affront.

Shawar did not keep his side of the bargain. Shirkuh instructed me to take half our force and occupy Bilbais. I did as I was asked. Shawar appealed to Amalric for help, and Shirkuh joined me with the remainder of our army. For three whole months, Ibn Yakub, we kept the Franj outside the city. Three whole months in Bilbais. It was not my idea of a good life. Then Nur al-Din, realising we could not resist for much longer, took the Franj by surprise, and confronted them outside the fortress of Harim, near Antioch. It was a famous victory. The Franj were crushed, losing ten thousand men. Their leaders, Baldwin of Antioch and the Count of Tripoli, were captured. The news of this defeat frightened Amalric. He sued for peace. We did not lose face. The mountain lion led us back to Damascus.

Before this I had no idea of what a war entailed. Having observed Shirkuh in command of an army, I had learnt a great deal, but I was totally exhausted. For the first week after my return I spent most of my days in the baths, being rubbed with oils. In the evening I went to enjoy poetry and wine in the tavern. Then, you know, Ibn Yakub, something strange happened to me. I became restless. The aimlessness of my daily existence began to nauseate me, and I yearned for the comradeship of the battlefield. I had seen the Franj face to face, and now, suddenly, all the childhood stories I had heard of the time when they first invaded and occupied our lands came back to me. How fate had smashed us as if we were tiny pieces of glass. The shards had scattered.

I remembered Shadhi's voice descending into a frightening whisper: "Sons of Ayyub, do you know what the Franj did in Ma'arra? They captured Believers and placed them in cooking-pots filled with boiling water. They roasted little children on spits and ate them grilled. These are the wild beasts who have devoured our country."

To tell you the truth, I never really believed Shadhi. I thought he was making all of this up to frighten us, so that we never missed a riding lesson, but it was the truth. The pure truth, unadulterated by invention. I have read the manuscripts of the infidel chroniclers. You have as well? Good. Then you understand the anger that expanded my chest when I first caught sight of the Franj in Misr. This anger was not mollified by women rubbing oil on me or the joys of the Taif grape, not to mention the delights of fornication. I felt that all of this was as nothing compared with the tasks that lay ahead.

Before Nur al-Din took Damascus, there was no sultan who understood the burning need to drive out the Franj, to recover the Dome of the Rock and the Temple of Solomon for the People of the Book. Before Nur al-Din, our emirs and sultans were happy to make their peace with the enemy. "Kiss any arm you cannot break," as they say, Ibn Yakub, "and pray to Allah to break it." But that was not the attitude of our Prophet. Did he not say, "Pray to Allah, but make sure you have tied your camel first!"

Pleased with himself, the Sultan burst out laughing. Naturally, I had heard him laugh before, but always in a restrained fashion as befitted a prince. Now it was uncontrolled. The saying of the Prophet, at best mildly amusing to myself, made him laugh and laugh. Tears poured down his face. When he recovered, and had wiped away the tears from his face and beard, he explained himself.

"You look surprised, scribe. I just thought of what could have made the Prophet say such a thing, and an image flashed past my mind of the early Believers who had come to pray. Trusting in the power of Allah, they left their camels outside, only to discover that they had been stolen. This could not have enhanced their faith in Allah, could it, scribe? Enough for today. I have to discuss the late collection of the taxes with al-Fadil, who thinks that this could lead to a national calamity."

I pleaded for one more hour. "The line contained in the Sultan's narrative today is very straight and clear. I fear that if we stop now we might never return to this part again. Could Your Highness not finish with the fall of Shawar and your return to Cairo?"

Salah al-Din sighed and then a frown crossed his forehead. Finally he nodded and continued, but not in his usual relaxed fashion. He began to gallop, and my fingers had to race to keep up. Usually there are at least five scribes present to note the words of the Sultan. After he has finished, they compare notes and we end up with one agreed version. I was alone.

Shirkuh never forgot Shawar's treachery. He burned for revenge. He would often remark: "That goat-fucker Shawar used us to win power, and used the Franj to neutralise us."

It was time, Nur al-Din said one day as he addressed a council of war, for Shirkuh and Salah al-Din to return to Misr. This was the first time he had mentioned me in the presence of all the emirs. My chest expanded with pride. My father, too, was much pleased, though his face, as usual, showed no emotion. Shirkuh bowed.

And so began our great adventure. Our spies reported that Shawar had concluded a deal with Amalric against us. This, dear friend, was the state of our world. Believers joined infidels against other Believers. Shawar and Amalric had joined forces and were waiting for us just outside Cairo. Shirkuh, who taught me everything I know about making war, was a brilliant commander. He refused to fight on the ground they had chosen. Instead we crossed the Nile. We marched northwards from Cairo and set up our tents near the pyramids of Giza. The great river separated us now from the enemy.

From this position Shirkuh sent Shawar a message. I see him now, roaring like a lion, as he reads the message first to our own soldiers. "The Frankish enemy is at our mercy. They are cut off from their bases. Let us unite our forces to exterminate them. The time is ripe and this opportunity may not rise again for a long time."

Our men roared their approval. For a long time, or so it seemed that day, there were loud cries of Allah o Akbar, so loud that the pyramids appeared to shake. Every soldier volunteered to take the message to Shawar. Every eye was strained. Who would Shirkuh pick?

His choice fell on his favourite bodyguard, Nasir, a young Kurdish archer whose sharp eyes had saved Shirkuh's life on more than one occasion.

Shawar received the message and showed it immediately to his ally, Amalric. To prove his loyalty to the Franj, he had Nasir executed. His head, wrapped in filth, was returned to Shirkuh. I don't think I have ever seen my uncle so angry as he was that day. The sun was setting and soldiers were making their ablutions before the evening prayers. Shirkuh interrupted them. He was naked except for a piece of cloth that covered his loins. He grabbed Nasir's head and ran like a madman, showing it to everyone. Nasir was a much-loved man, and tears filled so many eyes that evening that the level of the Nile itself must have risen.

Loud cries rent the camp. Shirkuh, still holding the head, climbed on his stallion. The last rays of the sun caught his hair as he screamed in rage: "I swear on the head of this boy, who like me came from the mountains. I swear that Shawar's head will fall. Nothing can keep him alive. Neither his Franj, nor his eunuchs, nor his Caliph. I swear this in front of you all, and may my soul rot in Hell if I fail."

There was complete silence as we drank in the import of his words. For a long time none of us spoke. We were thinking of Nasir's death, of cruel fate, and of how far we were from home. We were also thinking of ourselves. Shawar had declared war. Who would win this war? Even as we were thinking, the plaintive sounds of a flute floated through the air and, following it, the voices of the Bedouin who sang a lament for Nasir. The Nile rose again.

That night, after we had finished our meal, my uncle Shirkuh could be seen pacing up and down outside his tent, like a man possessed. I was sitting on the sand, dreaming of Damascus and watching the shooting stars. I have never seen such a sky as one glimpses lying at the feet of the pyramids. A messenger interrupted my dreams. It was a summons from Shirkuh.

The emirs and commanders were already assembled when I arrived. Shirkuh pointed to an empty place on the floor. I sat down not knowing what to expect. To everyone's amazement, Shirkuh told us that he was not going to confront Shawar and Amalric outside Cairo, or even here where we had set camp. He was planning to take the port-town of Alexandria instead. Everyone gasped at the audacity. By the light of lamps, Shirkuh sketched out his plan in the sand, giving each of us detailed instructions. He was aware that Amalric was marching to encircle and destroy us. Shirkuh knew that we had to fight a battle before reaching Alexandria. I was given command of the centre and ordered to retreat the minute the enemy charged. Unlike me, Shirkuh left nothing to chance. That is why, Ibn Yakub, I still believe that he was the greatest of our military leaders. I am nothing as compared to him. Nothing. Nothing.

We met the enemy at al-Babyn. When Amalric and his knights charged towards me, I feigned fear and led a retreat. The Franj unfurled their banners and accepted the challenge. The chase began. They had not realised that the left and right flanks of our army had been placed to circumvent a Frankish retreat. At a given signal, I stopped our forces, turning round to confront the knights. Soon they realised how exposed and isolated they were, but it was too late. Very few managed to escape, Amalric, alas, one of them.

Shirkuh did not permit us to celebrate the victory. That same day we began our march northwards across Misr, in the general direction of Alexandria. It was the first time I had seen the sea. I could have sat there for hours, breathing in its air and drinking its beauty. Shirkuh had given us no quarter. We were exhausted in body and mind. The sight of all that water soothed our nerves. I felt calm again. A few days later we entered Alexandria. We were showered with flowers and greeted with great acclaim by the people of the city. They had strongly resented Shawar's alliance with the Franj.

The pride in Shirkuh's face, the tears on mine, and the joy, the sheer joy of being greeted as saviours, these are what I remember. Shirkuh did not speak for long that day. He knew we didn't have much time. Yet the whole city had gathered to welcome us. He had to offer them a message of hope. His face was tired. He had not slept for two nights, just managing to catch the odd nap while he rode. The sight of the people aroused him. He stood on a wall outside the citadel. The crowd fell silent. Shirkuh spoke.

"Looking at you now, I can count the stars on your foreheads. What I am doing, what we are doing, everyone is capable of doing. Once our people understand this simple truth, the Franj are lost. I speak to all of you, not just the Believers. You are all under my care, and we will defend you. But the Franj are already on their way. Let us celebrate, but let us also prepare."

This was my uncle who had taken Alexandria. This was my uncle who had spoken these simple but meaningful words. I was overcome by emotion. As he stepped down, I hugged him and kissed his cheeks. He spoke a few kind words in my ear, telling me that he was getting old and soon I would have to fight in his place. Telling me that he was proud of how I had fought. What else would he have told me had not messengers arrived with news of the Frankish response?

Shawar and Amalric were shaken by the speed with which we had travelled from south to north. They were mustering a large army to crush us. Now Shirkuh missed my father's presence. He needed someone to plan the defence of the city, to take measures to withstand the Frankish siege, to ensure that food was saved and equally distributed, to make certain that flame-throwers were stationed in the port – to deter Frankish vessels from disembarking knights behind our backs. In my father's absence, I was assigned all these tasks.

As you know, Ibn Yakub, that siege has now entered our books of history. I have nothing more to add, except to confess to you that I was prepared for death. Fear, which haunts us all, had disappeared completely. We were surrounded by Frankish ships behind us, and their knights were outside the city walls, their catapults hurling fire and stones. I wanted to die a noble death, as did our army. I did not want us destroyed by famine or diseases, both of which were spreading as the city was paralysed. Once again it was Shirkuh who refused to contemplate either surrender or a thoughtless battle in which, hopelessly outnumbered, we would all die.

Shirkuh's daring had no equal. He placed me in command of the city and then, taking two hundred of our best fighters, he left under cover of darkness, galloped at full speed through the surprised ranks of the enemy, and headed for Cairo. Shadhi went with him and used to tell of Shirkuh going to villages, appealing to the peasants in a language they understood and appreciated – describing Shawar and Amalric as camel and horse droppings and making them laugh. In this fashion, he convinced the younger men among them to join his army.

The Franj, worried by this diversion, agreed to lift the siege, and we left Alexandria without losing a single soldier. The Franj, too, withdrew. Shirkuh, realising we were outnumbered, took us all back to Damascus. In his report to Nur al-Din, delivered in my presence, he predicted that within a year Shawar and Amalric would be at each other's throats. That, he suggested, would be the best time for us to return.

And it happened, just as he had said. Shawar refused to pay Amalric the booty he had been promised, and the Franj decided to teach him a lesson.

One day a messenger reached us from Cairo. He was a spy that Shirkuh had planted in Shawar's ranks. He had been present at the negotiations between Amalric and Shawar's son. The Franj had demanded Bilbais in return for the help he was prepared to provide Shawar for use against us.

Shawar's son, angered by this outrageous request had shouted: "Do you think Bilbais is a piece of cheese for the eating?" to which Amalric had responded: "Yes, it is cheese, and Cairo is the butter."

These proved to be more than empty words. Amalric took Bilbais, killed and enslaved its population, and burnt it to the ground. Then he marched onwards to capture Cairo. To delay his old friends, Shawar burnt the old city to the ground. The people fled to where we are now, the new centre of Cairo. The fire raged for one whole month. Shawar again tried to appease Amalric. He offered him gold and a free hand in the rest of the country, but still there was no change.

At this point the Caliph al-Adid sent a messenger to our Sultan. Nur al-Din summoned me, and told me what was taking place. He sent me to Homs to fetch

Shirkuh. When we returned, Nur al-Din ordered us to return to Cairo. I was reluctant. I could still see the suffering on the faces of the people at Alexandria. I did not want to experience another siege. Shirkuh took me aside.

"Are you the son of my brother or the son of a dog? Do you think I enjoy suffering? This time we will take Cairo. I need you at my side. Go and prepare your horses."

I did as he asked. On hearing of our departure, Amalric had decided to withdraw. He had already seen that the Cairenes would resist him all the way despite the manoeuvres of Shawar. It was winter 1169 when we entered the city. As in Alexandria the previous year, we were welcomed, and the horses on which my uncle and I rode into Cairo were fed the most amazing dishes. We met Shawar in this very room, Ibn Yakub. He rose as Shirkuh and I entered, and pretended to welcome us, but his eyes would not meet my uncle's. He fell on the floor and kissed Shirkuh's feet. We asked whether the Caliph was expecting us, and Shawar nodded mutely.

"Then take us to him, you goat-fucker," said Shirkuh with a cruel laugh.

He led us to the Caliph's palace, through vaulted hallways and an endless number of ornamented chambers, each of them empty. Brightly coloured birds from Ifriqiya were making a terrible noise. We passed through a garden which contained tame lion cubs, a bear and two black panthers tied to a tree. Shirkuh was unmoved by all this, yet it was difficult not to be impressed. I tried to mimic my uncle and pretended that I, too, was unaffected. Then we entered a large room with a vaulted ceiling. It was divided by a thick silk curtain of the deepest red, on which circles of pure gold had been sewn, and jewels the size of eggs.

Shawar bowed before the curtain and laid his sword on the floor. We did not follow suit. Slowly the curtain rose and al-Adid emerged.

So, I thought to myself, this pathetic and frightened figure, barely eighteen years of age, his dark eyes shadowed by the signs of over-indulgence, surrounded by eunuchs and a great display of inordinate wealth, this was the Caliph of the Fatimids. The Caliph asked Shawar to leave his presence, and the defeated vizir slunk away like a smelly animal.

Shirkuh did not waste time. "You requested us to save Cairo. We are here. Before anything else, I ask for Shawar's head. It is he who has brought death and destruction to our people."

The Caliph of the Fatimids nodded. He spoke in a strange choked voice as if he too, like most of those who surrounded him, had been castrated.

"We welcome you to Cairo. We take great pleasure in appointing you as our vizir."

Shirkuh bowed his acceptance, and we left the palace. The very next day, with the written permission of their Caliph, I personally separated Shawar's head from his shoulders, throwing it on the ground at Shirkuh's feet. My heart trembled, but my hand was strong.

"Now our Nasir is avenged," he said, in a voice softened by the memory of his favourite archer.

Two months after this day, the heavens darkened. A terrible tragedy befell our family. My uncle Shirkuh passed away. I was not the only one who wept as news spread through the ranks of our army. Shirkuh was a much-loved commander, and even the emirs of Damascus, who made fun of the way he spoke the language of the Koran behind his back, were subdued by grief. Who would lead us now that Allah had taken away our mountain lion?

In our lives we are all prepared to die at any time, but Shirkuh's death was not necessary. It was his appetite that led to his downfall. He had been invited to a feast where they ate for nearly three hours. Whole sheep had been roasted, goats grilled on an open fire, quails and partridges and every imaginable delicacy had been laid out before us. Shirkuh loved food. Even when he was very young, my grandmother often had to drag him away by force from the food. As I watched him, I remembered the old stories. He used to boast that he could eat and drink more than any other man in his army. Now he could not stop himself. It was a sad and an unpleasant sight. On three occasions Shadhi tried to restrain him, whispering warnings in his ear, but my uncle Shirkuh was in his own world. He choked on his food and began to suffocate. Shadhi hit him hard on the back and made him stand up, but it was too late. He lost consciousness and died in front of our eyes.

Shadhi and I hugged each other and wept. Throughout the night we kept guard over his bathed and shrouded body, which lay on a simple bed. Shirkuh's soldiers, many of them veterans who had fought by his side while I was still a child, came in small groups and made their farewell. It was a strange sight to see these hardened soldiers, for whom the loss of a life was all part of a day's work, weeping like children.

After midnight, we were left alone. Shadhi would remember an old episode, long before I was born, and begin to weep again. I remembered Shirkuh, his flashing eyes full of laughter as he sang to his own children and to us just as we were approaching manhood. Once when he discovered that I had been going secretly to a tavern, he called me into his room. His face was stern and I was scared. He had a terrible temper. "You have been drinking?" I shook my head. "Don't lie, boy!" I nodded. He roared with laughter and recited the sayings of Ibn Sina, which he forced me to recite after him:

> *Wine is a raging enemy, a prudent friend,*
> *A small amount is an antidote, too much a snake's poison,*
> *In excess it leads to no small injury,*
> *But in a little there is much profit.*

Alas, it was not a lesson he learnt himself. His death was the price he paid for over-indulgence in meat and wine. Ever since the day when I saw him die, I have been repulsed by the presence of too much meat on my table. Now do you understand why I insist on a balanced diet, Ibn Yakub? I felt the other day when we broke bread together that you really did not appreciate the meal. We shall discuss all this another time. Let us continue.

The next day, after Shirkuh's burial, the emirs of Damascus remained aloof from me. They were huddled in little groups whispering to each other. I did not appreciate the cause of their disaffection till much later that evening.

The advisers of the Caliph of the Fatimids saw me as young, inexperienced, and weak – someone who could be easily manipulated by the court. I was invited to the palace and given the title of al-Malik al-Nasir – victorious king. How they must have laughed amongst themselves, thinking that in me they had found a pliant instrument. I was conscious of the honour, but felt lost without Shirkuh. I felt like a re-channelled river, momentarily disoriented as I observed the new landscape.

I needed to talk to Shirkuh or, failing him, my own father, who was in Damascus with Nur al-Din. As I thought about our great Sultan, I wondered what he would make of my elevation. His proud emirs, men of noble lineage, were clearly upset that a lowly Kurd from the mountains, who, in their eyes, could not speak the divine language properly, was now Vizir of Misr. I determined to send a message to Nur al-Din reaffirming that he, and not the Caliph of the Fatimids, was my commander. The last person in the world I wanted to be sharply pitted against was Nur al-Din.

The vizir's white turban, embroidered with gold, was placed on this head, a sword decorated with jewels was placed in my hand, and a beautiful mare with a saddle and bridle encrusted with pearls and gold was given to me. I then marched at the head of a ceremonial procession with much music and chanting. We came, eventually, to this palace and to this room – here, where we are seated. It is a good place to be, and it is a good time to end our labours for the day, Ibn Yakub.

I'm glad you insisted that we finish this particular story, but I can see that your fingers are stiff. Your wife will need to rub ointments on your hands tonight, and my loyal al-Fadil must be very angry with me. I have never kept him waiting so long.

TEN

I meet Halima in secret to hear her story; she tells of her life in the harem and the brilliance of the Sultana Jamila

The next day a messenger arrived from the palace. He brought with him a large basket of fruits and other delicacies for my wife and child, and a message for me. The Sultan and the Kadi had left the town for a day or two and I was to be permitted a respite from my tasks. I was somewhat put out. I felt I might have been given the option to decide whether or not I was to accompany them. Where had they gone and why? Perhaps the Kadi was punishing me for having kept Salah al-Din to myself for so long the previous day. How could I write a proper account of the Sultan if I was excluded in this fashion from his daily work?

There was much rejoicing in the house after the messenger's departure. For weeks I had barely seen Maryam, and there was much anger that I had arrived late for the feast in honour of her tenth birthday a few weeks ago. Even Ibn Maymun had rebuked me on that occasion. Rachel was, of course, delighted by my temporary leisure. Relations between us had returned to normal, but she still resented the amount of time I spent at the palace. Yet she showed no signs of resentment at the unsolicited gifts arriving regularly at our house. These came not from the palace but from merchants and courtiers, who believed I had a great influence with the Sultan.

Ever since I had started my work as Salah al-Din's personal scribe, we had not spent a single dinar on food or oil. Add to this the satins and silks which were normally beyond the reach of people like us. Both Rachel and Maryam were now dressed in the fashion of the court nobility. On one occasion, when I taxed Rachel with all this, she laughed without any sense of shame, and replied:

"The pain of our separation is undoubtedly relieved by the receipt of all these gifts, though I still think that if I was to put you at one end of the big scales in the market and all the gifts on the other, the balance would still favour you."

Later that afternoon, as all three of us were wandering aimlessly through the streets, observing what was on offer at the various stalls, a woman I did not recognise handed me a note, slipping rapidly away before I could question her. The message was unsigned, but it asked me to present myself at the palace library the next day. Rachel and I both assumed it was a message from Shadhi, acting on the orders of the Sultan, but I was puzzled by the choice of messenger. Something in me told me that the message had originated with neither Shadhi nor the Sultan.

The next day, upon entering the library, I was told by an attendant that Salah al-Din and al-Fadil had still not returned from the country. As I sat waiting for the person who had sent me the note, I heard a slight noise behind me, and turned to see the wooden shelves in one wall moving. Slightly nervous, I stepped forward to see a flight of stairs beneath the ground and a figure slowly ascending them. It was Halima. She smiled at my astonishment. The executed eunuch Ilmas had told her of the existence of a secret passage from the harem to the library. It had been built by al-Adid's grandfather, a Caliph who did not object to his wives or concubines having access to the library. Subsequently the palace had been given to the vizir, and the passage had fallen into disuse.

It was dangerous to talk in the library. Halima wanted to meet in the room of a friend near the public baths, later that afternoon. The same woman who had handed me the message would meet me within a few hours, and guide me to her presence.

I was entering stormy waters. If I met her and did not inform the Sultan, my own neck could soon lie beneath the sword. If I did tell Salah al-Din, would Halima's life be worth living? Perhaps I should disregard her invitation. While walking through the courtyard, I saw Shadhi, who hugged me with real warmth. I had not seen him for some time. He too was annoyed with Salah al-Din for having left without him, but informed me that he was due back in the palace tonight.

We sat in the sun and talked. It was as if we had always been close and trusted friends. He asked how the Book of Salah al-Din was progressing, and I told him where the narrative had stopped. His memory confirmed Salah al-Din's account of the circumstances that led to Shirkuh's death. The memory saddened the old man. Taking my fate in my hands, I told Shadhi of my meeting with Halima. To my surprise he chuckled.

"Careful of that mare, Ibn Yakub, careful. She's dangerous. Before you know it you will have mounted her, and she will have galloped across the desert with you tied to her back. She has Kurdish blood, and these mountain women, let me tell you, are very strong-willed. I know not what she has in store for you, but whatever it may be she will not let you resist. Once women like her have decided to do something, they do not permit mere men to stop them."

I protested Halima's innocence and my own.

"She just wants to tell her story. Is that not my job?"

The bawdy look on his face indicated that he was not convinced.

"Go meet her. Don't be frightened of the Sultan. If he finds out, say you told me and assumed I would have passed on the information. These things do not worry Salah al-Din. It is only if others in the harem discover your secret that Halima will be in danger. And you, my friend, be careful. She is very beautiful, but she is also carrying the Sultan's child."

The news stunned me. I was bathed in a wave of jealousy and anger. Why should a ruler, however benign, have the right to appropriate the body of any woman he finds temporarily desirable? I noticed Shadhi looking at my transformed features, and nodding with a sympathetic, understanding smile. I recovered my composure, regretting my illogical reaction to the news. As I walked towards the palace gates I thought I heard Shadhi's whisper in my ears: "Careful, be careful, Ibn Yakub." But it was my imagination.

Ibn Maymun maintains that in a state of heightened emotions, one sees and hears imaginary things related to the subject of the emotions. He told me once of a man whose favourite horse had been killed as part of an old blood-feud. He used to catch a glimpse of the horse in the oddest places. It is the same with the object of one's love, regardless of whether that love has ever been spoken. Suddenly I had no desire to see Halima. I wished she was dead. This feeling did not last longer than a few minutes at most and, as I waited at the agreed spot near the public baths, just behind the Street of the Bookbinders, I felt ashamed of myself.

The messenger-woman saw me from a distance and beckoned me to follow. She was swift of foot and, fearful of losing sight of her, I lost all sense of geography. When she entered the courtyard of a modest house, I had no idea of the quarter. The house was empty. I was directed to a small room and, seeing that I was sweating and out of breath, an attendant provided me with a jug of water. I did not look at him too closely till he spoke, in a strange voice, which made me wonder whether he was a eunuch.

"Would you like to rest for a while?"

"No, no, I'm fully recovered."

I waited. The attendant continued to stare at me in a familiar fashion. His insolence annoyed me, but I managed a weak smile. He burst out laughing and removed his headgear, revealing the light red tresses of Halima. She had come disguised as a man.

"Even you, Ibn Yakub, who stared at me so long that day in the palace when I was telling my story, even you did not recognise me. This gives me hope."

She showed her pleasure by clapping her hands, like a child. Then she laughed, a throaty deep laugh, the sound of which struck me like a waterfall and increased the pace of my heart. I was glad she disappeared for a while after this performance. I needed a little time to recover. When she returned, in a brocaded green and blue silk robe with large sleeves and gold bracelets, she reminded me once again of those legendary princesses of the Caucasus. Whatever anger I may have felt earlier was soon dispelled. One could not be angry for long with such an exquisite treasure.

"Have you been struck dumb, scribe?"

I smiled and shook my head.

"Why do you think I have summoned you to my presence?"

"I assumed there was something you wished to communicate to me. You see I have brought my equipment with me so that I may transcribe your every utterance."

She ignored my display of servility.

"Why did you not stay till the end of the shadow-play? Ilmas told me you left before the final act."

I sighed.

"The public humiliation of our Sultan was not pleasing to my eyes or ears. I have grown to like him."

Her face changed suddenly. Lightning flashes from her wrath-laden eyes burnt me to the core. I was speechless in the face of her rage. She sipped some water and counted thirty cross-sections on the fingers of both hands. Thus becalmed, the softness returned to her features. She swayed gently from side to side.

"Can you play the lute, scribe?"

I shook my head.

"Then Mansoora shall play for us. When one is sad, the sound of the lute is like the noise of water to a thirsty traveller in the desert."

Her maidservant began to strum the lute, and a strange, magical peace embraced the room. Halima started speaking. Slowly she spoke, and my pen moved in perfect rhythm with her words. I was in such a trance that I barely knew what she was saying. Not till I returned home did I understand the import of what she had told me.

For the first few nights, I couldn't sleep. Salah al-Din would enter my chamber and possess me with a passion whose intensity was such that it excited me, even though I had no real feelings for him. After he had finished, I would leave his sleeping body and wash myself. I did not wish to bear his child.

I should speak the truth with you. After the first few nights I used to shut my eyes when Salah al-Din mounted me, and I would imagine that he was Messud. You seem shocked, scribe. Or is it that you think my immodesty might cost you your life? Do not worry. My lips will never speak of our encounter, but I wish you to know everything. Or are you worried that I have become too embittered with your Sultan and dream of revenge? Why should I? He saved my life and became my lord and master. For that I am grateful, but in my bed he is a man like any other.

The only man I have truly loved is Messud. Perhaps it is just as well that he is no more. If he were here, I would risk both our lives to lie in his arms once more. I used to dream that he would make me heavy with his child, and I would pretend it belonged to Salah al-Din. Can gold ever cure grief, scribe? I think of Messud all the time. I torture myself by imagining him in Paradise in the arms of a houri, a creature far more alluring than me. In my heart I am still with him. I tell myself that we have not separated. He disturbs my sleep often. His smiling eyes, his serene gaze, his comforting voice, the feel of his hands stroking my body, all this enters my dreams and I know it will not go away.

It was during the first few weeks, late at night, that I would hear the others talking loudly and anxiously about their own lives and futures, and about me. They were laughing at me. I suppose they thought that I loved the Sultan, and that when he moved on to feed himself in newer pastures, the blow would cripple me, leaving me alone to nurse my wounded heart. How wrong they were, and how little they knew me in those early days. It was only six months ago, Ibn Yakub, but it seems like an eternity.

The first few weeks were fine, though being the latest concubine in the harem was not a pleasurable experience. Salah al-Din's first wife, Najma, was a noble but ugly lady. She is the daughter of Nur al-Din. He told me he found her repulsive, but that did not prevent him planting his seed in her. The marriage, as you can imagine, was hardly designed for pleasure. It had only one purpose, and that was fulfilled when she bore him three sons in succession. She, too, felt her duty done, and never left Damascus.

Salah al-Din's visits, thanks be to Allah, became fewer and fewer, and once I was with child he stopped altogether. At this stage everyone became more friendly. I was surprised when I first entered the harem to discover that there were not many of us. Apart from myself, there were eighty other concubines and two wives, but there was no real distinction between us when it came to enjoying the privileges of the court – except that we had six attendants to serve our needs, while the wives had eight or nine.

I had realised in the very first week that there was one woman who dominated the harem. This was Jamila, a lute-player from Arabia, of noble birth. The Sultan's brother sent her as a gift, and Salah al-Din was entranced by her beauty and her skills. Since you will never set eyes on her, Ibn Yakub, let me describe her to you. She is of medium height, not as tall as me, dark-skinned and dark-haired, with eyes which change colour from grey to green, depending on where you catch sight of them. As for her body, what can I say? I embarrass you again. I will stop. If you think that Mansoora plays the lute like a magician, you should hear Jamila. In her hands the lute begins to speak. When it laughs, we smile. When it is sad, we cry. She makes it almost human. It is Jamila who keeps our minds alive. Her father was an enlightened Sultan. He adored her and insisted that she be educated, just like her brothers. He refused to tolerate any attempt to restrict her learning. What she has learnt she tries to teach us.

I was exhilarated when she started talking about us in a very bold way. Not us in the harem, but us women. Her father had given her a manuscript by the Andalusian Ibn Rushd, and she talked of him in a reverential tone. She told us of how Ibn Rushd had criticised the failure of our states to discover and utilise the ability of women. Instead, he argued, women were used exclusively for purposes of procreation, child-rearing and breast-feeding. I had never heard talk like this in my whole life and, judging by the expression on your face, nor have you, my dear scribe.

Jamila told us that many years ago in Cairo, one of the Caliphs of the Fatimids, Al-Hakim, had woken up one morning and decided that women were the well of all wickedness. He promptly passed a decree preventing women from walking in the streets and, in order to make sure they stayed at home, shoemakers were forbidden to make shoes for women. He had all the wives and concubines in his palace packed into crates and thrown into the river. Jamila said that though Al-Hakim had undoubtedly taken leave of his senses, it was interesting that his madness was directed exclusively against women.

Jamila and I have become close friends. We hide nothing from each other. My innermost secrets are hers and hers are mine. She has already borne Salah al-Din two sons, and now he rarely comes to her. At first, like me, she was upset, but now she sighs when he comes. It is not the other way round. How fickle our emotions can be! I wonder how I would have felt if the memory of Messud was not so strong in me. Jamila thinks that Messud is a fantasy that I nourish to keep myself sane. I know that the past loses power over the heart, but it hasn't happened to me yet, and in the meantime Jamila lets me dream. Sometimes she encourages me in this, for she never had a Messud. She also encourages me to stop shaving the hair on my pudenda.

My only other friend was Ilmas the eunuch. He had been in the harem for a long time. Long before Salah al-Din came here. The stories he used to tell, Ibn Yakub. Allah protect me, I cannot bring myself to repeat them, even to you. Perhaps if you had been a eunuch, but that is foolish. Forgive me. I had no right to speak like this to you.

Ilmas was really a poet. I still don't understand what devil possessed him. Why did he write that shadow-play? He was killed for telling the truth, for in the last act which you were too cowardly to watch – or was it your seventh sense that warned you it might be dangerous? – Ilmas described the love of one inmate of the harem for another. The love of a concubine for one of her maids. I think he had Mansoora in mind, because the lute figured prominently. He certainly could not have had me in his mind. I have not moved in that direction yet, though if I did it would be Jamila's warm embrace that would comfort me. A sign to her that I was ready to take such a step would be to stop removing my body hair. I am close to a decision. Misery-laden days are about to end.

Look at your face. Do I detect disgust? Surely a man of the world like you, Ibn Yakub, is not shocked by such details. Cairo and Damascus, not to mention Baghdad, are full of male brothels where beardless youths satisfy every conceivable need and desire of those who visit them. This is tolerated, but mention women smelling the musk of each other's bodies and it is as if the heavens were about to fall.

I think I should stop. You look as though you're about to choke on your own anger, and your friend Ibn Maymun would never forgive me if I was responsible for making you ill.

I'm disappointed in you, scribe. I don't think I shall summon you again.

Before I could reply, Mansoora had ushered me to the door and straight into the courtyard. I turned back to catch a last glimpse of Halima, but there was no sign of her. My last memory of her remained a strange, obstinate, half-contemptuous gaze which was her farewell.

I walked into the street, upset and disoriented.

ELEVEN

Shadhi and the story of the blind sheikh;
Salah al-Din tells how he overcame his rivals

My clandestine meeting with Halima had shaken me to the core. I felt abused, though when I recalled her exact words there was nothing in them to upset me. I suppose I was taken aback by her decision that henceforth all men, except Messud, were out of bounds. My reaction was nothing personal. I was shocked on behalf of all males, or, at least, that is how I consoled myself.

Shadhi was not so easily convinced. He was waiting for me anxiously at the palace. The Sultan was back, but would not be able to see me till later in the afternoon. Shadhi wanted to hear of my meeting with Halima and so I obliged him. He was not in the least bit perturbed.

"I could tell you stories of harems which would make you die of shame on their behalf," he chuckled. "Not that I ever died. I have lived long enough to know that of all Allah's creations, we human beings are the least predictable. Do not plague your heart with the problems of women, Ibn Yakub. Leave Jamila and Halima to be happy. They will never be as free as you or me."

I was astonished by Shadhi's carefree attitude, but also relieved. I had told him everything. If the Sultan ever discovered our secret, both of us would share the blame. My fear, which had given me a sleepless night, evaporated and I became cheerful again. I saw Shadhi laughing to himself. When I inquired as to the cause of his merriment, he spat loudly before speaking.

"There is a blind sheikh, who preaches his nonsense a few miles outside the Bab-al-Zuweyla. He's the sort who makes a living out of religion. He uses his blindness as a pretext to feel every part of the men with soft voices, all the time reciting the *hadith*. People leave him gifts of food, clothes, money and sometimes jewellery. Six months ago a trader brought him a beautiful shawl to keep him warm during the evenings. The sheikh loved this shawl. He would put one end of it through a tiny ring and then pull it out with one sharp tug, to show his disciples the unusual character of the wool. One evening, just after he had finished his prayers, a man entered his house. The sheikh was seated on a rug on the floor playing with his beads and muttering invocations and prayers and whatever else these charlatans mouth to gull the poor.

"The man who entered muttered a few prayers and placed a little bundle at the feet of the preacher. Pleased with his present, he asked the stranger's name, but received no reply. For a while they prayed in silence. Then the stranger spoke.

"'Tell me something, learned teacher. Are you really blind?'

"The sheikh nodded.

"'Completely blind?'

"The sheikh nodded more vigorously, this time with a touch of irritation.

"'So, if I were to remove the shawl from your shoulders,' the man's voice was gentle and reassuring, 'you would never know who I was?'

"The sheikh was amused by the suggestion and smiled, while the enterprising young thief lifted the shawl and calmly walked from the house. The holy man rushed out after him with his stick. The mask disappeared as he began to scream abuse at the thief. Mother-fucker. Sister-fucker. Twice-born-camel-cunted-son-of-a-whore. And worse, Ibn Yakub, words that I would not

want to repeat to you. Later it was discovered that the bundle which the thief
had left for the sheikh consisted of three layers of pigeon shit covered with
straw!"

Shadhi began to laugh again. His laughter was infectious, and I managed a
weak smile. But he could tell that I found the story only mildly amusing. This
annoyed him, and he spat in an elegant arc over my head to express his disapproval. Then stared into my eyes and winked. I laughed. Peace was restored.

It was late in the afternoon when the Sultan deigned to notice my insignificant
presence. He was in good spirits, and when I inquired if his trip with the Kadi
had been successful, he sighed.

"Convincing people to pay taxes to the state is not one of my duties, but al-
Fadil insisted that my presence was necessary in the North. As usual, he was not
wrong. My being there had the desired effect. In two days we collected taxes that
had not been paid for two years. So, let us continue with our story. Where did we
finish?"

I reminded him of how he had become the Vizir of Misr.

I had been worried that the Sultan Nur al-Din might have been misled by the
behaviour of some of the Damascus emirs. They scarcely bothered to hide
their envy and contempt for me. I had sent Nur al-Din a message, and now
eagerly awaited his reply. It came after a week. The form of address he had
chosen revealed his nervousness at my elevation. I was still the Emir Salah al-
Din, Chief of the Army. I quickly sent another message stressing that he, Nur
al-Din, was my Sultan and I was obedient to his instructions alone. I also
requested that my father Ayyub, and the rest of our family, might be permitted
to come and live with me in Cairo. Without them I felt lonely and homeless.
After several months, this request was granted. I had not seen my father and
mother for nearly a year. Great was our mutual joy at the reunion decreed by
Allah.

I told my father that if he would like to take the position of vizir, I would immediately transfer my position and power to him. He refused, insisting that Allah's choice had fallen on me. It would be wrong to tamper with his will. I did, however, persuade him to become the Treasurer, a key position. Without control of the treasury, it was difficult to wield real power.

The Caliph of the Fatimids and his courtiers were enraged by this decision. They had chosen me to be the vizir because they thought me weak and unprepossessing. Now they realised that power was slipping away from their hands. The Caliph al-Adid was a weakling, manipulated by eunuchs. One of these creatures, a Nubian named Nejeh, with a complexion as black as his heart, was a particular favourite of al-Adid. It was Nejeh who supplied his master with both opium and false reports.

The Caliph had harboured ambitions of becoming the vizir himself, but had felt it would be easier to retain power in the court by acting through me. The spies put in place by al-Fadil reported one evening that the Nubian eunuch Nejeh had sent a secret messenger to the Franj. The Caliph pleaded with them to attack Cairo as a feint. He knew I would ride out and give battle to the occupiers. Then, once I was fully distracted, Nejeh and his Nubians would thrust their daggers in our back.

On the advice of al-Fadil, I decided that Nejeh had to be dispatched as soon as possible. It was difficult to do this while he was in the palace without provoking a full-scale war. You must realise that tens of thousands of Nubians followed Nejeh as if he were a god. But we discovered that he had a male lover. He used to meet him regularly at a country house far from the palace. We waited for the right moment, and then, when the time had come, both Nejeh and his lover were consigned to hell.

My father had taught me that two armies under two different commands can never coexist for long. Sooner or later, Allah willing, one or the other must triumph. What was taking place in Cairo in these months was a struggle to achieve absolute power. I told the Caliph of the Fatimids that his men had established contact with the enemies of our Prophet. I told him that the eunuch Nejeh had been captured and executed. I told him that my Sultan Nur al-Din wanted Friday prayers in al-Azhar to be offered in the name of the only true Caliph, the one who lived in Baghdad.

On hearing these words, the pathetic boy began to tremble and shake. Fear had paralysed his tongue. He spoke not a word. I did not tell him that Nur al-Din wanted me to get rid of him without further delay.

The next morning, the Nubians came out on the Beyn al-Kaisreyn. Armed from head to foot, with their sharp scimitars glistening in the sun, they began to taunt my soldiers. We had many black soldiers in our army, but these Nubian brutes shouted insults in our direction. My father advised me to show no mercy to these devils. As they saw me, riding out to confront them, their ranks began to heave with hatred and a chant reached my ears:

"All white men are pieces of fat and all black men are burning coal."

My archers were ready to shoot, but first I sent the Nubians a message. If all white men were pieces of fat, I inquired, how come that Nejeh had been plotting treachery with the Franj? In the sight of Allah we are all equal. Surrender and give up your arms, or be crushed forever. One of the rebels struck my messenger on the face with a sword. Blood had been spilled and we gave battle.

The fighting lasted for two whole days, and the Nubians burnt streets and houses to slow our advance. On the third day it was clear that Allah had granted us another victory. When we burnt al-Mansuriya, the quarter in which most of the Nubians lived, they realised that further resistance would be foolish. It was a costly victory, Ibn Yakub, but the prize was worth every life we lost, for now Misr was under our sole control.

All our emirs wanted to topple the Caliph of the Fatimids and declare our immediate loyalty to the rightful Caliph in Baghdad. I sympathised with the emirs, but, in private, I consulted my father. His sense of caution advised against further bloodshed. He reminded me that it was the Caliph al-Adid who had placed the vizir's turban on my head. His motives may have been dishonourable, but it would be a greater dishonour to our clan to act ungenerously. I was not entirely convinced by his line of argument. I pressed my father further and finally, after making sure that no eavesdroppers had been stationed outside the chamber, he whispered in my ear:

"This wretched Caliph will help keep Nur al-Din at bay. Destroy the Caliph and you become the Sultan. What will Nur al-Din, the Sultan of Damascus and of Aleppo, think if you made such a leap? I know him well. He would ask himself: how is it that one of my youngest emirs, a jumped-up Kurd from the mountains, a boy whose uncle and father are my retainers, how come, he would ask, how come this upstart has arrogated to himself the position of Sultan without offering it to me first? Be patient, son. Time favours you. Now is the time to consolidate our power. Your brothers and cousins must be placed in all the vital positions of the state. So that when the Caliph of the Fatimids one day takes so much opium that he can only sleep the sleep that knows no waking, at that time we must make sure that the succession is smoothly handled."

"What succession?"

"Yours. The minute he dies, you will abolish this Caliphate, you will announce from the pulpit at al-Azhar that henceforth there is only one Caliph and he sits in Baghdad. All prayers are offered in his name and you, Salah al-Din, are his Sultan."

My father, may he rest in peace, was an inspired adviser. He was proved correct once again. The Caliph fell ill and I immediately instructed the Kadi to change the prayers. From that day on, the prayers were said in our city in the name of the only true Caliph. When the news reached Baghdad, there was great rejoicing. I received from the Caliph a ceremonial sword and the black Abbasid flag. It was a great honour.

A few days later, the last of the Fatimids died. I instructed Qara Kush, one of the shrewdest men in Cairo at the time and one of my advisers, to tell al-Adid's family that their time was over. For nearly three centuries the Fatimid Caliphs had ruled this country. They had done so in the name of their heretical Shiite sect. Their rule was finished, and I offered thanksgiving prayers to Allah and his Prophet.

I became Sultan, with the written authority of the Caliph in Baghdad. Nur al-Din accepted my elevation, but it would be an exaggeration to say that he was pleased. I received two requests to meet him in Damascus, but I was too busy fighting the Franj. They had become greatly alarmed when they saw that Misr was now under our control. I captured a number of their citadels, including Eyla, a necessary fortress from which to provide a safe-conduct to the pilgrims visiting Mecca.

Some of his advisers suggested to Nur al-Din that I was only engaged in skirmishes with the Franj to avoid obeying his instructions to return to Damascus. This was malicious gossip. The Franj were worried by the fact that we now controlled both Alexandria and Damietta, the two ports they most needed in friendly hands. They feared, and in this they were right, that I would use our control of these harbours to destroy their line of communications with Europe. In time, that would mean the end of their occupation of our lands. They would crumble into dust. Qara Kush suggested an immediate offensive, but we were not in a strong position. It was reported that the Emperor in Constantinople had sent over two hundred ships laden with soldiers to lay siege to Damietta.

We obtained regular reports as to how many moving towers were being built for the siege and the number of knights at Amalric's disposal. All this information was checked and sent by messenger to Damascus.

It is sometimes said about me, Ibn Yakub, that at critical moments I am not decisive enough. Perhaps this is true. I have inherited my father's caution, and there are many in my ranks who would much rather I had inherited my uncle Shirkuh's impulsiveness. I am conscious of this failing, and sometimes I try and combine the two. It is not always easy to make decisions which affect the lives of so many people.

What made Nur al-Din a truly great leader was his capacity to understand one important fact, namely, that unless the Franj were decisively defeated, our people would never be at peace. To make this possible, everything was subordinated to this single goal. That he was irritated by me was a minor irrelevance.

When my messengers arrived in Damascus, and informed him that we were in danger, he did not hesitate for a moment. He prepared a large army and sent it to Misr. We used this army to launch an offensive against the Franj in Palestine, diverting them from Damietta. Allah gave us victory. A sudden storm helped to sink the ships which the Emperor, whose sister was married to Amalric, had sent from Constantinople. The Greek ostrich had come here to find itself a pair of horns. It was obliged, instead, to return without its ears. Nur al-Din was a greater man than I could ever hope to be, and everything I have achieved I owe to him.

A strange smile, a mixture of elation, triumph, envy and sadness, came over his face as he uttered these last words. Perhaps he was thinking how ironic it was that he, Salah al-Din, and not his old master, was the ruler preparing to take Jerusalem. He was the man who would offer prayers at the Qubbat al-Sakhra, the Dome of the Rock, and return it to the care of the Believers.

I wanted to question him further. I wanted to ask him about Nur al-Din. But it was clear from his face that he was thinking of other matters. Suddenly he interrupted my thoughts.

"Go and break bread with Shadhi, but don't go away. Ride with me to the citadel this afternoon."

I bowed and made my exit. As I walked through the chambers to the court-yard I was struck by the simplicity of the man. He was surrounded by opulence. While he had stopped the elaborate court rituals of the Caliphs, there was still a great display of wealth and power, as if to show ordinary mortals like me that the two always went together. They were old bedfellows and nothing could ever change that reality.

Salah al-Din was known for his generosity. This was one reason for his great popularity with his own soldiers. Except on ceremonial occasions, he dressed simply. He was fond of riding his favourite steed without a saddle. There was nothing like the feel of a horse's sweat to encourage dreams of future glory. He told me that on one occasion, adding that it was on the bare back of a horse, galloping through the meadows or across the sand, that his military ideas fell into place. It was, he said, as if the rhythm of the stallion's gallop coincided with the necessary leaps in his own thoughts.

With Shadhi, I was soon eating a leg of lamb, stewed with beans of three different varieties and soft as butter. Shadhi claimed the credit for the meal. He had threatened to boil the cooks in their own olive oil if they served tough meat again. He had lost a tooth on one occasion. His threats had the desired effect. The tender meat turned out to be pure bliss.

I told Shadhi of Salah al-Din's strange smile when he had been talking of Nur al-Din, and asked him for his interpretation. The old man snorted like a horse with a strained heart.

"Sometimes our Sultan can be very sly. We all admired Nur al-Din. He was a pure man. Nothing stained his honour. But Salah al-Din resented his authority. On one occasion, I think it must have been the siege of a Frankish castle, Nur al-Din himself joined us, and our Sultan returned to Cairo. He claimed that there was a danger of a rebellion by the remnant of the Fatimids. This was true, but it was nothing that could not have been handled by his brothers. He simply ran away from Nur al-Din. He was frightened of meeting him face to face. Why? Because he knew that Nur al-Din might order him back to Damascus. Nur al-Din was annoyed by Salah al-Din's insolence, for that is how he saw the situation. A subordinate was behaving as an equal. He needed to be taught a lesson. He decided to march to Cairo.

"Let me now tell you something, my friend. I was present, as was Ayyub, at a meeting of the emirs and commanders of the army when the Sultan told us that Nur al-Din was on his way. Salah al-Din's favourite nephew shouted impulsively that Nur al-Din should be resisted just like the Franj. Salah al-Din smiled indulgently at his nephew, but Ayyub, sharp as a sword from Damascus, called the boy and slapped his face hard. Right there. In front of everyone. He then stood up and spoke to Salah al-Din. 'Let me tell you something, boy! If our Sultan Nur al-Din came here, I would dismount and kiss his feet. If he ordered me to cut off your head I would do so without question, even though my tears would mingle with your blood. These lands are his, and we are his retainers. Send him a message today, Salah al-Din. Tell him that there is no need for him to waste his energies in travelling here. Let him but send a courier on a camel to lead you to him with a rope around your neck. Now leave, all of you, but understand one thing. We are Nur al-Din's soldiers. He can do with us what he will.'

"Everyone left the meeting, all except Salah al-Din and myself. Ayyub rebuked him sharply for permitting his ambition to show in front of the emirs, who would like nothing better than to see him displaced. Salah al-Din looked desolate, as though his heart had been wounded by a careless lover.

"Ayyub watched him for a while, letting the misery colour his features. Then he stood up and hugged him. He kissed him on the forehead and whispered: 'I know Nur al-Din well. I think your letter of submission will work. If, for some reason, it fails to pacify him, I will fight by your side.'

"Now do you understand, Ibn Yakub? When you saw that smile on the face of the Sultan, maybe he was thinking also of the sagacity of his father. He is on his own now. Ayyub is with his Maker. Shirkuh is no more. Sometimes when I take him some mint tea in the mornings he says: 'Shadhi, you're the only one left from the old generation. Don't you go and die on me as well.'

"As if I would. As if I would. I want to see al-Kuds, Ibn Yakub, the city your people call Jerusalem. I want to be next to him when we pray at the Qubbat al-Sakhra. I don't pray much, as you know, but on that day I will pray. And have no doubt, that day will happen as surely as the sun rises and sets. Salah al-Din is determined to take the city, whatever the cost. He knows that it will strike a blow at the heart of the Frankish settlement. He also knows that if he succeeds, he will be remembered for ever. Long after our bones have enriched the soil, Believers will remember the name of this lame boy who I once trained to use a sword. How many will remember the name of Nur al-Din?"

TWELVE

*The Sultan visits the new citadel in Cairo but
is called back to meet Bertrand of Toulouse, a
Christian heretic fleeing Jerusalem to escape
the wrath of the Templars*

One reason why the Sultan did not encourage me to accompany him
on his tours of inspection, or on his regular visits to supervise the construction of the new citadel, was because he was painfully aware of the fact that
I could not ride. This aspect vexed him, since he could not appreciate that some
of us simply lack the skill or the desire to race a horse. As a result he never talked
much in my presence of horses. His understanding of the subject was immense,
rivalled only by his knowledge of the *hadith*. Several times he would interrupt
his stories and start describing a particular horse that had arrived as a gift from
his brother in the Yemen. He would start on its wretched genealogy, and then,
seeing my eyes become distant, he would sigh, laugh, and return to his story.

I was thinking of this as I rode in his entourage through the city. He had
placed experienced horsemen on either side of me, just in case the animal I was
riding took it in its head to bolt. It did nothing of the sort, and soon I even
became used to the unpleasantness of the experience. I knew my backside would
be sore at the end of the day, but I was pleased to ride with him.

He rode without effort.

This was not his battle-horse, but a lesser steed. Yet even for this horse, Salah al-Din's movements had become a habit. He let the horse move at its own pace, neither too fast, nor too slow. With a slight flicker of the Sultan's heel, the horse increased his pace, obliging all of us to keep up with him. Sometimes it seemed as though the horse and its rider were one creation, just like the make-believe creatures of which the old Greeks sang in their poetry.

We rode out of the Bab al-Zuweyla and were soon passing through streets thronged with people. They interrupted their labours to bow or salute their ruler, but he did not encourage servility and preferred to speed through the city. He wanted to avoid the supplicants and sycophants from the layer of merchants who dominated most of the streets.

Soon we passed the burnt ruins of the Mansuriya quarter, where the Nubian soldiers of the eunuch Nejeh had made their last stand before being driven from the city. The Sultan had ordered that the quarter should remain demolished, as a grim warning to all those who might contemplate treachery in the future.

Without warning, he reined in his horse. Our entire party consisted today of myself, three court scribes to take down the Sultan's instructions for transmission to the Kadi al-Fadil, and twenty carefully chosen bodyguards – carefully chosen, that is, by Shadhi, who, if the truth be told, only trusted Kurds or members of the family to guard his Sultan, who now beckoned me to join him. He was laughing.

"It pleases me to see you ride, Ibn Yakub, but I think that Shadhi should give you some lessons. Your good wife will need to rub special ointments tonight to ease your behind. I hope this journey does not impair any of your functions."

He laughed loudly at his own remark, and I nodded my agreement. He managed a generous smile. Then he surveyed the buildings of the burnt quarter and his mood changed.

"We were lucky to survive this revolt. If they had taken us by surprise, the story might well have been different. This permanent state of uncertainty is the devil's curse against the Believers. It is almost as if we are destined never to be one against the enemy. None of our philosophers or inscribers of history have been able to answer this question. Let us discuss this problem with our scholars one evening."

He bent over the saddle to stroke the horse's neck, an indication that our journey was about to be resumed. Soon we had left the swarming streets and there, at a distance, were the mounds of the Mukattam range. Here builders like bees were constructing the new citadel. Huge stones were being carried by humans and donkeys. Thousands and thousands of workers were engaged in the building.

I wondered whether anyone else observing the scene was reminded of the ancient monuments in Giza. They must have been built by the ancestors of those who were at work on this great fortress.

The man in charge of the work was the Sultan's chamberlain, the Emir Qara Kush, the only person Salah al-Din trusted to carry out his detailed architectural instructions and to supervise the building during his long absences. The sight of these labours pleased Salah al-Din. Again he touched his horse below the neck and the large creature bent to his will, galloping off at a pace which only his guards could match.

The three court scribes and myself followed at a more dignified speed. The court scribes, Copts whose fathers and grandfathers had served the Fatimid Caliphs for centuries, smiled at me and made ingratiating conversation. Underneath, I could see, they were burnt by jealousy. They resented my daily proximity to their master.

Salah al-Din suppressed a smile as he saw me dismount. My legs were aching as I walked up a ramp to a newly completed tower. Here the Sultan was discussing the brickwork with the Emir Qara Kush. This giant eunuch, with a fair complexion and hair the colour of coal, had once been one of Shirkuh's mamluks. He had been freed and made an emir by his master. Shirkuh had greatly valued his administrative skills, and it was the advice of Qara Kush to the Caliph of the Fatimids that had secured the position of Vizir for Salah al-Din.

Qara Kush was describing how some of the stones had been brought all the way from the pyramids of Giza. He showed how well they mingled with the local limestone. The Sultan was clearly pleased and turned to me.

"Write this down, scribe. The reason we are constructing this new citadel is to create an impregnable fortress which can resist any Frankish adventure. But if you look at how the walls and towers have been planned, you will notice that we could also withstand a local rebellion with some ease. I have never forgotten how close we were to defeat when the eunuchs and mamluks organised the Nubians to surprise us. Here we can never be surprised."

As we were talking, Qara Kush pointed down to the dust created by the speed of two horsemen riding in our direction. He was not expecting anyone, and was irritated by this unplanned intrusion. He frowned and instructed two of the Sultan's guards to await the horsemen at the foot of the citadel. Salah al-Din laughed.

"Qara Kush is so nervous. Do you think our old friends from the mountains have sent someone to dispatch me?"

Qara Kush did not reply. When the horsemen arrived, he waited impatiently for the guards to question them and bring them to him. The Sultan's light-hearted reference to previous assassination attempts had failed to distract the chamberlain. As the riders approached, we all relaxed. They were the Kadi al-Fadil's special messengers, trained to ride like lightning and supplied with a special breed of racing horses for this purpose. They were used only in urgent circumstances, and the relief at knowing their identity was coloured by worry at the message they might be carrying.

Finally they arrived at the platform where we were standing. They carried a letter for the Sultan from the Kadi. As Salah al-Din began to read the message his face became animated, and his eye began to dart about like a fish in the Nile. He was clearly pleased. The messengers and the guards were dismissed. He showed us the letter. It read:

A Knight Templar has just arrived in Cairo and asked for refuge. He comes from Amalric's camp and has much information regarding their movements and plans. The reason for his defection is mysterious, and he refuses to divulge his secrets to anyone in the absence of Your Highness. Judging by his demeanour I am convinced he is genuine, but the Emir Qara Kush, who is the best judge of human character and failings, needs to speak with him before you meet him. I await the Sultan's instructions. Your humble al-Kadi al-Fadil.

Salah al-Din's immediate response was to grab Qara Kush and myself by the arms, and to run down the mud-strewn path to the place where the horses were tethered. He was truly excited, behaving like a man possessed by demons. He mounted his horse and began to race back to the palace with his guards, who were barely able to keep up with him.

To my immense delight, the Emir Qara Kush was not an expert horseman, and he permitted me to accompany him and his entourage as we rode back. I had never spoken to him before, and his enormous knowledge of Cairo and the wealth contained in its libraries was impressive. He told me that the task I was performing would be of great benefit to historians, and I was pleased that he, unlike al-Fadil, took my work seriously.

The Sultan was waiting for us when we arrived. He wanted both Qara Kush and myself to be present when he questioned the Frank. He clearly had no desire to delay the proceedings, but the sun was already setting. He ordered us to repair immediately to the palace *hammam* to cleanse ourselves, and then to return to the audience chamber. Since we were both aware that Salah al-Din disliked the grandiose nature of this chamber, we smiled. It was obvious that on this day he wished the Frankish knight to be impressed by the majesty of his court.

Refreshed by the bath, I made my way slowly back, through rooms where mamluks held torches to illuminate our way, to the audience chamber. Here sat

Salah al-Din, dressed unusually in his robes of state with the Sultan's turban on his head, glistening with rare stones. I bowed and was assigned a place, just below the Sultan's throne. He was flanked on one side by Qara Kush and on the other by al-Fadil.

Seated in a semicircle on the floor were the most distinguished scholars of the city, including, to my delight, Ibn Maymun. At a signal from Qara Kush, a mamluk left the room. A few minutes later I heard a drumbeat indicating that the foreigner was on his way. We all fell silent. The Frank, preceded by a guard carrying a scimitar, entered and walked straight to the throne. He placed his sword at the feet of the Sultan and bowed low, not raising his head till permission had been granted. Qara Kush indicated that he should sit down.

"The Sultan is pleased to receive you, Bertrand of Toulouse."

The lips enunciating these words were familiar enough, but the soft-spoken voice had disappeared. The Kadi spoke with a firmness and authority that surprised me. This, I thought to myself, is how he must speak when he is handing down justice and awarding punishments to the guilty.

"You are in the presence of Yusuf ibn Ayyub, Sultan of Misr and the Sword of the Faithful. We are pleased that you speak our language, albeit in a primitive fashion. We are all eager to hear why you are here."

Bertrand of Toulouse was of medium height, with an olive-coloured skin that made him a few shades darker than our Sultan. He had dark hair and brown eyes, but an ugly scar across his left cheek had left his face badly disfigured, making it temporarily awkward to concentrate on his other features. The wound, probably the mark of a sword, could not have been more than a week old.

Bertrand was about to respond, when the Sultan spoke. His voice, I was pleased to hear, was normal.

"Like the others, we too are anxious to discover the reasons for your presence. But before you proceed, I want to know if, in my absence, you were made welcome. Have you broken bread?"

Bertrand nodded, with a slight bow.

"Then we offer you some salt."

An attendant proffered a silver plate with salt. Bertrand took a pinch and placed it on his tongue.

"Now you may speak, Bertrand of Toulouse," said the Sultan, simultaneously signalling that the Frank should be seated.

Bertrand spoke Arabic in a harsh, guttural voice, but the smiles soon disappeared as his impressive command of our language became clear to all present.

"I am grateful to Your Majesty for receiving me so soon after my arrival, and for taking me on trust. I am indeed Bertrand of Toulouse, a member of the Order of the Knights Templar, and for the past five years I have been with my Order in Jerusalem, which you call al-Kuds. We were under the command of our King Amalric, who is as well known to the Sultan as you are to him.

"What you are all wondering is why I have twice risked my life to escape from my kingdom and to enter yours. The first time was by fleeing from my Order under cover of darkness two nights ago. I was nearly captured, and the price of freedom is this wound on my face. The sword which marked me belonged to a knight who was close to the Grand Master himself. The second risk was to be killed by your men, who might not have been patient enough to either ask questions or to wait for my response. Speaking your language, even though I do so imperfectly and with much hesitation, helped me to survive the journey and to reach your court safely.

"Let me begin my story with a confession. In the eyes of my Church, I am a heretic. If heresy is another way of expressing the struggle for the real God, then I am a heretic and proud of the fact.

"I come from a small village near Toulouse, and it was there that I came under the influence of a preacher who denounced our Church and preached a new vision of God. He used to say that churches lacked congregations, that congregations lacked priests, that priests lacked reverence and virtue and, lastly, that Christians lacked Christ. He used to say that there were two Gods, a good

God and an evil God, and that there was a permanent struggle between these two powers which were both eternal and equal.

"He used to say that the Holy Trinity of the Christians was a manifestation of evil; the Holy Ghost represented the spirit of evil, the Son was the son of perdition, and the Father was none other than Satan himself. He used to say that there were two Christs. The Christ in the celestial spheres was good, but the Christ on earth was evil. He used to say that Mary Magdalene was the earthly Christ's concubine, and that John the Baptist was a forerunner of the Anti-Christ. The Devil was Christ's younger brother and the cross was God's enemy, a symbol of pain and torture. As such, it was an icon that should be destroyed rather than worshipped.

"Our entire village, some three hundred souls in all, joined this preacher and helped spread the word to neighbouring villages. To their amazement, they discovered that others had been there before them. We soon learnt that the Counts of Toulouse were sympathetic to these ideas, and this knowledge strengthened our village's resolve. When I was fifteen years old, almost exactly fifteen years ago to this month, we tore down every cross we could find. We either set them on fire or used the wood to fashion tools that could be of use to the village. This single act made us worse than demons and vampires, for these creatures of the dark are supposedly frightened by the cross, whereas we heretics were brazen beyond belief.

"In our sect, there are three stages of becoming a True Believer. We start off as Listeners, imbibing the new Truth and learning the dual art of debate and dissembling in relation to our Christian opponents. The next stage is that of a Believer. Now we have to prove ourselves by winning new adherents to our cause. After we have won fifty new Listeners, we become known as the Perfecti and can participate in the election of a Council of Five, which makes all the important decisions.

"I am a Perfectus. I was asked by the Council to penetrate the Order of Knights Templar, to dissemble and to win them over to our cause. Constantinople had urged the Grand Master to burn the bitter and evil falsehoods of the heretics in the fire of truth, and our Council felt we should be represented inside this Order so as to warn our followers of impending doom.

"Excessive fornication and the consumption of alcohol is not permitted by our Council. They believe that drink and carnality weakens our resolve and makes us vulnerable.

"I was betrayed by a Listener, who was in his cups and, unaware of the presence of the Master's henchmen, was boasting wildly of our successes. I was not made aware of this till he was in prison suffering torture. Because of our method of organisation, he could only name me and two others.

"I am told the Grand Master was outraged when I was so named. He refused to believe that this could be true. Fortunately I was warned of all this by a Believer in the Grand Master's entourage. I knew I was being observed and I broke off all contact with our people. After a few days, I was detained and subjected to five hours of continual question by the Grand Master. I denied all knowledge of the Council and expressed my full confidence in the Churches of Rome and Constantinople. I thought I had convinced them, since they released me. They appeared to stop following me and watching my every move.

"There were three other Perfecti in Jerusalem. We met one night and they advised me to leave and seek refuge in Cairo. I woke before sunrise the next morning, and was saddling my horse, when I was challenged by a knight. He had his own suspicions of me. He used a secret word which is only known to our sect. It was clear that he had obtained it by torturing the three Believers. It caught me unprepared and I responded before I could see his face in the dark. He drew his sword. I killed him, but not before he had marked my face. I rode like the wind, Your Majesty. If I had been caught, they would have killed me in the most ugly fashion.

"That is the end of my story, and I am now at the mercy of the great Sultan Salah al-Din, whose generosity is known to all the world."

While Bertrand of Toulouse had been speaking only three faces had remained impassive. These belonged to the Sultan, Qara Kush and al-Fadil. As for the rest of the company, and here I must include myself, we had been actively exchanging glances. The description of the heresy had seen several hands going to their respective beards. These had been nervously stroked, as if to quell the agitation disturbing their owners' heads.

"We have listened to you with great interest, Bertrand of Toulouse," said the Sultan. "Are you prepared to be questioned by our scholars?"

"With great pleasure, Your Highness."

It was the Kadi who asked the first question, this time in a honeyed voice.

"What the Church regards as your heresy is your opposition to the Holy Trinity and your hostility to icons. Our Prophet, too, did not favour the worship of icons or images. Have you ever studied the Koran? Do you know the message of our Prophet, peace be upon him?"

Bertrand of Toulouse did not flinch.

"One advantage you possess over all others is the impossibility for any person to doubt the existence of your Prophet. He was very real and, therefore, it is not possible to ascribe dual features to him. He lived. He married. He fathered children. He fought. He conquered. He died. His history is known. This magnificent city and all of you are one of the consequences of your Prophet's remarkable vision.

"Of course I have studied the Koran, and there is much in it with which I agree, but, if I may speak frankly, it appears to me that your religion is too close to earthly pleasures. Because you realised that you could not live by the Book alone, you encouraged the invention of the *hadith* to help you govern the Empires you had gained. But is it not the case that many of these *hadith* contradict each other? Who decides what you believe?"

"We have scholars who work on nothing else but the *hadith*," replied the Sultan quickly. He did not want his Kadi to dominate the discussion. "As a young man I studied the *hadith* with great joy and care. I agree with you. They are open to many interpretations. That is why we have the ulema to ascertain the degree of their accuracy. We need them, Bertrand of Toulouse, we need them. Without these traditions, our religion could not be a complete code of existence."

"Can any religion ever become a complete code of life when, within the ranks of the Believers, there is such disparity in interpretation? The followers of the Fatimid Caliphs, to take the most recent example, do not share your beliefs or those of the Caliph in Baghdad. The same applies to our religion or that of the Jews. He who rules, makes the rules."

"You truly are a heretic, my friend," laughed Salah al-Din, indicating that any of those present could speak to Bertrand if they so wished.

An old man, a much-respected scholar from al-Azhar, rose. He spoke in a weak and husky voice, barely above a whisper, but so great was his authority that everyone strained to hear each word.

"With the Sultan's gracious permission, I would like to explain one fact to our visitor. The greatest fear that haunts each human being, regardless of his religion, is the fear of death. It is a fear which oppresses us all. Every time we bathe and enshroud a corpse, we see in it our own future. In the days of Ignorance, and long before even that, this fear was so strong that many people preferred not to accept death as real, but to see it as a journey to another world. Islam has broken this fear of death. That alone could be counted as one of our great achievements, for without breaking this fear we cannot move forward. We are held back. It was our Prophet who understood the importance of this question before all else. That is why, Bertrand of Toulouse, our soldiers reached the edge of this continent and the heart of yours. That is why nothing can stop this Sultan from taking al-Kuds, your so-called Kingdom of Jerusalem."

Then Qara Kush spoke.

"With the Sultan's permission, I would like to ask Bertrand of Toulouse a single question. What in your opinion, O brave knight, is the single most important difference between your beliefs and those of our Prophet?"

There was not a moment's hesitation on Bertrand's part.

"Fornication."

There were several gasps amongst the scholars, but Salah al-Din smiled.

"Explain yourself, Bertrand of Toulouse."

"Only at Your Majesty's insistence. Ever since I came to these parts and learnt your language, I have been studying the *hadith* and also certain commentaries on the Koran. It appears to me that fornication, and the rules under which it should or should not take place, has occupied the Prophet and his followers a great deal. In your Koran, if my memory is correct, the sura entitled 'The Cow' overturns the traditional Arab taboo on coitus during fasting.

"Some of the *hadith* record the Prophet as saying that your Allah had preordained the share of every man's copulation, which he will do as fate requires. Each indulgence is thus predestined. The old scholar has just explained that your religion has removed the fear of death from the minds of its adherents. Is this not, at least partially, related to your conception of the Paradiso? Your heaven is the most voluptuous of all. Are not your knights who fall while fighting the jihad promised the most delicious pleasures in heaven? Erections which last for eternity and an unlimited number of houris to choose from, while they sip from rivers heavy with wine. Your heaven removes all earthly prohibitions. In these circumstances, only a man who had lost possession of his senses would fear death. All this flows from the self-confidence of your Prophet. He was a man of few doubts. Is it not the case that when your Prophet died, his son-in-law Ali cried out – and here Your Highness will forgive me since I only know the words in Latin – '*O propheta, O propheta, et in morte penis tuus coelum versus erectus est.*'"

The Sultan frowned, till the Kadi whispered a translation in his ear.

"The Frank refers to Ali's remark, as he gazed on the dead body of our Prophet: 'O prophet, O prophet, even in death your penis is erect and pointing to the heavens.'"

Salah al-Din roared with laughter.

"Our Prophet was made of flesh and blood, Bertrand of Toulouse. His virility was never in doubt. Even his sword was known as al-Fehar, the one that flashes. Our prophet was a complete man. We are all proud of his activities. It was only because we held on to the stirrup of our Prophet that Allah has rewarded our people. Would that we ordinary mortals were as blessed as our Prophet so that even in death he pointed towards heaven. I think, however, that you are wrong. The driving force of our religion is not fornication, but the relation between God and the Believer. If you wish you could say that our way of looking at the world is perhaps too much influenced by merchants and traders. You look surprised. It could be argued that Allah is like a master-merchant and everything in this world is part of his reckoning. All is counted. All is measured. Life is a trade in which there are gains and losses. He who does good earns good, and he who does evil earns evil, even on earth. The Believer provides Allah with a loan; he is in other words paying in advance for a place in our Muslim paradise. At the final reckoning Allah has a book of accounts from which the deeds of men are read and carefully weighed. Each is paid what is his due. This is our religion. It shows the influence of our world. A real world. It speaks a language which is easily comprehensible and that is the reason for its success.

"Enough of theology for one evening. Let us eat and drink. Tomorrow you will inform us of Amalric's plans, and we shall ask you many searching questions about the towers and battlements of al-Kuds. My emirs, you will discover, are less polite than our scholars."

THIRTEEN

Shadhi tests the Cathar hostility to fornication by spying on Bertrand of Toulouse; Jamila recounts how Salah al-Din defied the traditions of the Prophet by spilling his seed on her stomach

Shadhi and I had just finished eating and were relishing the morning in the palace courtyard, bathed in the sunshine of early spring. He had been talking of the military secrets that Bertrand of Toulouse had brought with him and which were now lodged safely in the Sultan's head. He did not enlighten me as to the nature of this information, except to wink and whisper that al-Kuds was already as good as ours.

The meeting had been confined to the Sultan, six of his most trusted emirs, and Shadhi, who had really taken to the Frankish knight. He had tried to convince him that there was sham and superstition in every religion, and corruption in each of the sects that composed any religion. False prophets and rhetoricians could be bought in the bazaar of Cairo or Damascus. The Frank had refused to accept that the Cathars – the name given to them by the Church – were degenerate in any way.

Shadhi had attempted to test the Cathar hostility to fornication. He sent one of the most beautiful serving-women from the harem, who was also one of the wiliest, to tempt the virtue of the knight. Shadhi had promised her rich rewards if she was successful. Bertrand, to Shadhi's exasperation, had resisted her charms and had firmly, but nicely, propelled the woman from his chamber. Shadhi's devious brain was now preparing another trial for the Sultan's most welcome guest. From a special brothel reserved exclusively for the nobility, a young male prostitute had been borrowed for the night and, since Shadhi had entrusted the master cook with his idea, news of the plan had spread throughout the palace.

Nowhere was tomorrow's dawn so eagerly anticipated as in the harem, and it was in that direction that Shadhi pushed me after we had digested our meal. In response to a request from the Sultana Jamila, he had obtained the Sultan's permission for her and Halima to meet me for a short time in a special chamber adjoining the harem. It was there that he led me, muttering and grimacing at the eunuchs, whose numbers increased as we neared the site of the harem.

Halima smiled to acknowledge my presence. It was no ordinary smile. It lit her entire face, causing my heart to quicken, even though the cause of her happiness was not the sight of this tired scribe, but the woman who stood at her side. It was the Sultana Jamila. She was a striking woman. Of that there could now be no doubt. I was observing her with my own eyes. She was taller than the Sultan. The hair on her head matched the blackness of her eyelashes, her thick, arched eyebrows and lustrous eyes. She was dark-skinned, just as Halima had described, but there was something about the way she moved, the way she met my gaze, and the way she spoke, which displayed a sense of confidence and authority not usually associated with the women in the harem – or at least, that is what I thought at the time. I was wrong, of course. The portrait painted by Halima and Jamila of their secluded quarters was to banish the old images from my mind for ever.

Jamila looked at me knowingly and smiled, as if to say: mind yourself, scribe, this young girl has told me all I need to know about you. I bowed to their presence, which made Halima laugh.

"Ibn Yakub," said Jamila, and though her voice was soft and unbroken, it possessed an easy confidence due, I suppose, to the fact that she was the daughter of one sultan and married to another. "How did Bertrand of Toulouse describe the corpse of our Prophet, peace be upon him? I ask you since you were present on that occasion. You may repeat the words in Latin, a language with which I am familiar."

I was speechless with embarrassment. It was not the question I had expected. Halima smiled reassuringly, nodding at me to encourage a response. I repeated the words ascribed to Ali by Bertrand in Latin. Jamila translated them for Halima and both women shrieked with laughter.

"Is it also true that the Frank regarded our religion as being too concerned with the details of fornication?"

I shook my head in affirmation.

They laughed again. I could not help observing the demeanour of these two women as they laughed and joked with each other. It was like the happiness of lovers during the first few months of bliss. It was strange to see the strong-willed Halima completely enthralled by this enchantress from the Yemen, who was now speaking to me again.

"Was Salah al-Din amused by Bertrand's observation?"

"He was, noble lady. He laughed and proclaimed that it was an honour for the Believers to have had such a strong and virile Prophet. A man in every sense of the word. He even mentioned the name of his sword in this regard."

"I am pleased to hear it," said Jamila, "for I have said the same to him for many years. Some of our scholars cook our history to make a camel taste like a lamb, which is unhealthy for the development of our intellects. Your Sultan may be well versed in the *hadith*, but not as well as I am. I remember one occasion, soon after I had become his wife. We were in bed and he suddenly decided to practise al-Azl, by withdrawing at the critical moment and spilling his seed on my stomach. I was slightly surprised, since the main purpose of our encounter had been for me to provide him with a son or even two.

"I told him that al-Azl was contrary to the *hadith*. At first he was taken aback, but then he threw his head back and laughed and laughed. I have never been able to make him laugh like that again. He thought I had made up the reference to the *hadith*, but I gave him the reference from the Sahih Muslim and the number. It was 3371. I can still recall it. Salah al-Din refused to believe me.

"He shouted for a messenger and sent him with a note to al-Fadil. Can you imagine, Ibn Yakub, it was not yet light. The stars were still travelling in the night sky. Can you imagine a messenger knocking on the door of our venerable Kadi with an urgent question from the Sultan regarding a particular *hadith* concerned with al-Azl? What if the Kadi had himself, at that very moment, been engaged in this unlawful practice? Within an hour the messenger was back with an answer. Al-Fadil confirmed the accuracy of my knowledge.

"For the next two years Salah al-Din rode me as if I were his favourite mare. Our seeds intermingled in abundance. I gave him first one son and then another. Then he left me alone. He would come and see me often, as he still does, but it was usually to discuss affairs of the state or poetry or the *hadith*, but never anything intimate. It was almost as if, in his eyes, the knowledge I possessed had transformed me into his equal. I had become a temporary man.

"Do you know how the Franj refer to al-Azl?"

Knowledge of this sort, alas, was not stored in my head, and I lifted both hands to the heavens in a gesture acknowledging my ignorance. Jamila smiled.

"It is far more poetic than us. The flight of the angels."

Her laughter was infectious, and I found it difficult to restrain a smile, which pleased them both. It was at that point that I understood how and why Halima had fallen under the spell of this woman, and I forgave them both. The cobwebs had suddenly disappeared from my head. My heart was wiped clean. They looked at me and observed the change, and became aware that they could now trust me to be their friend.

For a while they ignored me and spoke to each other. Jamila asked Halima about a third woman, whose name I had not heard before. She was clearly miserable because Allah had not blessed her with a child.

"She is like an orange tree," said Halima, "which pleads with the wood-cutter to chop it to pieces because it can no longer stand the sight of its fruitless shadow."

The two women discussed how to lighten this unfortunate woman's load. After they had devised a way of easing the pain suffered by their friend, Jamila looked at me.

"Do you think there is life after death, Ibn Yakub?"

Again the Sultana took me unawares. Ibn Maymun and I had often touched on this question, but even on our own we were careful to talk in parables. To question the central tenets of her faith was more than heresy. It bordered on insanity. She looked straight into my eyes with an intense, teasing gaze, as if to dare me to reveal my own doubts.

"O Sultana, you ask questions of which ordinary mortals dare not even think, lest their thoughts accidentally betray them. We are all the People of the Book. We believe in the after-life. For asking a question like this our Rabbis, the Christian Popes and your Caliph in Baghdad would first have your tongue removed and then your life extinguished."

She refused to accept my caution.

"In my father's court, O learned scribe, I discussed questions of life and death without any restriction. What makes you so nervous? Our great poet Abu Ala al-Maari questioned everything, including the Koran. He lived to a ripe old age in Aleppo. He never allowed any authority to set limits to the kingdom of reason.

"Ibn Rushd and his friends in Andalus, who have studied, understood and developed Greek philosophy, are also inclined to doubt. Divine revelation in all our great Books is one type of wisdom. It relies on tradition to create a set of rules, a code of conduct, by which we must all live. But there is another kind of wisdom, as the ancient Yunanis taught, and that is wisdom which can be demonstrated to all without recourse to the heavens. That wisdom, my tutor at home once taught me, was called Reason. Faith and reason often clash, do they not Ibn Yakub? I'm glad we agree. Unlike reason, divine truth can never be proved. That is why faith must always be blind, or else it ceases to be faith.

"I will now return to my initial question. Do you agree that after death there is nothing? What you see are men and women, who live and die and who, after death, turn to mud or sand. No long journeys to heaven or hell. Do you agree, Ibn Yakub?"

"I am not sure, Lady. I am not sure. Perhaps the foolishness of God is wiser than men. Surely it gives you some comfort that, if you are wrong and there is a heaven, the seventh heaven, of which your great Prophet spoke, is, surely, the most delightful heaven of them all."

This time Halima, her eyes flashing, responded angrily.

"For men, Ibn Yakub. For men. Shadhi, if he gets there, will have seven-year erections and a choice of virgins, like apples from a tree, but both our Book and the *hadith* are silent on the question of what will happen to us women. We can't be transformed into virgins. Will there be young men available to us, or will we be left to our own company? That may be fine for Jamila and myself, but not for most of our friends in the harem. And what about the eunuchs, Ibn Yakub? What will happen to them?"

The Sultan's familiar voice startled all of us.

"Why should anything happen to the poor eunuchs? What are you three talking about?"

Jamila summarised her case and my reply. The Sultan's face softened, and he turned to me.

"Do you not agree, good scribe, that Jamila would be a match for any scholar in Cairo?"

"She would also make a wise ruler, O Commander of the Loyal."

Jamila laughed.

"One of the problems of our great religion is that we exclude half the population from enriching our communities. Ibn Rushd once remarked that if women were permitted to think and write and work, the lands of the Believers would be the strongest and richest in the world."

The Sultan became thoughtful.

"There are some who argued this during the time of the Caliph Omar. They told him that our Prophet's first wife, Khadija, was a trader in her own right and she hired the Prophet to work for her, some time before she wed him. After the Prophet departed, his wife Aisha took up arms and fought, and this was accepted at the time. But there are many *hadith* which contradict such a vision and . . ."

"Salah al-Din ibn Ayyub! Don't start me off on the *hadith* again."

He laughed, and then the conversation moved on to a much lighter subject. We began to talk of the fate that awaited Bertrand of Toulouse tonight. Shadhi's tricks had reached every corner of the palace. Halima and Jamila were as intrigued as the Sultan himself. They too were curious to see if the knight would be ensnared by Shadhi's latest ruse.

The chamber in which the knight was lodged was one in which the occupant was spied on from two corners of the adjoining room. It had been built by one of the Fatimid Caliphs who enjoyed watching his concubines coupling with their lovers. Even though the unfortunate women were later executed, the sight excited him much more than mounting them himself.

FOURTEEN

The death of Sultan Nur al-Din and the opportunity of Salah al-Din

I was in the palace library, absorbed in a study of al-Idrisi's map of the world. The Sultan had sent me to consult the map, to ascertain whether Toulouse was marked on it. If it was, I was to take it to him immediately.

I had not completed my task when Shadhi walked into the library. There was an evil, triumphant grin on his face. It was obvious he had won the duel of wills with Bertrand. I congratulated him.

"I do not wish to shock you, Ibn Yakub," he said in solemn tones. "You are a great scholar and scribe, and many of the ways of this world are unknown to you. I will not dwell on the details of the events which took place last night in the bedchamber currently occupied by our knight from al-Kuds. It is sufficient to inform you that he likes young men, but he insists on a violent ritual before he uses them. That poor boy's body was tested to the extreme last night. He has bruises and whip marks on his tender skin, and our treasury has had to pay him triple the amount we had agreed because of the strange ways of these Knights Templar. Our spies have described what took place and have not spared me any detail. If you like . . ."

Before the old devil could finish, one of the Sultan's attendants appeared to summon me to the royal presence without any further delay. I ignored Shadhi's wink and hurried back to the Sultan's chamber, having failed to find Toulouse on al-Idrisi's otherwise superbly detailed map. He was disappointed, but soon settled down to dictation. Shadhi, irritated at my lack of interest in the night-time activities of Bertrand, had followed me here. One look at the Sultan's face told him that now was not the moment to dwell on the habits of Bertrand of Toulouse. He settled down in the corner like a faithful old dog. Salah al-Din ignored his presence and began to speak.

Death surprises us in many ways, Ibn Yakub. Of these the battlefield is the least worrying. There, you expect to die. If Allah decides that your time has not yet come, you live on to fight and die another day.

Our great Sultan Nur al-Din became ill during a game of *chogan*. They say that one of his emirs had cheated him of a hit, and the Sultan lost his temper. His rage was such that he fainted. They carried him to the citadel in Damascus, but he never recovered. His personal physician wanted to bleed him, but the proud old man refused with a disdainful look, saying: "A man of sixty is never bled." He died a few days later. Our world suffered a heavy blow with his passing. He was truly a great king, and a worthy follower of our Prophet. He had begun the jihad against the Unbelievers and, for this, all our people loved him dearly. Mischief-makers, most of them eunuchs with nothing better to do, would come to me with stories of how Nur al-Din was preparing a big army to take Cairo and reduce me to the status of a vassal, but I ignored such talk, for it was based on rumour.

Our differences – and yes, these existed – were not the result of petty rivalry. He knew a war against me could only benefit the Franj. Where we disagreed was on the nature of the offensive to be launched against the enemy. Nur al-Din was a just and generous king, but he was impatient. I had often told him that the time to strike must be carefully judged. If we were wrong our entire cause would be consigned to the flames. But these were not disputes between enemies, but disagreements within the camp of the Believers.

While he had been alive, I was proud to dwell underneath his giant shadow, but his death transformed the landscape. If Cairo and Damascus were left unlinked, the Franj would, through a mixture of bribery and war, take advantage, isolate one from the other and destroy both. In their place, I certainly would have attempted such a plan. Before I go into battle, be it political or military, fought with words or swords, I always place myself in the enemy's mind. My good al-Fadil compiles a dossier detailing the activities of the enemy we are preparing to confront. We have reports on his strength or weakness of character and purpose. We have a list of his advisers and kinsmen, we know how they think and of the differences amongst them. With all this information in my own head, I then put myself in my enemy's place and work out how they would try and outwit us. I'm not correct every time, but often enough to know that this simple method has much to recommend it.

Now think, Ibn Yakub, just think. Nur al-Din is dead. In Damascus, Aleppo and Mosul, those who wish to succeed him are making plans to elbow rivals out of the way. They are expecting me in Damascus for the funeral. But I remain in Cairo. I let them make the first move. Nur al-Din's son, es-Salih, is only a boy. They are trying to use him to grab the throne. I still remain aloof.

Then a messenger arrives with a letter for me from Imad al-Din, one of Nur al-Din's most trusted advisers, as he is now mine. The letter appeals to me to protect the young boy from the vultures with greedy eyes who watch the citadel day and night. I send an ambassador to Damascus and pledge my loyalty to Nur al-Din's son. I also warn the emirs of Damascus that if they make the kingdom unstable, they will have to face the wrath of my sword.

I often ask myself how it has happened that strong rulers usually leave behind weak dynasties. Is it the curse of our faith that Allah has condemned us to a state of permanent instability and chaos? The first Caliphs were not chosen on the hereditary principle, but by a decision of the Companions of the Prophet. The dynasties established by the Umayyads and the Abbasids have led to disasters. Sultans and viziers nurture the growth of kingdoms for their children, but what if their children are incapable of ruling, as we have seen so many times since the death of our Prophet? I sometimes think we should have a Council of the Wise consisting of men like al-Fadil and Imad al-Din. These wise men should determine the succession. You smile. You think the wise men would, in time, unleash their own dynasties of wise children and grandchildren? Perhaps you are right. Let us continue this discussion some other time. Our friend Shadhi is already fast asleep.

Despite Shadhi's loud snoring, I resisted this suggestion. I knew that his mind was now totally concentrated on one objective, the reconquest of Jerusalem. The information given him by Bertrand of Toulouse had enhanced his confidence. He now believed that he could overpower Amalric.

I suggested that perhaps we should continue the story of his triumph in Damascus, subduing all his rivals and making himself the most powerful ruler amongst those who swore allegiance to Allah and his Prophet. Soon he would be engaged in new battles. We would have little time, and memories of previous encounters might fade away.

Salah al-Din sighed and nodded in agreement.

"You are too delicate to mention another possibility, Ibn Yakub. I might be killed in battle. and then your story would remain half-finished and untold. Your case has much merit. Let us continue, though there is a danger of which I must warn you. I am now speaking of events which excited a great deal of passion. My enemies spoke of my conquests as acts of personal ambition. I was a lowly mountain Kurd in a hurry. I was only concerned with leaving behind a dynasty and enriching my clan. I say this to you because if ever you feel that I am straying into the land of deceit, you must feel free to question me as you wish. Is that understood?"

I nodded, and he continued.

*

The most disturbing news from Damascus came one day in the shape of an old soldier. He had left the city of his birth with his family, his herd of camels, and all his belongings, and made his way across the desert to Cairo. It was Shadhi who saw him one day, a supplicant outside the palace. This old man had served with my father and uncle. He was a brave and dependable soldier and had become very attached to my father's person. Shadhi did not waste time, but brought him in immediately to see me. We found quarters for his family, though he had not come here to ask for favours.

He informed me that the emirs in Damascus had paid a great deal of gold to the Franj to buy their good will. This act of treachery had been multiplied a hundred times over in an exchange of letters in which the Franj had been asked for help against me. Can you imagine, Ibn Yakub? They were so frightened at the thought of losing their own power that they would rather hand their city over to the enemy. The same city where the grief-stricken populace had only recent buried Nur al-Din, who taught us all that the first task was to rid our land of these locusts, who worshipped icons and two pieces of wood stuck together.

I was livid with anger. At that moment I decided that we had to make sure that the Franj never entered Damascus. Fate helped us. Since Nur al-Din's death, the three great cities – Damascus, Aleppo and Mosul – had become divided. The eunuch who ruled Aleppo kidnapped Nur al-Din's son and made him a pawn on the chess-board that was once his father's kingdom. The nobles of Damascus became panic-stricken. They had lost the pawn to their rival. They appealed to Saif al-Din in Mosul, but he was engaged in his own plans and refused to help them.

At that point they turned to me. It was winter. We would have to ride through the night-cold of the desert, never a pleasing prospect. I called my commanders, and we prepared a force of a thousand carefully picked soldiers.

At these critical moments, timing is everything. Even a short delay and victory withers to defeat. We left the very next day and rode as if on our way to heaven. We took a spare horse for every soldier, enabling us to rest the beasts though not ourselves. Often we slept as we rode. Within four days I had reached the gates of Damascus. You see, O trusted scribe, the reason for my speed. Those who had, in desperation, invited me to save them were just as easily capable of changing their mind if another alternative in the shape of the Franj had appeared outside the city walls. I did not want to give them that opportunity.

As we entered the old city I found tears streaming down my face. This was the city of my youth. I went straight to my father's house. The streets were crowded with people who were cheering our arrival. There were loud acclamations and the nobles, their faces hard as a camel's behind, bowed before me and kissed my hands. They would have done the same to Amalric, though not in public. Our people would have hidden in their homes if the Franj had ever entered our town. I speak now not simply of the Believers, Ibn Yakub. Your people have always been with us, but even the old Christians of Damascus, who call themselves Copts, were not inclined to welcome the Knights Templar.

It was a joyous day, and many old friends came to see me. Imad al-Din, fearful of the nobles and their self-serving intrigues, had left the city and sought refuge in Baghdad. I sent for him. He is the al-Fadil of Damascus. These two good men are my conscience and my head. If every ruler possessed men like them, our world would be better governed. I left my younger brother, Tughtigin, in charge of Damascus and went to complete the task I had assigned myself, the task of reuniting Nur al-Din's kingdom.

The winter was getting worse, there were reports of big snowfalls in the highlands. But I was intoxicated by the support of the people of Damascus. I decided not to waste more time. Often our rulers are so busy celebrating one victory, they fail to see that the revelry is costing them their kingdom.

The Sultan stopped speaking suddenly. I stopped writing and looked up at him. Exhaustion had swept his face and he was deep in thought. It was difficult to know what it was that had distracted him. Was it the thought of yet more wars and bloodshed? Or was he perhaps thinking of Shirkuh, whose advice would have been so useful at this stage?

I sat there paralysed, waiting for him to dismiss me, but he had a distant look in his eyes and appeared to have forgotten my presence. I was undecided when I felt Shadhi's hand on my shoulder. He signalled that I should follow him out of the royal chamber, and both of us crept out quietly, not wishing to disturb Salah al-Din's reverie. He saw us leaving and a strange, frozen smile crossed his lips. I was concerned for his health. I had never seen him like this before.

When I reached home, I realised that I, too, was debilitated by the day's work. I had been sitting cross-legged, writing continuously for four hours. My legs and my right arm and hand were in need of care. Rachel heated some oil of almond to massage my fingers. Later, much later, she heated some more to soothe my tired legs and excite what lay, limp and inert, between them.

FIFTEEN

The causes of Shadhi's melancholy; the story of his tragic love

"You were worried last evening, Ibn Yakub. You thought Salah al-Din had been taken ill. I have seen that look on his face. It comes when turmoil takes over his mind. Usually this boy is very clear-headed, but he is assailed by doubts. Even when he was very young he could go into a trance, like our Sufis in the desert. He always recovers and usually feels much better. It is as if he has taken a purge.

"Yes, this old fool who you take as an illiterate clown from the mountains knows much more than he reveals, my good friend."

Shadhi was not his usual ebullient self this morning. He had a sad look in his eyes, which upset me. I had come to feel very close to the old man, who knew his ruler better than anyone else alive. It was clear that the Sultan loved him, but Shadhi, whose familiarity with Salah al-Din puzzled many, including the Kadi, never took advantage of his position. He could have had anything: riches, fiefdoms, concubines, or whatever else had taken his fancy. He was a man of simple tastes. For him happiness lay in close proximity to Salah al-Din, whom he regarded as a son.

I asked him for the cause of his melancholy.

"I am getting older by the day. Soon I will be gone and this boy will have no shoulder on which to shed his tears, no person to tell him that he is being foolish and headstrong. As you know I rarely pray, but today I fingered a few beads and prayed to Allah to give me strength for a few more years so I can see Salah al-Din enter al-Kuds. The fear that this wish might not be granted upset me a little."

For a while he said nothing, and I was touched by this uncharacteristic silence. His recovery, which was sudden, took me by surprise.

"Salah al-Din will not talk any more of his troubles, when he was subduing the heirs of Zengi and Nur al-Din. I think the memory of those days brings him pain. They were difficult times, but you should not imagine that he was a complete innocent. Hearing him talk to you yesterday one could get the impression that he was surprised by what finally happened. Not true.

"His father, Ayyub, had patiently and prudently prepared him for the day when Nur al-Din would pass away. I recall very well Ayyub warning him that impatience to secure Nur al-Din's kingdom would be fatal. He had always to act in the dead Sultan's interests, or that is what he should allow people to feel. He assimilated his old father's advice and when the time came he acted on it, and acted well. The day when we entered Damascus, and the people of that city wept tears of joy and threw flowers at us, was what decided him that the time was now ripe. He needed to secure these lands and prepare for the great encounter with our enemy.

"It was exactly ten years ago today that he defeated the joint armies of Mosul and Aleppo. We were outnumbered five to one. To buy time, Salah al-Din offered our opponents a compromise, but they imagined that our heads were already in their saddle-bags. They dreamed of showing our Sultan's head to the people of Damascus. They turned down our offer of truce. Then the Sultan became angry. His face was twisted with contempt for these fools. He spoke to his men, tried and tested veterans from Cairo and Damascus, who had fought many wars against the Franj. He told them that victory today would seal the fate of the Franj. He told them they were to fight against other Believers who were traitors to the cause of the great Nur al-Din. He, Salah al-Din, would take up the black and green colours of the Prophet and cleanse these lands of the barbarians.

"We had taken up a position on the hills known as the Horns of Hamah. Below was the valley watered by the Orontes. Salah al-Din's voice carried below, as did the acclamation of his soldiers, but the peacocks from Mosul and Aleppo were so sure of success that they took no notice of military tactics. They led their troops through the ravine, and we destroyed them. Many of their soldiers deserted their masters and swelled our ranks. Their defeated leaders pleaded for mercy and Salah al-Din, always mindful of his father's caution, accepted a truce. It gave him everything he wanted except the actual citadel of Aleppo. That too would belong to him, but later.

"This was no ordinary victory, my good scribe. It made your Sultan the most powerful ruler in the land. It was at this time that he declared himself the Sultan of Misr and Sham. Gold coins were cast in his name and the Caliph in Baghdad sent him the documents which sanctified his new position. He also sent him the robes which he would wear as a Sultan.

"But that was not the end of the story. No, far from it. The wounded pride of the nobles of Aleppo caused them to make one last attempt to rid themselves of this meddlesome Kurd. They sent a message to Sheikh Sinan, the Shiite, who lived in the mountains. The Sheikh was surrounded by a band of men trained in the art of tracking and killing particular individuals. He was a supporter of the Fatimids and had his own good reasons for seeking to dispatch our Sultan.

"The fact that the request came not from the remnants of the Fatimids, but from Sunni nobles, strengthened Sinan's resolve. Imad al-Din, who I hope you will meet one day soon, informed the Sultan that Sheikh Sinan's followers were accustomed to smoke a large amount of *banj* or hashish before they went on their special missions. Only thus intoxicated, and dreaming of other pleasures, could these *hashishin* kill on the orders of the Sheikh. They made two attempts on the life of the Sultan. On one occasion they overpowered his guards and surrounded his bed. Had an alert soldier not given the alarm, and had not Salah al-Din been wearing his special quilted jacket to protect himself from the cold of the night desert, he would have been dead. Only one dagger touched him before his assailants were taken.

"It was after these assassination attempts that he finally met Sheikh Sinan and agreed a truce. Indeed, on one occasion, when Sinan was threatened by some rival, we even sent soldiers to defend him. He never tried again. All sorts of stories were spread about the truce. Some said that the Sheikh had magical powers and could make himself invisible. Others said that, when surrounded by our soldiers, the Sheikh had the power to defend himself by exerting a mysterious force around himself which protected him against all weapons. These were tales spread by the *hashishin* to promote myths of their invincibility. But one thing I must tell you, Ibn Yakub. Whether it was the hashish or dreams of paradise, there is no doubt that Sheikh Sinan's men were extremely efficient and capable of reaching any target. We all sighed with relief, and gave thanks to Allah, after Salah al-Din and Sinan agreed to respect each other.

"A few months later, the Sultan entered Aleppo and was recognised as the Sultan of all the territories over which he ruled. He appointed Nur al-Din's son, es-Salih, as the governor of Aleppo. He confirmed Salih's cousin, Saif al-Din, as the ruler of Mosul, and he agreed to keep the peace for six years. I think he took caution too far. He was behaving as his father would have advised, but I thought that he needed more of his uncle Shirkuh's spirit on this occasion. He should have removed es-Salih and then taken on the dogs of Mosul, men so sly that they would not have hesitated to piss on their own mothers.

"Yes, I told him that, but he smiled, his father's smile. He had given his word, and that was enough. This Sultan never broke his word, even though his enemies often took advantage of this fact.

"The Franj, for instance, believed, good Christians that they are, that no promises made to infidels were binding on those who had pledged their word.

Those arse-fucking icon-worshippers broke treaties whenever it suited them. Our Sultan was too honourable. I think it was his origins. In the mountains, a Kurd's word, once given, is never taken back. This tradition goes back thousands of years, long before our Prophet, peace be upon him, was brought into this world.

"Amalric, King of Jerusalem, had died and had been succeeded by his fourteen-year-old son Baldwin, a poor boy afflicted with leprosy. Bertrand of Toulouse had given us information about Raymond, the boy's uncle, the Count of Tripoli. He became the real power in the Kingdom of the Franj. Salah al-Din concluded a two-year peace with Baldwin. He did not want to be outflanked in Misr while he was shoring up Syria.

"The Sultan's brother, Turan Shah, was left in charge of Damascus, and the Sultan, myself and his bodyguards returned to Cairo. We had been away for two whole years, but there were no problems. The Kadi al-Fadil had administered the state in the Sultan's absence.

"He had done it so well that Salah al-Din, congratulating him, asked: 'Al-Fadil, tell me something. Is there a real need for a Sultan? It seems to me that this state runs perfectly well without a ruler!' The Kadi bowed with pleasure, but reassured the Sultan that without his authority and prestige he, the Kadi, could not have managed anything.

"As for me, Ibn Yakub, I think they were both right. You know something? In the mountains of Armenia, the father of Ayyub and Shirkuh commanded the loyalty of people because they knew he was one of them. He would defend them and their sheep and cattle against raiders from neighbouring villages.

"I know I'm getting very old and I may be simple-minded, but it seems to me that if you can maintain peace and defend your people, what title you give yourself is of no great importance."

I looked at this old man closely. The wrinkles on his face seemed to have multiplied since I had first met him. He had only eight or nine teeth left in his mouth and was totally deaf in his left ear. Yet in his head lay decades of unsuspected wisdom, truths he had learnt through the rich experience which life had brought him. His tongue was always out of control and respected neither Sultan nor mamluk.

It was this capacity to speak whatever came into his mouth that made him indispensable to Salah al-Din, and before him to Ayyub and Shirkuh. It is often assumed that people in positions of power prefer sycophants and flatterers to those who speak unpleasant truths. This only applies to weak rulers, men incapable of understanding themselves, leave alone the needs of their subjects. Good rulers, strong sultans, need men like Shadhi who fear nothing.

As I observed him slowly chewing nuts in the winter sunshine, I felt a surge of affection for him sweep through my whole being. All of a sudden I wanted to know more about him. I knew his pedigree, but had he ever married? Did he have children? Or was he one of those men who always prefer their own sort to the presence of any female? I had wondered about this in the past, but my interest had waned and I had never questioned the old man. Today, for some reason unconnected with him, my curiosity had been aroused.

"Shadhi," I said, speaking to him in a soft voice, "was there ever a woman in your life?"

His face, relaxed in the sun, acquired an alertness. The question startled him. He glared at me, a frown casting a giant shadow across his face. For a few minutes there was an oppressive silence. Then he growled:

"Has anyone been telling you stories about me? Who?"

I shook my head.

"Dear, dear friend. Nobody has spoken to me of you except with affection. I asked you a question because I wondered why someone as alive and wise as you are never built a family. If the subject is painful, forgive my intrusion. I will leave you alone."

He smiled.

"It is painful, scribe. What happened took place seventy years ago, but I still feel the pain, right here in my heart. The past is fragile. It must be handled carefully, like burning coals. I have never spoken about what happened all those years ago to anyone, but you asked me with such affection in your voice that I will tell you my story, even though it is of interest to only me and affects nothing. Shirkuh was the only one who knew. I must warn you, it is not an unusual tale. It is simply that what happened burnt my heart and it never recovered. Are you sure you still want to hear me?"

I nodded and pressed his withered hand.

"I was nineteen years old. Every spring my sap would rise and I would find a village wench on whom to satisfy my lust. I was no different from anyone else, except, of course, for those lads who had difficulty in finding women and went up the mountains in search of sheep and goats. You look shocked, Ibn Yakub. Recover your composure. You asked for my story and it is coming, but in my own fashion. When we were children we used to tell each other that if you fucked a sheep your penis grew thick and fat, but if you went up a goat it became thin and long!

"I see that none of this amuses you, but life in the mountains is very different from Cairo and Damascus. The very function of these big cities is to curb our spontaneity and impose a set of rules on our behaviour. The mountains are free. Near our village there were three mountains. We could just lose ourselves there and lie back and watch the sun set, and permit nature to overpower us.

"One day my real father, your Sultan's grandfather, raided a passing caravan and brought the plunder home. Part of what he had pillaged were a group of young slaves, three brothers aged eight, ten and twelve, and their seventeen-year-old sister.

"They were Jews from Burgos in Andalus. They had been travelling with their family near Damascus, and had been captured by bounty-hunters. The father, uncle and mother had been killed on the road, their gold taken by the traders. The children were being brought to the market in Basra to be sold.

"The sadness in the girl's eyes moved me as nothing had done before, or has done since. She had clasped her brothers to her bosom and was awaiting her destiny. They were clothed, fed and put to bed. Our clan adopted them and the boys grew up as Kurds and fought many of our battles. As for the girl, Ibn Yakub, what can I say? I still see her before me: her dark hair which reached her waist, her face as pale as the desert sand, her sad eyes like those of a doe which realises that it is trapped. Yet she could smile, and when she smiled her whole face changed and lit the hearts of all those fortunate enough to be close to her.

"At first I worshipped her from a distance, but then we began to talk and, after a while, we became close friends. We would sit near the stream, near where the lilies with the fragrant scent grew, and tell each other stories. She would often start weeping as she remembered how her parents were murdered by the bandits. I could think of nothing else, Ibn Yakub. I asked her to become my wife, but she would smile and resist. She would say it was too soon to make such important decisions. She would say she needed to be free before she could decide anything. She would say she had to look after her brothers. She would say everything except that she loved me.

"I knew she cared for me, but I was annoyed by her resistance. I often became cold and distant, ignoring her when she came up to me and attempted to talk, ignoring her when she brought me a glass of juice made from apricots. I could see her pleading with her eyes for more time, but my response remained cruel. It was hurt pride on my part, and for us men of the mountains, dear scribe, our pride was the most important thing in the world.

"All my friends were aware that I was losing my head over her. They could see me going crazy with love, like characters we used to sing about on moonlit summer nights when we talked of conquering the world. My friends began to mock me and her. This made me even more determined to hurt her and offend her sensitivities and her feelings.

"How many times have I cursed this sky, this earth, this head, this heart, this ugly, misshapen body of mine, for not having understood that she was a delicate flower that had to be nurtured and protected. My passion frightened her. Soon her delight on seeing me turned to melancholy. As I approached, her face would fill with pain. She had become a bird of sorrow. Even though I was only twenty years old myself, I began to feel that I was fatal for all those who are tender and young.

"All this happened a long time ago, my friend, but have you noticed how my hand trembles as I speak of her? There is a tremor in my heart and I am beginning to lose my strength. I want to sink into the ground and die, for which the time cannot be too far away, Allah willing. You are waiting patiently for me to reach the end, but I am not sure if I can today. Now you look really worried. Let me finish then, Ibn Yakub.

"One evening a group of us young men had been drinking *tamr*, date wine, and singing the *khamriyya* and becoming more and more drunk and, in my case, unhappy. It was a really warm summer's night. The sky was glittering with stars and the dull light of a waning moon was reflected in the water. I walked away from my group to the edge of the stream where she and I used to meet and talk. At first I thought I was imagining her presence. But my eyes had not deceived me. Feeling the heat of the evening, she had discarded her clothes. There she was, naked as the day she was born, bathing in the moonlight. The sight turned my head. I felt my senses taking leave of me, Ibn Yakub. May Allah never forgive me for what I did that night.

"I see from your frightened eyes that you have guessed. Yes, you are right, my friend. I was in the grip of an animal frenzy, though most animals are kinder to each other. I forced her against her will. She did not scream, but I could never forget the look on her face, a mixture of fear and surprise. I left her there by the stream, and made my way back to the village. She never returned. A few days later they found her body. She had drowned herself. You would have thought that an animal like me would have recovered, found other women, married and produced fine sons. Yet perhaps with her death the animal in me also died. My heart certainly did, and I think of it as buried near that little stream in the mountains of Armenia. I had discovered and lost a priceless treasure. I never looked at or touched another woman again. Alcohol, too, was banished from my life. Allah has his own ways of punishing us."

Usually after one of his stories, Shadhi would wait for my reaction, discuss further details, and answer questions. Often we would share a glass of hot water or milk with crushed almonds, but not today. Today he slowly raised himself to his feet and limped away, probably cursing me inwardly for having compelled him to recall painful memories. He had said that the past was always fragile, and as I saw his back recede as he walked away, I thought of how he symbolised those very words in his own person.

I was stunned by his story. Forcing women was not an uncommon occurrence, but the punishment Shadhi had inflicted on himself was truly exceptional. This old man, to whom I was already greatly attached, now grew further in my estimation.

SIXTEEN

I meet the great scholar Imad al-Din and marvel at his prodigious memory

As was my habit, I entered the palace library to browse while I awaited my call from the Sultan. To my surprise, the person who came to fetch me today was the great scholar and historian Imad al-Din himself. Even though he was approaching his sixtieth year, there were not many white hairs on his head or in his beard. He was an imposing man, a good measure taller than both the Sultan and myself. One of his books, *Kharidat al-kasr wa-djaridat ahl al-asr*, an enlightening anthology of contemporary Arab poetry, had just been published, to great acclaim.

Usually he preferred to live in Damascus, but the Sultan had summoned him to Cairo, to help in the final preparations of the new jihad. Imad al-Din was regarded as a great stylist. When he recited poetry or read an essay, his reading was punctuated by appreciative remarks or exclamations. I respected his work greatly, but for myself, I prefer the simplicity of the scriptures. Imad al-Din's constructions were too flowery, too elaborate, too precious and too lacking in spontaneity, to appeal to my slightly primitive tastes.

As we walked through several chambers, he told me that he had heard much good said about me. He hoped, one day, to have the time to read my transcription of the Sultan's words.

"I hope you improve our ruler's words even as you take them down, Ibn Yakub. Salah al-Din, may he reign for ever, does not pay much attention to style. That is your job, my friend. If you need my help, please do not hesitate to ask."

I acknowledged his kind offer with a smile and a nod. Inwardly I was angry. Imad al-Din was a great scholar. Of this there could be no doubt. Yet what right had he to impose his will on the Sultan's own very personal project, with which only I and no one else had been entrusted? We had reached the Sultan's chamber, but only Shadhi was present.

"Please sit and relax," said the old man as he shrugged his shoulders. "Salah al-Din has been called to the harem. It seems that Jamila has created a crisis of some sort."

There was an awkward silence. Imad al-Din's inhibiting presence meant that I would not ask and Shadhi would not volunteer any information regarding Jamila. It was well known that Imad al-Din did not care for women in any way. For him true satisfaction, intellectual and emotional, could only be derived from the company of men.

As if aware that we were both tense, Imad al-Din cleared his throat, which I took as indicating that he required the attention due to a person of his standing. Shadhi, no respecter of persons at the best of times, broke wind loudly and deliberately as he left the room, and I was alone with the great master.

As I racked my brains for a way to open a conversation with this illustrious scholar, I felt embarrassed and intimidated. It was said of Imad al-Din that he only need see or hear something once for him never to forget. If one had told him a story several years ago and, forgetting that fact, began to repeat it in his presence, he would remember the original so perfectly that he would immediately point out the discrepancies between the two versions – to the great embarrassment of the story-teller.

He could recall not only the time of day or night when a particular incident had taken place, but all the circumstances as well. Once the Sultan had asked him how he could remember so much. He explained that his method was first to recall details such as the tree under whose shade the listeners were resting when the story was told, or the boat trip they were taking, the sea-shore and the time of day: then everything would become clear. I had been present during this discussion several months before, but had been unable to write it down. I had become so fascinated by Imad al-Din's way of talking and his soft, enticing voice that I had forgotten all else.

"With respect, O master, it is said that your intention was not to become a secretary in the Sultan's chancery, but to concentrate your great powers on writing your own works. Would such an assumption be accurate?"

He looked at me coldly, making me feel like an insignificant insect. I regretted having spoken, but his familiar voice reassured me.

"No. It is not accurate. When I studied the texts and letters formulated by al-Fadil in Cairo, I realised that we could do the same in Damascus. I had thought that this might be a difficult task, but Allah helped me. I threw off all the old ways of composing a letter of state and developed an entirely new style. This, my dear young man, astounded rulers such as the Sultan of Persia and even the Pope in Rome. The late Sultan Nur al-Din, may he rest in peace, was so pleased with my work that he made me the *mushrif*. I was now in charge of the entire administration of the state. This annoyed many people who felt that I had been promoted above their heads. They tried to make my life difficult.

"I recall one occasion. An envoy had arrived from the Caliph in Baghdad with a letter to Nur al-Din. My small-minded enemies had not invited me to the reception for the envoy. The old Sultan noticed that I was not present. He ordered a halt to the entire proceedings till I had been fetched. The Sultan handed me the letter to read, but al-Qaisarini, who was standing in for the Vizir that day, snatched the letter from my hand. I humoured him, but throughout his reading I corrected his mistakes and guided him whenever he went astray. I remember afterwards, when we were alone, Nur al-Din laughed at what had taken place – and this was a Sultan who rarely found time to appreciate a joke. That day he laughed and complimented me on my diplomatic skills."

He was about to continue, when our conversation was interrupted by the Sultan's entry. I stood and bowed, but Salah al-Din pushed Imad al-Din's shoulders downwards to stop him rising.

"You've been educating Ibn Yakub?"

"No sir. Not I. I have simply been correcting a historical misapprehension regarding my own past."

The Sultan smiled.

"You must not tire your memory, Imad al-Din. Sometimes I feel you memorise too much. I need you to be ready for the wars we are about to fight. It is possible that I might fall. You alone will be able to recall each and every detail of the jihad and make sure that it is diffused amongst the Believers."

The secretary bowed his head, and the Sultan indicated that he could leave. Once we were alone, he began to speak.

"As you know, I appreciate the Sultana Jamila and her enormous intelligence. Yet sometimes I wonder how such a capable woman can create such a mess. It would appear that she and Halima have separated themselves from most of the other women. Jamila has a group of six or seven women, and she educates them and trains them in her own ways. This creates tension and hostility, since neither Jamila nor Halima bother to conceal their contempt for those who prefer to enjoy the pleasures of life by refusing to exercise their minds at all. They live for pleasure and pleasure alone. They are not concerned either with the jihad or the philosophy of Ibn Rushd. For this Jamila seeks to punish them. I was forced to reprimand her and insist that she does not impose her will on the others. She accepted my injunction in front of the others, but with bad grace. I left immediately afterwards, but have no doubt, Ibn Yakub, she will try and bend both your ears and mine before this week is over. That woman never accepts defeat. I am not in the mood to dictate today. We will speak again tomorrow.

"As you leave, could you please ask Shadhi to send al-Fadil, Imad al-Din, and Qara Kush to my chamber? You look surprised. There are important decisions to be made over the next few days."

I was despondent at being asked to leave, and for the first time I spoke my mind.

"I will do as Your Grace asks, but it would seem more logical if I, too, could stay. It is I who have been chosen to write the Sultan's memoirs. I will remain silent and take notes, and the accuracy of these could be checked by the Kadi."

He looked as amused as he would have if his favourite steed had dislodged him from the saddle.

"There are some things, Ibn Yakub, which are best left untold. Do not imagine that I am unaware of your unease when I ask you to leave before meetings where the highest matters of state are discussed. This is as much for your safety as for our security. All my enemies are aware that you see me every day. They are also aware that you are sent out of the chamber when we plan our tactics for the next phase of the jihad.

"Nothing that happens in this palace is secret. Within a few hours the stories reach the harem, and rumours travel swiftly from there to the city. If it became known that you were part of the innermost councils of the state, your life might be in danger. That is the reason. However, tonight's meeting is completely unplanned. So tonight you can sit at a distance, observe and take notes, but it will not be al-Fadil who checks them for accuracy but Imad al-Din. He will remember everything."

I bowed to show my gratitude as I left the chamber. I was pleased that I had found the courage to challenge his decision and, for some unfathomable reason, this tiny victory gave me a gigantic amount of pleasure. Outside I met Shadhi and informed him of the Sultan's directives. He summoned a messenger to inform the three men that they had to return to the palace without further delay. Then he turned to me.

"And what make you of our great scholar, the noble Imad al-Din?"

"I think highly of him, but perhaps not as highly as he thinks of himself." Shadhi laughed.

"That son of a whore, al-Wahrani, has written a new song about him and his lover."

"Who is his lover?"

"That pretty boy with curly hair. The singer. You know who I mean? I think his name is al-Murtada. Yes, that is his name. Anyway, the song goes like this:

> *"Our great scholar Imad al-Din knows*
> *that his favourite text is al-Murtada,*
> *but without any clothes.*
> *They fornicate like dogs, each one on all fours,*
> *And drink wine from the navels of slave-girls and whores."*

Even as we were enjoying the joke, Imad al-Din walked past us in animated conversation with the Kadi al-Fadil. The sight of him sobered me immediately, but Shadhi was by now completely out of control. He laughed till the tears ran down his cheeks. I left him in that state as I followed the two men back to the Sultan's chamber. Behind him I heard the gentle tread of the trusted Qara Kush. I waited for him to catch up, and we walked together to the Sultan's chamber.

The discussion had clearly been taking place for several days. The main issue to be decided was the Sultan's departure for Damascus. It was felt that since Cairo and the rest of the country was stable, now was the time for the Sultan to return to Damascus, where there were serious problems which needed attention.

Imad al-Din reported that Salah al-Din's nephew in charge of Damascus, Farrukh Shah, was not a good administrator. His tastes were lavish, he refused to consider the needs of the jihad as a whole, and made decisions that depleted the funds held by the treasury. Imad al-Din argued strongly for the court to shift from Cairo to Damascus.

Qara Kush resisted the move, but was unconvincing. Unable to give a single serious reason for his argument, he descended to merely singing the praises of the Sultan, arguing that without his serene and noble presence he was fearful that the country might degenerate.

Remarks of this nature irritated the Sultan. He admonished his steward in sharp tones, pointing out that the sole basis for any major decision was the answer to one simple question: would it bring closer the defeat of the enemy and the capture of al-Kuds? He refused to countenance any other criterion.

Then al-Fadil spoke. He explained that if the Sultan's standard of judgement was to be the only one then the move to Damascus was unavoidable. Al-Kuds would not be taken using Cairo as the centre of operations. At the same time he expressed some worry as to what could happen here in the Sultan's absence.

Salah al-Din let them speak for a while, before interrupting them with a gesture of the hand.

"I think the arguments for strengthening Damascus and the other cities of Sham are irrefutable. If we are to take al-Kuds, I must be sure that all my cities are in safe hands. We cannot trust either to luck or the hope that the Believers will not betray us. As I never cease telling our people, this has been the curse of our faith. We shall leave exactly ten days from now. You, Ibn Yakub, will come with us to Damascus, together with your wife and daughter, for Allah alone knows how long we shall be away.

"We shall return to Cairo after our tasks, Allah willing, are accomplished, and not before. I am fond of this city. There are good memories to treasure.

"Your job, Qara Kush, is to make sure that, by the time I return, the citadel will be finished. That is where I will stay. As you know, I am not greatly attached to these old palaces."

Everyone present smiled, but Imad al-Din's face clouded, and when he spoke there was a trace of anger in his voice.

"That you sleep best in citadels is known to all, O Sultan, but I must plead with you to keep Qara Kush under some control. He is busy selling all the books in the palace libraries. Some of the fools buying them are so ignorant that they purchase according to weight rather than content. I am aware that Qara Kush is contemptuous of learning, but what he has been selling is our heritage. We have the most complete collection on medicine and philosophy in the library of this palace alone and . . ."

Before he could finish, the Sultan interrupted him.

"Qara Kush! I do not like this. Will you please make sure that Imad al-Din is consulted before any more books are sold."

Qara Kush nodded to acknowledge the instruction.

"One more thing. Bertrand of Toulouse has expressed a desire to return to his country. He will help us from there, and keep us informed on the movements of the Franj leaders. I want him given a safe-conduct and an escort on a merchant ship. Give him everything he needs. Will you see to this yourself, al-Fadil? I want this knight to return safely to his family."

The Kadi acknowledged the order, and Salah al-Din clapped his hands. Three attendants, familiar faces to me since they were permanently positioned outside the Sultan's chamber, entered and prepared the table. They served us a frugal meal, whose contents I had inwardly predicted. As I had suspected it was bread and three varieties of bean stew. No concessions were made to the presence of Imad al-Din, whose tastes in food were well known. His banquets consisted of several courses and always included a new dish that left his guests gasping in astonishment. I watched the face of our greatest living historian. It did not betray a single emotion. Like all of us, he followed the Sultan and dipped his bread in the stew. The Sultan looked at him.

"Does this humble meal meet with your approval, Imad al-Din?"

Answer there was none, but the great man touched his heart to convey his approval and gratitude. It was only as we left the chamber that I heard him whisper to al-Fadil:

"One should only eat with Salah al-Din if afflicted with constipation and an urgent need to move the bowels."

SEVENTEEN

I arrive home unexpectedly to find Ibn Maymun fornicating with my wife

A chamber had been assigned to me at the palace and usually, after a late night, I did not bother to return home. It was well past the midnight hour and, had I not heard al-Fadil grumbling earlier that because of the Sultan's meeting he had to cut short a consultation with Ibn Maymun, I would have stayed at the palace. Instead I began a brisk walk home. I had not seen Ibn Maymun for a long time, and I wanted him to be present when I told Rachel that we were all moving to Damascus.

As I reached the courtyard inside my house I was surprised to see the lamps still burning. Not wishing to wake either our guest or my family, I crept in quietly. Imagine my surprise when I entered the domed room to see Ibn Maymun lying flat on his back with his robe pulled above his stomach and covering his face while Rachel, my very own Rachel, sat astride him and kept moving up and down as if she were taking a leisurely morning ride on a tame pony. She was stark naked, her breasts moving in rhythm to the rest of her body. I stood paralysed. Anger, shame and fear combined to stun me. I was horrified. Could it be an apparition? A bad dream? Was I still asleep in my palace chamber?

I stood in the darkened corner of the room silently observing the fornication progress. Then I coughed. She saw me first, screamed as if she had caught sight of the devil himself, and ran from the room. I approached our great philosopher, who had just managed to cover his erect penis.

"Peace be upon you, Ibn Maymun. Did Rachel make you welcome? Were you demonstrating a particular section from your *Guide to the Perplexed* just for her benefit?"

He did not reply, but sat up and hid his face in his hands. Neither of us spoke for a long time. Then his choked voice managed to mutter an apology.

"Forgive me, Ibn Yakub. I beg your forgiveness. It is a lapse for which I deserve to be severely punished. What more can I say?"

"Perhaps," I asked him in a calm voice, "I should simply cut off your testicles. Honour would then be restored, would it not?"

"None of us are infallible, Ibn Yakub. We are only human. Would you have resisted had Halima invited you into her bed?"

I was startled and angered by his audacity. Before I could control myself, I moved forward, grabbed him by the beard, and slapped his face, first on one side and then the other. He began to weep. I left the room.

Rachel was sitting on the mattress, wrapped in a blanket, as I entered. She was too ashamed to look me in the eye. Anger had dumbed me. I spoke not a word, but removed a blanket and left the room. I entered my daughter's room and lay down on the floor, beside her mattress. Sleep refused to visit me that night or the next.

Rachel wept for two whole days, pleading with me to forgive her. To my surprise I did so, but I also knew that I did not wish her to go with me to Damascus. I merely informed her that the Sultan had asked me to accompany him and I would be away for an indefinite length of time. She nodded. Then I asked her the question that had been burning my mind since I saw her mount Ibn Maymun.

"Was it the first time? Speak the truth woman!"

She shook her head and began to weep.

"You never forgave me for not giving you a son. Was it my fault that after our daughter was born I could never conceive again? You abandoned me for the Sultan and life in the palace. Ibn Maymun became my only source of consolation. I was lonely. Can't you understand?"

I was shaken. No reply formed itself on my lips. I was filled with a blind rage and, had I not left the room, would have struck her several blows. I staggered to the kitchen and drank two glassfuls of water in order to calm myself and bring my emotions under control. Then, recalling that this was one of Ibn Maymun's prescriptions for controlling one's temper, I smashed the glass on the floor.

For the next week, while I was preparing to leave, I did not speak to her. At first I wanted revenge. I thought of lodging a complaint with the Kadi. I wanted to accuse Rachel of adultery, and Ibn Maymun of being her accomplice. This thought did not stay long in my mind. I considered hiring a few men to murder the guilty couple. Then I calmed down. It is strange how fickle emotions of this sort can be, and how anger, jealousy and revenge can rise and fall within the space of a few moments.

I bade a fond farewell to Maryam, my twelve-year-old daughter, who, if the truth be told, I had neglected for far too long. Surprised by my display of affection, she hugged me in turn and wept copiously. I looked at her closely. She was on her way to becoming a beautiful young woman, just like her mother. The resemblances were stark. I could only hope that in a year or two she would find a suitable husband.

It was my last night in Cairo. I broke my silence. Rachel and I sat up and spoke for half the night. We talked of the past. Of our love for each other. Of the day Maryam was born. Of the laughter that used to resound in the courtyard of our house. Of our friends. As we talked, we became friends again. She admonished me for having put the needs of a sultan before my own work. I acknowledged the justice of her criticisms, but explained how my own horizons had expanded through my life at the palace. She had always accused me of leading far too sedentary an existence. Now I was about to travel. She smiled, and there was a special pleading in her eyes. My heart melted. I promised that once Jerusalem had been taken by the Sultan, I would send for her and Maryam. We parted friends.

To his great irritation, the Sultan's departure from Cairo became the occasion for a mass display of public emotion. Salah al-Din would have preferred an unannounced departure, but both al-Fadil and Imad al-Din insisted, for reasons of state, that it had to be a public event. Courtiers, poets, scholars and sheikhs, not to mention several waves of the local people, had gathered near the old lake to bid their Sultan farewell. Qara Kush and his men were keeping a path open from the palace for the Sultan and his immediate entourage, which included myself and, of course, Shadhi.

The reason for the excitement was obvious. Everyone was aware that Salah al-Din was going away for a long time. He would not return till he had defeated the Franj outside the gates of Jerusalem. The people wanted their Sultan to succeed, but they were also aware that the expedition was full of risks. The Sultan might perish, as he had almost done a year ago in some preliminary skirmishes with the enemy. On that occasion he had found a camel, clambered on its back, and found his way back to the city with a handful of warriors.

The Cairenes liked their Sultan. They knew that his tastes were modest and, unlike the Caliphs of the Fatimids, Salah al-Din had not taxed the people to accumulate a personal fortune. He rewarded his soldiers handsomely. His administrators had made sure that the country had not been plagued by famines. For all these reasons and many others, the people and their poets and musicians wanted Salah al-Din to think of them when he was away. They wanted him to return.

As we rode down the streets from the palace they were shouting: "Allah is Great," "Victory to the Commander of the Valiant," "There is only one Allah and Mohammed is his Prophet," "Salah al-Din will return victorious." The Sultan was touched by this reception. We were moving slowly, to give ordinary people the chance to touch the Sultan's stirrup and bless his endeavours.

As we reached the site of the old lake, the nobles of the court were gathered in all their finery. Salah al-Din quickened the pace. It was clear that he was becoming impatient with the ritual. At the heart of the dried lake, he reined his horse to a stop. Farewells were spoken. On a raised platform, a young, clean-shaven poet rose to declaim some lines. The sight was too much for Shadhi, who belched in anticipation of early relief.

The Sultan's face betrayed nothing as the following lines were recited:

> *"May Allah never bring you sorrow*
> *May Allah never disturb the tranquillity of your sleep*
> *May Allah never make your life a cup of bitterness*
> *May Allah never melt your heart with grief*
> *May Allah give you strength to defeat all our enemies*
> *We bid you farewell with heavy hearts*
> *Whose load can only be lightened with your return."*

Not to be outdone, an older man, his grey beard sparkling in the hot sun, took the stage and recited:

> *"Spring is the season that turns the year*
> *Yusuf Salah al-Din's greatness is our eternal spring*
> *Sincerity rules his heart*
> *Iron rules his mind."*

At this juncture the Sultan signalled to al-Fadil that it was time for him to leave. He saluted his nobles and kissed al-Fadil on both cheeks. There were tears in many eyes and these, unlike the poetry, were genuine. Just as we were leaving, an old man approached to kiss his hand. He was so aged that he did not have the strength to reach the Sultan's stirrup. Salah al-Din jumped off the horse and embraced his well-wisher, who whispered something in his ear. I saw the Sultan's face change. He looked at the old man closely, but his face, now wreathed in smiles, taught Salah al-Din nothing. Shadhi rode up to the Sultan.

"What did the old man say?"

Salah al-Din's face was downcast.

"He said I should bid the Nile a fond farewell since it was written in the stars that I would never see it again."

Shadhi snorted, but it was clear that the discordant note had eclipsed the preceding good will. Bad omens displease all rulers, even those who claim not to believe in them. Our departure was abrupt. Salah al-Din turned his horse sharply and we rode out of the city.

Our party numbered three thousand men, most of them soldiers who had fought at the Sultan's side for many years. These were tried and trusted swordsmen and archers, each of them adept on horseback. I noticed three veterans, who had, till our departure, been attached to the School of Sword-Makers. There they had taught both the art of sword-fighting and the skill required to make a sword. All three were from Damascus, and were pleased to be returning to their families.

Jamila and Halima, together with their retinue, had left Cairo three days ago, though many of the former slave-girls who had produced the Sultan's children were not accompanying him to Damascus. I wondered what he was thinking. The Sultan spoke little while he rode, a habit inherited from his father rather than his uncle Shirkuh who, according to Shadhi, found it difficult to keep his thoughts to himself regardless of the circumstances.

News of our departure was hardly a secret. The Franj were aware of what was happening and had their soldiers on the borderlands waiting to pounce on us. So to avoid an ambush, Salah al-Din had ordered the Bedouins to plan a route which avoided the Franj. He was not in a mood for either a show or a test of strength. He was a man possessed with only one idea in his head. Everything else had to wait till it had been accomplished.

As in the past, however, local rivalries would not permit him to concentrate his energies on freeing Jerusalem.

Later that evening, as we reached the desert and made camp for the night, Salah al-Din summoned the emirs to his tent. Shadhi and I were left free to admire the stars. The old man was in an affectionate mood, but even so I was surprised by the turn our conversation had taken. After talking about his impending death, he suddenly changed tune.

"I hope you have truly forgiven your wife, Ibn Yakub. I know that in Allah's scale, adultery is never treated lightly, but in our lives you must understand that what took place between her and Ibn Maymun was not of great importance. I've startled you. How do I know? One of the Kadi's spies keeps a watchful eye on the movements of the great physician, for his own protection, you understand. He appears to have watched him a bit too closely. A report was made to the Kadi, who informed the Sultan in my presence. It was Salah al-Din who decided that you should not be informed. He made me swear an old mountain oath to that effect. He values you greatly and did not want you upset. At one stage we even discussed finding you a new woman."

I was silent. It was cold comfort that these people knew everything about me. I was not concerned about Shadhi. I might even have told him myself, but the Kadi and the Sultan? Why did they know? What right had they to spy on anyone? I was gripped by anger. Inwardly I cursed Rachel for having betrayed me. Above all, I felt shamed. In their eyes now I was not just a scribe, but also a cuckold. I took my leave of Shadhi and walked for a while. In front of me the desert was like a dark blanket. Above me the stars were laughing in the sky.

And this was just the first day of our journey. There were to be thirty more. I looked back in the direction from whence we had come, but all I could see was the dark and bitter cold of the night desert. I clutched the blanket tightly around my body and covered my head as I bade farewell to Cairo.

DAMASCUS

EIGHTEEN

*I meet the Sultan's favourite nephews and hear
them talk of liberating Jerusalem*

It seemed as if we had arrived in Damascus only a few hours ago. In reality we had already been here for two weeks, but it had taken that long for me to recover from the torment of the four weeks that preceded our arrival. The journey had proved uneventful for everyone else, but not for me. I was now capable of riding and controlling a horse, but the activity was not greatly pleasurable. My face had been badly burnt by the sun and, had it not been for the ointments carried by our Bedouin scouts, the pain alone would have killed me.

I could only thank my stars for having been born a Jew. If I had become a follower of the Prophet of Islam I, too, would have been compelled like the bulk of the soldiers and emirs to turn towards Mecca and say my prayers five times a day, usually in the heat of the desert sun. The Sultan, whom I had never thought of as a deeply religious man, was, in his role as commander of his troops, very insistent on observing the rituals of his religion. The lack of water for the ablutions posed no problem. Sand became an easy substitute. Shadhi pleaded old age to avoid the mass prayers. One day as he saw the Sultan lead the prayers he whispered: "It is just as well there are no Franj in the vicinity. The sight of three thousand good Believers with their arses in the air might prove too easy a target."

Leaving aside the physical rigours of the journey, I had been compelled on several evenings to sit in the Sultan's tent and listen to Imad al-Din's monotonous voice recite the stories of the Caliphs of Baghdad. This became a torture of the mind for me, since the tales he was repeating had been lifted from works with which I was only too familiar.

To be fair to Imad al-Din, he did not attempt to claim the *Muraj al-Dhahab* and the *Kitab al-Tanbih* as his own works. He credited al-Masudi, the author, but it was his own style of recitation which imparted a false sense of authority. Perhaps it was all in my imagination. Perhaps I was so exhausted by the day that having to listen to stories I had already read did not appeal to me greatly at the time.

Two weeks of total rest in this most beautiful of cities revived me completely The joy of being able to bathe every day, the delight of the food that was served by the kitchens in the citadel, and the respite from the sun was all that I needed

The Sultan, bless his heart, took a great deal of interest in my recovery. He, too, was pleased to be in Damascus, but for reasons that were different to mine This had been his home for many years. It was here that he had learnt the arts of war and the delights of a woman's bedchamber. He felt safe in this city, and his appearance at the great Umayyad Mosque on the previous Friday had demonstrated how much he had grown in stature in the eyes of the ordinary people Shadhi had told me that he had seen by the Damascenes as a raw youth, given to the pleasures of the wine-cellar and fornication. News of his conquests had reached them from afar, and now they barely recognised their Sultan. He had become an even greater leader than the pious and much-loved Nur al-Din.

I could detect the excitement on the faces of many during the Friday congregation. The white-bearded scholar who had taken the pulpit had called on Allah to give Salah al-Din a long life and help him drive the Franj into the sea. He had referred to the Sultan as the "sword of Islam" to the acclaim of the assembly, which responded with one voice: "There is only one Allah and Mohammed is his Prophet."

The citizens here seemed to be more deferential, less audacious than their equivalents in Cairo. In my city it was not uncommon to hear criticisms of the Kadi or even the Sultan, and the shadow-players usually spoke for a much larger public. I was reflecting on the differences between the two cities, and the temperament of their inhabitants, when a person unknown to me knocked on the door and entered my room.

From his dress, he appeared to be a retainer, and yet the look on his face expressed a certain familiarity which surprised me. He bowed and introduced himself as Amjad al-Islam. He was tall, very tall, extremely well-fed and clean-shaven. He informed me that he had been in the service of the Sultan since he was ten years old. He claimed that "Uncle" Shadhi had taught him all he knew of this world.

"The Sultan wishes you to dine with him tonight and Uncle Shadhi wishes you a good appetite. He will eat with you tomorrow."

With these words a self-satisfied and grinning Amjad left my chamber. I smiled at Shadhi's message. The old man had been in his element during our march from Cairo to Damascus, but he was suffering from tiredness and ill-humour. Since our arrival he had kept to his own quarters. I was delighted to hear that he was well, and looked forward to our meeting. I had already bathed and had thought of writing a detailed account of the desert for my own book, but once again Salah al-Din had interrupted my labours.

He was seated with two men whom I had seen in his company a great deal since our arrival here. From their demeanour they appeared to be emirs, which they certainly were, but they were also the Sultan's favourite nephews, Farrukh Shah and Taki al-Din. They were brothers, sons of the Sultan's oldest brother, Shahan Shah, who had died when Salah al-Din was only ten years old. He loved both of them and each competed with the other in audacity on the field of battle.

They reminded him of Shirkuh, and in them he had invested a great deal of love and trust.

He introduced me to them in turn, and both stood to embrace me.

"Our future depends on you," laughed Taki al-Din. "If you write badly of us we will be forgotten, but if you write truthfully the memory of what our clan has achieved will remain till our Maker decides that the time has come to end this world."

"Tell me, master scribe," asked his brother, "is there any such thing as absolute truth? Do you report different versions of the same event? Do you consult more than one source? After all, much of what you are writing comes to you from the lips of our esteemed uncle. Naturally he will not talk of those events in which he disappointed himself."

I looked at the Sultan, who burst out laughing.

"I may not, but Shadhi, as we all know, can always be relied upon to make up for my deficiencies. And now that we are in Damascus, Ibn Yakub has two extra informants in the shape of you devils. Kindly do not forget that he is engaged in writing my memories and these can only be experienced by me."

This little family exchange made a reply from me redundant. I smiled, as good scribes sometimes do, but remained silent. The arrival of the food provided another diversion. The younger men looked at my face as I observed the variety of dishes being placed before us and burst out laughing. Farrukh Shah exchanged a meaningful look with me.

"I can tell you're not used to meat at our uncle's table! He will just eat a bowl of broth tonight followed by fruit. What we have before us is lamb marinated in herbs and freshly grilled. It was our great-uncle Shirkuh's favourite dish, and today is the day of his birth. We owe it to ourselves to remember him in the fashion he would have appreciated."

The Sultan frowned at the frivolity.

"Better you eat it on his birthday rather than to mark the day he died. I saw him die and it was a painful sight. Mimic his capacities as a great leader of men and a fighter of tremendous spirit, but avoid his vices. All our great men of medicine have warned against over-indulgence on any front."

Salah al-Din's annoyance sobered his nephews. They bowed their heads to acknowledge his warning. The rest of the meal was virtually silent, but after the food had been cleared and mint tea served, I realised that this was not a casual gathering. As he prepared to speak, the Sultan indicated that I should ready my pen.

"What I say about the sons of my dead brother, Taki al-Din and Farrukh Shah, I wish to say in their presence. I feel closer to these two men than anyone else in my family. They are not just my nephews, but also two of my ablest generals.

"My own sons are young, and if anything were to happen to me I would expect Taki al-Din and Farrukh Shah to protect my children from the vultures that will start circling the cities we have made our own. If I die soon, I want Taki al-Din to sit in Cairo and Farrukh Shah to rule Damascus. The other places should be divided amongst my brothers and their children, but Damascus and Cairo are the real jewels of our kingdom. Without them we are reduced to nothing. They are the cities which will enable us to drive out the Franj.

"For almost ninety years, the Franj have been prowling on our lands like wild beasts. Few, if any, now remember a time when they were not here. When they first arrived we were unprepared. We panicked. We betrayed each other for gain. Later we made alliances with the Franj against our own brethren. Sultan Zengi and the great Sultan Nur al-Din understood that the only way to drive out the Franj was to unite ourselves. As is known this unity does not come without the sacrifice of much blood.

"Look at the situation today. The Franj still occupy many towns near the sea as well as al-Kuds. I want to divide our armies into three carefully organised, well-knit instruments under the command of myself and my two brave nephews. I will concentrate on taking either Aleppo or Mosul, though preferably both. That will make us the mightiest power in these our lands. At the same time

I want you, Taki al-Din, to strike at the heart of the Franj in Palestine. Let them think that this is part of a big push to take al-Kuds, their beloved Kingdom of Jerusalem. Inflict defeats, but do not delay too long in one place. Strike fear in their hearts. I want them fully preoccupied so that they have no time to even think of helping our enemies in Aleppo and Mosul.

"Farrukh Shah, you will stay here and guard this city and its borders with your life. I have received reports of your extravagant style and your propensity to leave the treasury depleted. I never wish to hear any such complaint again. Your father and grandfather were men of simple tastes. I have learnt that to win the respect of the people and, in particular, our soldiers, one must learn to eat and dress like them. We are the lawgivers, Farrukh Shah. We must observe each law and set an example. I hope I have made myself clear. Never forget that even though we rule, we are still seen as outsiders. It is only now that the Arabs are beginning to accept me as their Sultan. The future of our family depends on how you behave and how you rule. Never forget that a man is what he does.

"If you hear that the Franj are sending exploratory expeditions to test our defences, go out and crush them. We will talk again tomorrow, but make preparations for our departure within a week.

"Our destination must be kept a secret. I do not wish you to even tell your wives where we are headed. If people ask, reply: 'The Sultan is still making up his mind.' If, in my absence, which I hope will be brief, Damascus is seriously threatened, inform me without delay. We must never lose this city. Go now and rest. I wish to speak with Ibn Yakub on my own."

The nephews, chastened by the Sultan's words, bent and kissed their uncle in turn on both cheeks. He rose to his feet and hugged them both. They shook hands with me and departed.

"I wanted you to come with me, Ibn Yakub, but I am worried by Shadhi's health. He has always accompanied me on my campaigns, but, as you can see, he is getting older and frailer by the day. Any day now Allah could summon him to heaven. He is my only link with the older generation. All the others have gone.

He is, after all, as you know, my grandfather's son. I have such happy memories of him. He was a great influence on my youth and I have always relied on him a great deal. Allah has blessed me with good and strong advisers, men like al-Fadil and Imad al-Din. No Sultan could ask for more, but even they find it difficult sometimes to resist some of my more irrational decisions.

"Shadhi alone never fears to speak the truth and call me an obstinate ass and talk me out of some foolish notion that had entered my head. Shadhi is not a scholar, but he has a strong instinct for what is right or wrong in the field of politics and of war.

"There are times in our lives, Ibn Yakub, when we are unhappy in love or sad because a dear friend has been killed in a battle or we have lost our favourite steed. At times like this, when we feel we are on the edge of an abyss, hare-brained advisers and sycophants can unwittingly push us over the edge. Men like Shadhi never permit that to happen. These are men of great integrity and our world, alas, has too few like them. Shadhi has saved me from myself on more than one occasion. That is why he has meant more to me than even my parents.

"You're surprised to hear me speak like this, and you're wondering why I do so, since Shadhi is still with us and recovering from the journey and might outlive us all. I used to think like you, but something very deep inside me is warning me that I will be far away when Shadhi dies. The thought upsets me greatly, Ibn Yakub. I know how much he respects and likes you and for that reason I am not taking you with me. It will make my decision not to take him much easier for him to bear if you are with him. Do you understand?"

I nodded.

"I want him to rest. I have directed Amjad, the eunuch who earlier brought you my message, to make sure that Shadhi never wants for anything while I am away. Amjad answers to me and nobody else.

"Shadhi and Farrukh Shah are not close. Why? Because Shadhi's tongue is no respecter of persons who, in his opinion, are not behaving as he thinks they ought to, and in the past he has subjected Farrukh Shah, who is not a bad person, to a very severe lashing with his tongue. It was in the presence of other emirs, and his pride suffered a blow. Farrukh complained bitterly to me, but what could I do? Can you imagine me reprimanding Shadhi? The problem is that Farrukh has still not forgotten the insult. I'm sure he will do nothing to hurt Shadhi, but that is besides the point. What the old man needs at this time is friends and a great deal of attention.

"I hope my fears are misplaced. I pray that when Allah brings me back to Damascus, Shadhi will still be here with detailed information on the mistakes I made during the campaign, which Imad al-Din will have reported to both him and you.

"Perhaps what is also worrying me is not just Shadhi's death, but my own. Till now Allah has been kind to me. I have escaped death on several occasions, but if you lead an army into war as frequently as I do, and my person is the main target of the enemy, then it is only a matter of time before an arrow pierces my heart or a sword cracks my skull. I am feeling a little bit fragile, Ibn Yakub. I want you to know that your family is well looked after in Cairo, and I have left instructions for you to be paid regularly while you are here. After we achieve our objective, and Allah has spared me, I will present you with a tiny fief outside your beloved Jerusalem. If I fall, I have left instructions with al-Fadil and Imad al-Din that you are to be given a village wherever you desire."

To my surprise I felt tears roll down my cheeks. The Sultan's generosity was no secret, but I was simply a lowly scribe. I was overwhelmed by his giving thought to my future as well. When I rose to take my leave of him, he rose too and embraced me, whispering in my ear a last command.

"Keep the old man alive."

NINETEEN

Shadhi presides over the circumcision ceremony of Halima's son; the death of Farrukh Shah

The Sultan had been gone just over three weeks. It was the height of summer. Damascus had become unbearably hot. Every creature, human or animal, was constantly in search of shade and water. It was on one such day that Amjad the eunuch came rushing to my quarters in the early afternoon and disturbed my sleep. He was smiling as he woke me up to announce that the Sultana Jamila had summoned me. I had not seen either her or Halima since our arrival. I thought of them often, but felt that perhaps the reason for this was the stricter social rules that operated in Damascus, which was less open than Cairo.

Still feeling drowsy, I followed Amjad blindly to the harem. Halima had given birth to Salah al-Din's son. Naturally I did not see her, but was led to an antechamber where Shadhi, watched by Jamila, was reciting the *qalima* in the ear of the newborn babe. The infant was carried by a wet-nurse, a slave girl of incredible beauty, who I had not seen before. The child was named Asad al-Din ibn Yusuf. This was the Sultan's tenth son, and Shadhi's instinctive ribaldry led him to offer a prayer to Allah to control the Sultan's seed, lest the weeds outnumber the flowers. Jamila laughed loudly, and whispered her agreement to the old man.

Shadhi was still in excellent spirits three days later, after the circumcision ceremony. He appeared to have recovered completely from his recent fatigue. The local emirs and Farrukh Shah were the new targets of his lacerating wit. It was difficult not to laugh out loud and draw attention. Shadhi's hatreds were always pure and usually justified, but there were times when I did worry that there were many tale-carriers in the citadel who would like nothing better than to please a master by informing on Shadhi. When I shared my apprehensions with him he chuckled, and refused to take me seriously.

One reason for his anger was the fact that, like me, he was excluded from the innermost councils of the court. This was hard for him to tolerate, given his closeness to his nephew. Both of us felt the absence of the Sultan. It was strange being without him. I was surprised at the intensity of my own feelings. I had been in his service for only five years. How much more aggrieved must Shadhi have felt at being deprived of his traditional place, close to the Sultan in war and in peace. Habits and routines are hard to dislodge from one's system. Sometimes I found myself wandering thoughtlessly and in a semi-daze to the Sultan's chamber and then making my way slowly back to my own, almost as if I were a loyal dog left behind by an uncaring master.

In recent years, in very different ways, our lives had revolved so completely around the person of Salah al-Din that it was difficult to accept that he was not present here in the citadel, and that we were not by his side wherever he happened to be.

"It is that peacock on heat, Imad al-Din, who must be writing all the Sultan's dispatches," Shadhi muttered one day. "Why don't you ride out and join Salah al-Din? You can tell him I forced you to leave Damascus. You can also tell him that Allah has restored my health, and I don't need you by my side waiting for death to strike."

This was a difficult order. Salah al-Din's movements were still unclear. Even f one knew where he was, it was perfectly possibly that he would be somewhere completely different by the time one reached him. We had not received news for some weeks. Neither pigeon nor courier had arrived, and Farrukh Shah was slightly concerned. Other reports of Franj activity, not far from Damascus, had been received two days ago. Even as Shadhi and I were talking, an attendant summoned us to Farrukh Shah's presence. He had returned earlier that day from a skirmish with a small group of Franj knights about half an hour away from Damascus.

Farrukh Shah was not the most intelligent of rulers, but his generosity and courage were well known. Imad al-Din's complaints regarding his extravagance were not exaggerated, but they underplayed the fact that little of the money was spent on himself. He rewarded loyalty, and in this he was not unlike his uncle, except that Salah al-Din's austere tastes and habits were so well known that even the poorest of the poor never believed that he spent much on himself. Some rulers are motivated by artistic pursuits, others are addicted to hedonism, others still to the pursuit of riches as an end in themselves. The Sultan was only concerned with the well-being of others.

It was a moonlit sky as we crossed the ramparts to the audience chamber. We had been excluded from it ever since the departure of Salah al-Din. The emirs were already gathered as we entered. I bowed to Farrukh Shah, who looked exhausted, as if he hadn't slept for many days. Shadhi glared at the Sultan's nephew, who ignored the old man completely, but he came and welcomed me with a display of real warmth.

"I'm glad you could come, Ibn Yakub. A letter has just arrived from my uncle, and we are instructed that you and old man Shadhi are to be invited when it is read to the council."

I bowed again to thank him. Shadhi sniffed loudly and swallowed his phlegm. One of the younger court scribes, a pretty, fair-skinned boy with golden hair and curled eyelashes, probably no more than eighteen years of age, had been selected to read the letter.

"Look at this shameless hussy," whispered Shadhi, looking at the scribe. "He's probably just walked here from Farrukh Shah's bed, and he's still busy making eyes at him."

I frowned at my old friend, hoping to control his bitterness, but he grinned at me defiantly.

The boy spoke in a cracked voice.

"Castrated," muttered Shadhi.

"Silence!" shouted Farrukh Shah. "Silence when a letter from our Sultan Salah al-Din ibn Ayyub is being read to the court."

The scribe began to speak, at first with a certain nervousness, but then, as Imad al-Din's prose gathered its own momentum, with much greater confidence.

"This letter is addressed to my dear nephew Farrukh Shah and all our loyal emirs of Damascus. We are outside Aleppo and desirous, as ever, of avoiding the unpleasant sight of Believer killing Believer, I have offered the emirs an honourable truce, provided we occupy the citadel. I am not sure that they possess the intelligence to appreciate our generosity.

"One of them rode out to meet us yesterday. He was full of flowery words and grand flourishes, hoping to flatter me into withdrawal, offering me untold treasures and swearing eternal loyalty to us on the Koran. 'We are your friends, O great Sultan, and we will be at your side on that day which is about to come, the day when you take al-Kuds and drive the Franj out of our lands.'

"These fine words made no impact on me, since only three days previously our spies had reported that the nobles of Aleppo had sent urgent messages to the Franj and the *hashishin* in the mountains, offering them money if they could keep me out of the city.

"I replied to him as follows: 'You claim to be my friend. For me friendship is a sacred trust, Acred, but tell me something: who are your enemies? Name your real enemies and I will name your friends. For me friendship means, above all, common animosities. Do you agree?'

"The fool nodded. At this point I showed him a copy of the letter his master had sent to the Franj. He began to sweat and tremble, but I contained my anger. Shadhi, bless his heart, would have advised sending this rogue's severed head back to Aleppo, and I was greatly tempted, but I rose above my anger. Anger is never a good emotion when one is determining a higher strategy. We sent the Emir back to Aleppo with a severe warning that, if they persisted in their defiance, then I would have no alternative but to take their city by storm. I warned them not to imagine that, in these circumstances, all their citizens would rush to defend them.

"We wanted to send you a dispatch after the armies of Mosul, backed by their allies, decided to meet us on the plain of Harzim, just below Mardin, but we waited for them in vain. They may have advanced like men, but they vanished like women. We were tempted to chase them, but instead I decided to isolate them completely from the neighbouring towns.

"Two days ago we took the city of al-Amadiyah, without too much resistance, though too much time was taken by our soldiers in piercing the massive black basalt walls. This was a pleasurable victory because of the surprising treasures contained in the city. We have, as a result of this victory, succeeded in capturing many weapons, enough to create two new armies. Both al-Fadil, who was here for the siege, and Imad al-Din, were interested only in the library, which contained a million volumes. These were loaded on seventy camels and are, even as I write, making their way to Damascus. Ibn Yakub should be placed in charge of ensuring that they are placed safely in our library till Imad al-Din returns. They include three copies of the Koran which date to the time of the Caliph Omar.

"The Franj will not be able to resist their offer, and that is the main reason for this letter. The aim of the Franj will be to prevent me from assembling a large army. I think they will attempt a diversion in both Damascus and Cairo. If my instincts are justified then you need to forestall such a move by taking the offensive.

"You have done well, Farrukh Shah. I have detailed reports of your recent victories, but we need Aleppo and Mosul under our control if the Franj are to be dislodged from our world and returned over the sea to their own.

"Tomorrow we march back to Aleppo. The mountain air has done us all much good and has dispelled our tiredness. The soldiers know that the sun in the plains will be like the fires of Hell, but our Heaven will be Aleppo. It will take us fifteen days to reach it and, Allah willing, we shall take the city this time. Only then will I return to Dimask to make our final preparations for the jihad. Be on your guard against surprise attacks by the Franj."

The chamberlain indicated that the meeting was over, and as Shadhi and I rose to leave the chamber, we bowed in the direction of Farrukh Shah. But there was something wrong, and suddenly his attendants, too, realised that he had fainted. The room was cleared, and the physicians summoned. It is to the credit of all the emirs present that there was no sense of fear or panic, of the kind which usually accompanies the illness of a ruler. Perhaps this was due to the fact that Farrukh Shah was not a Sultan, but acting on his behalf.

Shadhi was dismissive, refusing to take the illness seriously.

"He probably had too much to drink or extended himself too far when fondling that foolish boy who read Salah al-Din's letter. Go to bed, Ibn Yakub."

I did go to bed, but I was too worried to sleep, so I got up again, put on my robe and walked outside. The moon had set and the stars had changed places. I walked slowly in the direction of Farrukh Shah's bedchamber, only to be greeted by his favourite attendant who was weeping like a child, loudly and uncontrollably. I feared the worst, but he was still alive, though still in a swoon.

The next morning, Farrukh Shah's condition weakened. He never recovered. Even as the Sultan was marching towards Aleppo, loud screams and wailing rent the citadel in Damascus, announcing to all of us that his nephew had breathed his last.

We buried him the next day, with all the honours due to his person. It was not just a gathering of nobles. Thousands of ordinary people, including several hundred vagrants, came to offer prayers at the side of his grave. This was the clearest indication to me that perhaps Shadhi's hostility to the dead man had been misplaced.

TWENTY

Halima abandons Jamila and the latter is heartbroken

In the absence of the Sultan my daily routine had been transformed. I would spend most of the morning in the library, studying any manuscript I could find which related to my own work. Here in Damascus there was a private collection in the possession of a great scholar, Ibrahim ibn Suleiman, now nearly ninety years of age. I had first heard of him and his library from someone whose memory even now brings me pain. My only image of him is that of an animal satisfying his lust on my wife's body. I shall not dwell on him again, or so I have hoped.

Ibrahim was the oldest Rabbi in the city. I used to see him nearly every day as I made my way to the synagogue, behind which his library was situated. On most days he could be found there. Old age had not yet affected his mental faculties. On the few occasions when I needed to ask him for some advice, he revealed the splendours of his mind, making me feel somewhat sad and inadequate. He had heard a great deal of the intellectual prowess of the man I have no desire to mention again, and one day he sat me down and wanted to know everything I could tell him about Ibn Maymun.

The spell is broken. The accursed name has again darkened these pages. And yet . . . And yet, I could not deny Ibrahim ibn Suleiman the information for which he yearned with all the eagerness of an eighteen-year-old scholar.

So, against my will, and to please this great and generous old man, I talked of Ibn Maymun and of the work on which he was engaged. I mentioned why he was writing *The Guide to the Perplexed*, and, as I spoke, the wrinkled map that was Ibrahim's face was suddenly wreathed in a smile so pure that I was shaken by the change. This was the face of true wisdom.

"I will die happy now, Ibn Yakub. Another has done what I wanted to, but could never achieve. I will write to Ibn Maymun, and give you the letter. You can use your position as the Sultan's favoured scribe to have it sent to Cairo immediately. I will also enclose with the letter some of my own work on the subject which he might find of some use. How well do you know him?"

How well did I know him? The question echoed and re-echoed in my mind. A deep pain, which I thought I had transcended, gripped my insides once again, as the memory of that awful night burst like a thunderstorm that drowned me in the moment. I did not realise that tears were pouring down my face. Ibrahim wiped them with his hands and hugged me.

"He brought you grief?"

I nodded.

"You may tell me if you wish, even though I may not be able to help."

And so my heart poured out its long-repressed agony to this patriarch in his robes. He sat listening, as Musa must once have listened to the troubles of his children. When I had finished, I realised that the pain had disappeared. This time I felt it had gone forever. It would never return.

The comfort Ibrahim offered was written on his face. His alert, intelligent eyes did not flicker. He understood. He did not need to say anything. I understood. In the scale of suffering that our people had undergone, my personal experience was a grain of sand. Nothing less. Nothing more. All this had been suggested by his presence alone. As if through a miracle my head had suddenly cleared. The residual pain had disappeared. My inner balance was restored. Everything could be seen through a different, centuries-old perspective. I wanted to laugh out loud, but restrained myself. He noted the change.

"Your face has cleared, Ibn Yakub. The lines on your forehead have evaporated. I hope the dark clouds inside your head have once again given way to the sun."

I nodded my head. He smiled.

As I made my way back to the citadel, the sun was at its zenith, piercing the black muslin robe that I wore. I was beginning to sweat and feel uncomfortable. The minute I had reached my destination, I headed straight for the baths. I lay in the cold water for a long time. Slowly the heat and discomfort in my body gave way to a cool calm. I dried myself and returned to my chamber fully restored. I drank some water and lay down to rest. My dreams were very clear, as they usually are during the afternoon sleep. Because one is sleeping lightly, the memory is clearer. I was dreaming of the domed room in Cairo, and I saw my wife and daughter sitting in front of a vessel containing water, which they were pouring over each other. How the dream would have developed, I do not know. I felt myself being shaken out of my slumber, and raised my eyelids to see the grinning face of Amjad the eunuch.

"The Sultana wishes to see you now, Ibn Yakub."

I sat up in bed and glared angrily at him, but he remained unaffected.

"Which Sultana?" I asked.

He refused to reply, as was often his wont, merely indicating with an arrogant gesture that I should follow him. In some ways he reminded me of the eunuch Ilmas in Cairo, who had come to a bad end.

It was Jamila who awaited me in the antechamber which led to the harem. She dismissed Amjad with a flicker of an eye. She was not her usual ebullient self; her languid eyes were unhappy. She had been crying, and had clearly not slept well for many a night. What could have upset this woman whose piercing intelligence and strength of character had dazzled the Sultan himself? She stared at me for a long time without speaking.

"The Sultana appears distracted. Can a humble scribe help in any way?"

"Your old friend Halima has betrayed my trust, Ibn Yakub. In her I thought I had found a worthy friend. She shared my criticisms of the way we lived. For many months, as you know, we were inseparable. We lost count of the days we spent together. She learnt to appreciate Andalusian philosophy and the satirical poetry of our wits in Cairo and Damascus. We used to laugh at the same things. Even our animosities were matched. For fear of offending your delicate sensitivities, I will not describe our nights together, but believe me, Ibn Yakub, when I say that they move me still. We played together like the flute and the lyre. Need I say more? When, looking at me, she used to smile, her face flowed like a freshwater spring, radiating goodness and tempting one to bend down and drink its refreshing waters. When she smiled it was as though the world smiled with her.

"Since the birth of her son, something has transformed her completely. She behaves in a strange fashion. She shuns my company. She listens to the ravings of superstitious old witches whose only task is to frighten us into submission. Amjad tells me that some of the old maids in the harem have filled her head with nonsense of every sort. He says that they told her that the Sultan favoured her son over my boys; that her son could become Sultan one day, but only if she broke away from me. They told her that I was a malign influence, that I had led her astray, away from the true path decreed by Allah and his Prophet. They filled her ears with falsehoods about my past. All this Amjad told me, and his sources are always accurate.

"Halima has begun to believe that the world is full of demons. The other day I heard her anxiously asking a maid whether the *udar* ever attacked children. Do you know what the *udar* is supposed to be, Ibn Yakub? It is a creature the Bedouin invented centuries ago to frighten away their rivals in the desert.

"The udar is supposedly a monster who rapes men and leaves them to roast in the desert, but only after he has made sure that worms have built nests in their anuses! If an uneducated person believed in all this rubbish I would simply laugh, but I have spent months teaching the finer points of philosophy to Halima. I thought she understood. Instead she now thinks that the *udar* is real and Ibn Rushd and Ibn Sina are false. It is as if her brain has been eclipsed by a dark cloud, which refuses to be blown away.

"When I try and speak with her she looks at me with fear-filled eyes, as if I was a demon or a witch. She refuses to let me pick up her child. She will not let me touch her. Three nights ago she told me that everything we had done together was evil, sinful and repulsive. She said that Allah would punish us by throwing us to the mercy of djinns and other demons. I wanted to scream at her, to pull her hair, to shake her roughly till she saw sense again, but I contained myself, trying instead to understand what had happened to her.

"Only once, when I surprised her alone in the bath, did she seem like her old self. She was on her own and I, too, slipped off my clothes and entered the bath beside her. Neither of us said a word. I took a piece of cloth and began to gently massage her tender, slender shoulders. It must have stirred some memories.

"For the first time in months, she turned round to look at me. Then she smiled. Her teeth were gleaming like polished ivory and her face lit up again. It was the old Halima. My heart melted away and I stroked her head, before lowering my arms and rubbing her breasts.

"Then it was as if she had been struck by a thunderbolt. Her entire demeanour changed. Her face grew stern. She glared at me with anger, removed herself from the bath and fled. She screamed for her attendants, who rushed to her side with towels. I sat in the bath, Ibn Yakub, and watched silently as my tears increased the volume of the water.

"Now I am broken-hearted and distressed beyond reason. Yes, beyond reason, and that hurts me for I feel that I, too, am being dragged away from calm, rational, elevated thoughts, and from a love whose purity is deep.

"She was my closest friend. We talked about everything, including Salah al-Din's weaknesses in the bedchamber. Now that I am estranged from Halima there is nobody with whom I can discuss matters that are close to my heart. thought of you, because you were once her friend. She spoke well of you and told me that you were a good listener. To find an intelligent listener these days is not easy, especially if you happen to be married to the Sultan.

"How do you explain Halima's evolution? Surely, Ibn Yakub, it could not simply be the outcome of childbirth. I have provided Salah al-Din with two sturdy boys, with no such effects. How is it that she can live in a world totally composed of fantasy?"

I was shaken by Jamila's story. It was difficult to believe that Halima, a free spirit if ever there was one, a woman who the Sultan once described to me as being strong-willed as a pedigree horse, could be the frightened, pathetic creature of Jamila's description. A thought flashed through my head. Perhaps Halima had decided to end her unnatural relationship with the older woman, and the only way she could do so was by rejecting not just Jamila, but everything associated with her, everything she had taught and everything she stood for in this world. If that were the case, however, surely Halima would not need to descend so low as to believe in monsters and evil spirits. Or again, was she putting on an act to convince Jamila that everything was over, and that she Halima had changed for ever? Aloud I said:

"I was deep in thought, Sultana, trying to fathom the mysteries of the change you have described. To me it appears unreal, as if Halima were in a trance. I do not think it has much to do with child-bearing, but it could be that meddlesome women, jealous of her friendship with you, have sought to poison her ears."

"That was tried in Cairo as well, Ibn Yakub, but she scattered the trouble-makers with words so rude that they must have scorched their ears. So why should she be more vulnerable in Damascus? I wrote a great deal for her. Stories, poems, letters to express my passion. In return I received but one little piece of paper a few weeks ago. It contained these words: 'I am what I am. I wish you another, who is better than me. I no longer deal in happiness like a trader in a caravan. I love only Allah and I follow the way of his Prophet.'

"Does this make any sense to you at all, Ibn Yakub? Nor to me. It is like being stabbed in the heart and hearing her voice say 'Die!'"

"I have a request to make of you. Will you please speak to Halima, and see for yourself whether or not I am mistaken? Perhaps where I have failed, you might succeed. The Sultan does not object to either Halima or myself meeting with you as often as we like. This is a well-known fact, there would be nothing secretive about such a meeting. If you have no objections, I will arrange it. Amjad will fetch you at the agreed time."

Before I could agree to her proposal, she swept out of the chamber. It was not a request, but an instruction.

For a week or more I walked about in a daze. It was almost as if I had been infected by Jamila's sadness. Her words had left a deep mark on me, yet I could not believe that Halima's transformation could have been as profound as she had suggested.

I waited impatiently for Amjad the eunuch, and one morning he came to fetch me. His smile always irritated me, but I noticed that he could not help himself. It was a sign of nervousness on his part. I followed him eagerly through a long corridor to the same antechamber where I had met Jamila several days ago.

Halima was already seated on a large cushion draped with brocades. She saw me and managed a weak smile. I was stunned by her appearance. Her face was pale and the life seemed to have gone out of her eyes, which appeared hollow. Her voice was subdued.

"You wished to see me, Ibn Yakub."

I nodded in silence.

"Why?"

"I wanted to congratulate you on the birth of your son and to inquire as to your own thoughts and preoccupations. If I may be so bold, can I ask why you appear so changed? Was the birth difficult?"

"Yes," she replied in a voice so soft that I had to strain to hear her words. "It was very difficult. They put a special stone in my hand to ease the pain, and wound a snake-skin round my hips to speed up the birth. You ask whether I have changed, Ibn Yakub. I have. My son was born healthy only because of three spells that were written by a man of medicine. These involved a renunciation of my entire past and especially my relations with Jamila. The birth changed me completely. Even if the spells had not been cast, I would have wanted to thank Allah for giving me a son by not deviating from the path he has determined for us through our Prophet, may he rest in peace.

"It was not easy for me. As you know, Jamila and I used to spend all our time together. We used to joke, laugh and blaspheme in the same breath. If I were to tell the Kadi some of the things she used to say about our Prophet, peace be upon him, the Sultan himself would not be able to save her neck.

"Everything she taught me was false. She wanted me to doubt the word of Allah. She said that the wisdom contained in the writings of al-Maari, Ibn Rushd and Ibn Sina far exceeded that contained in our Holy Book. Allah forgive me for listening to such dangerous rubbish. I have repented, Ibn Yakub. I am no longer a sinner. I pray five times a day, and Allah will forgive me and protect my son. As for Jamila, I wish we did not have to stay in the same quarters. Her presence is a constant reminder of my sinful past. I know this will shock you, but I wish she were dead."

All this had been uttered in a listless voice devoid of passion. Even her last sentence was spoken in a melancholy whisper. The change in Halima went very deep. I could see that now, and it upset me greatly. I had been wrong to doubt Jamila. This was not just a case of Halima deciding to break her friendship. She had turned her entire life upside-down. I made one last attempt.

"Lady Halima, if someone else had told me that you had undergone such a complete change I would have laughed in their face. Surely you must accept that not everything the Sultana Jamila taught you was evil. Did she not teach you to appreciate poetry? Are the songs that I heard you sing in Cairo defiled because she taught them?"

For a moment her face softened and I caught a brief glimpse of the Halima I had once known. But her features quickly hardened again.

"Her influence on me was evil. I thought she loved me, but all she wanted was possession. She wanted me to belong to her and to nobody else. I must belong to myself, Ibn Yakub. Surely you can understand my desire to become myself again."

"You forget that I knew you before you met Jamila. Have you forgotten Messud? Can you not remember the way you spoke to the Sultan when the Kadi brought you to the palace in Cairo? It is true that you had not then been subjected to Andalusian philosophy, or to the erotic poetry of Wallada, but your mind was ready for a leap. Jamila, too, noticed that and helped to show you a new world."

"Jamila played on me as if I were a lute."

This was a travesty of the truth, and I felt constrained to defend the motives of the Sultana.

"Even though I resented her power over you, she played well. The music that the two of you made together was the envy of the palace. The eunuchs talked about you all over the city. They talked of two queens who cared for nothing but the truth. They described how your eyes were like a furnace when you denounced those unfortunates who believed in djinns and other imaginary creatures. Your fame spread everywhere. That was a kind of freedom, Halima. I say that to you as a friend."

"You talk like a fool, scribe. True freedom lies in the commands of Allah and his Prophet alone. Why should we be so arrogant and assume that we alone, a tiny minority, speak the truth, while a majority of Believers who refuse to doubt are, by virtue of this refusal, prisoners of prejudice? Let me tell you something. I now know that Jamila's blasphemies were like a breeze from Hell. You look shocked, Ibn Yakub. I should not be so surprised. How could a Jew ever understand the ways of our Prophet?"

I looked at her face. She averted her gaze. Everything between her and me ended at the moment. She had fallen for the honeyed words of false prophets and the bitterness of those who make a living by casting spells.

I rose, gave her an exaggerated bow and left the chamber. I was angry. Halima was a lost soul. Now I understood Jamila's despair. It was not simply the sorrow of a forsaken and rejected lover. Jamila was sad not just because of the gulf that had now opened up between them, but because, together with their entire relationship, the knowledge and understanding of the world that she had so patiently imparted to her friend had also been rejected. Something terrible had happened. Both Jamila and myself had recognised the change. Halima's thirst for understanding had disappeared. Birds were no longer singing. Flowers died.

I reflected on that conversation for several days. Her words swirled through my mind continuously and, in my head, I argued with her over and over again, to no avail. Halima was a ship that had sunk to the bottom. I reported my distress to Jamila, and a bond that had been lacking in the past grew between us, a closeness brought about by a common sense of loss, a bereavement for a friend in whom wisdom had petrified. She was surprisingly philosophical.

"I have been thinking a great deal on this matter, Ibn Yakub. I have come to the conclusion that the loss of a close friend, with whom one shared everything and in whom one had complete trust, is a far greater blow than being deprived of physical contact. Even as I say this to you, I ask myself whether I really believe this or whether by telling you I am trying to convince myself that the love between friends is of greater value than erotic love. There are times, increasingly few, when I believe the exact opposite. Times when it seems that my mind is on fire, and the flames must spread to my body. Times when I would sacrifice friendship for just one last passionate embrace.

"You see, Ibn Yakub, how even someone like me, strong and sure of myself, can be afflicted by love. It is a terrible disease which, as our poets never cease to tell us, can drive us insane. I know that you, too, were once in love with her. Is that why a veil of sadness covers your face as well?"

It was not the memory of Halima, who I pictured at her strongest, defiant in her love for Messud, her eyes blazing with passion, as she confessed her adultery to the Sultan in the presence of the Kadi, that had come over me. I felt troubled by the sight of Jamila, who was anxiously awaiting my reply to her question.

"It is seeing you in such a dejected state that makes me unhappy, O Sultana. My own passion for Halima did not last long. It was a childish desire for something unattainable, not uncommon in men of my age. It faded many months ago. What I do ask myself is why you remain unhappy. Anger, bitterness, desire for a cruel revenge, all this I could understand, even though it would be unworthy of you. But it does not behove a woman of your intellect to mourn for someone whose transformation is so complete that it makes one question one's earlier judgements and ask whether this was always the real Halima. Was what you and I once saw simply a mask, designed above all to please you, not unlike those deployed by the shadow-puppeteers in Cairo?

"I also wonder whether what you really miss is the love and friendship, or something else. Perhaps what truly upsets you is that you have lost something that you regarded as a possession. Halima was always precious, but she had rough edges. In smoothing those down, and giving her a vision of a world much larger than the palace or even the city, an exciting world of ideas where nothing was forbidden, you brought out the best in her. All those who saw you together, including the Sultan, marvelled at the close affinity that marked your friendship. In other words she became your proudest possession, and possessions are not permitted to run away. Could it be this that has really upset you?"

Her eyes flashed fire, transcending the misery, and I saw the old Jamila once again.

"Listen to me scribe. Neither you nor that toothless old dog, Shadhi, nor those wretched eunuchs who report to him, have any idea of what it was like between Halima and me. It was not a one-sided friendship. I learnt a great deal from her, about other worlds and about the way people less privileged than me lived, but even that is unimportant.

"You and your beloved Sultan live in a male world. You simply cannot understand our world. The harem is like a desert. Nothing much can take root here. Women compete with each other for a night with the Sultan. Sometimes they ease the pain of their frustrations by finding eunuchs who will crawl into their rooms at night and fondle them. The lack of a penis does not always impair the capacity of the eunuch to provide pleasure.

"In these conditions it is impossible for any woman to have a serious friendship with a man. My father was very exceptional in this regard. After my mother's death he became a true friend with whom I could discuss a great deal. As you know full well, I'm fond of Salah al-Din. I know that he takes me seriously. I'm not simply a mound of flesh on which he occasionally fornicates. He recognises the existence of my mind. Despite this, I could not in honesty pretend that ours is a profound relationship. How could it be in these times and in these conditions? With Halima I enjoyed something that was complete on every level. It has nothing to do with possession. After all, we are all possessions of the Sultan.

"You see, Ibn Yakub, I still think that she will return one day. Not to me, but to her senses. That will be sufficient. My hope is that one day she will teach other women what I have taught her, so that our time together will not have been wasted. Now I want nothing more from her. Nothing more! Her heart no longer responds to my voice. Everything is over. She is dead to me and for me. I will grieve alone. Sooner or later, solitude brings its own calming wisdom. My serenity will return and I will be happy again. Do you understand?"

I nodded, and a small, sad smile appeared on her face as she left the chamber slowly, with measured steps, almost as if she did not wish to return to the site of her pain.

I thought of Jamila a great deal after that meeting. If our world had been different, we could have become close friends, and it would have been me who benefited from the experience. She, more than any other woman I have met, exemplified Ibn Rushd's complaint to the effect that the world of those who believed in Allah and his Prophet was disabled by the fact that half its people, namely the women, were excluded from functioning in the field of commerce or the affairs of state.

When one is cut off from what is happening in the world beyond the citadel, then events like the transformation of Halima acquire an importance that is undeserved. The minute the couriers, their clothes and faces coloured by a red dust, arrived with dispatches informing us that Aleppo had fallen without a battle, I recovered completely. Everything fell into place. The first courier who brought the good news was embraced by everyone. The fool who had resisted the Sultan had been forced by the populace to flee and return to Shinshar, the city of his birth.

Outside Aleppo, the soldiers who had guarded the city rode past the Sultan with their heads lowered in tribute. The people of Aleppo had loved Nur al-Din, and remained loyal to his successors, but they knew that in Salah al-Din they had found a conqueror who would both defend them and their city and also refuse to let anything stand in the way of the jihad.

The fall of Aleppo sent a wave of excitement through Damascus. There were celebrations on the streets. The taverns in all quarters of the city were packed with young men determined to drink their fill. It was as if our whole world had changed with the news. People felt this in their bones. Our Sultan was now the most powerful ruler in the land.

The next day my joy was circumscribed by the news that an inimitable voice had fallen silent. Ibrahim had died peacefully in his sleep. Our friendship was new, but I wept for him as one does for a father. Even the most hardened faces were wet the next day at his funeral. He had left me a small collection of books from his private library. They were accompanied by a note. I did not read it till later that evening in the privacy of my own chamber.

"The service of great kings may carry its own rewards, but the service of truth goes unrewarded and is, for that very reason, worth far more."

TWENTY-ONE

*Jamila leaves Damascus and, hoping to regain
her serenity, returns to her father's palace;
Salah al-Din falls ill and I hasten to his side*

Two days later, Amjad the eunuch brought me a letter from Jamila. He was neither grinning nor eager to offer information. He simply placed the letter in my hands and left the chamber.

I was startled by the beauty of her handwriting. I had never seen such exquisitely crafted letters except in the calligraphy of the great masters of the art. Whoever had taught her to write like this must have been a master or the descendant of one. As I write these lines I have the letter in front of me. Even as I transcribe her words I can once again hear her clear voice the way I heard it that day when Halima first introduced me to her. Her voice echoes in my ears, and her strong features appear in my mind's eye.

Good friend, Ibn Yakub,

This is to let you know that I am leaving Damascus for a few months, perhaps longer. I am returning for a while to my father, who is now nearly eighty years of age and has not been well for

some time. I wish to see him before he dies, and the Sultan, bless
his heart, has never placed any impediments against my desire to
travel.

Once many years ago I spent some time in Baghdad. That was a visit
to improve my mind. I went to listen to the teachings of a great
philosopher and poet. It was he who taught me the importance of
reason. I can still see him stroking his white beard as he made me learn
the following exchange between our Prophet and Mu'adh ibn-Jabal, the
Kadi of al-Yaman.

Prophet: How wilt thou decide when a question arises?
Mu'adh: According to the Book of Allah.
Prophet: And if thou findest naught therein?
Mu'adh: According to the sunnah of the messenger of Allah.
Prophet: And if thou findest naught therein?
Mu'adh: Then shall I apply my own reasoning.

When I returned, I reminded Salah al-Din of this and he began to use
it a great deal, especially when he was dealing with the theologians of
the Fatimid Caliphs in Cairo. I felt then that I had achieved something,
and that journey always stayed with me.

Now I leave in order to restore my state of mind. I have suffered a
terrible blow, and I am convinced that in Dhamar I will not be troubled
by the memories of Cairo and Damascus.

I want to smell once again the fragrance of the blossoms in the unique
garden created by my grandfather, surrounded by the most beautiful
wall that I have ever seen, a wall out of which grow the most lovely
plants and flowers. I always used to think that heaven would be like our
garden. Here I used to spend many hours in the silence among the trees,
watching the birds coming down from the wall to drink water from a
stream that had been contrived to create the impression that it was
natural.

It was here that dreams were formed. I used to sit there in the shade for hours and dream, wondering what the world must be like outside Dhamar. Merchants would talk of Baghdad and Cairo and Damascus, of Basra and Calicut, and the strange and wonderful things that happened in these cities, and I would rush to my father and insist that I be allowed to become a merchant when I grew up so that I could go as far as China.

When I was fourteen, I often rode with my father. Sometimes we would go and watch the sea. How calming it is to watch the gentle waves and admire the work of nature. My father, too, used to pull up his horse next to mine, leaving our retinue of attendants way behind. Most of them were frightened of the water, which they believed was inhabited by djinns in the shape of giant fish, who ate humans. I remember galloping in the sand and then riding my horse through the shallow water, which splashed me as well.

My father would look at the sea and say: "Here, everything will outlast us and those who come after us. This same breeze will be felt by people several hundred years from now and they will marvel at nature just as we do. This, my child, is the voice of eternity."

I did not fully understand what he meant till much later. Then I realised how lucky I was to have a father not given to believing that the world would end before his children grew old. Many people genuinely believed that Allah would bring the world to an end, and that the angels would open their ledgers and read out an account of our lives. My father was very different.

I was sad to leave my home and my friends, but I had no choice in the matter. Nor did Salah al-Din. It was an alliance deemed necessary by his father and mine, and blessed by the great Sultan Nur al-Din, may he rest in peace. I liked Salah al-Din's company, but I never enjoyed the pleasures of union. I bore him two sons and after that he never troubled me again. We became friends, and I discouraged him from spending the

night with me. This is only my personal experience, and perhaps I would
have reacted to any other man in the same way. Perhaps my body was
never intended to be defiled by a man. Pure love and happiness I found
only with Halima, but you know that old story well.

When Nur al-Din's widow, Ismat, married Salah al-Din, she was for
many months in a state of total disbelief. I think after the ascetic Nur al-
Din, who probably mounted her out of duty, she found Salah al-Din as
frisky as an untamed horse. I remember the day she told me that she had
never realised that coupling could actually give her pleasure.

I say this so that you do not judge your Sultan's performance in this
field solely on the basis of my experience. That would be unfair to him.
Ismat's version is much more reliable, and borne out by the reports of
many others in the harem. Halima, like me, was an exceptional case. For
her the memory of Messud was so strong that she was quite open. She
admitted to me that when the Sultan first took her she shut her eyes and
imagined it was Messud, simply to ease the burden.

Perhaps I will not stay long in Dhamar. Perhaps it is futile to search
for a lost past or imagine that one can cure the pain of the present by
reliving one's childhood and youth. There are aspects of life in Dhamar
which displease me. The constant glorification of the old way of life of
the desert tribes leaves me cold. The exaggerated stories of Bedouin
triumphs against nature and their human enemies leave me completely
unmoved. My father, too, never encouraged any of this. Yet it exists and
the courtiers indulge themselves by writing bad poetry in praise of the
unwearied pace of pure-bred camels, or a Bedouin encampment being
surrounded by wolves and hyenas, or hunger and drought and the
delights of camel milk.

If any of this goes on for too long, I will return soon to Damascus
cured forever. But there are people I want to see. My mother's sister who
brought me up after my mother's death and who became a close friend.

She would confess all her worries and secrets. In return, I would tell her of my worries. She came once to visit me in Cairo, but I was so enamoured of Halima in those days that I had no time for my poor aunt. She went back unhappy, thinking, no doubt, that I had become arrogant and inconsiderate. Now I wish I had taken her into my confidence and explained the state of my mind at the time.

It is not good to be trapped by one's emotions, Ibn Yakub. Do you not agree? And yet it is difficult to break free of them. From that point of view my return to Dhamar will be helpful, and I will return to Damascus restored and my old self again. Then we shall sit, you and I, and discuss philosophy and the history which we are living through every day. If Salah al-Din embarks on another adventure while I am away, tell him that Jamila insisted that he leave you behind. Peace be upon you.

I had barely had time to reflect on Jamila's letter when Shadhi limped into the room. I hid the letter from him simply to avoid answering any lewd questions, but he cackled.

"Amjad the eunuch has already alerted me to the contents of her letter. It is not of great interest. So she's going. Perhaps she has another woman in Dhamar. Salah al-Din will probably be relieved, since her harsh tongue always frightened him a little. I have displeased you?"

Before I could reply, the chamberlain who had crept in on us unnoticed spoke in his booming voice.

"I bring sad news, Ibn Yakub. I've come to tell you to pack your belongings and your pen and inks and writing books. The Sultan was on his way back, but was taken ill in a village two days' distance from here. It is not good. He has summoned both of us. We leave in a few hours."

Shadhi began to weep, insisting that he, too, would accompany us to the village where the Sultan lay ill, but he looked so frail that we had to refuse the request. I

romised to keep him informed as I hurried away to pack my belongings. I had
now become accustomed to riding a horse, but the thought did not give me
great pleasure.

We rode out of Damascus in the hush of the twilight, when all was quiet save
the noise of the cicadas. Our party consisted of twelve riders, eight of whom
were soldiers sent for our protection. The other two, apart from the chamberlain
and myself, were retainers who carried the food for our journey.

What worried me was the failure of the Sultan's physicians to have him carried to Damascus, where he would be in greater comfort and other physicians
could attend on him. The only possible reason for this was that he was too ill to
be moved. I was also puzzled as to why he had sent for me, since Imad al-Din
had been with him throughout this last campaign. If he wanted to dictate a testament, the great scholar would have been better qualified than me to take down
his master's last wishes.

It was late in the night when we stopped to make camp in a tiny oasis. I was
too tired to eat or converse with the chamberlain, whose great loyalty to the
Sultan was not matched by his intelligence. In fact it was painful listening to him,
since his only interests were horses and brothels, neither of which held any
attraction for me.

Earlier on the journey he had described a strange Damascene brothel, to the
delight of the soldiers. Here, according to the chamberlain, prostitutes were
tied with chains and whipped by their customers before being freed and inflict-
ing the same pain on them. This alone provided immense gratification to all
concerned. I looked at the chamberlain closely. His ugly smile confirmed the
question forming in my mind. He had been there himself. I made a mental note
to question Shadhi as to the suitability of the chamberlain on my return.

We woke early, well before sunrise, and resumed our journey. To my surprise
we reached the village when the sun was at its zenith. I had assumed that we
would be riding for at least another six hours, but two of the soldiers were from
this village and had brought us here along a much shorter route.

Our arrival had been eagerly awaited, and we were taken immediately to a small house. Here the Sultan lay, covered in white muslin sheets, with two attendants keeping the flies away from his face. His eyes were shut, but I was startled at how thin his face had become. His voice was weak.

"I know what you're thinking, Ibn Yakub, but the worst is over. Your journey was unnecessary. I am feeling much better again, and tomorrow I will ride back with you. Imad al-Din is in Aleppo and when I summoned you I thought I would not live long. I wanted to set out my exact plans for the jihad so that my successor could carry through what Allah in his infinite Mercy had decided was now beyond me. Fortunately the Almighty changed his mind and I am still alive. We buried four emirs in this village only a week ago. I think I have survived simply by dint of sucking the juice out of the lemons which hang from the tree outside. I cannot think of any other reason, for I was as ill as those who died. Do you think the lemon has curative qualities? My physician thinks I am cured because he bled me, but he bled the emirs who died. Write to Ibn Maymun and ask him for his opinion. And from now on I must always have lemons wherever I go."

The Sultan smiled as he sat up in the bed. His eyes looked clear. He had survived. I had taken all this talk of lemon juice to be nothing more than delirium brought about by the fever, but now I wondered whether it could all be true.

He wanted to know what was going on in Dimask and questioned me in great detail, appearing irritated when I could not answer all his questions. I tried to explain that in his absence I was not present at the meetings of the council, and therefore my knowledge was limited to what had been reported to me directly. This increased his annoyance, and he summoned the chamberlain to demand why, despite his express instructions to the contrary, I had been excluded from meetings where important decisions of state were taken.

The chamberlain had no excuse and bowed his head in a shamed silence. The boastful frequenter of special brothels had suddenly lost his tongue. The Sultan dismissed him with an angry gesture.

The next day, when the sun was beginning to set, we began our return journey to Damascus. The size of our party had increased a hundredfold. When we camped for the night, the Sultan sent for me and questioned me first about the state of Shadhi's health. When I had reassured him that all he was now suffering from was the rigours of old age, he asked after Halima and Jamila. I was taken aback. Should I simply mutter a few half-truths about both of them being in good health, to face his wrath when he subsequently discovered my deception, or should I confess all that I knew?

Unfortunately, he was more alert than I had expected and noticed my slight hesitation. He spoke in a stern voice as his eyes, shining in the light of ten candles, fixed on mine.

"The truth, Ibn Yakub. The truth."

I told him.

TWENTY-TWO

The Sultan declares his undying hatred for Reynald of Châtillon; the death of Shadhi

Salah al-Din was not a vindictive or cruel man. He did not harbour grudges. He usually counselled against vengeance. I heard him say once that to act purely out of revenge was always dangerous, like drinking an elixir which becomes a habit. It was impolitic and did not differentiate Believers from the barbarians. He expressed these views often, though quietly, but when his commanders or emirs defied his advice and could not control their baser emotions, he never punished them. Instead he would sigh and shake his head in bewilderment, as if to indicate that the ultimate arbiter was not the Sultan, but Allah and his angels.

There was, however, even in Salah al-Din's case, one remarkable exception. There was a Franj knight, by the name of Reynald of Châtillon, and the time has come to write of this abomination, for we are now not so far from the last battles of the Sultan against the Franj, and we will soon meet this wretch in person.

The Sultan's hatred for Reynald was pure. It was unsullied by any feelings of forgiveness, generosity, kindness or even arrogance, which might have led to regarding this man as a worm beneath the contempt of Sultans. Reynald was a poisonous snake whose head must be crushed with a rock. I had myself heard Salah al-Din in open council swearing before Allah that, if the opportunity ever arose, he would decapitate Reynald with his own sword. Remarks of this sort always pleased his emirs, who felt much closer to their ruler when he expressed emotions akin to their own. The fact was that ever since the Franj had first arrived and stunned our world with their barbaric customs and habits, our side too had become infected, imbibing some of the worst of the traditional practices of the Franj.

It was the Franj who, over a hundred years ago, during a siege, had roasted their prisoners on an open fire and eaten them to assuage their hunger. The news had travelled to every city, and a sense of shock and shame had engulfed our world. This we had never known before. Yet only thirty years ago, the great Shirkuh had punished one of his emirs for permitting the roasting of three Franj captives and tasting their flesh. The ulema had soon been prevailed upon to acknowledge the practice and denounce it as a sin against the Prophet and the *hadith*.

The argument that finally settled the issue was a view expressed by the Kadi of Aleppo, who had stated after Friday prayers that eating Franj flesh was repugnant to Believers, since the Franj consumed large quantities of pig-flesh. This meant that their own flesh was polluted. Curiously enough this statement had a much greater effect in curbing the practice than all the pious references to the *hadith* and the convenient discovery of new traditions just when they were needed.

I had never been told of the reasons that lay behind the Sultan's revulsion for Reynald. It was something that was just accepted, like the landscape. One day I ventured into the library of Imad al-Din and stayed waiting for the great man to arrive. His first reaction on seeing me was to frown, but his face changed rapidly as he donned a mask exuding good will.

"I am sorry to intrude in this fashion, Master, but I wondered if you could spare me a tiny portion of your precious time?"

He smiled with his lips, but his eyes remained hard.

"How could I refuse any request from the Sultan's personal scribe? I am at your service, Ibn Yakub."

"You honour me, sir. I will not take up too much of your time. Could you perhaps enlighten this ignorant scribe on the reasons for the Sultan's burning hatred for Reynald of Châtillon?"

Imad al-Din laughed, a deep, throaty chuckle which was completely genuine. He was delighted at my ignorance and only too pleased to enhance my knowledge on this as on any other subject.

"Good friend, Ibn Yakub, you have begun to understand the ways of our Sultan, but even I, who have been with him much longer than you, am sometimes surprised at the way he arrives at a decision. For me, the method is all-important, but for him it is always instinct, instinct, instinct. If my method and his instinct coincide then all is well, but there are occasions when the two are opposed. Then his instinct triumphs and, as a loyal counsellor, I bow before his will.

"How should we deal with the Franj in the course of the jihad? This is a subject on which we have never disagreed. There were some hot-headed fools for whom the jihad meant a state of permanent war with the Franj, but Salah al-Din was never sympathetic to such a view. He understood that the enemy, like us, was usually divided. Just as our belief in Allah and his Prophet never stopped us from cutting each other's throats, so, in the same fashion, the Franj, despite their worship of idols and their loyalty to their Pope, were rarely able to rise above petty disputes with each other.

"The Sultan now rules over Cairo, Damascus, Aleppo and Mosul. From the Nile to the Euphrates there is one authority, except where the Franj rule. No other ruler is as powerful as he is, yet despite our strength, he agreed a truce with Amalric's boy, Baldwin the Leper, who rules in al-Kuds. Baldwin may have been weak in body, but his mind was strong. He knew that the Sultan kept his word and the peace was helpful to him as well. The result of the truce was that our car-

avans travelled freely between Cairo and Damascus, often stopping at Franj
villages to sell their wares.

"Four months ago, as you know, the poor leper-King died, insisting that his
six-year-old son be placed on the throne as Baldwin the Fifth. Our spies send
us weekly reports from that city which, Allah willing, will soon belong to us
again.

"The Sultan is well informed. He knows that there are two major factions
within the Franj in al-Kuds. One of these is led by the Count of Tripoli,
Raymond ibn Raymond al-Sanjili, descended from Saint-Gilles. To look at him
he could be an emir from Damascus. His complexion is much darker than the
Sultan's. He has a nose like a hawk and he is fluent in our language.

"The Sultan is very fond of him and would like him to win the struggle for
power. Were you aware that in order to help him we freed many knights from
Tripoli who we had captured at different times over the last few years? That is
a measure of the seriousness with which the Sultan regards the outcome of the
factional struggle in that city. A battle which is taking place even as I speak with
you, Ibn Yakub.

"Now I come to the question which you asked me earlier. Reynald of
Châtillon! A more bloodthirsty monster was never born, not even in the world
of the Franj. He was captured by Nur al-Din, and spent twelve years in the pris-
ons of Aleppo. He was only released after Nur al-Din's death. The Franj paid a
large ransom to obtain his freedom. Better instead that his head had rolled in the
sand.

"He is a man who enjoys killing for its own sake. He takes special delight in
killing your people, Ibn Yakub. He believes that Isa was sold to Pilate by the
Jews. We come second in his hatred. I am told that he specialises in disembow-
elling all Jewish prisoners and feeding their insides to his dogs. I say all this so
that you can appreciate that, even if he had not directly offended the Sultan, he
would still be a figure who inspired hatred. But he did upset Salah al-Din by
breaking the terms of the truce that had been agreed with Baldwin the Leper.

"Two years ago he attacked a merchant caravan on its way to our holy city of Mecca. All the merchants as well as those travelling with them were brutally dispatched. Mercy, in Reynald's eyes, was a vice. A sign of weakness. Among those who lost their lives that day was Samar, four score years of age and desperate to see Mecca before she died. Instead what she saw was the grim visage of the Franj. She was the Sultan's last surviving aunt, his father's younger sister.

"I drafted a very strong letter on his behalf to Baldwin the Leper. We asked him to punish and control his wild vassal. Baldwin confessed his powerlessness. As if this was not enough, Reynald led a raid on Mecca itself and desecrated our Holy Shrine. His horses defecated in the mosque. News of this outrage stunned Believers throughout the world. A very rude message arrived from Granada and other cities in Andalus to the Caliph in Baghdad, offering help in the shape of gold and men to aid the capture of the Franj beast. Prayers were offered in every mosque in the land, demanding retribution in the shape of Reynald's severed head.

"The Sultan sent an urgent dispatch to his brother al-Adil in Cairo. It contained one sentence: the criminals must be punished. He did as he was asked, and most of the criminals were captured and taken to Mecca and publicly beheaded. An exemplary punishment for those who dared violate our holy places, and a warning to those who attempted such a sacrilege again. Alas, Reynald, one of the most accursed and wicked among the Franj, had escaped us again.

"To my surprise the Sultan smiled when this fact was reported to him. 'Allah is saving the devil for me, Imad al-Din. I will kill him with my own hands.'

"Does that answer your question, Ibn Yakub?"

"More thoroughly than it could ever have been answered by anyone else in the whole kingdom, O learned master."

He was pleased by the flattery, but not enough to prolong my audience and so, after thanking him again, I took my leave. As I reached the door, his voice arrested me.

"I have just prepared an order for the gratuity you are now due from the Treasury and which will be paid to you regularly till you die. The Sultan instructed me to prepare it many weeks ago, before he fell ill, but it was in the midst of war, and I was so busy taking down the names and details of the prisoners we had captured, that your case escaped my mind. Forgive my neglect.

"There is another surprise awaiting you today. I think it will please you, and that, too, is the result of an order issued directly by the Sultan. If you see the chamberlain on your way out, he will provide you with the details. Your welfare concerns the Sultan. He must be pleased with you."

Was there a slight touch of envy in the way he spoke those last words, or was it just my imagination? I had little time to think of Imad al-Din and his sensitivities, for the chamberlain's news stunned me into such speechlessness that I had to sit down and drink some water. The Sultan's motives were pure, but I wish he had consulted me in advance.

My wife and daughter, together with all our possessions and my library, had been transported from Cairo to Damascus. A small house, not far from the citadel, had been provided for our use, and a retainer was leading me in its direction. I walked in a daze, like those who have inhaled more *banj* than their bodies can contain. The retainer from the citadel left me just outside the house. The door was open and the courtyard glistened in the afternoon sun.

It was Maryam who saw me first from a window and rushed down to hug me. I had not seen her for nearly four years. Tears wet my beard as I held her close to me and then pushed her gently away so I could see how she had changed. She had matured, but not beyond recognition. For what I saw before me was a beautiful young woman of sixteen, her eyes the colour of honey. Her pitch-black hair nearly touched the ground. I had seen this before.

She was the exact image of her mother Rachel when I had first espied her walking with her friends to fetch water from the well. As I drank in the sight, I felt a touch on my shoulder, which burnt me. I turned to embrace Rachel. She had aged. Her face was lined and there were streaks of grey in her hair. My heart missed a beat, but all the poison had gone and I kissed her eyes. It was wise of the Sultan not to have asked me before sending for them. I might have refused and suffered a great deal as a consequence.

It would be strange living in a house again. I had become accustomed to the luxury of the citadel, where all my elementary needs had been satisfied. The permanent proximity to power had stimulated me. Yet I was not displeased with the opening of a new phase in my life. Maryam would be married soon. Rachel and I would be alone again as we had been for four years, before Maryam was born. In those days we were so desperate for children that we fornicated at every possible opportunity. All that labour had produced only Maryam. A son was denied me. What would we do after Maryam had left home?

It was strange that this question arose in my mind so soon after Rachel's arrival, but I was distracted by a messenger from the citadel. I was to return immediately. Rachel smiled patiently.

"It will be just as it was in Cairo. Go, but do not stay long. It is our first night together for many years, and last night in the desert caravan I saw the most beautiful crescent moon."

I did not return home that night. I had been summoned to Shadhi's bedside. The old man lay dying. He smiled weakly as I entered his chamber.

"Where is my Salah al-Din? Why is my boy not with me in these last hours?"

I held his hand and stroked it gently.

"The Sultan is fighting the Franj, my good friend Shadhi. Please don't leave us yet. Just a few more months."

"Allah has finally summoned me, but listen to me now. Just listen. When al-Kuds falls and you enter the gates next to my boy, think of me, Ibn Yakub. Imagine I am riding next to the Sultan, whispering encouragement in his ear just as I did when he fought his first battle. It was not granted to me to see my boy's victory, but I am sure it will come. As sure as I am that I will not be there by his side. His name will live forever. Who will remember Shadhi?"

"He will," I whispered, the tears cascading down my cheeks. "And I will. We shall never forget you."

He did not reply. His hand went cold in mine. My throat was tight with fear. Shadhi had gone. This old man in whose company I had spent countless hours, who had enriched my life immeasurably, was dead.

I remembered our first meeting. I had been a bit frightened of him, not knowing how to respond to his disregard for authority. Yet even on that day, at the end of our first conversation, I was praying for a second one. I had realised that he was an invaluable source for the secret history of Salah al-Din and the House of Ayyub.

Shadhi was no longer with us, but he would live inside me. There could be no permanent separation. I tried to peer into the future. His voice, his laughter, his mocking tones, his spirit often clouded by arrogance, his refusal to tolerate fools or pompous religious scholars, his bawdy jokes and the tragic story of his own love. How could I ever forget him? I would hear his voice as long as I lived. Memories of him would guide me as I completed the chronicles of the Sultan Salah al-Din and his times.

We buried him early the next morning. The Sultan's oldest son, al-Afdal, led the mourners, who had been restricted to the Sultan's immediate family. Amjad the eunuch and I were the only outsiders. Amjad had looked after Shadhi, tended his needs during the last few months. He, too, had fallen under his spell and was sobbing uncontrollably. As we comforted each other, I felt close to him for the first time.

I had not slept all night. After the funeral prayers were over I went home. I thanked my stars for having my wife and daughter in Damascus. It would ease the pain of Shadhi's loss.

Rachel knew what Shadhi had meant to me. I had talked of him often enough during the first weeks of my employment in Cairo. She knew that he had been my only true friend in the Sultan's entourage. Words were unnecessary. I fell asleep weeping in her lap.

TWENTY-THREE

A traitor is executed; Usamah entertains the Sultan with lofty thoughts and lewd tales

Ten days after Shadhi's death, Salah al-Din returned to Damascus. A courier had informed him of the event, and since receiving the news he had, uncharacteristically, not spoken to anyone after giving the orders to lift the siege and return home. He insisted on being completely alone when he stopped to pray at Shadhi's grave before entering the citadel.

I was summoned to his chamber in the afternoon. To my amazement he hugged me and wept. When he had recovered his composure he spoke, but in a voice heavy with emotion and barely audible.

"One night during the siege the sky grew dark and it began to rain. As we covered our heads with blankets, several soldiers approached me holding a tall, dark man captive. The prisoner, who was groaning, had insisted on pleading his case before me. My men had little alternative but to agree to his request, since my battle orders are very firm on this question. Any prisoner condemned to death has the right to appeal directly to the Sultan. I asked them why they were intent on killing him. A short soldier, one of my best archers, replied: 'Commander of the Brave, this man is a Believer. Yet he betrayed us to the enemy. If it were not for him we would have taken Reynald's castle.'

"I looked at the prisoner, who stared down at the earth. The rain and the wind had stopped, but the evening was still black. No stars had appeared in the sky. I looked at his bloody, bearded face and became angry.

"'You are an apostate, wretch. You betrayed the jihad, you betrayed your fellow-Believers to this devil, this butcher who has killed our men, women and children without mercy. You dare appeal to me for your life. By your actions you have forfeited my grace.'

"He remained silent. Once again I asked him to explain himself. He refused to speak. As the executioner was preparing the sword to decapitate him, the traitor whispered in my face: 'At the exact moment that your swordsman removes my head from my body, someone very dear to you will also die.'

"I was enraged and walked away, refusing to dignify his death with my presence. I am told, Ibn Yakub, that Shadhi died that same evening, leaving us alone to count the empty days that lie ahead. He was more than a father to me. Long years ago he never left my side during a battle. It was as if I possessed two pairs of eyes. He guarded me like a lion. He was friend, adviser, mentor, someone who never shied from telling me the truth, regardless of whether or not it gave offence. Now he has fallen victim to death's cruel arrow. Men like him are rare and irreplaceable. I wish we could bring him back to life with our tears.

"How had that blasphemer, punished before the eyes of Allah, known that Shadhi, too, would die? It was as we were riding back to Damascus that one of the soldiers told me that the prisoner we had executed had turned to treachery because Reynald had raped his wife before his eyes and had threatened to invite a hundred others to do the same before he killed her. Naturally I was sad on hearing this tale, but I did not regret the punishment. During a war, good scribe, we have to be prepared for every sacrifice. And yet I respect him for not recounting his wife's ordeal himself. Reynald, too, will be punished. I have taken an oath before Allah.

"Death has become a garland round my neck.

"I want to be distracted tonight, scribe. Send for Usamah and let him enter-
tain us or, at the very least, stimulate our brains. A session. Let us have a session
tonight after sunset. I do not wish to sleep. Let us remember Shadhi by doing
something that always pleased him. He loved testing his wit against that of
Usamah. Is the man in Damascus or has he deserted us for the delights of
Baghdad? He's here? Good. Send a messenger, but please eat with him on your
own. I am not feeling in a mood to watch him devouring meat like a wild beast.
You look relieved."

I smiled as I bowed myself out of the royal chamber. Not sharing the Sultan's
meal was indeed a relief. I dispatched the chamberlain to fetch Usamah ibn
Munqidh as the Sultan had directed, but I wondered whether the old man might
not be too tired for a sudden exertion. Usamah was born not long after the Franj
first came to these lands. He was ninety years of age, but as well preserved and
as solid as ebony. He showed no trace of infirmity, though his back was bent and
he walked with a slight stoop. He spoke in a deep, strong voice. I had last seen
him in Cairo in the company of Shadhi.

He had been in his cups while we had sipped an infusion of herbs, pretending to keep him company. Usamah had consumed a whole flask of wine, all the
while smoking a pipe filled with *banj*. Despite the stimulation he had not taken
leave of his senses and regaled us for most of the night with anecdotes relat-
ing to his Franj friends, who were numerous. They often invited him to stay
with them and Usamah would return with a sackful of strange and wonderful
stories.

That night in Cairo he had discussed the Franj's filthy habit of not shaving
their pubic hair. He described a scene in the bath when his Franj host had called
in his wife to observe Usamah's clean-shaven groin. The couple had marvelled
at the sight, and there and then summoned a barber to shave off their unwanted
hair. "Did not the sight of a naked woman, having the hair below her belly
removed, excite you, my Prince?" Shadhi had asked. The question appeared to

have puzzled him. He puffed on his pipe, looked straight at Shadhi and replied: "No, it didn't. Her husband was far more attractive!"

Shadhi and I had roared with laughter till we saw his surprise at our mirth. Usamah was in total earnest.

Usamah was a nobleman with an ancient lineage. His father was the Prince of Shayzar, and so the son was brought up as a gentleman and a warrior. He had travelled widely and was in Cairo when Salah al-Din became Sultan. The two had become friends from that time onwards, but all of Salah al-Din's attempts to draw on Usamah's age and experience to acquire an understanding of Franj military tactics ended in failure.

The Sultan was genuinely perplexed, till one day Usamah confessed that he had never fought in a single battle, and that all his training had come to nought. He was, he said to the Sultan, a traveller and a nobleman, and he liked to observe the habits and customs of different peoples. He had been taking notes for thirty years and was working on a book of memories of his life.

Later that evening I was still recalling the past, when Usamah arrived and greeted me with a wink. I had been waiting to eat with him, but he had already taken his evening meal. I gave up mine and we walked slowly to the Sultan's audience chamber later that evening. His stoop had become more pronounced, but otherwise he had changed little over the last few years. He acknowledged Imad al-Din's presence with a frown – the two men had always disliked each other – and bowed to Salah al-Din, who rose to his feet and embraced him.

"I am sad that Shadhi died before me," he told the Sultan. "At the very least he should have waited so that we could go together."

"Let us imagine he is still with us," replied Salah al-Din. "Imagine him sitting in that corner, listening to every word you utter with a critical smile. Tonight I really need your stories, Usamah ibn Munqidh, but no tragedy, no romance, only laughter."

"The Sultan's instructions are difficult, for there is never a romance that is not preceded by laughter, and why is a tragedy a tragedy? Because it stops laughter.

So with great respect I must inform the Sultan that his desires cannot be fulfilled. If you insist simply on laughter then this tongue will fall silent."

It was a useful opening move by the old magician. The Sultan raised his hands to the heavens and laughed.

"The Sultan can only propose. Ibn Munqidh must dispose as he chooses."

"Good," said the old storyteller, and began without further ado.

"Some years ago I was invited to stay with a Franj nobleman, who lived in a small citadel near Afqah, not far from the river of Ibrahim. The citadel had been constructed on the top of a small hill, overlooking the river. The hillside was a cedar forest and the whole prospect afforded me great pleasure. For the first few days I admired the view and relished the tranquillity. The wine was of good quality and the hashish even better. What more could I want?"

"If Shadhi were here," muttered the Sultan, "he would have replied: 'A pretty young man!'"

Usamah ignored the remark and continued.

"On the third day my host informed me that his twenty-year-old son was seriously ill and asked me to take a look at him. I had met this boy once before and had taken a strong dislike to him. As the only son he was greatly over-indulged by his parents. He used his position as the son and heir of the Lord of Afqah to have his way with any wench who caught his eye. Several months ago he had killed two peasant boys who attempted to protect the honour of their twelve-year-old sister. To say that he was loathed by his father's tenants would be an understatement. Perhaps some of the stories about him that travelled from village to village were exaggerated during the journey. Perhaps not. It is difficult for me to say.

"Yet I could not turn down the request of my friend to look at the boy. I was not a trained physician, but I had studied all the medical formularies and my closest friends had been celebrated practitioners. After their deaths I was often consulted on medical matters and surprised myself by my own knowledge and prescriptions, which were often successful. My reputation had grown.

"I ordered the sheets to be removed and inspected the bare body of this boy. There were abscesses in both legs, which had spread and could kill him within a few weeks unless drastic measures were taken. It was too late for poultices and a severe diet. I told the father that the only way of saving the boy was to sever both legs from the thighs. My friend wept. His wife's anguished screams softened even the hardest heart present in the boy's chamber.

"Finally the father gave his approval, and I supervised the removal of the legs. The boy, not unnaturally, fainted. I knew from past experience that once he returned to awareness he would not realise his legs had been removed. This is an illusion which remains for a few days after an organ has been cut off. His father told me to ask the poor boy what his greatest wish was in this world, and he would do all in his power to make sure it was granted. We waited for him to recover. We waited for over an hour. When he opened his eyes, he smiled because the old pain had gone. I whispered in his ear: 'Tell me, son, what would you like the most in this world?' He smiled, and a chilling, lecherous grin disfigured his face. I bent down so he could whisper back in my ear. 'Grandad,' he said mockingly, and I was surprised that even in this state his voice was marked by viciousness. 'What I really want more than anything else is a penis that is larger than my leg!'

"'You have it, my boy,' I replied, slightly ashamed at my own pleasure. 'You have it.'"

At first, the Sultan looked at Usamah in horror. Then he began to laugh. I could see that the story was not yet finished. Usamah's body movements indicated that a few embellishments, last-minute treats, still awaited us, but the Sultan's laughter became uncontrollable and began to take on a character of its own. He would stop. Usamah would make as if to continue, but the Sultan would be overcome by a new fit of laughter. I had caught the infection and joined him, discarding a time-honoured court ritual. At this juncture, Usamah, deciding that his isolation was now complete and that his story was destined to remain unfinished, decided to forgo the ending and joined in the merriment.

The Sultan, having recovered his composure, smiled.

"What a marvellous storyteller you are, Usamah ibn Munqidh! Even Shadhi, may he rest in peace, would not have been able to resist a laugh. I understand now that humour only amuses when it is twinned to something else. Have you anything else for us this evening?"

The Sultan's praise pleased Usamah. The lines on his face multiplied as he smiled to show his pleasure. The old man took a deep breath and his eyes became distant as he recalled another episode from his long life.

"Many years ago, some time before you were born, O Sultan, I found myself one evening in a tavern in the Christian quarter of Damascus where only lofty subjects were discussed on the day of the Christian Sabbath. I was nineteen or twenty years of age. All I wanted was to enjoy a flask of wine and think again of a Christian girl who had been occupying my mind for several months.

"I had come to this quarter on that particular day for one reason alone. I wanted to catch sight of her coming out of church with her family. We would exchange glances, but that was not the sole reason for my journey to this quarter. If the scarf was white it was bad news, and meant we could not meet later that day.

"If, however, she was wearing a coloured headscarf it was a sign that we would meet later that evening, at the house of one of her married friends. There we might hold hands in tender silence. Any attempt by me to stroke her face or kiss her lips had been firmly rebuffed. Last week she had taken me by surprise, by responding warmly to my lukewarm effort to go beyond holding hands. She had not merely kissed me, but guided my hand to feel her warm and trembling breasts. Having set me on fire, she had refused to put out the flames, leaving me frustrated and in a state of considerable despair.

"'One citadel at a time, Usamah. Why are you so impatient?' Having whispered these words in my ear she had fled, leaving me alone to cool myself. It was this change in her attitude that had given this particular day its importance. I was dreaming of conquering the citadel that lay hidden under that perfumed forest of hair between her legs.

"She emerged from the church, wearing a coloured scarf. We exchanged smiles and I walked away, surprised at my own self-control. I wanted to jump up and down and shout to all the other people on the street that exquisite raptures awaited me that afternoon. Happy is the one who has experienced the torments, tempests and passions of everyday life, for only he can truly enjoy the fragile and tender delights of love.

"I waited for her at the house of her friend, but she did not arrive. After two hours a servant-boy came with a letter addressed to her friend. She had made the mistake of confiding her growing love for me to her older sister, who, overcome by jealousy, had informed their mother. She was worried that her parents would now hasten her marriage to the son of a local merchant. She pleaded with me not to act rashly, but to await a message from her.

"I was desolate. I wandered the streets like a lost soul and wandered into the tavern of lofty thoughts with only one thought, namely to drown my sorrows. To my amazement they were not serving wine that day. The innkeeper informed me that they never served wine in his establishment on the Sabbath. I found this odd, since alcohol had always been part of their pagan church ritual, symbolising as it did, the blood of Isa.

"I protested and was informed in a cold voice that the prohibition had nothing to do with religion. It was simply the day designated for lofty thoughts. I was welcome to repair to a neighbouring tavern. I looked around and realised that the clientele, too, was unusual. There were over fifty people, mainly men, but a dozen women. Most of them were old. I think, leaving me aside, the youngest person present must have been forty years of age.

"The arrogance of these people attracted me to them while simultaneously distracting me from my more immediate concerns. I asked whether I could participate in their discussion and was answered by a few affirmative nods of the head, mainly from the women present. The others looked at me with cold indifference, almost as if I were a stray dog desperate for a bone.

"It became a matter of pride. I decided to stay, to melt their coldness and pierce the cloud of aloofness that surrounded them like a halo. From their expressions I could see that they saw me as a shallow youth with nothing to teach them. They were probably correct, but it annoyed me and I became desperate to prove them wrong. This whole business had begun to distract me from the blow I had suffered earlier that afternoon, and for that I was immensely grateful.

"I took my seat on the floor. The subject for that evening's discussion seemed relevant enough to my problems: 'The escape from anxiety.' The speaker was Ibn Zayd, a traveller and a historian from Valencia in Andalus.

"I should have known. Only the Andalusians were capable of dissecting the meanings of concepts and words that we took for granted. The distance from Mecca had given their minds a freedom greatly envied by our own scholars.

"The Sultan may frown, but what I say is acknowledged by all our scholars. Even our great Imad al-Din, who disapproves of my habits and way of life, would confirm this well-known fact. It is true we have had our share of sceptics, and one was even executed on the orders of the Sultan, but not on the scale of Andalus. We can discuss scepticism another day.

"With the Sultan's permission, I will continue the sad story of my youth. Ibn Zayd must have been in his late forties. Only a few grey hairs were visible in his raven-black beard. He spoke our language with an Andalusian lilt, but despite the strangeness of his accent, his voice was like that of the singer-boatmen of the Nile, both soft and deep at the same time.

"He began by informing us that the talk he was about to give us was not original, but based on the *Philosophy of Character and Conduct*, by Ibn Hazm, in front of whom even the greatest intellect is abashed. He, Ibn Zayd, had his own criticisms of the master-work, but without it nothing could have been possible.

"He spoke of how Ibn Hazm wrote that all human beings are guided by one aim. The desire to escape anxiety. This applied equally to rich and poor, to Sultan and mamluk, to scholars and illiterates, to women and eunuchs, to those who crave sensuality and dark delights as well as ascetics. They all seek freedom from worry. Few follow the same path in achieving this aim, but the wish to escape from anxiety has been the common purpose of humanity since it appeared on this earth.

"He then took out from his little bag a book with a gilded cover, but which must have been read many times, for it was faded. Ibn Yakub and Imad al-Din will understand that nothing affords a book greater delight than being passed from hand to hand. This was one such book, the *Philosophy* of Ibn Hazm. He had marked a passage which he now read to us in his quaint Arabic.

"Subsequently I, too, obtained a copy of the book and read that passage many times, with the result that, like passages from our own divine Book, it is now imprinted on my mind:

"'Those who crave riches seek them only in order to drive the fear of poverty out of their spirits; others seek for glory to free themselves from the fear of being scorned; some seek sensual delights to escape the pain of privations; some seek knowledge to cast out the uncertainty of ignorance; others delight in hearing news and conversation because they seek by these means to dispel the sorrow of solitude and isolation. In brief, man eats, drinks, marries, watches, plays, lives under a roof, rides, walks, or remains still with the sole aim of driving out their contraries and, in general, all other anxieties. Yet each of these actions is in turn an inescapable hotbed of new anxieties.'

"That is all I can recall today, though some years ago I could recite the entire passage. Our traveller from Andalus developed Ibn Hazm's argument further, and the more we heard the more entranced we became. Before this I had never been exposed to philosophy, and suddenly I could see why the theologians regarded it as pure poison.

"It soon became obvious that Ibn Zayd's criticisms of Ibn Hazm's philosophy would never come to light, for the simple reason that he had none. He worshipped the works of Ibn Hazm but thought it prudent to dissociate himself from them, just in case the Kadi had sent a few spies to report on the meeting. The essence of Ibn Hazm's philosophy lay in his belief that man could, through his own actions alone, rid himself of all anxieties. He did not need any help."

"Heresy! Blasphemy!" shouted the Sultan. "Where is Allah and his Prophet in this philosophy?"

"Exactly so, my Sultan," replied Usamah. "That is what the theologians asked as they burnt Ibn Hazm's books outside the mosques. But that was many years ago, before the Franj polluted our soil. Our knowledge is much more advanced now, and I am sure our great scholars like Imad al-Din would prove Ibn Hazm wrong in the space of a few minutes."

Imad al-Din glowed with anger, and stared at Usamah with undisguised hatred. He did not speak.

"What was the point of this story, Usamah?" asked the Sultan. "Did you finally get the Christian girl?"

The old man chuckled. He had put the choicest morsels of Arab philosophy before the Sultan, and all he wanted was the story of the girl.

"I did not get the girl, Commander of the Ingenious, but the ending of that day in the tavern of lofty thoughts took me by surprise, as it will you if I have permission to finish."

The Sultan nodded his approval.

"At the conclusion of the meeting I asked several questions, partially because the Andalusian had aroused my genuine interest, and partially to show the others present that I was not an ignorant fool intent simply on hedonism. It would be too wearisome to recount my own triumph and, unlike Imad al-Din, I rarely make notes of all my encounters. But let it be said that my remarks made a deep impression on Ibn Zayd. He became more and more animated and soon we repaired to a tavern which served a brew more potent than lofty thoughts. We talked throughout the night. We were both in a state of modest inebriety. At this stage he extended his hand and clasped my penis. The expression on my face surprised him.

"'You seem anxious, my young friend. Do we not agree that anxiety should be expelled from our spirit?'

"I replied: 'My anxiety will only be dispelled if you ungrasp my penis immediately.' He did not persist, but began to weep.

"Out of pity I guided him out of the Christian quarter and back into ours. There I left him, happily occupied in that male brothel which is frequented by many from the citadel. Do you remember the street where it is situated, Imad al-Din? My memory escapes me again. The price of old age."

Once again Imad al-Din did not reply, but once again the Sultan began to laugh as he congratulated Usamah.

"I think the moral of your story is how easily even men with the most lofty thoughts can degenerate into a debased sensuality. Am I correct, Usamah ibn Munqidh?"

Usamah was delighted with the praise, but refrained from endorsing the Sultan's view.

"That is certainly one possible interpretation, Commander of the Wise."

TWENTY-FOUR

The Caliph's letter and the Sultan's reply,
mediated by Imad al-Din's diplomacy and
intelligence; Jamila's discourse on love

The Sultan, dressed in his formal robes of office, was seated cross-legged on a raised platform, surrounded by the most powerful men in Damascus. I had been summoned earlier, but he had no time to speak with me and I stood in a corner waiting for the ceremony to begin.

The chamberlain clapped his hands twice and Imad al-Din ushered in the ambassador from the Caliph in Baghdad, who fell on his knees before the Sultan. Rising slowly, he presented him with a letter from his master on a little silver platter. The Sultan did not touch it, but signalled to Imad al-Din, who bowed to the ambassador and accepted the royal communication.

Normally any such letter was read aloud before the court so that the message could be made known to a slightly wider public. But Salah al-Din, presumably to express his irritation with Baghdad, dispensed with tradition and dismissed the court. Only Imad al-Din and myself were asked to remain behind.

The Sultan was not in a light mood that morning. He frowned at his secretary of state.

"I suppose you know what the letter contains?"

Imad al-Din nodded.

"It is not a well-written letter, which means that Saif al-Din must be ill or otherwise engaged. The letter is long, and full of inept flattery and clumsy sentences. It refers to you as the 'Sword of the Faith' on four separate occasions, but its purpose is expressed in one sentence. The Commander of the Faithful wishes to be informed as to when you intend to renew the jihad against the unbelievers. He also asks whether you will find time to make the pilgrimage to Mecca this year and kiss the Ka'aba."

The Sultan's face grew dark.

"Take my reply, Imad al-Din. Write it as I speak. You too, Ibn Yakub, so we have another copy immediately. I know that Imad al-Din will coat my words with honey, and for that reason we shall compare the two versions at my leisure. Are you ready?"

We nodded, and dipped our pens in the ink.

"To the Commander of the Faithful. From his humble servant, Salah al-Din ibn Ayyub.

"You ask when I intend to renew our war against the Franj. I reply when, and only when, I am sure that there is no dissension within our own camp, and when you will use the authority vested in you by Allah and the Prophet to warn all Believers who collaborate with the Franj for petty gain, to desist from their acts which harm our cause. As you know full well, I have been trying to tame some of the princes whose citadels are not far from the Euphrates. On each occasion they have refused to accept your authority, and have gone hands outstretched to plead for money and support from our enemies. If you can keep vermin of this sort under control, I will take al-Kuds within the next year.

"I have fought so many battles in recent years that my cheeks have become permanently scorched by the sun. Alas, many of these wars have been against Believers, which has weakened our cause.

"Reynald, that visitor from Hell, under whose cold and emotionless gaze so many of our women and children have died and whose terror has even silenced the birds, whose name is used to frighten recalcitrant peasants, that Reynald still lives, while his puppet in al-Kuds who they refer to as 'King Guy' refuses to honour the terms of the truce. Our soldiers still rot in the dungeons of Karak, in open violation of all that was agreed between both sides.

"I say this so that the Commander of the Faithful realises that it is some of the so-called Faithful who have prevented me from fulfilling our aims this year. Fortunately for us the Franj, too, are divided. The noble Raymond of Tripoli, who, I hope, will one day become a Believer, has sent me much valuable information. Be reassured that the jihad will be resumed very soon, provided the Commander of the Faithful plays his part in the campaign.

"I share your worry regarding my inability, till now, to make the pilgrimage to Mecca. I ask Allah's forgiveness each time I offer prayers. I am so busy as the 'Sword of the Faith' that I have not yet found time to kiss the Ka'aba. I will make up for this lapse soon, after I have taken al-Kuds, and given thanks for our victory to Allah at the Dome of the Rock. I pray for your health."

The Sultan had barely left the chamber to relieve himself when Imad al-Din exploded.

"This letter is a disgrace, Ibn Yakub. A disgrace. It will have to be rewritten from beginning to end. A letter from the most powerful Sultan in the land to the Caliph, whose authority is great but whose power is weak, must be dignified as befits the position of Salah al-Din.

"What you have transcribed will give offence, but without being effective. It is couched in crude language, its tone is petulant, and it fails to deploy an irony that would deceive the Caliph, while simultaneously alarming his more astute advisers.

"It has one serious factual error. Our Sultan is besotted with Count Raymond of Tripoli. It is true that Raymond has helped us in the past, but precisely because of that he was accused of treachery and collaboration with the enemy. Our intelligence reports suggest that he has now made his peace, sworn an oath of loyalty to the so-called King of Jerusalem, and is pledged to take arms against us. The Caliph must be informed of this fact. The Sultan's hope of converting Raymond could, in the circumstances, appear as a serious misjudgement. If you don't object, Ibn Yakub, I will take your copy as well and have a new version prepared tomorrow."

Despite the Sultan's express instructions to the contrary, I could not resist the great scholar's logic. I meekly handed him my copy of the letter. He marched out of the chamber with a triumphant smile, leaving me alone to confront the wrath of my master. When Salah al-Din returned he was, to my pleasure and relief, accompanied by the Sultana Jamila, whose return to Damascus had been reported to me by Amjad the eunuch earlier that day. The Sultan gave me a knowing smile, as if to indicate that he was not surprised at Imad al-Din's absence. I bowed before the Sultana, whose complexion had fed on the sun. She was much darker now, but the lines of worry that had marked her forehead and the space below her eyes had disappeared.

"Welcome back, Princess. The citadel was dark without your light."

She laughed, and immediately I knew that she had recovered from the pain of Halima's betrayal. It was her old laugh, and her shoulders shook as she watched me.

"A compliment from you, good friend Ibn Yakub, is as rare as a camel with a scented behind. I, too, am glad to be back. It is wonderful, is it not, how distance from pain can heal our innermost wounds better than anything else?"

The Sultan was clearly pleased by her return, though I was surprised by her openness in his presence. He read my thoughts.

"Jamila and I are now good friends, scribe. We have no secrets from each other. Do you know what this woman has been reading in her father's palace?"

I shook my head respectfully.

"Blasphemy. Cursed philosophy. Scepticism."

Jamila smiled.

"He is not wrong this time. I have been devouring the writings of al-Farabi. He has reinforced my instinctive belief that human reason is superior to all religious faiths, ours included. His writings are more convincing than the works of Ibn Hazm."

The Sultan grimaced and took his leave, but told me to stay.

"I am preparing the orders for the last battle of this jihad, Ibn Yakub, to show that our religious faith is superior to that of the Franj. You are welcome to listen to Jamila's stories, but I forbid you to be convinced by her. Heads may roll if you do."

"I am only the storyteller, O great Sultan."

Jamila had lit a pipe of *banj* and smiled at my surprised expression.

"I permit myself this indulgence once a week. It was more than that when I arrived at my father's palace, but it helped to deaden the pain. It relaxes me, yet if I smoke a pipe more than once a week it slows down my brain. I find it difficult to think or concentrate my attention on a book."

"It is good to hear the Sultana laugh again as she used to in the old days. I hope you are fully recovered, and that the hurt you suffered is now firmly in the past."

She was touched by my concern.

"Thank you, my friend. I thought of you often while I was away. Once I even had an imaginary conversation with you which was very soothing. It is strange how our deepest and most heartfelt emotions can be so transient. In Arab and Persian literature, if the river of true love is diverted, it must perforce travel through a valley of madness. A lover deprived of his beloved loses his mind. This is sheer nonsense. People love. Their love is rejected. They suffer. Do you know of a single case where any person has really lost his or her mind? Has this ever happened, or is it a poet's fantasia?"

I thought for a long time before a reply worthy of her question came to mind.

"Love is the music that is first heard by our soul and then transferred slowly to the heart. I have known instances where a deprived lover enters into a deep decline and his entire life-pattern is transformed. He suffers from a dull headache that never leaves him, and his mind is numbed by the sense of loss. One such person was Shadhi, who is now no more."

She interrupted me.

"I am sad that he is dead, but there are limits, Ibn Yakub. You talk of love as the poetry of the soul, and in the same breath you talk of Shadhi, a crude, uncouth mountain goat. Is this a callous joke? Are you mocking me?"

I told her then of the tragedy that had befallen Shadhi, of how the only woman he had ever loved had taken her own life, and of the price he had paid for his cruel mistake. The tale astonished her.

"Strange how you can see a person every day, but not know his real story. I'm glad you told me, Ibn Yakub. So, the old goat did have a heart, but surely you agree that the permanent loss of his love did not make him go mad. One of the more reassuring things about him was his ability to distance himself from events and individuals and look at both with an indifferent rationality. The sign of a totally sane person."

"Madness can take many forms, Sultana. Our poets paint a picture of the distressed lover as a long-haired youth, whose hair has greyed prematurely and who wanders the desert talking to himself, or who sits at the edge of a stream and stares endlessly at the water, seeing in it the images of his lost one. In reality, as you know even better than me, madness can make you bent on a cruel revenge. You conceal your feelings by wearing a polite mask. You talk to your friends as if nothing had happened. Yet inside your blood boils with rage, with anger, and with jealousy, and you want to skewer those who have caused you pain and burn them on an open fire. You can only do so in your imagination, though even that helps to ease the torment, and slowly you are able to rebuild your strength."

She looked at me, and the old sad smile reappeared.

"How many times did you burn Ibn Maymun, my friend?"

She, too, knew my story.

"I was not talking of myself, Sultana. Let me give you another example. The case of our young poet Ibn Umar, all of nineteen years old, yet he produces verses that make grown men weep. The whole of Damascus sings his praises. Cups of wine are drunk in his honour in every tavern. Young men talk to their lovers in Ibn Umar's language . . ."

"I know all about this boy," she said impatiently. "What has happened to him?"

"While you were away, he fell in love with a married woman, several years older than him. She encouraged his attentions and the inevitable tragedy occurred. They became lovers. Her husband was informed of what was taking place and he had her poisoned. Simple solution to a simple problem. Ibn Umar and his circle of friends, however, refused to let the matter rest in the grave. One day, while in their cups, they planned their revenge. The husband, a decent man by all accounts, was ambushed and battered to death on the street. The Kadi arrested Ibn Umar, who confessed everything.

"The city was divided. Those under forty years of age wanted the poet released. The rest demanded his execution. Ibn Umar was indifferent to his fate. He carried on writing, till the Sultan intervened."

"Ah, yes, the judgement of Salah al-Din," she said with a laugh. "Tell me about it."

"Ibn Umar has been sent to join the Sultan's son in the army which is assembling near Galilee."

"Typical." she muttered. "The Sultan has lost interest in poetry. Twenty years ago he could recite whole poems with real passion. Sending poets to fight in wars is like roasting nightingales. I will have that boy returned."

TWENTY-FIVE

I dream of Shadhi; the Sultan plans his war

"In the mountains the cowherds used to suck the vagina of the cow while she was being milked. They claimed it improved the quality and the quantity of the milk. As boys we used to watch them and get excited. Which part of your wife excites you the most, Ibn Yakub? Her breasts or her behind?"

It was typical of Shadhi. He often asked a question without waiting for my reply. This time he began to laugh. Noisy, crude, laughter.

I was dreaming. The only reason I remember this trivial dream is that it was brutally interrupted by a deafening and insistent knocking at the front gate. Rachel was still asleep, but my sudden leap out of bed disturbed her and she began to stir. I opened the shutter. It was still not morning, though signs of dawn were visible on the horizon in the shape of a single, thin stripe of red. I pulled on my gown and hurried through the courtyard to open the gate.

I was greeted by the familiar smile of Amjad the eunuch. His smile, which so often irritated me, now seemed reassuring.

"The Sultan wants you in the council chamber before the day breaks. Should we return together?"

"No!" I replied, my voice harsher than I had intended, something I immediately regretted. "Forgive me, Amjad. I have only just risen from bed and need a few minutes to recover and prepare for the Sultan. I will follow you very soon."

He smiled and went on his way. It was strange how he rarely took offence. During my first few months in Damascus I had been rude to him for no other reason except that I disliked his facial expressions. Yet Shadhi had liked him, and Jamila trusted him completely. It was this combination that had changed my own attitude.

Rachel was wide awake when I returned to our bedchamber. She was sitting up in bed drinking water. Her nakedness stirred me, and watching her breasts sway as she moved made me laugh. I told her of my dream. She saw the lust in my eyes and, throwing off the sheet that covered the rest of her body, she smiled and extended her arms, offering me an embrace and possibly something more.

"The Sultan is waiting," I began apologetically, but she interrupted me.

"I can see that for myself," she replied as she jumped out of bed and put her hand between my legs. "The Sultan is erect and ready to mount for battle."

Reader, I succumbed.

I ran most of the way to the citadel. The city was still asleep, though the muezzins were clearing their throats as they prepared to call the faithful to prayer. Here and there a dog stood outside a front gate and barked at me as I hurried to the Sultan.

"You are late today, Ibn Yakub," said the Sultan, but without any note of displeasure. "Your wife's embrace kept you from us?"

I bowed low before him in silent apology. He accepted it with a smile and indicated with a gesture that he wished me to be seated just below him.

My eyes had been so completely fixed on the Sultan that when I now observed the room I was taken aback by those who were present. This was no ordinary gathering. Apart from the Kadi al-Fadil and Imad al-Din, all the emirs were present who commanded different segments of the Sultan's armies. No, not all.

Taki al-Din and Keukburi were absent. The Sultan had referred to them as his "two arms" without whom he was powerless. It was his way of stating publicly that he trusted both men with his life.

As far as Taki al-Din was concerned this was no surprise. He was Salah al-Din's favourite nephew and he treated him as he himself had once been treated by his own uncle Shirkuh. In fact, Taki al-Din's presence caused the Sultan to shed the instinctive caution he had inherited from Ayyub, his father. He had once told me that in times of crisis there was a battle for his soul between Ayyub and Shirkuh, and it was pure luck as to which of them won. Taki al-Din reminded him of his own youth, and in some ways he wished that this nephew rather than al-Afdal, his own son, could succeed him. This he had confessed, not to me but to old Shadhi, who had eagerly passed on the information. On this question he agreed enthusiastically with Salah al-Din.

Emir Keukburi was a different matter altogether. There had been a time, only three or four years ago, when Salah al-Din had provoked widespread incredulity and ordered his arrest. It was the time when he was consolidating his empire to prepare for the day that had now arrived. It had taken the Sultan three days, with the help of Keukburi and his men, to ferry his troops across the Euphrates. He had then marched on to Harran. There, he had spent a morning playing *chogan* with his host. When the game was over, the Sultan's bodyguards had placed the Emir Keukburi under arrest. Pigeons carried the news to Cairo and Damascus.

The Kadi al-Fadil was on one of his tours of inspection around Cairo. He was stunned by the news and immediately wrote a powerful and moving plea to Salah al-Din. He has given me a copy of the letter for my book. It read as follows:

Most Gracious and Generous Sultan:

    A letter from Imad al-Din informs me that you are angry with Keukburi and have had him arrested. I remember well the heat and dust of Harran, which affects us all, and I have little doubt that your kindness

and generosity will once again prevail over your anger. I know you have
Imad al-Din by your side, but if you feel that my presence, too, might be
useful or desirable, I will banish my dislike of Harran. I will make way
by mule, endure the wretched heat without a tent, and be at your side
very soon. I am disturbed and slightly confused by what I hear. I think
the Sultan has made an error of judgement.

Emir Keukburi regards you as a father. He has always been loyal and
has proved himself by persuading his brother to back you against the
Lords of Mosul. He was an example to all who wished to serve your
cause. The intimacy you have shown him has undoubtedly gone to his
head. He is like a young pup who, when stroked too often by his master,
sometimes bites him. Yet the bite expresses an overflowing affection
rather than anger. I would be prepared to offer my own head to the
executioner's blade if Keukburi ever betrays our interests. He is young,
ambitious, and wants to prove himself in battle by your side.

Imad al-Din writes that you were retaliating because Keukburi had
promised 50,000 dinars to the Treasury the day you reached Harran, and
then reneged on his pledge, claiming that it had been made by an envoy
who had not consulted him. Since the money is for the jihad, I know how
angry this must have made you, but your generosity is the source of all
the pure, sweet water that flows in our lands. Forgive him and I can
assure you that he will have learnt his lesson.

Your humble servant, al-Fadil.

Keukburi was pardoned and never offended the Sultan again. But the cause
was not simply the confusion over the payment of 50,000 dinars. The Sultan told
me that the matter had been far more serious. Keukburi had been the intermedi-
ary between his brother, the Emir of Irbil, and the Sultan. In return for his
loyalty, Keukburi had negotiated extra lands for his brother. Once the Sultan was
in complete control of the region, Keukburi had suggested that the lands given

to his brother should be transferred to his own estate. The proposal had enraged
Salah al-Din, for whom family loyalty was a critical test of a person's character.
He had contemptuously rejected the suggestion and begun to doubt Keukburi's
loyalty to himself.

These facts were not divulged to al-Fadil by Imad al-Din for the simple
reason that the great scholar had become infatuated with the Emir of Harran. He
was, if the truth be told, a strikingly handsome specimen, though not inclined to
the pleasures favoured by our worthy bibliophile.

After a few months, Keukburi was pardoned. He was never to fall out of
step with Salah al-Din again. He learnt, as al-Fadil had so wisely predicted, that
there were some things in this world more precious to the Sultan than all the
wealth of China and India. These included keeping one's word to both friend
and foe. On this he could never be challenged, let alone be convinced of an alternative course of action.

Keukburi had earned back his Sultan's trust, and now, even as we gathered in
this assembly, he and Taki al-Din were camped in the valley of Galilee, patiently
awaiting Salah al-Din's arrival. Only then could they finalise their plans.

I realised that I had been invited, for the first time, to observe a council of
war. The Sultan had clearly been speaking for some time. The interruption of
my late arrival over, he continued to persuade them with a mixture of guile and
flattery.

"Our desires are always disappointed by reality. That, as good Imad al-Din
will tell you, is a fact of life. There are few of us who can say that everything
they wished has come to pass. My enemies, of which there are not a few, say to
the Caliph: 'Salah al-Din prefers to attack us and forget the infidels.' They say
that all I am interested in is establishing my own family in power and amassing
wealth. What they accuse me of is what they do themselves. It is much easier, I
suppose, to burden me with their guilt. Yet before this year is over, these tongues
will be silenced forever.

"I know that some of you are reluctant to attack the Franj at this particular time. Perhaps you are correct to be apprehensive, but those who delay too long, those who only go halfway, usually end up digging their own graves.

"Let me speak plainly. We do not have more time. Allah alone knows how much longer I have in this world. As I look at you, I see men who have fought so many battles that nature has prematurely aged them. I see grey hairs in all your beards. None of us has a great deal of time.

"Our spies report that the Franj have between twelve and fifteen thousand knights and twenty thousand soldiers on foot to defend their Kingdom of Jerusalem. We must prepare an army which will destroy their backbone. An army of Believers that will scale the walls of al-Kuds and ensure that the familiar and reassuring cry, 'Allah is Great', is heard once again in that great city.

"This time we must cut them so deep that they leave our lands and never return. Our army is the only army that can achieve this aim. Not because Allah has given us more brains or more strength, but because we alone pursue such an end. It is our determination that will give strength to those who fight under our banners. Soon we will wipe out the stain of our defeat at the hands of these barbarians for ever. I am not given to proud boasts, for they have been the downfall of Believers. Yet I am burning with confidence.

"Our soldiers from Misr and Sham alone could defeat the enemy, but everyone now wants to be on our side. The Emirs of Mosul, Sinjar, Irbil and Harran all want to be represented in our army. The Kurds in the mountains beyond the Tigris are promising us a band of warriors. In the past, they often resented the successes of my father and my uncle Shirkuh. Now they have pledged themselves to join in the battle for al-Kuds or to die in the attempt. Their messenger came yesterday and told me that they will only fight by our side if they are allowed to be the first to take the city. Strange, is it not, Imad al-Din, how the smell of success travels so far and so fast?"

The great scholar, whose eyes had been shut for most of the Sultan's speech was clearly not asleep.

"It is not simply the scent of victory in their nostrils that sends them to us, O

Commander of the Victorious. They feel in their bones that our history is about to be refashioned. They want to tell their children and their grandchildren that they fought with Salah al-Din on the day that is about to happen."

Salah al-Din, usually deaf to coarse flattery, was not displeased by Imad al-Din's remarks.

"Tomorrow I leave Damascus to join the army, gathering for our last big effort. We will all leave at different times and by separate routes, just in case the Franj have prepared an ambush. If something happens to me before or during the battle, I do not wish you to waste any time in mourning. Finish the work that Allah has given us, and never let the enemy think that the death of one single person could disorganise our force. Now leave, and may Allah give you the strength we need for victory. There is only one Allah and Mohammed is his Prophet."

The emirs dispersed, but not before each of them had come forward to embrace the Sultan and kiss his cheeks. With the ritual over, the Sultan turned to the Kadi al-Fadil, and to Imad al-Din and myself.

"I want all of you to be at my side. Imad al-Din to compose letters demanding total surrender, al-Fadil to ensure that I make no mistakes in dealing with our own emirs, and Ibn Yakub to inscribe everything on parchment. Whatever Allah has decreed for us, be it victory or defeat, our children and their children will never be able to forget what we sacrificed for their future."

This was the first occasion on which the Sultan had mentioned me in the same breath as al-Fadil and Imad al-Din. To write that I was flattered would be a terrible understatement. He recognised my worth, that alone was sufficient to make me feel I was in heaven. I could not wait to rush home and tell Rachel, but my pace slowed as I realised that this would be another long parting.

Before I could leave the citadel, the light-haired figure of Amjad the eunuch appeared before me. I groaned. He laughed.

"This time the call is from the Sultana Jamila. She requires your presence. Follow me, if you please."

I never regretted a conversation with Jamila, which usually improved my knowledge of our world and my understanding of human emotions. But on this day, bursting with news of my little triumph, I wanted to share my joy with Rachel. It would have mitigated the sorrow of parting, but I was nothing more than a scribe and I obeyed orders. So, like a faithful dog, I followed Amjad the eunuch to the special chamber where the Sultana met male visitors. Her face was glowing with pleasure, and she smiled as I entered. The smile melted my heart and I felt guilty at having wished to avoid her. This was only the second occasion since her return from the lands in the South, and it confirmed me in my opinion that she was now fully recovered.

"Welcome, Ibn Yakub, and congratulations. I am told that you are to be one of the three wise men who will accompany the Sultan and observe the mother of all battles. And I will be the only woman, wise or otherwise."

She saw the look on my face, and began to laugh.

"He resisted and resisted, but I won. I have your Sultan's permission. I will have my own tent, and my special guard of eunuchs under the leadership of Amjad, and a number of well-trained mamluks.

"Keukburi must not know till we arrive. You know he is married to my younger sister. If she knew she would move the stars in an attempt to share my tent. But Salah al-Din forbade me to tell anyone except you, for when you are not busy writing we shall keep each other company. I have much to relate, but we can talk during the journey. We leave tomorrow and it is nearly midday. You must have time with your wife and daughter."

I thanked her and was about to take my leave, when she began to speak again. She had something else to tell me. I settled down on the cushion at her feet.

"I met Halima last night. We ate together. She has permission to take her son to Cairo, where she will await the Sultan's pleasure. I was surprised when she sent me a message asking for a meeting, but it did not disturb my calm. What was it you once told me that your old friend Ibn Maymun had written on emotions?"

Hearing the mention of Ibn Maymun took me aback, but I, too, remained calm.

"I think what he wrote was to the effect that emotions of the soul affect the functioning of the body and produce significant and wide-ranging changes in the state of our health. Unless emotions that cause upset and disorders are smoothed out, we remain ill at ease with ourselves and all those who come into contact with us."

She laughed again.

"Your Ibn Maymun is a truly great philosopher. He pierces the inner depths of our hearts and souls. You can tell him that he is correct. I feel well again. The emotions that tormented my soul have disappeared forever.

"When I met Halima I was not sure how I would react. I did not know what to expect from her or myself. In the event it was like meeting a stranger. She left me cold, Ibn Yakub. She apologised to me at length for having maligned me to her retainers and friends, the lowest of the low in the harem. She wanted us to be friends again and, with a pitiful smile, she tried to reach my heart by saying that the demons had finally abandoned her mind and she was her old self again.

"I had no desire to be cruel or flaunt my indifference, so I smiled and told her I understood, but we could not recreate what had been lost. She looked sad and her eyes filled with tears, but with my hard heart I felt nothing. The place which she had once filled in my life had become occupied by other things, including the works of the great al-Farabi. So, I wished her well, and hoped she would find good friends in Cairo and bring up her son to be a decent, educated human being. With these words I left her. Do you think I was overly harsh, Ibn Yakub? No dissembling. Speak plainly."

I thought for a moment and spoke the truth.

"It is difficult for me since I knew both of you at the peak of your happiness. I saw how you were with her and she with you. I envied both of you. And then when she became ill in her mind, it was not simply you that she rejected. I too was discarded, for I reminded her of the satanic past. In your place I would have done exactly the same, O Sultana, but I am not and never was in your place. If she asked me, I would resume my friendship with her. She needs friends."

"You are a good man, scribe. Now go to your wife and make your farewells. We leave at dawn tomorrow."

I was not thinking of Halima and Jamila as I walked back from the citadel to our house. My head could not rid itself of Ibn Maymun. Jamila's reference to him had not hurt at the time, but now it reopened old wounds. My bitter anger was no longer directed at Rachel, but against her greatly venerated seducer. If I had seen him on the street, I would have picked up a stone and burst open his head. The violent character of this thought upset me greatly, yet it also calmed me as I reached the outer courtyard of our house.

Rachel greeted me with news. Our daughter had become engaged to the son of the cantor in the synagogue. The father I knew well, an intelligent and well-read man. As for the son, Rachel informed me that he was a bookbinder by trade.

"Does he read what he binds?"

"Ask your daughter!"

One look at Maryam's face was enough to tell me all I needed to know. The child was clearly very happy with her mother's choice. My question became redundant. It was a strange sensation. Soon this girl around whom we had built our lives would leave our house and enter that of another man. How would it affect relations between Rachel and me? Would we painlessly grow old together, or would we grow apart? I could not think too much because they were insisting that I go and meet the boy. I had not yet told them my own news, but given my departure it was necessary that I inspect the young man who was to take my daughter away. It was with difficulty that I prevented Rachel from accompanying me.

The cantor embraced me as I entered the synagogue. He took me to his home, where his daughter made us some tea. The mother had died some years ago and the eldest girl was in charge of the household. News of my arrival must have travelled fast. We had barely drunk our tea when the young man in question burst into the house and stood motionless before me. I rose and embraced him. Goodness appeared to be written on his face. My instincts told me he was a good boy, yet Shadhi's warnings resounded in my ear. "The nicer they seem the more brutal they are . . ." But the old man had been talking of the Franj, and this was the son of a friend.

Later, back at home, I gave my approval of the match. When the excitement finally subsided, I told Rachel that I was leaving the next day, on the express instructions of the Sultan. She took the news well. Mother and daughter both hugged me when I insisted that the wedding must go ahead as soon as possible. They should not wait for my return.

That night in bed, Rachel whispered in my ear.

"Can you imagine a grandson, my husband? I could never give you a boy, but our Maryam will, and soon, I'm sure."

With imaginary grandsons on the way, I understood why news of my departure to a war in which I might be killed had not caused greater sorrow. I understood, but it would be a lie if I said that I was not a little hurt.

JERUSALEM

TWENTY-SIX

The Sultan pitches camp and soldiers begin to assemble from every quarter of his empire

The journey itself was uneventful. It took us two days to reach Ashtara, nothing compared to the agonies I suffered when we made the journey from Cairo to Damascus. It was, however, unbearably hot. Once we had abandoned the green fields and rivers outside Damascus, the trees became fewer and fewer. My mood began to get correspondingly worse. The disconcerting thing about the desert is that no birds sing to greet the dawn. Morning comes suddenly, and before one has time to wake fully and stretch, the sun is already beginning to hurt.

The Sultan had decreed that we should pitch camp at Ashtara, a small city surrounded by large plains. Here mock-battles could be fought and we would be blessed with an unlimited supply of water – always a crucial consideration, but a hundred times more so in times of conflict. For the next twenty-five days, we prepared for the battles that lay ahead.

Soldiers, archers and swordsmen began to assemble from all corners of the empire. Slowly our encampment grew and grew until the entire town was overwhelmed by the great city of tents that had sprung up in its midst. A hundred cooks, assisted by three hundred helpers, prepared food for the army. The Sultan insisted that everyone should eat the same meal. He told his emirs and secretaries that this simple rule recalled the earliest days of their faith. It was necessary to show both friend and enemy that, in a jihad, all were equal in the eyes of Allah.

To the great amusement of the emirs, Imad al-Din found it difficult to conceal his chagrin. He muttered under his breath that the early days of their religion were long past, now it should be just as important to let the Franj observe the richness and variety of the Damascus cuisine. The Sultan's frown ended the frivolity. Imad al-Din's tastes were very special and could only be satisfied by the cooks in two establishments in Damascus. For most other people the camp was well stocked with everything. There were several dozen cooks, each of whom had thirty cooking pots under his command. One of these pots could hold nine sheep-heads. In addition special baths had been dug in the ground and lined with clay. The Sultan knew that the stomach and hygiene of an army were crucial in maintaining its morale.

The camp routine was established from the first day, and newcomers were initiated from the moment of arrival. Trumpets and a roll of drums, punctuated by the cry of the muezzin, woke the whole camp at sunrise. This was the only call for collective prayers, except for Christians and Jews, who were exempted, though they had to rise at the same time. This was followed by a substantial breakfast, whose function was to keep the soldier strong till the evening meal. A short recreation followed, utilised mainly for purposes of defecation. Rows and rows of men went outside the town to empty their bowels in ditches dug for the purpose and covered with sand every second day to moderate the stench. A second drumroll summoned the men to carefully organised bouts of swordfighting, archery and horse-riding. The foot-soldiers had to run for two hours every day.

Not a day passed without some excitement. The colours of the Caliph arrived, to be received by the Sultan amidst general acclaim and shouts of "Allah is great". This did not stop al-Fadil whispering comments to Imad al-Din, loud enough to reach my ears:

"At least he has sent the Abbasid banners, but he will be sick with fear if our Sultan takes al-Kuds. That will make Salah al-Din the most powerful ruler in Islam."

"Yes," chuckled the great man of letters, "and his astrologers are already telling him to beware of him who prays first at the Dome on the Rock, for he will come to Baghdad and be greeted as the real Caliph."

That the Caliph was jealous of our Sultan was hardly a secret. Every merchant travelling from Baghdad to Damascus came replete with court gossip, much of it exaggerated, but some of it confirmed by other sources, namely the spies of Imad al-Din, who sent him regular reports from the first city of the faith. What was surprising was the contempt with which the two men closest to the Sultan regarded the Caliph.

We had been at Ashtara for barely a week and it already felt like home. The reason for this was not the comfort of our surroundings but the general feeling of solidarity which suffused the atmosphere. Even the Kadi al-Fadil admitted that he had never experienced anything like it during previous campaigns. Soldiers spoke to emirs as virtual equals without threatening the discipline of the army. The emirs, for their part, and under the explicit orders of the Sultan, made a point of eating the evening meal with their men, dipping bread in the same bowl and tearing meat off the same bone.

It was in this spirit that one morning the colours of the Kurds were seen in the distance. A messenger rushed to inform the Sultan, who was out riding with Taki al-Din and Keukburi. I, on my poor horse, was trying to keep up with them. The three men were discussing whether their traditional tactics of charge and retreat, which owed a great deal to the Parthians, and were ideal for small formations of highly trained and skilled horsemen, could be applied with such a large army as was being assembled at Ashtara.

At this crucial juncture, the messenger announced the arrival of the Kurdish warriors. The three generals burst out laughing, for the indiscipline of the Kurds was well-known. Shirkuh was the only leader who had succeeded in taming their wilder instincts. Most of them had, till now, refused to fight under Salah al-Din. They claimed that he lacked his uncle's audacity and his father's cunning. This was why their arrival was greeted with joy by the Sultan, and we rode back ferociously to the camp.

The Kurds had arrived and cheered the Sultan's arrival in their own language. Their leaders came forward and kissed Salah al-Din fiercely on both cheeks. He turned to me with a tear in his eye. I went close up to him and he whispered in my ear.

"I wish Shadhi were here to witness this day. Many of them remember him well."

That night the spirit of fermented apricots dominated the camp. Even the Sultan was observed taking a sip from a flask covered in leather worn shiny with use. Then the Kurds began to sing. It was a strange mixture of lover's laments, combined with chants of hope and love. An older warrior, who had imbibed too much potent apricot water, interrupted everyone with a lewd song. He sang of the woman he wanted, that she might have a vagina that burned like a furnace. Before he could continue, his sons took him aside, and we did not see him again till the next day.

The evening ended with a Kurdish war-dance which entailed several pairs of fighters leaping over the camp-fire with unsheathed swords and fierce expressions, and the carefully orchestrated clash of swords.

As I was walking back to my tent, I saw the Emir Keukburi and Amjad the eunuch in animated conversation with a man of medium height who I did not recognise. He was clearly a nobleman, probably from Baghdad. He was wearing the colours of the Caliph, and a black silk turban which matched his flowing beard. Even in the starlight a precious stone the colour of blood, set in the centre of the turban, shone splendidly. I bowed to the party, and Amjad introduced me to the stranger. It was Ibn Said from Aleppo, who had lost his power of speech as a child and could only communicate with gestures.

"What did you think of the Kurds, Ibn Yakub?" asked Keukburi.

"They provide the Sultan's army with much-needed colour," was my polite reply, but the mute from Aleppo began to gesticulate wildly. Amjad the eunuch nodded sagely and translated Ibn Said's hand movements for our benefit.

"Ibn Said wants you to know that the Kurds are only good for stripping a city clean. They are the vultures of our faith and should be used sparingly."

Keukburi frowned.

"I am sure Ibn Said is aware that the Sultan himself is a Kurd and, for that reason, I cannot accept the insult lightly."

Once again the stranger began his hand movements, which included touching the stone in his turban. Amjad watched every movement like a hawk, nodding all the while.

"Ibn Said says that he is only too well aware of the Sultan's origins. He says that all precious stones are rough before they have been shaped and polished. The Sultan is such a precious stone, but the men from the mountains still require a lot of work."

Keukburi smiled and was about to comment when Taki al-Din hailed him and took him away from us. They were both invited to sip tea with the Sultan. As they left I, too, began to move, when suddenly the mute Ibn Said began to speak.

"I knew I had deceived Keukburi, Ibn Yakub, but I thought your powers of observation were sharper."

The voice was familiar, but the face . . . and then Amjad was laughing and I knew that the beard and turban were a disguise. Underneath lay the familiar features of the Sultana Jamila.

We all laughed and I was invited to the tent of "Ibn Said" to sip some coffee with her and Amjad the eunuch. Jamila could not live without her coffee, and the beans were sent regularly by her father and, lately, her sister in Harran. It was certainly the most delicious coffee in Damascus, and she was probably right in claiming that it was the best in Arabia and, therefore, the world.

We sat outside her tent savouring the aroma and watching the stars. None of us felt much like speaking. I had noticed this on previous days as well. Soldiers and emirs often sat quietly, deep in thought, before they went to sleep.

What were they thinking? What thoughts were crossing their minds? Were they, like me and Jamila and Amjad, thinking of the battles that lay ahead? Victory or defeat? Both were possible. The feeling of deep solidarity that existed in all these men when they marched together was undeniable. That solidarity was created by the knowledge that if they succeeded in driving the Franj out of al-Kuds, this army of which they were a part would be remembered throughout history.

This solidarity gave them a collective identity when they thought only of victory, but these soldiers were also individual human beings. They had mothers and fathers, and brothers and sisters and wives, and sons and daughters. Would they see their loved ones again? True this was a jihad, and that meant they would go straight to heaven without any accounting by the angels. But what if people close to them failed to win entry to heaven? What then? It was thoughts of this sort that dominated their minds as they savoured the night sky before closing their eyes. I know this because I spoke to many of them and heard their stories.

"If we lose," said Jamila, "and Salah al-Din is killed, I will take my sons and return to my father's home. I do not wish to sit in Damascus and watch more wars whose only aim is to determine who succeeds him. I suppose pessimism is natural on the eve of a war. My instinct, however, says the opposite. I feel strongly that he will win this war. Let us retire for the night, Ibn Yakub, and careful you do not betray my secret."

I bade goodnight to the bearded Jamila, but the Sultan clearly had other plans for me. Just as I was walking to my tent, one of his bodyguards waylaid me with instructions to attend to the Sultan without delay. I rushed to my tent to collect my pen and ink and sheafs of paper.

The Sultan's tent was surprisingly modest. It was only slightly bigger than mine, and the bed in the corner was no different to that on which I slept. The only sign of rank was a large silk carpet which covered the sand and on which he sat, leaning against a pile of cushions. Next to him were the Emir Keukburi and Taki al-Din. The Sultan was in a light mood. He looked at me and winked.

"Who is this Ibn Said from Aleppo who insults my Kurdish warriors?"

"A man of no importance, Commander of the Victorious."

"I hope you are right. Keukburi is convinced that he is a spy of some sort."

"Spies," I replied, "are usually keen to ingratiate themselves with the enemy. They flatter shamelessly the better to deceive. The stranger from Aleppo is one of nature's sceptics, with a whip for a tongue and a brain so sharp that it could slice a camel in two."

The Sultan laughed.

"You have just described the Sultana Jamila."

Everyone laughed at this sally, and Keukburi, unaware that he was the butt of the joke, louder than most, to show that he really appreciated the dig at his sister-in-law.

Before Keukburi's ignorance as to the real identity of Ibn Said could be further exploited, the tent flap opened and the Sultan's oldest son, al-Afdal, all of seventeen years, walked in and bowed to his father, acknowledging the rest of us with a patronising smile. He had grown since I last saw him over a year ago. His beard was neatly trimmed and his whole demeanour suggested a person of authority. I remembered him and his brothers as small boys being taught to ride in Cairo. I had seen this boy being taught how to fight with a sword on horseback and on foot.

Assuming that father and son wished to be alone, Taki al-Din, Keukburi and myself rose to leave. The Sultan permitted the other two to leave, but waved me to stay seated. After the two men had departed, he allowed his son to sit down.

The boy had fought his first battle several weeks ago and had sent his father a glowing account, comparing his first war to the deflowering of a virgin, an analogy that had greatly displeased Imad al-Din. He had muttered rudely that, whatever else he might become, al-Afdal could never be a prose stylist. Salah al-Din was a loving but stern father. Since the arrival of his son, his mood had changed. His face had taken on a severity which did not augur well for the young prince, who realising this just as I did, frowned at my presence. I smiled at him sweetly and he turned his face away, not looking his father in the eyes.

"Look at me Afdal! We are about to fight a battle in which I might die. Our spies tell us that the Franj King, Guy, has offered a large reward to the knight who lances me in the heart."

The boy was moved to tears.

"I will be at your side always. They will have to kill me first."

The Sultan smiled, but his face did not lighten as he continued.

"Listen to me, boy. You are still young. Understand one thing. In the field of battle, respect must be earned. I was given a chance by my uncle Shirkuh to prove myself early in life, just like you, except that I exercised no power whatsoever till much later. Shirkuh never believed in inherited authority.

"I was grateful to him, even though at the time I felt like a man who does not know how to swim but is thrown into a river. He has to learn how to swim and reach the other side at the same time. You think because you are the son of the Sultan that the soldiers and the emirs will respect you. They may want you to believe that, but you would be a fool to do so. Once you have fought by their side, eaten sand and tasted blood, then they might begin to see you as their equal. After you have fought with them several times, they might begin to respect you. The right to give orders does not win respect.

"Imad al-Din and al-Fadil have educated you well. I am aware that you are well acquainted with the history of all the great wars we have fought since the days of our Prophet, may he rest in peace, but that knowledge, important though it is, will not come to your aid in the battlefield. In wars, experience is a much better teacher.

"What you learn from books you can just as easily forget, unless you are blessed with the memory of Imad al-Din. What you experience yourself stays with you till you die.

"I summoned you because it has come to my attention that some weeks ago you challenged the authority of your cousin and my brother's son, Taki al-Din, in front of the emirs, ordering him to carry out an instruction contrary to what he had already decided. He was disciplined, and did as you asked. In his place my uncle Shirkuh and I would have slapped your neatly bearded face. Fortunately your orders did not lead to disaster, otherwise I would have had to reprimand you in public.

"I want to be clear on one point. Taki al-Din is my right arm. I trust his judgement. I trust him with my life. If, in the course of the battle, Allah decides that my time has come, Taki al-Din is the only emir genuinely respected by the soldiers, who could still lead our side to victory. I am leaving orders to that effect. You can learn a great deal by observing your cousin and staying by his side, but that is a decision for you alone. Tomorrow morning I want you to go to him, apologise for what you did, and kiss his cheeks. Is that plain? Now go to bed."

The Sultan's chosen heir was in chastened mood as he bowed to both of us and left the tent.

"Do you think I was too harsh, Ibn Yakub?"

"Not having a son myself, O Sultan, I am not the right person to comment on relationships between a father and his son, but as a leader of men, what you said was totally justified. He was hurt, but mainly because of my presence. He would have taken it better without me, but a young prince who aspires to be a good ruler must learn to make his own way in this harsh world."

"I could not have put it better myself, scribe. I wanted you to be present so that you could inscribe it and it will remain part of our family history. If he turns out to be a good Sultan he will appreciate these words, for he might need to use them to his own son. Leave me now. I think I will spend the night exploring the mind of Ibn Said. I shall send for our sceptic from Aleppo to warm my bed and stimulate my brain."

I looked at him in surprise. There was a twinkle in his eye, but how would Jamila receive the news of the intended exploration? She had not shared the Sultan's bed for many years, and the look on his face made it clear that this was what he had in mind.

TWENTY-SEVEN

The story of Amjad the eunuch and how he
managed to copulate despite his disability

Ashtara, three days' journey south of Damascus, lies on a plateau that crowns a large hill. We had been there for almost a month. The Sultan was delighted with the progress being made by the soldiers. While there would always be differences between the units gathered under his command, he now felt that they understood how he wanted to fight the war. Much time had been spent explaining the meaning of different signs and sounds. Each unit assigned a member to watch the Sultan's tent. For troops at a distance, the ability to understand what the shifting banners signified was as much a matter of life and death as a correct interpretation of the drumroll was for soldiers in closer proximity to the Sultan. All this took time to explain to the emirs and nobles in command of the different units and squadrons of Salah al-Din's armies.

One day after morning prayers, he breakfasted in his tent with only Taki al-Din and myself in attendance. He looked his nephew in the eye, saying with a laugh: "The dust that rises when my army marches to al-Kuds will eclipse the sun!"

This was the only time that I saw him excited by the prospect of war. He had embarked on the conflict at this particular moment, not because military strength favoured him, but for reasons of state. He had behind him the most united army of Believers ever raised to defeat the infidel. There were Jews and Christians as well, but their numbers were small. Many of them were simply waiting for an opportune moment to convert to the faith of the Prophet of Islam. Not the Copts, however. Their strong beliefs and implacable hostility to Rome and to Constantinople made them Salah al-Din's natural allies.

I was walking away from the Sultan's tent when Amjad the eunuch took me by the arm and whispered: "Ibn Said, the mute, desires your attendance."

I followed him without a word. I had still not become used to Jamila's new identity. Only when her eyes twinkled did I recognise the woman behind the disguise. That and her voice, which could only be heard in the secrecy of her tent.

"Salah al-Din tells me that he shocked you, confessing the desire for me that was filling his loins a few nights ago. True?"

I could never get used to this woman. She invariably took me by surprise. Amjad the eunuch laughed at my discomfiture. How in heaven's name could I reply?

"The truth, Ibn Yakub. As always, the truth!"

"I was not shocked by the Sultan's announcement that he wished you to share his bed again. That was normal for him. You are very beautiful and . . ."

She became impatient.

"And I'm the only woman in the camp. Yes, yes, I am aware of this fact, but what was it that shocked you, master scribe?"

"It was the thought of how degrading it might be for you if you were compelled to submit to the desires of a man."

She smiled and stroked her false beard.

"I thought as much, and it was noble of you to feel a sense of shock at my predicament. As you can see, I survived the experience. I am used to your Sultan. I could not have submitted my body to any other man – or, for that matter, a eunuch."

Amjad the eunuch flinched as if he had been touched by fire. He appeared upset by her remark. Realising this, she stroked his head and whispered an apology, immediately putting him on the defensive.

"Trying to persuade Amjad to talk about his past is like pulling a tooth from the mouth of a crocodile."

The eunuch smiled, pleased with her attention. She continued to press him.

"Who knows whether any of us will live or die over the next few weeks? Today you must tell us your story, Amjad. We have the advantage of the scribe's presence. Ibn Yakub will write it all in his little book, and you will be immortalised for the future. What say you to this, my red-haired friend?"

It was now for the first time that I observed Amjad's features. The reddishness of his hair was emphasised by the whiteness of his skin. His eyes were grey. He was much taller than me, and I am taller than the Sultan. I had never been interested in him as a person, but his closeness to Shadhi and Jamila mirrored my own affections. I too appealed to him directly.

"Amjad," I said. "Shadhi often spoke with me about you. He had a high regard for your intelligence and yet, despite this, we know little of each other. Who are you? When did you come to Damascus, and how did you end up in the citadel as a retainer of the Sultan?"

His eyes became melancholic and he sighed, before speaking in his soft, unbroken voice.

"The reason I have resisted the Sultana's previous injunctions to speak of myself is because I know very little of my past. I am a *saqalabi*, that much is clear from my appearance, and I am a eunuch, which almost reduces me to the level of a caged animal.

"As you are both no doubt aware, people like me come in different shapes and sizes. There are some eunuchs whose entire penis has been removed. This variety is popular amongst those kings and sultans who watch their women like tigers, ready to pounce on them at the first signs of betrayal. They imagine that a eunuch whose organ has been completely removed can, for that reason, be trusted completely. Strange how the degree of trust for some nobles and emirs is dependent on the degree to which a eunuch has been mutilated. If they really wanted to avoid all physical contact between a eunuch and a woman they would have to eliminate more than a poor penis. Fingers, toes and the wonderfully agile tongue would also need to be removed. But I have long given up studying the inconsistencies of emirs and sultans.

"There are others like me, who are simply castrated and sold to churches. We are taught to sing in praise of Isa, and in our spare time we gratify the carnal desires of priests and bishops. Fate favoured me. I did not undergo any such ordeal. I was castrated when I was four or five years old, bought by Jewish merchants in the lands of the Bulgars, and sold in the market in Andalus. Here I was bought by another trader, who believed in Allah and the Prophet, and brought me to Damascus. All this I was told by the family to whom I was sold at the age of seven.

"As the Sultana is aware, our faith expressly forbids the castration of boys or men. So the only way in which the demand for eunuchs can be met by our sultans and emirs is through buying them from churches or freeing them from the tyranny of the priests, after a city has fallen to the followers of the Prophet. Then we become faithful and willing converts to Allah, because we have never been treated better or permitted so much influence and power.

"The Sultana understands well that intelligence resides not in the penis, but in the brain of a man. To regard eunuchs as powerless purely on the basis of their emasculation is foolish, as many rulers, the late Sultan Zengi amongst them, have discovered to their cost.

"I know of at least three different cabals of eunuchs in the citadel alone. They are loyal to the Sultan, yet after he dies they will take different sides in the struggle for the succession. I belong to none of them and, for that reason, am both trusted and mistrusted by all. It is a happy position because they tell me what I wish to know, but keep secret their plots. That also pleases me. If I was aware of any plan to kill al-Afdal, I would inform the chamberlain without hesitation.

"You, wise and good Ibn Yakub, asked of my childhood memories. Alas, I have no recollection of my parents or when and why they sold me. Perhaps they were poor peasants and needed money. There are several eunuchs in Damascus who have told me stories of how they were castrated by their own parents, and sold to merchants acting on behalf of the Patriarch of Constantinople.

"I have no memory of the voyage from the land of the Bulgars to Andalus, or from those parts to Damascus. I was sold by the trader who had bought me in Andalus to the merchant, Daniyal ibn Yusuf. His family treated me kindly. I was taught how to read and write as if I was their own child. They clothed me and made sure I was well fed. I always knew I was different from the rest of the family because I did not sleep in the house. I lodged in the quarters allocated to the cook. They were always hot and dominated by an offensive odour, which emanated from the body and clothes of the cook. He never mistreated or abused me and, since he was a good cook, I forgave him the unpleasant smell.

"By the time I was sixteen, the master commented that I had a natural ability with figures and he took me out of the house. Every morning I would accompany him to his work in the suk, where he owned two shops. The first sold expensive cloths and rugs: satins and brocades from Samarkand, silk from China, muslin and shawls from India, and Persian rugs.

"The neighbouring shop sold only swords, and these, too, were of the highest quality. The master told me that one of the swords of the Sultan Salah al-Din had been bought from his shop, though later Shadhi told me that this could not have been the case. All the Sultan's weapons were specially made to measure by craftsmen attached to the armouries established for this purpose in Cairo and Damascus.

"What is undoubtedly true is that the cloth shop was visited one day by the Sultana Ismat, may she rest in peace, and her retinue. I am talking now of the time when she was married to the great Nur al-Din and not to our Sultan. I was in the shop that day, and she was impressed by the way I spoke to the ladies who waited on her. I refused to haggle and stuck firmly to the price that had been fixed by my master. I had no idea who these grand ladies were or from whence they came.

"The Sultana laughed at my impudence and within a week she had me transferred to the citadel. When she discovered I was a eunuch, she was overjoyed. I was attached to the harem as her special messenger to the world outside. After Nur al-Din's death, she married our Sultan. The rest you know. I am sorry that my life has been so uneventful."

I could now see why Amjad was so highly valued by those who trusted his discretion. He knew many of the darker secrets of life in the citadel, but had refused to divulge them. Perhaps it was my presence that inhibited him. Perhaps he did not wish to speak out of turn while Jamila was present, for then she might think that if he could talk about others in front of her he could easily do the same about her to others, and trust would be destroyed.

That same day, following the evening meal, I resisted all attempts to make me join the various games with which the soldiers amused themselves. I was not in a mood to enjoy the company of my fellow men. Morbid thoughts had begun to crowd my mind. I returned to my tent and began to meditate on the stage my life had reached. Might it not be prematurely cut short in the weeks and months ahead?

The tent itself began to feel oppressive and, anxious to rid my head of cobwebs, I decided to walk out into the night, to regain my inner calm by breathing the cold night air and watching the movement of the stars.

I had sat down on a little mound and was thinking of Rachel, when a hand tapped my shoulder. I had thought I was alone and the touch sent a shock-wave of fright through my body. In times like this, one thought of Franj spies, but the voice was familiar.

"My heartfelt apologies for frightening you, Ibn Yakub. I, too, found the camp very restricting tonight and decided to follow you here. I should have made my presence known earlier, but I felt you needed to be alone for a while."

It was Amjad. Relief dissipated the anger I had felt at being followed in this sly fashion. He had done so for a purpose.

"I could feel that you did not fully trust the account of my life that I gave you and the Sultana this morning."

I reassured him that this was not the case. I had no reason to doubt his veracity. My dissatisfaction, for it was nothing more, had arisen because I felt instinctively that he knew a great deal more than he had cared to divulge. Jamila had felt this more strongly than myself, and had been irritated by what she characterised as Amjad's refusal to take sides on any issue. The eunuch smiled when I informed him of her annoyance.

"I know why she was angry. In the past I have told her everything. What used to interest both her and the Lady Halima was my inability to enjoy the delights of the bedchamber.

"One day their intense questioning led to an insistence on both their parts that I bare what remained of my genitals so that they could examine them closely. I was reluctant, but their pressure became relentless. Ultimately I acceded to their outrageous demand. Their inspection did not last long, but they used the fact to blackmail me. Unless I kept them informed of all the activities in which the other ladies in the harem were engaged, they would tell the Sultan that I had shown them the remains of my penis. It was Halima who half-threatened me in this fashion. Jamila saw the fear on my face and immediately sought to reassure me that it was a joke and instructed me to forget everything that had taken place.

"Nonetheless I was regularly questioned by Halima about the other women, and I had to feed her with the odd crumb of information. Often I made something up for her amusement. All was well as long as Halima and Jamila remained close friends. Serious trouble only erupted when their relationship had come to an end. Halima told some of her new friends what I had said about them, and one evening five of them, watched by Halima who had incited them in the first place, surrounded me, and proceeded to whip me on my bare back. I still bear the marks of that humiliation.

"Two people helped me greatly after that ordeal. When I told him what I had suffered, Shadhi became so angry that he wanted to tell the Sultan. I had to use all my wiles to stop him, but I think he sent a message to Halima warning her that if she carried on in this fashion she would be spending the rest of her days in a tiny hut in a remote village.

"Jamila, too, was genuinely shocked and upset. As a result we became close friends and, in her presence, I pledged in the name of Allah and our Holy Prophet that I would never tell tales again.

"Till a few weeks ago Jamila helped me honour this pledge. Then suddenly one evening, and without any warning, she began to question me about Halima. I kept quiet and shook my head. My silence upset her and we did not speak again till this morning. Presumably she thought that in your presence my tongue might loosen. I am aware of what she wishes to know and I understand her motives, but I am bound by a vow before Allah. I had no alternative but to disappoint her."

Listening to him that night under the stars I could understand how Shadhi and Jamila had been seduced by the soft voice of this eunuch. Now he had me under his spell. I was intrigued by his teasing references to Halima. What could he know? What did he know?

"I too am dismayed by your story, Amjad. I can see why Shadhi wanted to tell Salah al-Din. It would have ended the matter immediately. I fully respect your vow not to tell tales, and I have no desire that you breach your oath. Yet surely what Jamila wished to know was the truth about Halima. Your pledge concerned inventions and lies. Am I not correct?"

He did not reply for some time, and suddenly the majestic silence of the desert night became oppressive. I was about to rephrase and repeat my question, when he began to speak again.

"You are correct, as usual, Ibn Yakub, but what Jamila wanted to know involved my own person. If I had told her the whole truth it would have killed her regard for me, which means a great deal. In fact, I treasure it more than anything else in this world. The sad truth is that one night, when I was fast asleep,

Halima entered my bedchamber. She removed the gown that covered her nakedness, lay down beside me, and began to stroke my body and fondle that which she and Jamila had once, long ago, inspected from a distance.

"In the name of Allah, I swear to you, Ibn Yakub, that for quite some time I thought I was dreaming. It was only when she mounted me and began to move up and down on this little dateless palm-tree between my legs, that I realised it was all real, but by then, even if I had wished, it was too late to resist or complain. Even the strongest doubts can be drowned by pleasure. After it was over she left. We had not managed to exchange a single word. I felt like an animal. Perhaps she felt the same disgust that overcame me, but perhaps not.

"She returned several times, and we coupled in silence. It ended as it had begun. Abruptly. Afterwards we used to avert our eyes whenever we saw each other, but she avoided me and, as I later heard, used to mouth obscenities at my expense to her new friends. One of them, who later fell out with her, told me that Halima had confessed to all of them that mounting me was the only way she could rid herself of the spectre of Jamila which she encountered everywhere.

"Nothing remains secret in the harem. I am convinced she was followed and malicious tongues informed Jamila, who, not unnaturally, wanted a confirmation or denial from my own lips. I could not oblige her, Ibn Yakub. It would hurt her a great deal and demean our friendship. For me, one afternoon spent in conversation with Jamila is worth all my nights with Halima. They are not even delights I could measure on the same scale. Jamila's intellect affects me like an aphrodisiac. When she laughs with me the sun shines on my heart. She is the one I truly love, and I would happily die at her command. Now you know it all. My guilty secret is out at last."

I was stunned by Amjad's confession. Where I had failed, a eunuch had succeeded. I looked at the stars, silently praying for the heavens to fall. I wanted to smother all memories.

That night I was awakened by a dream. I was being castrated by a woman whose face was disfigured by an ugly leer. It was Halima.

TWENTY-EIGHT

Divisions within the Franj are brought to our notice

Two of our spies within the Franj camp, both merchants of the Coptic persuasion, had informed Taki al-Din of developments within the Kingdom of Jerusalem. It was being torn asunder by a furious battle between the two principal knights of King Guy. Count Raymond of Tripoli was advising the King to be cautious and defensive, which meant staying in Jerusalem and not marching out to fall straight into the trap being prepared by Salah al-Din. The King himself was more inclined to the view championed by Reynald of Châtillon. This knight had smelt blood. He questioned the integrity of Count Raymond, accusing him of being a friend of Salah al-Din and a false Christian. Reynald believed that the balance of strength favoured the Franj. He argued that their knights and foot-soldiers could outmanoeuvre and outflank the Sultan's armies.

At one stage the two men had almost come to blows. They would have fought each other there and then had not the King grabbed a wooden cross and put his own person between them. He had compelled the two knights to swear an oath that they would cease quarrelling and fight together to defeat the Saracen infidels.

Taki al-Din questioned the two spies in detail. He asked them about the exact size of Guy's army, the amount of supplies they would need to survive outside their city, the names of the men who would command the Templars and Hospitallers, and the length of time it would take us to receive information about the exact whereabouts of the Franj army, if, that is, they were foolish enough to abandon the Holy City and come out to meet the Sultan on his own ground. The merchants looked at each other and laughed. It was the older one who spoke.

"The Emir need not worry on that count. My own brother is responsible for maintaining the supplies needed by Guy and Reynald. He will inform us the moment he has the necessary information. The pigeons are prepared."

Taki al-Din smiled.

"My uncle always complimented me on being a good judge of character. You have never supplied me with false information or disappointed the trust I have placed in you. For this the Sultan will reward you generously. Your tent is prepared. You have had a long journey. Please rest and recover your strength till the evening meal."

Two days later the news we had been waiting for reached us. Reynald of Châtillon had won the battle for Guy's ear. The Franj were even now preparing to march out of the Holy City, to fight on our terrain. The Sultan's face lit up when he heard the news. He insisted that it be checked and double-checked. We had to wait another day before confirmation arrived from another source. Only then did Salah al-Din order a review of all his troops to be held the next morning, six miles north of Ashtara at Tell Tasil, situated on the main road to the valley of the Jordan river.

"I want to stand on a mound and observe the whole army, Ibn Yakub," he said. "Radishes come like men, in different shapes and sizes," our friend Shadhi used to say. Apart from my own squadrons, most of these men are new. They are radishes from fields I have not ploughed. Let us see how they compare to our variety."

News that the Franj had moved out of the Holy City to give us battle swept through the entire camp within half-an-hour. News of this nature can never be kept secret for long. The effect was a complete change in the mood of the men. If they had, till now, been relaxed and slightly over-confident, the information that they might now be engaged in real combat within a few days made them nervous, somewhat edgy, and yes, even fearful.

The Sultan was well aware of how fluctuating morale can dampen the ardour of even the best army on the eve of battle. He ordered the camp to be dismantled. I had never seen him like this before. He appeared to be everywhere at the same time. One minute I could see him and his emirs rushing to inspect the storage and alert the supply-masters of the decision. With their gowns flying in the wind, they looked from a distance like giant ravens. They gave orders for the camels, supply mules and wagons to be made ready, for tent-pegs to be loosened that night, to be rolled and packed at the crack of dawn. The next minute the Sultan himself, to my amazement, clambered up on a newly constructed siege tower to test its solidity. I was alarmed at the needless risk, but young al-Afdal, who stood by my side watching his father, laughed away my worries.

"We are used to him behaving like this before a battle. He insists on taking risks. He says it inspires confidence in the men. If the Sultan can die then so can they."

"And will he let you risk your life, my young prince?"

The neatly bearded face changed colour.

"No. He says I have to stay alive in case he falls. So my task in the battle is to convey his orders, and to stand by his tent and his banner at all times. I went to my cousin Taki and asked to fight by his side, but he too has his orders. It is not fair. I have already fought in two battles, but this will be the most important."

"Patience, Ibn Yusuf. Your time, too, will come. You, too, will live without misfortune. You will govern and judge and raise your sons as you have been raised. The Sultan acts in your best interests. A sapling has to be protected from hot winds so that it too can grow and bear fruit."

The heir to the Sultanate became petulant.

"Ibn Yakub, please don't try and act like Shadhi. There was only one of him."

With these haughty words, the young man left me to my own devices, though not for long. Amjad the eunuch, uncharacteristically long-faced, whispered in my ear that Ibn Said, the mute, was awaiting my presence. As we walked to her tent, Amjad warned me that the Sultana was in a foul mood and he would leave me alone with her. The reasons for Jamila's ill-humour soon became clear.

"Salah al-Din has ordered that I am not to be permitted to march with the army. He says the danger is too great and my presence is unjustifiable. I explained to him patiently that he was talking like a man whose brains had been replaced by the anus of a camel. This annoyed him greatly, and he pushed me aside. He has even instructed Amjad to prepare my return to Damascus. So while all of you are marching to take al-Kuds, the eunuchs and one woman will be heading towards Damascus.

"I am warning you in advance, Ibn Yakub. I will not obey him this time. Amjad, poor fool, is frightened out of his wits. He dare not disobey Salah al-Din. I've told him I am quite capable of looking after myself. I ride better than most of you, and I have often shot at the mark with an arrow. What is your opinion?"

She was in a rage, and I followed Ibn Maymun's advice in these situations and offered her some water. She sipped slowly from a glass, which calmed her a little.

"Sultana, I feel honoured and privileged to be your friend, but I beg of you not to resist the Sultan's will on this occasion. He has enough to think about without worrying about your safety. I know it is not in your nature to accept orders blindly. Your first response is always to resist his command, but I know how much he loves you and how seriously he always considers your advice. I have often heard him say that you, not he, are in possession of a powerful brain. Indulge him just this once."

She smiled.

"So, you can be sly as well. That is a revelation. I am prepared to accept your advice provided you answer one question truthfully. Do we have a deal?"

I was so taken aback by this odd request that, without further thought, I eagerly nodded my agreement.

"When Amjad walked with you into the desert night a few days ago, did he tell you how many times he let Halima fuck him?"

I had been led neatly into a giant trap. She had taken me by surprise, and she did not need me to utter a single word. My guilt-ridden features told her all she wished to know.

"Amjad!" I heard her shout. "You disgusting whore. They should have cut it all off when they had the chance. Come here!"

I thought this might be an opportune moment to slip out of her tent unobserved.

Early next morning, in the light of a rosy hue which is the desert dawn, we rode out to Tell Tasil. Spirits were high, but the odd note of laughter, a shade too loud and over-enthusiastic, testified to the nervousness felt by some of the emirs, for it was they who laughed in this fashion. It did not take us long to reach Tell Tasil. Usually, Salah al-Din reviewed his army when stationed on a mound, and always on horseback. This time he broke with tradition. He instructed the foot-soldiers to push a siege tower to where he stood. He invited me to climb up with him, but the look on my face made him laugh and withdraw the invitation. Instead he took al-Afdal up with him. I stood at the base of the large wooden construction which would usually be deployed to scale the walls of enemy citadels.

Once he was in position, he raised his arm. The trumpeters blared out their message, and a drumroll began the proceedings. Then, preceded by the black banners of the Abbasid Caliphs and by the Sultan's own standard, Taki al-Din and Keukburi, looking fierce in their armour and with swords raised, led the troops past the tower. It was a remarkable sight. The 10,000 horsemen were followed by archers on camels, and then by the long line of foot-soldiers.

Even the Kurdish fighters had managed to curb their unruly instincts. They rode past the Sultan in exemplary formation. It took over an hour for everyone to march past, and the dust became a thick cloud. Salah al-Din looked pleased as he came down from the tower. For once he was deeply affected by the sight of what we had witnessed. The experience seemed to have dispelled his customary caution.

"With this army, Allah permitting, I can defeat anyone. Within a month, Ibn Yakub, your synagogue, in what you call Jerusalem, and our mosque, in what for us will always be al-Kuds, will be filled once again. Of this I have no doubt."

That same day, a Friday, the day usually favoured by the Sultan to launch a jihad, we marched in the direction of the Lake of Galilee. We reached al-Ukhuwana just after sunset. Here we set up camp for the night.

TWENTY-NINE

The eve of the battle

The Sultan had received word from his advance scouts that the Franj were assembling their knights and soldiers at Saffuriya. Some of his emirs wanted to draw them out a bit further, but Salah al-Din shook his head.

"Let them stay there for the moment. You shall cross the river and wait for them on the hills, near Kafar Sebt. They will come running when I take Teveriya. They will be enraged, and anger on this terrain can be fatal. Once you receive news that Allah has rewarded us with a shining victory, you will move through this area and place guards near every well, stream and river. Then, wait where you are with your lances poised like the claws of a lion. Taki al-Din will come with me. Keukburi will command the army here. Remember that the lands of the Franj are covered in forests. The shade is never far away. Allah will show them the strength of the sun. Let them bake inside their mail till they cannot bear its touch."

The emirs could not conceal their admiration. They sighed with delight and began to hum praises in his honour.

"Those who place their hopes in you are never disappointed. You are the only one who protects all his subjects against the Franj. In you we have . . ."

The Sultan silenced them with an irritated gesture.

News spread quickly that the Sultan had decided to take Teveriya, the city that the Romans called Tiberias. There was no shortage of volunteers to take this Franj stronghold. Situated on the southern tip of the Lake of Galilee, it had been left alone in the past because of the truce agreed between Salah al-Din and Count Raymond of Tripoli. Now that Raymond had joined the Franj forces in Saffuriya, we were free to take the city.

The eagerness of the men to fight was motivated not so much by the greater cause, the need to combat error and defend truth, the desire to crush the infidel and to strengthen the Believers, as by the hope of a quick victory. They hoped above all that some of the riches of this perishable world might fall into their hands. Salah al-Din did not accept volunteers. He picked his own tried and tested soldiers.

"They are the burning coals of our faith. With them I will take Teveriya by surprise."

While he marched to take the old Roman fortress, Keukburi crossed the river. After a few hours he set up camp, ten miles to the east of the Franj encampment, on a small plateau, south of a village which bore the name of Hattin. To my considerable annoyance, I had been instructed by the Sultan to stay with the main army. I can only assume that he did not want any unnecessary baggage and wished to limit his strike force to seasoned warriors. I could appreciate the logic, but it did not deaden my disappointment.

The decision to camp here had been taken two days earlier following reports received from the advance scouts. They spoke of two large streams bubbling with cool fresh water and surrounded by fruit and olive orchards. We arrived here with the sun at the zenith. The heat had exhausted man and animal alike. Sweat poured off the Emir Keukburi's face and merged with the lather of his steed.

As soon as we had reached the site, Keukburi stripped bare, drinking some water before entering the stream. He shut his eyes as the water travelled over his body. We watched, desperate to follow his example, but whereas the Sultan would have gestured to the whole army to join him, his favoured commander maintained his reserve. After a long time, or so it seemed on that day, he put his head under the water and then quickly re-emerged and clambered up the bank. Two retainers draped his body in white cloth and dried him from head to foot. He retired to his tent, which had been pitched in the fragrant shade of orange trees.

The minute he disappeared from sight there was a muffled cry of relief. We did not wait for permission. Everyone headed towards the water, to soothe their parched throats, to lie in the path of the flowing stream, and to recover from the rigours of the journey. A fair proportion of the new soldiers had not yet lived to mark their sixteenth or seventeenth year. It was reassuring to observe their care-free frolicking. Sounds of laughter mingled with the comforting noise of the water.

The more experienced veterans of the jihad bathed silently, keeping their thoughts to themselves, trying, no doubt, to avoid too many thoughts of the future. Many were not yet thirty years of age, but they had seen enough horrors to last them in this life, and beyond. Some had seen the destitute inhabitants of town and village, ruined and driven out of their homes by the Franj knights. They had experienced battles whose final memory was the bodies of their companions piled high upon each other before the mass burial. They had seen a close friend struck down by an arrow, his liver torn in two. Many had lost brothers and cousins and uncles. Others had witnessed sons crying for their fathers and fathers weeping for their sons.

Having bathed and dried myself, I was sitting in the shade of an olive grove thinking stray thoughts. My daughter was expecting a child. Would it be a boy? Jamila must be safe in the citadel in Damascus. Had she become embittered with Amjad the eunuch, and how was she punishing him? As always, Shadhi occupied my mind, and we were about to commence an imaginary discussion when a retainer coughed politely. My master demanded my presence.

Before separating from us earlier that afternoon Salah al-Din had given his soldiers a brief period to prepare themselves for the journey. As he drank water and half-heartedly chewed some dried dates, he appeared thoughtful. I also detected a touch of sadness in his eyes. He had told me on previous occasions that after Shadhi's death a loneliness would often grip his soul, a loneliness that remained even when he was in the company of men who stimulated his mind. I knew this mood.

"What does Allah have in store for us, Ibn Yakub? Battles are rarely won by the superiority of arms or men. It is the motivation, a sense of belief in being engaged in Allah's mission, that is decisive. Do you think the soldiers realise the importance of the next few weeks?"

I nodded.

"Commander of the Victorious, let me tell you what Shadhi would have told you. He always wanted to be with you on this day. He knew it would come, and what you would ask, and this was his reply: 'I know our soldiers,' he said. 'They understand only too well what it means to retake al-Kuds. They are prepared to die for this cause.' I have listened to them talking to each other, and Shadhi would not wish me to change a word."

The Sultan smiled and stroked his beard.

"That is the impression that I, too, have gained. Let us hope that their belief in the righteousness of our cause will be sufficient. Let us pray that the cruelties of fate and random misfortunes do not unite to aid the Unbelievers. Tell Keukburi to make sure that the men are fed well tonight."

There had been no need to pass on this message to the Emir Keukburi. Unlike his commander, he loved eating. He was capable after a single mouthful, or so it was faithfully reported, of discerning every herb and spice that had been used to flavour the meat. He had already instructed the cooks, and just before sunset the scent of cooked meat wafted through the camp, inflaming our appetites. Even the Sultan, whose aversion to meat was well-known, remarked on the unusual fragrance of the aroma.

The cooks had prepared a beef sikbaj, a stew much favoured by the boatmen on the Euphrates. It was sweet and sour, cooked with fresh herbs soaked in vinegar and honey. Its effects were soporific. Even the Kurds with their addiction to grilled meat were forced to admit that the sikbaj they ate that night had been prepared in heaven.

A drumroll awoke us next morning. The exhaustion had disappeared and the soldiers seemed relaxed. Keukburi, to the great relief of most of the men, did not insist on morning prayers. He wanted to join the Sultan in Tiberias. He refused to wait for the supplies to be loaded, and left the camp with a thousand horsemen and myself in attendance.

We had been riding for under half an hour when a cloud of dust moving towards us made everyone tense. Keukburi sent two of his scouts to ride out, to ascertain the number and strength and the banners of the approaching horsemen. If they were Franj knights, we would have to give battle and send out another scout to inform Salah al-Din. We waited, but the scouts did not return. The dust moved steadily in our direction.

Keukburi and three of the emirs who rode at his side conferred with each other, and divided our force into three wedges. Suddenly we heard loud cries of "Allah o Akbar". Everyone smiled and began to breathe again. Those approaching were friends. Then our scouts galloped back, to inform the Emir that Salah al-Din had taken Tiberias and was riding back to join us.

Keukburi roared with delight, and we rode forward to meet the conqueror of the city that had just fallen. The dust subsided. Keukburi jumped off his horse and rushed to the Sultan to kiss his robe. Salah al-Din, moved by the gesture, dismounted and embraced the young Emir with a fierce tenderness. The triumphant chants of the Believers rent the air around the two men.

"They will come now to try and retake their city, and they will take the shortest route, the road that leads from Acre straight through the plain of Hattin. The virtue we must preach to ourselves today is patience. Even my uncle Shirkuh with his monumental impatience would, were he alive today, agree with me. Let us return to the camp and find a pleasant place from where we can observe Guy with his Templars and Hospitallers. The sky is clear, the sun burns like a furnace, and we control the water."

THIRTY

The battle of Hattin

Salah al-Din knew that the noble Raymond of Tripoli would try to devise an alternative, more defensive plan. His wife was in the citadel of the captured city. Raymond would be aware that Salah al-Din had yet to confront the Franj when they were in a strong and entrenched position. The Sultan was depending on the rashness and stupidity of the Franj leaders. He was confident that the blind mistrust and hatred of the Count of Tripoli felt by Guy and Reynald of Châtillon would lead them to ignore any plan that Raymond might suggest.

On the third day of July, a Friday, the scouts who had been watching the movements of the Franj rode back to our camp in great excitement. Keukburi accompanied them to the entrance of the Sultan's tent. He was resting, and I was teaching one of his guards the basic moves of chess. Here, underneath the lemon trees, we all waited for him to finish his rest.

The faces of the two scouts were lined with dust. Their eyes were dark with lack of sleep. Their posture suggested that the news they carried was important. They were under strict orders from Taki al-Din to speak directly with

Salah al-Din. It was I who suggested that the Sultan might be happy to be disturbed, and Keukburi entered his tent. Salah al-Din walked out bare-chested, a
cloth round his waist.

The scouts whispered their message in his ear. It confirmed his predictions. A
much-relieved Sultan allowed his emotions to show. He roared with delight.

"Allah o Akbar! They have abandoned the water and are in the grip of Satan.
This time I have them."

Trumpets and drumrolls alerted emir and soldier alike. The speed with which
our army made ready for war was a sign of the high morale and discipline that
had been achieved during the weeks of training at Ashtara. The fall of Teveriya
had a feverish effect on those who had stayed behind. The Sultan, fully dressed
in his armour, his green turban in place, and his sword strapped on by attentive
retainers, was giving his final orders to Taki al-Din and Keukburi. The two
men bowed and withdrew after kissing his cheeks.

Like beasts awaiting their prey, the Sultan's archers prowled anxiously on the
ridge. Their impatience for the kill made them simultaneously nervous and
eager. Despite my best efforts to remain calm I could not control my excitement.
I broke bread that day with the great Imad al-Din. He was hard at work writing
his account of the battle that was about to begin. As he left the tent to relieve
himself I read and copied his opening paragraph: "The vast sea of his army surrounded the lake. The ship-like tents rode at anchor and the soldiers flooded in,
wave upon wave. A second sky of dust spread out in which swords and iron-
tipped lances rose like stars." He wrote with such ease, the words flowing from
his pen quicker than the ink that gave them shape. It did make me wonder, once
again, why the Sultan had chosen me and not him to compose this work.

At midday, we caught our first sight of the enemy. The sun was reflecting on
the heavy armour of the Franj knights, and the flashes pierced the dust.

As the Franj moved towards the ridge, the Sultan gave the signal. Taki al-Din
and Keukburi took their squadrons on a flanking manoeuvre that should not
have surprised the Franj. They surrounded the enemy, cut them off from their

water supply, and blocked all possible retreats. The Sultan continued to hold the ridge.

I had remained on the ridge next to al-Afdal, near the Sultan's tent, far from the fighting. Salah al-Din would ride away to observe the battle from different positions, listen to first-hand reports, and then return to his banner where we stood. Then he would send out new instructions. His eyes shone like lamps and his face was free of worry. He was clearly satisfied, yet his caution never deserted him, not for a moment. I had occasion to observe him closely that day.

He was not an interfering commander. He had planned the battle carefully, and provided his orders were carried out he saw no reason to intervene. Throughout the day messengers on horseback, their faces full of dust, would come to him with information and return with orders. One of the most important victories in the annals of Islam was a surprisingly calm affair.

The sight of our dead and wounded soldiers touched me deeply. It upset me that neither the Sultan nor the Emir – nor, for that matter, the men themselves – seemed to show much sympathy for those who had been lost that day. It is strange how, even after one day of war, it is difficult to remember what normal life was like before the battle and all its afflictions.

As the Franj knights slumped and fell, the only emotion I felt was one of relief. By temperament, I am not a vengeful person, but as I saw the sand darkened by the blood of the Franj I recalled the accounts of what they had done to my people in Jerusalem and other towns. I offered a silent prayer pleading with the Almighty to hasten the victory of our Sultan. Not that he needed my prayers that day. His tactics had worked well and, though none of us realised it at the time, it won him the battle of Hattin. Unlike the Franj, we lost few men on that first day. We could have followed them, and finished the job by the evening, but the signal given by al-Afdal from outside the Sultan's tent was to let them retreat. They had nowhere to go. Every exit had been sealed. Every well was under our control. The supplies on which the Franj had been relying had been diverted, and some of them were already being unloaded at our camp.

The Franj had thought that, as in the past, their knights would charge and break through the encirclement, opening up a path for their entire army to retreat. But they underestimated the size of our army. What they wanted to do had become impossible.

That night, as both sides made camp, neither was aware that the battle was over. On our side, the Sultan conferred anxiously with the emirs. He wanted the names of the skirmishers from each squadron. He demonstrated his own prodigious memory by naming the archers he wanted in position the next day. He had carefully watched the new archers at Ashtara and noted the names of those who hit the mark most often. They were given 400 loads of arrows. The Sultan watched the supplies being distributed and addressed his favourite archer by name.

"Tell your men, Nizam al-Din, that, despite the temptation, they must never waste arrows by aiming at the knights of the Franj. Their armour cannot be pierced. But mark the horse, and aim well, so that the beast falls. A Franj knight without his horse is like an archer without a bow. Useless. Once you get the horses, Taki al-Din and our horsemen will ride like a wave and decapitate these infidels as they stagger nervously to their feet. Is that clear?"

The reply came from all the archers who had been straining their ears to catch the Sultan's words.

"There is only one Allah, and he is Allah, and Mohammed is his Prophet."

"I agree," muttered the Sultan, "but I don't want Him to welcome too many of you into Heaven too soon. This war is not over."

Before the battle began again, the Sultan gave firm instructions to his emirs regarding Raymond of Tripoli.

"He is a good man, who was once our friend. Even though he has been compelled by the worshippers of icons to fight against us, I harbour no ill-will against him. He must not be killed. I want him taken alive. If that is not possible, let him escape. We shall find him again."

It was our skirmishers who began the fight, testing the intentions of the enemy. The Sultan, flanked by Taki al-Din and Keukburi, waited awhile before committing his army to battle. The Franj charged the skirmishers and we suffered some losses, but Salah al-Din signalled to another group of mamluks to join the skirmishing. This time the Franj knights retreated. Imad al-Din, who was with me that day, laughed at the sight.

"The lions have been transformed into hedgehogs," he said, but a look from the Sultan silenced him. Shadhi had taught Salah al-Din that celebrating a victory before it had been won always brought bad luck.

Salah-al-Din ordered his two wings to begin their outflanking operation and his trusted archers moved into position at the same time. Now, at his signal, their bows quivered and their arrows rained on the Franj, unhorsing many knights. A further signal was given and the scrub was set alight, enhancing the miseries of the Franj. The flames were almost invisible in the bright light. The terrified knights and their horses surged to and fro, feeling they could not remain still, wanting to do something, but they confronted an impossible situation. The smell of scorched flesh, human and animal, began to waft in our direction with the breeze of the late afternoon. Those Franj knights who rode through the fire and charged desperately up the wadis found the Sultan's archers waiting for them. Some collapsed from sheer exhaustion. Others were burnt alive. The Sultan received the news without emotion. Only once did he speak to me directly, and that was to remark that some of the finest-pedigreed horses of Arabia had perished and this was a cause for regret.

I heard with my own two ears the desperate cries of the Franj soldiers. Crazed by thirst and burnt by the sun, they pleaded for water, praying to their God and then to Allah, much to the disgust of their knights who belonged to the Orders of the Templars and the Hospitallers.

I could see one of their commanders, that impure and infantile adventurer, Reynald of Châtillon, of whom I have already written. He had a frightening scar across his face, a permanent reminder of the skills of one of our unknown swordsmen. Reynald was riding on his sweaty black steed, which snorted arrogantly just like its master. He pulled his horse to an abrupt halt. The roar of the soldiers began to die down. A messenger rushed to the commander. Reynald dismounted and the man whispered something in his ear. Then I lost sight of him completely. Suddenly, and before our very eyes, the Franj lost their formation and appeared without aim or direction.

They moved instinctively towards the lake of Tiberias, but our soldiers barred their way. Hundreds of Franj soldiers gave themselves up to the Sultan, falling on their knees and chanting "Allah o Akbar". They converted on the spot to the religion of the Prophet, and were given food and water.

Thousands of these soldiers climbed to the top of a small hill, effectively deserting their King. They refused orders to come down. They were thirsty and could not fight without water. Most of them were killed by being hurled over the rocks by their own side. Some were taken prisoner by us. It was clear to every-one that the Franj had been defeated.

Salah al-Din received news of these victories with an impassive face. He was watching the tents which surrounded the symbolic Cross of the Franj. These housed the King and his immediate bodyguard, and had not shifted throughout the battle.

As we watched, young al-Afdal began to jump up and down, shouting: "Now we have beaten them." He was quickly silenced when a Franj charge drove our soldiers back, causing a frown to occupy the Sultan's forehead for the first time during this battle.

"Be silent boy!" he told his son. "We shall not defeat them until that tent falls."

Even as he pointed to the tent of King Guy, we saw it fall. We saw our sol-diers capture the "True Cross". Now Salah al-Din embraced his son and kissed him on the forehead.

"Allah be praised! Now we have beaten them, my son."

He ordered the victory drumroll, and cries of joy erupted on the hills and plains around the village of Hattin. Taki al-Din and Keukburi came riding up, their arms filled with Franj banners. They threw them at the Sultan's feet and leapt off their horses, their eyes filled with tears of joy and relief. They kissed Salah al-Din's hands, and he lifted them both to their feet. With his arms round their shoulders, he thanked them for what they had achieved. Then Taki al-Din spoke to him.

"I allowed Count Raymond to escape, O Commander of the Victorious, just as you had instructed, even though my archers were straining to unhorse him."

"You did well, Taki al-Din."

Now it was Keukburi's turn.

"Commander of the Victorious, we have captured most of their knights. Their so-called King Guy and his brother, Humphrey of Toron, Joscelin of Courtenay and Reynald of Châtillon are among our prisoners. Guy wishes to speak with you."

The Sultan was moved. He nodded appreciatively.

"Pitch my tent in the heart of the field where this battle was won. Place our banners in front of the tent. I will see Guy and whoever he chooses to accompany him in that tent. Imad al-Din! I want an exact tally of how many men we have lost and how many were wounded."

The great scholar nodded sagely.

"It will not take too much time today, O great Sultan. Compared to the Franj whose heads cover the ground like a plague of melons, our casualties are light. We have lost Emir Anwar al-Din. I saw him go down when the Franj charged us just before their final collapse."

"He was a good soldier. Bathe his body and send it back to Damascus. None of our men should be buried in Hattin, unless they belonged to this region."

"Who would have thought," continued Imad al-Din in a more reflective mood, "that the success of your military tactics would transform Hattin, this little insignificant village, into a name that will resound throughout history?"

"Allah decided the fate of the Franj," was the Sultan's modest reply.

Imad al-Din smiled but, uncharacteristically, remained silent.

In the distance, we observed the Sultan's tent established on the plain below. He spurred his horse and our whole party – al-Afdal and a hundred guards, with Imad al-Din and myself bringing up the rear – galloped past corpses already beginning to rot in the sun and stray arms and legs to the place where the tent had been pitched.

Such was the feeling of euphoria that had gripped us all that the only thought to cross my mind was that the wild beasts would be having a feast tonight.

Imad al-Din as his chief secretary and I, the humble chronicler of his life, sat on either side of his chair. He told a guard to inform Keukburi that he was now ready receive the "King of Jerusalem". And so it happened. Guy, accompanied by Reynald of Châtillon, was brought in by Keukburi, who spoke now with a formality which surprised me.

"Here, Commander of the Victorious, is the self-styled King of Jerusalem and his knight, Reynald of Châtillon. The third man is their interpreter. He has just decided to become a Believer. I await your orders."

"I thank you, Emir Keukburi," replied the Sultan. "You may give their King some water."

Offering Guy hospitality was the first indication that he would not be beheaded on the spot. Guy drank eagerly from the cup, which contained cooled water. He passed the cup to Reynald, who also took a sip, but the Sultan's face became livid with anger. He looked at the interpreter.

"Tell this King," he said in a voice filled with contempt and disgust, "that it was he, not I, who offered this wretch a drink."

Guy began to tremble with fright and bowed his head to acknowledge the truth of Salah al-Din's words. Then the Sultan rose and looked into Reynald's blue and ice-cold eyes.

"You dared to commit sacrilege against our Holy City of Mecca. You further compounded your crimes by attacking unarmed caravans and by your treachery. Twice I swore before Allah that I would kill you with my own hands, and now the time has come to redeem my pledge."

Reynald's eyes flickered, but he did not plead for mercy. The Sultan drew his sword, and drove it straight through the prisoner's heart.

"May Allah speed your soul to Hell, Reynald of Châtillon."

Reynald collapsed on the ground, but he was not yet dead. The Sultan's guards dragged him outside and, with two blows from their swords, they removed his head from his shoulders.

In the tent there were wrinkled noses as a terrible stench arose. The Franj King, frightened by the fate of his knight, had soiled his clothes.

"We do not murder kings, Guy of Jerusalem," said the Sultan. "That man was an animal. He transgressed all codes of honour. He had to die, but you must live. Go now and clean yourself. We will provide you with new robes. I am sending you and your knights to be shown to the people of Damascus. I will set up camp outside al-Kuds tonight, and tomorrow what your people once took by force will be returned to the People of the Book. We shall sit where you sat. Yet unlike you we shall dispense justice and avoid tasting the elixir of revenge. We shall repair the injuries that you did to our mosques and to the synagogues of the Jews, and we shall not desecrate your churches. Under our rule, al-Kuds will begin to flourish again. Take the prisoner away, Keukburi, but treat him well."

Thus it was that Guy and his chief nobles left for Damascus. Even as they were being led away, they could see three hundred knights of the two military orders of the Hospital and the Temple being led to their execution.

They must die, the Sultan had decreed, for if we let them live they will only take arms against us once again. It was the deadly logic of a conflict that had long poisoned our world. All I could think of was the moment we would enter Jerusalem.

THIRTY-ONE

The Sultan thinks of Zubayda, the nightingale of Damascus

Salah al-Din permitted only a modest celebration on the night of our great victory. Couriers were dispatched to Baghdad and Cairo, carrying news of the battle that had been won. The count of the Franj dead had revealed that they had lost 15,000 men. Imad al-Din confirmed the figure, and wrote that the prisoners numbered 3,000 nobles, knights and soldiers.

The letter to the Sultan's brother al-Adil in Cairo also carried a command. He was to bring the army of Egypt to Palestine, where it was needed to complete the jihad.

The Sultan was happy, but, as always, he permitted nothing to overwhelm his caution. He told Taki al-Din that Hattin was not a decisive victory. A lot more needed to be accomplished, and he warned against overestimating our strength.

He was worried that the Franj would regroup and rally outside the walls of Jerusalem, and he embarked on a careful plan. A great sweep along the coast would destroy every Franj garrison. Then the Holy City would fall into his lap like a ripe plum from a tree that is gently shaken.

The soldiers were drunk with victory. They cheered when the Sultan rode through their ranks and told them of his new plans. They dreamed of the treasure that was waiting to be taken.

Only Imad al-Din and myself, exhausted by the encounters of the last few days, were desperate for the Sultan to grant us leave. We had both spoken of returning to Damascus – we would rejoin the swollen army once it marched in the direction of Jerusalem – but the Sultan was not inclined on this occasion to indulge our wishes.

"Taken together," he told us, "you are both sincere, learned, eloquent and generous men. You, Ibn Yakub, are cheerful and without arrogance and false pride. Imad al-Din is cheerful and easygoing. On account of these merits I need you both by my side."

He wanted Imad al-Din to write letters of state, and he wished me to observe and note his every move. Earlier he had promised me that every night after the battle he would dictate his impressions of the day. In the event, this proved impossible, for he spent hours engaged in discussions with his emirs before bathing and retiring to bed.

Four days after our victory at Hattin, the Sultan's armies stood outside the walls of Acre, a wealthy citadel held by the Franj ever since they had first polluted these shores. He was sure that the city would surrender, but he gave them but a single night in which to make up their mind. From their ramparts the Franj saw the size of the army and sent envoys to negotiate a surrender. Salah al-Din was not a vindictive man. His terms were not ungenerous, and they were accepted on the spot by the envoys.

When the Sultan entered the town, the city appeared lifeless. Imad al-Din commented that it was always the same when new conquerors entered a town. The people, overcome by fear of reprisals, normally stayed at home. Yet there could have been another reason. That day the sun was unrelenting, and those of us who rode through the gates of Acre felt its pitiless heat and sweated like animals.

It was a Friday. The Sultan, his son al-Afdal riding proudly by his side, rode with his emirs to the citadel. As he dismounted, Salah al-Din looked towards the heavens and cupped his hands. While we stood silent, he recited the following verses from the Koran:

> *You give power to whom You please,*
> *and You strip power from whom You please;*
> *You exalt whom You will,*
> *and You humble whom You will.*
> *In Your hand lies all that is good;*
> *You have power over all things.*

Afterwards they bathed and changed their clothing. Then with smiling eyes and dust-free complexions they celebrated the fall of the city, offering prayers to Allah in the old mosque. The Franj had used it, for a very long time, as a Christian church.

After the Friday prayers, the Sultan embraced his emirs and returned to the citadel. He had called a meeting of his council for later that evening, and al-Afdal was sent to ensure that everyone attended. He wanted to remind everyone that this war was not yet over. Alone with Imad al-Din and myself, he dictated a letter to the Caliph, informing him of the victory at Acre. Then, without warning, his whole face softened and his mood changed.

"Do you know what I would really like to do tonight?"

We smiled politely, waiting for him to continue.

"Listen to a singing girl, sitting cross-legged and playing the four-stringed lute."

Imad al-Din laughed.

"Could it be that the mind of the Commander of the Victorious has recalled the delights and merits of Zubayda?"

The Sultan face paled slightly at the mention of the name, but he nodded.

"She still resides in Damascus. She is not as young as we all once were, but I am told that her voice has not changed much. If the Sultan will permit, I will make some inquiries in this city to ascertain . . ."

"No, Imad al-Din!" interrupted the Sultan. "I spoke in a moment of weakness. This is a city of merchants. Nightingales could not survive here. Do you really believe that there could ever be another Zubayda? Go now both of you and get some rest. I require your presence at the Council and, as a special favour to Imad al-Din, I will not oblige you to eat with me beforehand."

I had not known the Sultan in such a relaxed mood since our early days in Cairo. Since his return to Damascus he had usually been tense and preoccupied with matters of state.

Later, as the great master of prose and I were being scrubbed by attendants in the bath, I questioned him about Zubayda. He was surprised that Shadhi had never mentioned the object of Salah al-Din's youthful passions. As we were being dried in the chamber adjoining the baths, he provided me with an account that, once again, revealed his startling capacity for recollection.

"It was the love of a sixteen-year-old boy for a thing of great beauty. You smile, Ibn Yakub, and I know what is passing through your mind. You are thinking how can I, of all people, appreciate beauty in a woman. Am I wrong? You smile again, which confirms my instincts. I understand your doubts. It is true that the sight, even of your unwieldy body, excites me more than that of any woman, but Zubayda was exquisite because of her deep, throaty, voice. It touched the souls of all who heard her sing. Truly, my friend, she was unrivalled in perfection.

"I have no idea of her lineage. It was rumoured that she was the child of a slave woman who had been captured in battle. Zubayda herself never once talked about her past. She did not speak much in company, though al-Fadil, who was also charmed by her, told me once that her conversation sparkled when she was in the presence of just one or two people at the most. That privilege was denied me.

"I was present, however, when young Salah al-Din, his spirit clouded by arrogance, saw her the first time, in the presence of his father Ayyub and his uncle Shirkuh. Of course, Shadhi, too, in those days, was everywhere. It was in the house of a merchant, a man desperate to please Ayyub. He had, for that reason, obtained the services of Zubayda. This was the first time we had heard her sing. Salah al-Din was captivated at once. One could almost see his heart inflamed, by a passion so pure that it could burn everything.

"Zubayda had not yet reached her thirtieth year. Her complexion was fair, her hair was dark, and her large eyes shone like two lamps from heaven. Her teeth when she smiled put pearls to shame. She was slightly built, and if I may say so, she reminded me of a beautiful boy I had once loved in Baghdad. At times her eyes would move away from us, as if she were in a dreamlike trance. Her face then reminded me of a soft moon-entangled cloud. I wish she had been a boy, Ibn Yakub, but I must not digress.

"She was dressed that night in a silk robe, the colour of the sky. It was richly patterned with a variety of birds. The nightingales were embroidered in gold thread. Her head was covered by a long black scarf, with a circular red motif. A silver bracelet hung loosely on each of her wrists. All this one forgot when she played the lute and her voice accompanied the music. It was heaven, my friend. Pure heaven.

"Salah al-Din had to be taken home that night by force. His uncle Shirkuh offered to buy Zubayda for him, but the very thought that she could be bought offended his love. His face paled as he walked away, the blood pulsing in his veins, the ever-protective Shadhi by his side. From that night on, he never missed an opportunity to hear her sing. He sent her presents. He declared his love for her. She would smile with sad eyes, gently stroke his head, and whisper that women like her were not meant to grace the beds of young princes. He began to write poetry underneath the thick, forking pear tree in the courtyard of Ayyub's house. He would send her couplets, one of which later came to my attention. He spoke of her as more beautiful than the full moon in heaven's vaults because her beauty survived the dawn. The quality of the poems, as you can imagine, was indifferent, but there was no doubt that they were deeply felt.

"Zubayda was touched by the boy's love, but she had her own life to live, a life which, of necessity, excluded Salah al-Din. He refused to understand what she was trying to tell him. He could not accept that he was being spurned and rejected. Believe me, Ibn Yakub, when I tell you that things got so bad that this sober, cautious Sultan threatened to take his own life unless he could marry her. His uncle Shirkuh settled the affair by taking him away to Cairo. The rest is known to you. Salah al-Din became a Sultan. Zubayda remained a courtesan."

Aware of Salah al-Din's strong will and his obstinacy, I expressed surprise that he had let the singer go so easily. He had obviously left her with regret, but surely he could have returned to her in rapture, and even married her at a later stage. The fact that she was a courtesan would not have bothered him a great deal. Everyone knew, after all, that usually it was the courtesans that made the most faithful wives.

What puzzled me was why Shadhi had never even referred to this tale. Not once. Either the great scholar was exaggerating a youthful obsession or there was another reason, which was still hidden from me. I pressed the Sultan of Memory further, and insisted on being told the whole truth.

Imad al-Din sighed.

"Alas, my friend, she was the keep of his father Ayyub. When Shirkuh made Salah al-Din aware of this terrible fact, something died in the young man. I am firmly of the opinion that after learning of this he diverted all his energies towards warcraft. When I am turned down by a lover all my efforts become concentrated on the books I am preparing for publication. For Salah al-Din it was sword-fighting and riding. It was as if the love he wished, but was not permitted to bestow on Zubayda, was transferred to horses. You may smile, Ibn Yakub, but my observation was not designed to provoke levity on your part.

"Zubayda's rejection pierced his young heart like a knife. It took him a long time to recover. The consequence was, as you are no doubt aware, that he married much later in life than most men of his position. Once the children began to arrive he became as active as his favourite steed. He took one concubine after another, and produced more sons than his father and uncle put together.

"Despite the growth of his families, nobody was permitted to mention Zubayda's name in his presence. Her memory was banished. Perhaps that is why Shadhi never told you. He realised it was a painful subject.

"Today I took a big risk. I just knew Salah al-Din was thinking about her. He wanted to share his triumph with her, to tell her: 'Look at this man, Zubayda. He has achieved much more than his father.' I felt this instinctively and that is why I took the liberty of mentioning her name. I was truly surprised when the Sultan responded in the way he did. He might have sent me out of the room. I think the pain has finally disappeared. We shall see if he sends for her when we return to Damascus."

I was now overcome by a burning desire to cast my eyes on Zubayda, to listen to her voice and to hear her play on the four-stringed lute. I determined to see her on my return to Damascus. Perhaps she might add to the story. Perhaps it had meant little to her in the first place. Could it be that Salah al-Din, so cautious in war, had been equally cautious in love? I could not let the matter rest. Imad al-Din had told me all he knew, but I felt that there was something more to the story. I would uncover the truth. If Zubayda was not forthcoming, I would question Jamila. She was the only living person who could exhaust the Sultan with her questions till he told her what she wanted to know.

Shadhi, the only person who might have told me the real story, had betrayed me. As I made ready to attend the Council of War, Shadhi entered my head and we had an imaginary argument.

THIRTY-TWO

The last council of war

Even though Imad al-Din had confided in me that the Sultan regarded the council of war as the most important gathering of this jihad, I was inclined to disbelieve him. I assumed that Imad al-Din was revealing this to me simply to heighten his own importance as the Sultan's trusted adviser. On this occasion I was wrong.

I had thought that the council of war would be a mere formality, a victory celebration during the course of which the Sultan would announce our departure for Jerusalem. There are some thoughts that one just has to laugh away. This was one of them.

As I entered the crowded chamber where the emirs were gathered, I detected uncertainty and tension. From the back of the chamber I could see the Sultan at a distance, engaged in a conversation with al-Afdal, Imad al-Din and Taki al-Din. The latter appeared to be speaking, with the others nodding vigorously. The emirs made way for me to go through to the Sultan, but they did so as one does for a favoured pet of the ruler. There was no sign of affection or encouragement on their faces. Even Keukburi appeared to be upset.

It was not till I reached the platform where the Sultan was seated that I understood why the emirs were angry. What was being finalised by Salah al-Din and his closest family members was the division of the spoils, always a delicate moment after a city has been captured.

Salah al-Din's own inclinations were hardly a secret to the emirs. He would have ordered some of the money to be kept for the jihad and the rest shared out equally amongst all those Believers who had marched into the city. But his son reminded him of another tradition followed by rulers during a holy war. Leaving everything to their sons.

Under great pressure, the Sultan had presented the town and all its estates to al-Afdal. The sugar refinery was a gift to Taki al-Din, and the great man of letters had been given a large house. Al-Afdal had already announced all this to the emirs, which was a mistake. They would have grumbled, but accepted the information with considerably more grace, if the Sultan himself had addressed them. Imad al-Din was hostile to the whole idea, and suggested that everything should be put into the war chest to fund the wars that were still to be fought.

"Have no doubt, O Sultan," he whispered to Salah al-Din, "the Franj will send for help across the water and more knights will arrive. We will need money if they launch their third 'Crusade'!"

Salah al-Din expressed agreement but shrugged his shoulders in resignation. Then he rose to speak to his emirs. For a moment, the silence was only broken by the cicadas outside.

"I know what some of you are thinking. You are wondering why I am delaying the march to al-Kuds. Let me explain. I do not ever want al-Kuds to fall to the infidels again. If we took it tomorrow – and we might do so without too much trouble, with Allah's help, since the Franj have lost their best knights in Hattin – that would be a crude mistake. Think, and you will understand what I'm saying. The Franj still occupy the coastal towns. It is in these towns and harbours that the ships will arrive from their distant homes, with more knights, more weapons, more crosses, more alcohol. They will all gather together with the infidels still here and lay siege to al-Kuds. It is simple.

"For that reason we will divide our forces and take all the towns on the coast. As you know I am never happy when our army is divided and when emirs divide to lead squadrons in different battles. But that is what we are going to do before we reach al-Kuds. I want to shake the tree so hard that every orange lies on the ground, except one. That one we will pluck as if it were a rare and precious flower. Let us clear the coast of these infidels.

"For me, Tyre is even more important than al-Kuds. If we take the harbour in that town, we will have the Franj by the throat for ever. The knights who come over the water will feel our fire while still on their ships. You want to know my plan? It is very simple. Listen carefully, for here it is. Ascalon. Jaffa. Saida. Beirut. Jubail, Tartus, Jabala, Latakia, Tyre and then al-Kuds.

"If the Franj were our only enemy, with Allah's help we would have driven them out of these lands years ago. We have three enemies apart from the Franj. Time, distance and those Believers who prefer to remain in their towers, observing the battle from afar. Like hyenas in their lair, they are too frightened to come out and watch the tigers fight each other. It is these Believers who have heaped shame, cowardice and disgrace on the name of our Prophet, peace be upon him. Let them know that we will win and that they will be disgraced and despised in the eyes of all Believers. Allah will help us conquer them all."

The Sultan's words surprised the emirs. They were smiling and nodding as he spoke, and once he finished they chanted in one voice:

"There is only one Allah and He is Allah and Mohammed is His Prophet."

Keukburi was the first to speak.

"Commander of the Victorious, I am sure I speak for everyone present here when I say that truly you are favoured by Allah. I, too, had felt that we should not delay laying siege to al-Kuds. You have convinced me that I was wrong and that impatience is never a useful guide during a war.

"With your permission I would like to ask you one question."

The Sultan nodded his agreement.

"The only way we can conquer the coast rapidly is by dividing our forces, but . . ."

"I know your worries, Keukburi, and I share them. I am always fearful when I dispatch my family or my close companions on expeditions where they are on their own, but this time we truly have no alternative. Speed is essential. I want our soldiers to cover the coast like ants. You, much-trusted Keukburi, must clear the road from Teveriya to here in Acre. Take every village and town, starting with Nazareth where Isa was born. Take the Templars' castle at al-Fula. Hissam al-Din will take Sebaste and Nablus. Badr al-Din, you will move south and take Haifa, Arsuf and Kaisariya. Taki al-Din will march on Tibnin and Tyre, and I will take Beirut and Saida. Imad al-Din has worked hard and will give each of you an estimate of the resistance you are likely to meet in each of these towns. I think Nablus, where Believers outnumber the Franj by one hundred to one, is the only place where they might surrender. The Franj know of our successes, and elsewhere they might prefer to prolong their agony. In such cases give no quarter. Where they wish to negotiate a surrender, you must be generous, for it is not just Franj lives that are at risk. Allah be with you. We leave tomorrow."

On the following day, Salah al-Din, attired in a robe of honour and with a necklace of black and white pearls around his neck, made his way out of the city in a great procession. He was accompanied by all his emirs, who had come to say farewell before their own departures. The Sultan had selected his swordsmen, lancers and archers. They were men who had fought with him for several years. Imad al-Din and I rode by his side. Outside the gates of Acre we paused so that the Sultan could exchange a few last words with the emirs. Taki al-Din and Keukburi rode up to him, dismounted and kissed his robe. His expression became tender at the sight of these two young men, who had grown up before his eyes and who he trusted as much as he trusted himself. He smiled and told them to be on their way.

"We shall meet the next time outside the gates of al-Kuds."

Then his son, young al-Afdal, dressed in full armour and preening himself as seventeen-year-old boys are wont to do, came galloping on a coal-black steed. He had some difficulty in reining in the horse, and that amused his father, who suppressed a smile. Al-Afdal leapt off the beast and kissed his father's robe in an exaggerated fashion.

"Allah guide you to rule this city well, al-Afdal," said his father. "One day you and I will make the pilgrimage to Mecca together, but only after we have al-Kuds. Now go back to your city, but remember, we are all mortal, and rule only because the people let us rule. Avoid greed and never display ostentation. Rulers who behave thus only betray their own insecurity. I have placed my hopes in you, al-Afdal, and my biggest hope is that you will never disappoint me."

With these words the Sultan raised his right arm, and our army marched away from Acre.

THIRTY-THREE

Salah al-Din is hailed as the great Conqueror,
but he decides not to take Tyre, despite Imad
al-Din's advice to the contrary

We marched in comfort. The Sultan did not wish to tire his soldiers without cause. Villages and towns fell without a struggle and he added them to his conquests, which began to appear like a garland of pearls. Everywhere the inhabitants, be they Believers or Christians, or indeed of my own faith, would gather to stare at him with inquisitive eyes. Often children were brought to him so that he could bless them with a touch on their tiny heads. The Believers rejoiced, but there was no gloating. I have noticed how common it is for the populace to hurl curses at those who have been defeated, and to sing songs of praise in honour of the victors. This is a rule of war. It is the way in which the people defend themselves against uncertainties.

Yet in each village and town there are always those whose triumph rings false. In exhibiting their loyalty to the new conqueror, they defile the name of the old ruler, make tasteless jokes, and offend his reputation, like carrion to stray dogs. These are usually those very people who never offered resistance to the Franj, but, in the wake of their defeat, have become loud-mouthed avengers, creating new identities for themselves.

One would boast of how he found an isolated Franj knight near a stream and decapitated him so that the water ran red. Another would rival this tale with one even taller. He would speak of how, one night, he had caught a Franj knight violating the honour of a maiden, naturally a Believer, and driven his sword through the heart of the offender and then removed his testicles and fed them to the dogs.

After a few experiences of this nature, the Sultan ordered that any who lied about their exploits would be publicly whipped. Word spread that this Sultan did not look kindly on liars, and the number of boasters dwindled. Salah al-Din was angered by the sight of worthless braggarts climbing on the corpses of those who, whatever their faults, had at least fallen in battle.

As we approached Tyre, there was dissension in our ranks. Imad al-Din was of the opinion that the city should be taken immediately, despite its fortifications and although it would offer stiff resistance. He was backed by most of the emirs. They argued that since the Sultan himself had convinced them that the capture of Tyre was more important even than Jerusalem, it did not make sense to delay the attack.

I well remember that evening as we set up camp in the midst of orange groves and wild flowers. Their scent overpowers me even as I recall that night. There were dark clouds in the sky as Salah al-Din walked up and down the camp. He spoke to nobody. Occasionally he would pluck an orange from the tree, peel the skin, and consume the fruit. The sound of distant thunder distracted him. As he looked up, the rain began to fall.

He had been on his own for over an hour, while the emirs and Imad al-Din waited outside his tent. Now they all rushed in to take shelter.

What was he thinking? He looked at their faces for a long time. He knew what they were thinking. Then he walked purposefully to the door of his tent and peered outside. It was still raining. He came back in and informed them that he had decided, on this occasion, to bypass Tyre. We would march to Saida, and later move on to Beirut. Tyre would have to wait till our return journey to Jerusalem.

The disappointment was plain on every face, but nobody questioned the Sultan's judgement. Even Imad al-Din, who was normally outspoken in the extreme, was silent. He told me later that though he knew the decision was wrong, he did not feel that he possessed the degree of military competence necessary to challenge the Sultan. The Sultan's resolve had little to do with the needs of the jihad. It was an atypical act of pure sentimentality.

"I know they think I am wrong, Ibn Yakub," he confessed that night, soon after we had dined on his favourite bean stew. "The fact is that my old friend Raymond of Tripoli hides in the citadel in Tyre. I let him escape at Hattin. His pride will not let him surrender, and I still do not wish to kill him. Fate has conspired to make us enemies, but, for my part, I still feel close to him. Friendship is a sacred trust. My father and uncle taught me that when I was still a boy, and I have never forgotten. Now my head tells me I am wrong, but my heart will not permit a breach of trust. Do you understand? Or have you, too, like Imad al-Din, become so completely absorbed by our victories that trust and friendship have become empty words that no longer matter to you? It is always the same. We who do the fighting understand its limitations better than you who stay in your tents and scribble."

I took the opportunity he had so kindly provided to differentiate my opinions from those of Imad al-Din, but I told him that it was not just the great scholar who was upset. The emirs, and some of the soldiers as well, felt it was a mistake not to take Tyre. At this he became quietly thoughtful again, dispensing with my services for the rest of the evening.

There was a gentle breeze as I walked out of his tent into the night. The rain had stopped. The clouds had cleared and a carpet of stars hung in the sky. Suddenly, all my senses were assailed by a mixture of scents in that orange grove. Wild flowers. Jasmine. Oranges. Herbs. The wet earth. Each exuded its own special fragrance, but it was the combination that was overwhelming. I decided to go for a walk, but Imad al-Din would not permit me to enjoy the solitude. His retainer had been waiting for me to leave the Sultan's tent, and informed me that his master anxiously awaited my presence. What choice does a humble scribe have in the face of such powerful pressure? I gave up my walk and followed the retainer to Imad al-Din's tent. He was in a tetchy mood. Wars and the rough life of a camp did not suit the great man. He missed his comforts, his boys, his wine, his food and his Damascus. He growled as I appeared.

"Well?"

I feigned puzzlement at the question.

"Why in Allah's name has Salah al-Din decided to ignore Tyre? It is a very foolish decision!"

I smiled and shrugged my shoulders.

"I am only his scribe, master. He does not confide in me."

"You are a sly, lying son of a . . ."

I begged him not to complete the sentence.

"When, long years ago in Cairo, the Sultan decided to employ me, he made it clear that everything said to me was confidential. He also kept me out of the meetings of his war council because he feared that the Franj might kidnap me and torture me to learn the secrets of his war plans. I have no idea as to the military reasons for not taking Tyre."

Imad al-Din stood up, lifted his right leg, and passed wind very loudly.

"You have become a bit too clever for your own good. There is no military reason. It is sentiment that dictates this decision. His friend, Raymond of Tripoli, is in Tyre. We all know. If Raymond was his lover, I would still be critical of his decision, but my disapproval would be veiled with understanding. Friendship has no place in the midst of a jihad where the very future of our faith is at stake. His instincts misled him. His decision was misguided. The great Nur al-Din would never have tolerated such nonsense!"

"Perhaps what you say is correct," I replied. "Yet surely the fact is that the devout Sultan Nur al-Din, despite all his longing to do so, could not take Jerusalem. Our Sultan will not fail."

"I hope so," said Imad al-Din, "and I pray that what you say will happen, but I am not so sure. There are no certainties in history."

Two days later, Saida surrendered and we marched into the city. For the moment, the question of Tyre seemed forgotten. The Sultan was pleased that no lives had been lost. He wanted to leave a small force in the city, and then to march on towards Beirut the same afternoon. But he was prevailed upon by the nobles to grace their town, if only for a single night.

Salah al-Din had been reluctant to accept the invitation – he disliked these empty formalities – but Imad al-Din was horrified at any such thought. He bent down and whispered in the Sultan's ear. To turn down the offer would be offensive in the extreme. As in other matters of diplomacy, the Sultan sulked at the advice, but finally agreed. Everyone sighed with relief. The soldiers were hot and tired, and Saida was a seductive town.

The Sultan and his emirs, and Imad al-Din and myself, were taken to rest at the citadel. From there we could see the soldiers running to the edge of the water, removing their clothes and immersing themselves in the cool waves of the sea. The baths provided in the citadel were lukewarm and cramped by contrast.

That evening, while the Sultan retired early, Imad al-Din and I dined as guests of the notables of Saida. It was a magnificent feast. I had not eaten so many different varieties of fish since we left Cairo. The fish from the Nile, though cooked in different ways, tended to be from the same family. That night in Saida, the diversity of the sea was displayed in all its splendour. These dishes were not alone. The ever-full flasks of wine were served by beautiful young women who made no attempt to conceal their charms. Of course they left Imad al-Din unmoved, but they had a turbulent impact on the three emirs from Damascus. Soon they were dreaming of the enjoyment to come, and the night that lay ahead. I, too, would have liked to share in their pleasure, but the great scholar had no time for frivolities of this nature. Once the meal was over and we had sipped hot water flavoured with the essence of orange blossom, he rose, thanked our hosts and insisted that I accompany him to his chamber.

"I am sorry to disturb your evening, Ibn Yakub. I could see the lust in your eyes as you looked at those serving wenches, but I need to discuss something important with you tonight. In fact, I need your help. I am worried about Salah al-Din."

I had always assumed that Imad al-Din regarded me as nothing more than a lowly Jewish scribe who had somehow insinuated his way into the closed circle of the Sultan. In the past his tone was usually sarcastic or condescending. What could have brought about this change in him? I was puzzled, but also flattered by being treated as an equal.

"Why are you worried about the Sultan?"

"His health concerns me. He suffers from colic and Allah could take him from us any day. If he delays too long in taking al-Kuds, the prize might elude us forever. Once he dies, most of the emirs will be at each other's throats. The common enemy will be forgotten. This is the curse of my religion, Ibn Yakub. It is as if Allah, having guided us during the life of the Prophet, is now punishing us for our greed. I have told the Sultan, and al-Fadil has backed me strongly on this, that after we take Beirut he must not waste any more time on the coast. He must take al-Kuds. I want you to give the same advice."

I was stunned. Was he suggesting that I was the third member of the trinity?

"No time for modesty, Ibn Yakub. We know the Sultan values your advice greatly. Do not let us down."

Two days later we were camped in sight of the walls of Beirut, overlooking the sea. It was a humid day and the weather affected the Sultan. He was irritable and impatient. Imad al-Din, too, was ill. He reported severe pains in the stomach, followed by nausea. Marwan, the Sultan's physician, put him on a diet. He was treated with herb infusions and vegetables. Meat was denied him and his condition began to improve. But on the second day after the treatment the pains returned. Marwan suggested to the Sultan that the sick man be sent to Damascus. There his symptoms could be observed at leisure and properly treated. Marwan himself was a specialist in treating flesh wounds.

Salah al-Din, always more concerned about the health of his close friends than his own state, ordered a squadron to carry the ailing secretary to Damascus. Imad al-Din protested weakly, but I could see that he was delighted. As I bade him farewell he winked at me.

"Solitude, Ibn Yakub. I yearn for solitude. The jihad is necessary, but my work suffers. It is not easy to contemplate our past when the present appears so uncertain and death stalks us in the shape of the Franj. My absence will annoy the Sultan, but try your best."

I nodded and muttered a few sympathetic noises about seeing him soon, fully recovered, in Damascus. Yet as he was borne away in a litter, the voice of Shadhi echoed in my head.

"Doesn't like life in a war camp, does he? Needs solitude, does he? I'm surprised. That arse-lender and taker has been through so many young soldiers that I've lost count. His illness is over-indulgence, nothing more."

The Sultan had assumed that Beirut, like its coastal counterparts, would surrender happily and peacefully, but a messenger we had dispatched returned with bad news. The Franj were determined to fight.

Salah al-Din sighed.

"I had hoped that we would see no more corpses till we reached the ramparts of al-Kuds. Why do these fools want to fight, Ibn Yakub?"

Imad al-Din or al-Fadil would have had a ready reply to this question, but I was so used to listening to him and recording his thoughts that I rarely ventured my own opinion unless he pressed me. He frowned.

"Well? Have you no explanation?"

I smiled weakly and shook my head.

His voice rose.

"These fools imagine that if they put up a brief resistance against me, and sacrifice a few of their knights, they will be rewarded by their leaders. They want to show that they did not surrender easily. Send them a reply from me, Ibn Yakub. Tell them that unless they surrender immediately they shall suffer the wrath of Allah. We shall rain fire upon them and destroy their city. Tell them that their impertinence does not incline us to offer generous terms."

I bowed and retired to my tent. There I began to compose the Sultan's letter. I was honoured to have replaced Imad al-Din, but I was not sure whether to imitate the master's style or to develop my own. Imad al-Din had become so adept at writing the Sultan's letters that when Salah al-Din read them he was convinced that they had actually been written by him. He would, rather uncharacteristically, delight in the flattery that often followed the receipt of such a missive. Only al-Adil, his younger brother, dared tease him. Several months ago, after the evening meal, al-Adil asked Imad al-Din what he thought of the letter the Sultan had that very day dispatched to Raymond of Tripoli. The scholar thought for a moment and replied:

"It is not one of the Sultan's finer compositions."

While Salah al-Din looked surprised, al-Adil retorted: "Come now, Imad al-Din, modesty does not suit you."

I spent the whole night composing the terms of surrender. The document was short enough, but I rewrote it several times until I was convinced it was perfect. The Sultan saw it after the morning prayers and frowned.

"Too flowery. Too pedantic. Takes too long to get to the conditions we are offering them. Seal it and dispatch now."

I was hurt by his criticisms, but I knew they contained more than a grain of truth. I realised that I should not have attempted to copy Imad al-Din's style. Further reflections on this matter were however to be rudely interrupted by the approach of a messenger from the enemy. Our generous terms were rejected. The Franj nobles refused to surrender Beirut.

The Sultan's anger lit up the entire army. He ordered an immediate attack on the city, and siege towers began to be pushed forward, closer to the walls of Beirut. I was riding next to him, the first time that he had granted me this privilege, but I learnt little of what was passing through his mind. He was silent. Our tactics were tried and tested. The emirs in charge of the squadrons knew perfectly well what had to be done. Once again the defenders surprised us. Instead of staying inside the city and attempting to repel our advance from within, the Franj opened the gates and came out to fight us in front of the out-works. They were fearful of our sappers and wanted to prevent the mining at all costs.

Salah al-Din did not need to engage in the battle himself. His emirs inflicted heavy casualties and drove the defenders back behind their walls. This develop-ment had a disastrous effect on the morale of the populace. They thought that we had entered the town. This led to a crazed rush for the harbour and the safety of the sea. In the town itself, looting and general confusion reigned.

The Franj leaders, divided till now between the tigers, who wanted a brawl, and the sheep, who wished to surrender, realised that the sheep had been wise all along. Their messengers arrived, accepting the terms of surrender that I had drafted some days ago. The Sultan could have punished them for wasting our time, but he smiled benignly and accepted the city.

"Well, Ibn Yakub, it seems that the Franj were less critical of your document than me."

We rode into yet another conquered city, but the population here was largely sullen and silent. They were angry at the unnecessary deaths and the damage which was, in reality, the fault of their own leaders. But they preferred to burden us with the blame.

The town crier could be heard in the streets proclaiming the disaster.

"The great Sultan Yusuf Salah al-Din ibn Ayyub has entered our city. Listen now to the terms of surrender . . .!"

That evening, after he had bathed and rested, the Sultan and I stood on the ramparts of the citadel, watching the waves beat on the rocks below. The sun was about to set. His eyes looked at the horizon. The majesty of the sea had calmed him and he was deep in thought. For what seemed then to be a long time neither of us spoke. Then he turned to me with a strange, faraway look in his eyes.

"Do you know something, Ibn Yakub? If Allah permits the conquest of this coast, and once we have regained al-Kuds, I shall divide our empire. I shall leave it to my brothers and sons. I shall then visit Mecca for the pilgrimage, and take my leave of Allah.

"Then I shall prepare to cross this turbulent sea, whose calm, Ibn Yakub, is deceptive. I will go to the lands where the Franj live, and I will pursue these scoundrels till all of them acknowledge Allah and his Prophet. I will do this even if I die in the attempt. It is important, because others will then pick up my sword and finish what I could not achieve. Unless we strike at the roots of the Franj, they will continue to eat our flesh, like locusts that darken the sky and devour our crops."

THIRTY-FOUR

Halima dies in Cairo: ugly rumours hold Jamila responsible

The Sultan had not rested in Beirut. Once the Franj were disarmed, he nominated one of his emirs and several hand-picked squadrons to control the city. The rest of us rode on to Damascus with only the stars as our guide. We entered the city as dawn broke. I bade farewell to Salah al-Din as he rode up the incline to the citadel, and made my way home.

Rachel was not in our room. For a moment my heart began to race as I recalled that fateful day in Cairo, but our retainer, rubbing his sleep-filled eyes, set my mind at rest. She was with our daughter, and had not been expecting me back for many months.

I dispatched him to fetch Rachel, while I washed myself from the well in the courtyard. I was exhausted by the all-night ride. Even though I was now used to the horse, I could never fully relax like the Sultan. My backside was sore and my thighs were stiff with pain. The water helped. I went inside and lay on our bed.

It was midday when a small child's gurgle near my face startled me. I sat up to see the smiling faces of my wife and daughter. The boy was big and healthy,

but he screamed when I lifted him to my face and kissed his cheeks. Rachel res-
cued him as I first hugged his mother and then her mother, who whispered in my
ear: "This child is our reward for years of pain and trouble. You are alive and
well. God be praised."

"Perhaps, but the Sultan's victories helped a little to keep me alive."

We laughed. Then she spoke again.

"Maryam and I were thinking it would be nice to visit our house in Cairo and
spend the winter there this year. Her husband would come as well. He has many
friends in Cairo and has never seen the city. We were waiting for your permission."

"You have my permission, of course. I only wish I could accompany all of
you, but we leave in a few days for Jerusalem. The Sultan will not delay any
longer. He will pray at the al-Aqsa mosque before the month is over, and I shall
visit the site of the old synagogue. Afterwards, if he releases me for a few
months, I will join you all in Cairo."

Rachel smiled. She had always thought, because of what I had said a long
time ago, that because of my unhappy associations with the domed room,
never wished to set foot in that house again. But there is a limit to jealousy. If
had forgiven Rachel, and even forgotten the scale of Ibn Maymun's betrayal
how could I still bear a grudge against the house? The fault lay not within the
stones that formed those walls, but in ourselves. Later that afternoon, when we
were alone, I said all this to Rachel and much more. Serenity had returned. We
lay entwined in each other's arms and felt that the past had finally been buried

Alas, there was sad news awaiting me when I arrived at the citadel that same
evening. Amjad the eunuch had been impatiently awaiting my arrival and he
rushed and hugged me warmly. It was when he moved away that I noticed the
wetness on my cheeks.

"Halima died in Cairo a few days ago. The Sultan was mildly upset. He had
asked Ibn Maymun to conduct an investigation and send us a report before the
week is over."

The news stunned me. Halima had never known a day's illness in all the time I had known her. What could have struck her down? Images of her fluttered through my mind in rapid succession. I saw her face pale and motionless beneath the shroud. I wept.

"How did Jamila react to the news?"

Amjad remained silent.

I repeated the question.

"I broke the news to her. She looked straight into my eyes, but remained completely calm. Completely. Her face showed no emotion. Nothing. Perhaps she was wearing a mask to hide her pain. Perhaps."

The news of Halima's truncated life had stolen all my powers of concentration. I sat through the meeting of the council of war in a daze. The Sultan's soft voice, Imad al-Din and al-Fadil's impassioned interventions, the sense of excitement and expectation that radiated from every emir, were like background noises as far as I was concerned. I was desperate to see Jamila, to condole, to share common memories of Halima, to weep, to find out what she really felt at the death of someone who had meant so much to her and whose life she had greatly affected.

For the first time since I had been employed by the Sultan I did not fulfil the duties that kind ruler had assigned to me. Reader, I did not take any notes of that crucial meeting which decided the fate of Jerusalem. On that subject my notebook is a blank.

Later, I reconstructed that evening with the aid of Imad al-Din, but, as was his wont, he assigned the decisive role to himself and claimed that till he had spoken, the Sultan had been indecisive. I know for a fact that this was not the case, and for that reason I dismissed the great scholar's testimony as self-serving and unworthy of him. What did become clear in the weeks that followed was that there had been unanimity amongst all those who had comprised the council on that fateful night. They would take Jerusalem.

My mind was still tormented by the death in Cairo. I had asked to see Jamila, but it was not until two days later that she agreed to my request. An unusually sad and silent Amjad came to my house to fetch me.

She was waiting for me in the usual antechamber, the room where I had often met Halima. For a moment Jamila's features faded and mixed with those of the dead woman, but I clasped my hands so firmly together that they hurt. I was back in the present. I looked at her face and recalled Amjad's description. There was not a trace of sadness in her eyes.

"It was you who wished to see me, Ibn Yakub."

My only reply was to weep. I thought I saw her eyes flicker, but she recovered rapidly. She looked at me with a strange gaze.

"Sultana, I came to express my sorrow at her death. I know that your parting was grief-stricken, but . . ."

She interrupted me with an angry flash of her eyes.

"We parted without recriminations. She wished us to be friends. That was not possible, but we agreed to banish enmity and bitterness. You think I'm cold and unfeeling?"

I sighed.

"There are times when grief is useless, Ibn Yakub. Her death is painful. Her face appears to me, but is soon washed away. Hearts can turn to stone. Let me surprise you, Ibn Yakub. News of her death moved me in a strange way. It helped me discover an inner happiness. I thought you would be shocked, but it is the truth. I feel at ease with myself again. A painful chapter is now definitively over. All that remains are memories. Some of them are happy, most are sad. So you see, my friend, now I have a choice. What I think of her depends on me alone, on my mood, and that, I assure you, is a great relief. Ever since Halima and I parted, I found it difficult to write. Now I have started writing again, and one day I will let you read my manuscript."

Her callousness startled me. How could she be so indifferent to Halima's fate? She saw the question on my face and her eyes narrowed.

"I know what you are thinking, Ibn Yakub. You see me as a heartless creature, a woman without pity. You forget that, for me, Halima died a long time ago. I wept a great deal for her, and the pain of separation hurt me for many months. Sleep used to avoid my path completely. All that disappeared some time ago. When Amjad the eunuch, with streaming eyes, came to tell me of her death, I felt nothing. Do you understand?"

She looked into my eyes and smiled.

"I understand, Sultana, but for me what is real is the fact that she is no more. She is buried underneath the earth. We will never hear her laugh again. Surely this is different from the death imposed by your brain on your heart."

I had aroused her anger.

"No! Imposed by my heart on the brain. The last news of her that I received from Cairo revealed that she had once again abandoned the embraces of men. She had found a younger woman, closer to her own age than mine, and, or so my informants wrote, the two of them had become inseparable. A wave of jealousy and anger passed through me, but that was all. Nothing more. For me she was finished for ever. Dead. I am told that she was poisoned on the orders of her last male lover, a poor, deluded mamluk. He will suffer even more if Salah al-Din ever discovers the truth . . ."

Jamila's information turned out to be accurate. Ibn Maymun had performed an autopsy and his conclusion suggested a large dose of poison. Everyone pointed their finger in the direction of the mamluk, who pleaded his innocence, but he was executed on the orders of the Kadi. Only Amjad the eunuch was unconvinced.

"She was poisoned, Ibn Yakub. The poor woman was poisoned, but who gave the order? We will never know the truth. That poor mamluk was just like me, used by her to satisfy her physical needs. Nothing more. If she had been poisoned in Damascus they might have executed me! So I feel some sympathy with the poor man. In my heart I feel that Jamila dispatched the poison together with the instructions."

"Enough of this loose talk, Amjad! Your thought is worse than the poison that killed Halima. Expel it from your wicked heart before it kills you."

The eunuch's face paled.

"I have not confided my suspicions in any other living person. I needed to share them with you, but your advice is wise. If I do not quell these thoughts, I myself will perish. Rest assured, Ibn Yakub, I will quell them. No strain of martyrdom pollutes my blood."

Try as I might I could not banish Amjad's words from my own thoughts. That embittered eunuch had planted a poisonous seed in my mind as well. Could it be true? Could Jamila have ordered the poisoning of her detached ex-lover? The very idea seemed outrageous. After a few hours of agony I came to the conclusion that Jamila was innocent. Grief had poisoned Amjad beyond redemption.

I was interrupted by the familiar tones of Imad al-Din.

"You look preoccupied, scribe. I was hoping you would join me this evening in visiting the rooms of the purest Damascene nightingale. Remember? Zubayda? The woman who conquered Salah al-Din's heart when he was a mere boy, but refused to offer him her body?"

"How could I forget her?" was my reply. "You have caught me at an inopportune moment. I was mourning the tragic death of the Sultana Halima."

Imad al-Din's face became grave.

"There are ugly rumours floating on the Nile. Al-Fadil tells me that the mamluk who was executed for the crime insisted on speaking to him alone. When he agreed the condemned whispered in al-Fadil's ear: 'I administered the poison, but it was sent me by the Sultana Jamila, and she has pledged to look after my family.' Naturally, al-Fadil has not told the Sultan or anyone else apart from me. I tell you only because both women were close to you.

"Love has the capacity to drive us all mad. Jealousy is its most savage child. What Jamila did is unforgivable, unthinkable, and yet, if I am to be honest with you, I am not shocked by the news. To understand Jamila one has to have suffered the loss of a lover. Alas, you are a cold-water fish, Ibn Yakub. You never will. Come with me to hear the nightingale sing. Zubayda will make you forget everything."

I agreed to accompany him, but it was an oppressive evening and I begged his leave to return home so that I could bathe and change my clothing. Since Zubayda's house was not far from where I lived, he agreed to collect me within the hour. The cool of the night was yet to come and the lack of a breeze made me sweat profusely as I walked home. I told Rachel the story of Halima's death without naming the royal poisoner. I stripped in the courtyard and poured bucketfuls of fresh, cold water from the well on my head. Then Rachel brought me a towel.

I was distracted. There was only one person I wished to see that night. Jamila. I wanted to confront her with the accusations of Amjad and al-Fadil and Imad al-Din. I wanted to shout them in her face and observe her reaction. I wanted the truth, but I did not want to lose Jamila's friendship. I wanted her to spit in the face of those who spread such vile slanders. I wanted her to proclaim her innocence to me. After I was dressed I wrote a quick note and dispatched it to her, asking for an audience the next day.

Imad al-Din's retainer knocked on the door. I offered the great man some tea, but he touched his left cheek and shook his head. I had not noticed the swelling earlier that evening, but he appeared to be in pain.

"It is a bad tooth, Ibn Yakub," he groaned. "I have been sucking cloves to numb the pain, but it will have to be removed tomorrow. To tell you the truth I am not in a mood for anything tonight except the solitude of my bedchamber. Yet Zubayda has not sung for many years. It is an experience you will never forget, something you will tell your grandchildren."

The town crier preceded us on the narrow streets, often clearing a path through hordes of families and noisy children desperate for some air.

"Make way, make way for the great Imad al-Din, counsellor to the Sultan Yusuf Salah al-Din ibn Ayyub."

We saw familiar faces outside Zubayda's house. The Sultan's personal guards were on duty, swords raised as we approached, but lowered as they recognised us. The Nubian mute, who had been with the Sultan as long as me, grinned at our arrival and hastened to unfasten the door that led to the courtyard. It was to be an outdoor occasion. The courtyard was lit by lamps and the floor covered in rugs and cushions. There were no more than fifteen people present – among them, to my amazement, the Sultana Jamila. She smiled pleasantly to acknowledge my arrival. My heart quickened its pace.

We bowed to the Sultan, who smiled and indicated we should sit by his side. He introduced us to Zubayda. She was approaching her seventieth year, but her face radiated an attraction that surprised me. Her white hair shone in the darkness and illuminated her face. She had not washed it with henna to disguise her age. Her complexion was dark, not unlike that of Jamila, who I was trying to forget that evening and whose presence had shaken me.

Zubayda's eyes were large and lively, without a trace of sadness or regret. She had lived a rich life, that much was obvious, but had it been a life devoid of pain? Is any life completely without pain? She had been watching me observe her and suddenly she smiled. Her teeth, to my amazement, were as white as snow. How in Allah's name had she managed to preserve their youth?

It was as if she had heard all my questions.

"Salah al-Din has mentioned you to me, Ibn Yakub." Her voice was throaty and rich. "I know what you are thinking. Understand that my soul is quiet and tranquil. I want nothing. I regret nothing. I hope that death, when it comes, will be swift, like Salah al-Din's sword when it strikes the Franj."

"Umm Zubayda," the Sultan's voice was softer than usual. "We have come to hear you sing."

There were two musicians present, waiting patiently, fingering their lutes. She looked at them and put a finger to her lips. She wanted to sing tonight without any accompaniment. There was an expectant hush and then she sang. Listening to her was like entering heaven. Her voice was truly inimitable. I have not heard one like it before or since. It was a song she had written herself, and though it was simple and short, it took half an hour to complete, as each line was repeated several times, with musical variations.

ZUBAYDA'S LOVE SONG

On a warm night we drank some wine.
A soft breeze caressed my burning face.
He took me to the balcony and showed me the moon
And tried to make me believe he loved another.
I laughed. I wept.
I didn't believe him.
"You poor fool," I said, "you are young, you confuse reality with dreams."
He smiled. He left me.
A single salty tear wet my face and I knew
The confusion was all mine.
Yes, mine.
Mine. Mine. Mine. Mine. Mine.

Zubayda did not sing again that night. The musicians entertained us while we ate the food that had been carefully prepared in her kitchen. The Sultan was abstemious, but Imad al-Din's toothache did not appear to prevent him enjoying the four different varieties of meat that were laid before us.

After dinner there was more music, during the course of which Jamila prepared to depart. She asked me to accompany the litter in which she would be carried back to the citadel. The Sultan nodded his permission and I took my leave of the great singer, who invited me to visit her again so that she could tell me her story.

Jamila did not wait for me to speak.

"So you have heard all the evil talk?"

"Is it true, Sultana?"

"You know full well that my love is as pure as my hate. Jealousy is a poison that has to be removed in order to free more space in our heads for lofty reflections. That is all I will ever say on this subject."

I walked along in silence as the litter-bearers readjusted their burden slightly so as to ease their climb up the incline that led to the citadel. She dismissed me with a brutal laugh.

"You may return to your wife, Ibn Yakub. Enjoy her embrace, for tomorrow you leave for al-Kuds, and who knows what Allah has in store for all of you?"

Rachel, who has the most tranquil of temperaments, appeared nervous and tense when I reached our home.

"The Franj will make the Sultan pay a heavy price before they will give up Jerusalem," she said. "I fear that you might be part of that price. I have a terrible premonition that I will never see you again."

I comforted her fears. I told her of how Salah al-Din always made sure that I was kept away from any real danger. I mocked her superstitions. I tried to make her laugh, but failed miserably. It seemed as if nothing could dispel her worries. I wanted to love her, but she was reluctant, and so we lay mute in each other's arms till I fell asleep.

A retainer from the citadel woke me just before the break of dawn. Rachel had not slept at all. She sat up in bed and watched me dress. Then, as I took my leave of her, she almost suffocated me in a tight embrace and would not release me. Gently, I prised her hands away and kissed her eyes. "After the victory in Jerusalem I shall come to our house in Cairo so that we can celebrate together," I whispered in her ear. "I will write often." She did not reply.

THIRTY-FIVE

From the outskirts of Jerusalem I write an excited letter to my good wife in Cairo

 My very dear wife,

It is strange to think of you back in that old house with so many memories, most of them happy. I am sending this letter with the courier who is carrying royal dispatches from al-Adil to the palace, so you will get it sooner than if I used the caravans.

It is almost a month since you left, and this is the first opportunity that I have had to sit and write to you. We are living in tents within sight of the walls of Jerusalem. It is a strange sensation to be so close to the Holy City. The Sultan has offered them terms, but some of the fools want to die holding their infernal crosses.

You have by now probably heard from our friends in the palace why it has all taken so long. When we marched away from Damascus, the Sultan was overcome by one of his usual fits of indecision. Jerusalem could wait till he had cleared the coast. Once again he tried to take Tyre, but the resistance was strong. The emirs were now determined to take the city regardless of our casualties. They felt it had become a symbol of Franj resistance and should be erased from the map. Salah al-Din was annoyed that it had already taken up too much of his time. He decided to march away and we laid siege to Ascalon.

The Franj held out for nearly fourteen days, but the Sultan brought their King Guy from Damascus and offered to release him if they surrendered. They gave Guy authority to deal on their behalf, and he promptly agreed terms with the Sultan. We did not lose many men. The day we took the city turned cold all of a sudden when the sun's face was completely hidden. That very day a delegation of nobles from Jerusalem arrived in Ascalon. The Sultan offered them very good terms if they surrendered the Holy City, and they promised to recommend such an offer to the knights. When they got back, the Patriarch scolded them severely. The Church does not wish to surrender the city where Jesus was crucified without a battle.

The Sultan did not allow his spirits to lower when he heard the news. He is in a cheerful mood again, despite the setback at Tyre. The presence of al-Adil, who has remained his favourite brother since they were boys, is part of the reason. For the rest, Salah al-Din is now convinced that he will be in Jerusalem before the new moon, which gives him seventeen days to be precise.

On hearing that the Patriarch and knights such as Balian of Ibelin were now preparing to take up arms against him, the Sultan ordered all our soldiers in the region to march behind him and put up our tents just outside Jerusalem. He wants this to be a show of strength, but is prepared for a clash of arms if that is the only way. Yesterday we moved our tents to the eastern edge of the city. The Franj thought we were leaving altogether and waved ironic farewells from the ramparts, which amused al-Adil greatly. Instead we have our siege towers in place, just above the valley they call the Kidron. Here the walls seem less strong.

From where I am composing these lines I can see the Sultan's banners
fluttering in the breeze on Mount Olivet. Our men worked all night to
make sure the barbican was mined.

Ten thousand of our soldiers have now made it impossible for the
Franj to use two of their most important gates. Our archers are stationed
directly underneath the ramparts waiting for their orders. The Kadi al-
Fadil described their arrows as "toothpicks to the teeth of the
battlements". It is an accurate description, acknowledged as such even
by Imad al-Din, who, incidentally, was hoping that al-Fadil would stay in
Cairo so that he would be the only serious chronicler of the victory.

As you know, my dearest Rachel, they do not even deign to consider
your husband as a rival. For them I am just a pen-pusher who caught the
Sultan's eye at an opportune moment. That is Imad al-Din's public
attitude to me. In private he often tells me stories which he hopes I will
attribute to him, thus ensuring that he is mentioned in the "great book of
Salah al-Din". The Kadi al-Fadil is more subtle, more careful, but his
main concern lies in his own work. He barely thinks of me in serious
terms, but is always helpful when I need to check a fact or two with him.

Yesterday the Sultan was visited by Balian of Ibelin. His life had been
spared at Hattin and he had pledged never to bear arms against the
Sultan as long as he lived. Now he told us that the Patriarch had
absolved him of his oath.

"And your God," inquired the Sultan, "will He forgive you just as
easily?"

Balian remained silent and averted his eyes. Then he threatened Salah
al-Din. If our soldiers did not withdraw, the Franj would first kill their
own women and children and then set fire to the al-Aqsa mosque before
demolishing the sacred Rock. After this they would kill the several
thousand Believers in the city and then march out into the plain with
swords raised to die in battle against the infidels.

The Sultan smiled. He had vowed to take this city by force, but he offered the Franj a generous deal. All the Christians would be permitted to leave provided they paid a ransom to the treasury. The Christian poor would be set free with money from the King's treasure which was kept by the Hospitallers. Salah al-Din gave them forty days to find the ransom money.

"When you Franj first took this city, Balian, you slaughtered the Jews and Believers as if they were cattle. We could do the same to you, but blind revenge is a dangerous elixir. So we will let your people leave in peace. This is my last offer to your leaders. Turn it down and I will burn down these ramparts and show no mercy. The choice is yours."

Today it is Friday, the Holy Day of Islam. It is the second of October, but the twenty-seventh of Rajab in the Muslim calendar. On this day their Prophet dreamt his famous dream and visited this city in his sleep. And on this day, as even the least religious of them has been telling himself and others since daybreak, the Franj capitulated and signed the terms of surrender. As news of this spread there was a loud cry of "Allah o Akbar" and the amazing sight of thousands and thousands of men, falling to their knees in the dust and prostrating themselves in the direction of Mecca, to give thanks to Allah.

Then there was silence, a silence born of disbelief. We looked at each other in astonishment, wondering whether this had really happened or was it all a dream? After ninety years, Jerusalem, or al-Kuds, belongs to us again. All of us!

In exactly one hour the Sultan will ride into the city and I, my dearest Rachel, will be at his side. My thoughts at this moment are of you and our little family, but I am also thinking of my old friend Shadhi. This was a day he longed to see, and I know that his ghost will be riding just behind Salah al-Din, whispering in his ear as only he could: "Look straight ahead. You are a ruler. Don't lower your eyes. Remember, you are the Sultan who has taken back our al-Kuds, not the Caliph in Baghdad. Even as we march the so-called Caliph will be drowning himself in pleasure."

Shadhi would have said all that and I will think it, but I do not have the authority to say all this to the Sultan. Imad al-Din is on his way to Damascus and al-Fadil is not here. What will they advise him after he has taken the city?

I am alone with him and the responsibility is awesome. What am I to say if he seeks my advice? It is at times like these that I feel the most vulnerable and realise that, perhaps, I am nothing but a hired scribe.

I kiss your cheeks and hope to see you soon. Kiss our daughter and grandson. I am delighted to hear that another one is on the way. Perhaps you should come to Jerusalem. I think I will be here for some time.

Your husband,
Ibn Yakub.

THIRTY-SIX

*Salah al-Din takes Jerusalem; Imad al-Din
eyes a beautiful Copt translator; Jamila makes
her peace with Halima's memory*

We rode into the Holy City through the Bab al-Daud. The Sultan did not need Shadhi to tell him his head should be raised high. He rode straight to the Mosque, heavy with the stench of the Franj and their beasts. It was here the Hospitallers and Templars had stabled their steeds. Salah al-Din refused to wait till the holy precinct was cleansed. He jumped off his horse and, surrounded by his emirs, offered prayers of thanks to Allah. Then they began to clean the mosque.

As we rode back through the streets the Sultan was moved by the pathetic sight of Christians groaning and weeping. There were women pulling at their hair, old men kissing walls, frightened children clutching their mothers and grandmothers. He pulled up his horse and sent a messenger to fetch the Franj knight Balian.

While we were waiting the Sultan looked up and smiled. His flag was being raised on the citadel and the exultant chants and cheers of our soldiers momentarily drowned the noise of the distraught Christians. I thought again of Shadhi and so did Salah al-Din. He turned to me with a tear in his eye.

"My father and my uncle Shirkuh would not have believed that this could happen, but Shadhi always knew my banners would be raised one day in al-Kuds. At this moment I miss him more than anyone else."

We were interrupted by the presence of Balian.

"Why do they weep so much?" the Sultan asked him.

"The women weep, sire, for their dead or captive husbands. The old weep for the fear they will never see these sacred walls again. The children are frightened."

"Tell your people," Salah al-Din told him, "that we shall not treat them as your forebears treated us when they first took this city. As a child I was told of what Godfrey and Tancredi did to our people. Remind these frightened Christians of what Believers and Jews suffered ninety years ago. The heads of our children were displayed on pikes. Old men and women of all ages were tortured and burnt. These streets were washed in our blood, Balian. Some of the emirs would like to wash them again, but this time in your blood. They remind me that we all believe in an eye for an eye and a tooth for a tooth.

"I have quietened them and stilled their fears. I have told them that we are all the People of the Book, and this city belongs to all those who believe in the Book. Tell your women they are free to go even if they cannot afford the ransom.

"Alas, we lack the powers of your Prophet Isa and are not able to bring the dead back to life. We will release captive knights provided they swear an oath never to take arms against us again. You avert your eyes, Balian of Ibelin, and so you should. You, too, swore such an oath. An oath before Allah cannot be forsworn by any human, be he a Patriarch or a Pope. If that is understood, we will be generous. If you hear of any of my soldiers offending the honour of a single Christian woman, come and tell me. If you are told that any of your sacred shrines are being despoiled by my men, please let me know at once. It shall not be permitted. That is my word as a Sultan."

Balian fell on his knees and kissed Salah al-Din's robe.

"You have shown us a courtesy that we do not deserve, O great King. For this single act we shall never forget you. I, for one, do swear before Almighty God that I will never bear arms against you again."

Salah al-Din nodded, and our party rode through the streets to the citadel. The town criers were proclaiming our terms, and telling Christians that they were free to worship in their churches and shrines. People fell silent as we rode past them, looking at Salah al-Din with curiosity, tempered by fear.

That night I received a written message from a man who signed himself as John of Jerusalem. He was the grandson of an old Jew who had saved himself ninety years ago by shaving his beard and locks and pretending to be a Christian. In secret he had maintained his belief, and brought up his son as a Jew.

"I am not circumcised," wrote John of Jerusalem, "but my father was, and he was proud of his faith. It was impossible for me to be the same for fear of discovery. When I heard that the Sultan's scribe was of that faith, I had to write to you. It would be a great honour for my family if you would eat with us one day this week."

That was how I found myself in a small, two-roomed house, sipping wine with John and his beautiful, fair-haired wife, Mariam. Their son, who was probably ten years of age, observed me in silence. He was frightened.

"Our fear was plain enough. The last time, as you know better than me, Ibn Yakub, all our people had suffered horribly. The Franj killed us all. We have never forgotten that evil day, and nor have they. They thought that the Sultan and his army, poised outside the city, would exact a terrible revenge. The tears they weep are tears of guilt and fear. They rose to power on a mound of corpses, and they are fearful of joining that mound.

"When news came that the Franj nobles had accepted your terms, there was a strange silence on the streets. Nothing moved. The silence was broken by the sound of horses and marching feet, and by the shrill voices of their soldiers, whose internal equilibrium appeared to be somewhat disturbed. They were talking loudly and laughing, but without conviction. Poor fools. They were trying to convince themselves that it was a day like any other day. Have you noticed how people who feel insecure speak in loud voices and are cruel to those they regard as inferior to them?

"When your Sultan marched in through the Gate of David a wave of fear passed through the city. They are still in a state of shock. God has let them down and permitted Allah to triumph. They still find it difficult to believe that they are still alive and have been treated well. Some of them think it is all a plot and they will be executed soon. My own feeling, which may not be worth much, but which I would like you to convey to the Sultan, is not to trust the Franj. I have lived amongst them all my life. I know how they think, what they feel. They are sullen and embittered people. Better to keep them as hostages against the ill-fortune that will come, as surely as night follows day, from across the water. They will not show you mercy. Please pass this on to the Sultan from one of his humble admirers. I used to pray in secret for this day."

As news of our victory spread, there were rejoicings and prayers of thanksgiving were offered to Allah in all the dominions of the Caliph. Kadis and learned scholars began to arrive in Jerusalem in growing numbers.

Jamila was the first of the Sultan's wives to arrive. This time she did not travel alone or disguised as a man, but entered the city with her entourage of armed guards, eunuchs and maids-in-waiting. It was as if she was determined to show Jerusalem that she and none other was the Sultana closest to the Conqueror of the Holy City.

Salah al-Din, for his part, was personally supervising the cleaning of the Dome of the Rock and the al-Aqsa mosque, where the first *khutba* was due to be delivered in fourteen days' time. Many Christians had elected to remain in the city, though most of these were either Copts or belonged to denominations that had never sought or won the approval of the religious orders favoured by the Franj.

Imad al-Din was in his element. He was surrounded by six scribes and was

busy dictating dispatches to all the rulers in the world of Islam. One evening
I went to inform him that the Sultan needed his advice on a somewhat insolent
message that had belatedly arrived from Frederick I Barbarossa, the Holy
Roman Emperor, warning the Sultan not to even think of taking Jerusalem.
The letter, in Latin, had been read aloud in Arabic by the Sultan's new interpreter, an eighteen-year-old Copt by the name of Tarik ibn Isa, whose jocular
rendering had resulted in much merriment. The Copt had such a beautiful
face that even those of us who did not swim near the other shore were
bewitched by his presence. The great scholar, I knew, would find it difficult to
contain himself. I described the scene in some detail to Imad al-Din, and he
chuckled, but the question that formed itself on his sensuous lips related to the
Copt.

"Only eighteen years of age? Surprising. Is he a local boy?"

I shrugged my shoulders. I had no idea.

As we entered the Sultan's chamber the mood was light. Imad al-Din took the
letter from Tarik ibn Isa and began to laugh.

"Which passage amuses you the most?" asked the Sultan.

"It is his threats, O Commander of the Victorious. Just listen to them again:
'If you do not desist you will learn what it is to experience Teutonic anger. You
will experience the wrath of the Rhinelanders, the big Bavarians, the cunning
Swabians, the cautious Franconians, the Saxons, who sport with their swords,
Thuringians, Westphalians, the fiery men from Burgundy, the nimble-footed
mountaineers from the Alps, the Frisians with their javelins, the Bohemians who
die with smiles on their faces, the Poles, tougher than beasts of the forest, and
my own right hand is not so enfeebled by age that it can no longer wield a
sword.'

"What is interesting in this letter is that he could find no frightening words to
attach to the Tuscans and the Pisans. Perhaps we should question him about this
omission in our reply. As for the fiery Burgundians, does Your Grace remember
the knight from Burgundy who we met some years ago? The only fiery aspect

of his personality was his farting, which was so potent that you walked out of the tent, leaving my nose to bear the brunt of the explosion."

The Sultan began to laugh at the memory.

"I think there is no need to remind the German King of that unfortunate occurrence. Draft a reply now, Imad al-Din. This young man is also a scribe and will take down your words."

Imad al-Din looked at the boy and was overcome by desire. He caught his eye, but the Copt scribe looked hurriedly away. The Sultan's secretary began to dictate, all the while shamelessly eyeing Tarik's slender frame.

"To the Great King, Frederick of Germany, in the name of Allah, the Merciful, the Powerful, the Almighty, the Victorious.

"We thank you for your letter, but, alas, it is too late. With the blessings of Allah we are already in possession of al-Kuds, which you call Jerusalem. Three cities alone remain in Christian hands, Tyre, Tripoli and Antioch, but rest assured, powerful King, that we shall take all these as well.

"We could not help but notice that you have no words to describe the valour of the Tuscans, Venetians and Pisans, and this upsets us, for we are only too well aware of the qualities of the men who hail from these regions. They are beautiful in body and mind and have provided a great deal of pleasure to our Bedouins, starved of love and life in the desert. We look forward to seeing them again.

"If you want war, we await you, but understand this: once you are here there will be a sea between you and your lands. Nothing separates us from our people and our possessions. That is why we shall defeat you till the dawn of Judgement Day. This time we shall not be satisfied with your cities on our sea-coast, but will cross the water, and it will please Allah to take away all your lands, since your fighting men will be buried here, underneath the sand.

"This letter is written in the year 584 by the grace of Allah and his Prophet. It bears the signature of the conqueror of al-Kuds.

"Yusuf Ibn Ayyub."

Imad al-Din looked at the assembled company, enjoying the mirth that greeted his letter. What pleased him the most was the shy smile on Tarik's face, but the Sultan wanted something far more serious in tone. Salah al-Din had now become very conscious of his place in history. The delegations of scholars gathering in the city and the messages he had received from Believers all over the world, not forgetting, of course, the over-effusive greetings from the Caliph and his courtiers in Baghdad, had confirmed his belief in himself. For this reason he wanted all the dispatches sent in his name to bear the mark of his new status as the saviour of his faith. Imad al-Din was sent to his own office to rewrite the letter in more dignified terms and present it next morning to the Sultan for the attachment of his seal.

As I left the chamber, a hand tapped me on my shoulder. It was a Nubian eunuch, the old mute with white hair whom I had seen many times before at the citadel in Damascus. With exaggerated gestures of his hand, he indicated that I should follow him. He took me outside a chamber and withdrew.

"Come in, Ibn Yakub," said the only too familiar voice behind the latticed door. It was the Sultana Jamila.

I entered and bowed. She pre-empted my first question.

"Amjad? Alas, he is no longer with us. He spread so many calumnies to so many people that I had to ask for him to be sent away. The steward dealt with the matter. Do not look so worried. He is still alive."

Before I could express my relief, she had moved on to another subject.

"Does the heart have a language, Ibn Yakub?"

I smiled, but could not reply. From the brutal disposal of Amjad the eunuch she was transporting us into the intimate world of her philosophy.

"Come now, scribe, think hard. No? Perhaps your heart is mute. Most hearts speak a strange mixture of realities and dreams, though the exact proportion of each is always variable, since, ultimately, everything is determined by external circumstances. The heart is not a book which you can always open at the same place. If a heart is shattered to pieces it can bleed for many days, but then, suddenly, turn to stone. Do you agree?"

I nodded. I knew perfectly well what it was that had sent her mind wandering in this direction, but she wanted me to ask and so I posed the question.

"What has made you think of all this at such a time, Sultana? We are celebrating the fall of Jerusalem, and it surprises me that you are withdrawing deep into your inner self."

"My heart has undergone numerous transformations, Ibn Yakub. It has been light for many months, but a heaviness appears to have captured it again. Today, for example, I am crippled by remorse. I should have made my peace with Halima before she felt compelled to run away from my wrath and seek refuge in Cairo. She came to me once, her eyes filled with sadness, and wanted us to be friends again. I was hard-hearted, Ibn Yakub. I rejected her. I spurned her offer with contempt. Why? Because friendship, which has once coexisted with love and passion, is helpless on its own. To even strive towards it is the sign of an unsound mind. Those who think they have succeeded are, sooner or later, struck down by grief.

"Then she died. Evil tongues accused me of having sent the fatal poison. A base lie, spoken by a man about to meet his Maker and crazed with jealousy. That mamluk, incapable of enduring Halima's love for another woman, chose to blame me for his foul deed. As you know, I too was upset when I heard that Halima had found another woman, but it was inconceivable for me to punish her with death. I would have preferred to prolong her life so that I could find a delicious way to torture her. Though I will say something that might shock you, Ibn Yakub. It is all part of the language of my heart. When news of her death and its manner first arrived, I was not displeased.

"She had poisoned our love. She had killed what was precious to both of us. She had been poisoned in return. It was a cruel and unworthy reaction, but it was what my heart was saying at the time. This is the reason I have begun to investigate the connections between the heart and the mind. My paper on the logic of the heart will be finished before the first *khutba* in the Great Mosque. Do not judge me too harshly. This is a time for celebration. Salah al-Din has taken al-Kuds. My heart is full of joy."

I woke late the next morning to find the heat of the sun burning my face. I had not slept well. Jamila's words of the previous night were passing through my mind in a loop. Her callousness towards Halima had angered me greatly, but now, despite all my misgivings, I found myself admiring her fortitude and honesty. She was truly a woman who, unlike her esteemed and much-loved husband, did not believe in taking prisoners.

There were times when I wished that, just for a few months, a good djinn would transform this Sultana into the Sultan.

THIRTY-SEVEN

The Kadi of Aleppo preaches in the mosque;
the Sultan receives a letter from Bertrand of
Toulouse; my family are burnt to death in a
Franj raid in Cairo

Ten days later, we were all gathered in the great mosque of al-Aqsa. It had been thoroughly cleaned and the polished stones were shining with the glitter of paradise. All the emirs and kadis from the empire of Salah al-Din were present, as were his son al-Afdal, his nephew Taki al-Din and his favourite commander, the Emir Keukburi.

The pulpit, which had been constructed for this purpose on the orders of the late Sultan Nur al-Din, had arrived from Damascus.

The Kadi of Aleppo, dressed in black robes and wearing a green turban, climbed the steps hesitantly, and as he clutched the pulpit to steady himself those of us sitting near the front could see his hands trembling. He knew that the words he spoke this day would be remembered for a long time to come. He was also aware that the Sultan's patience was notoriously short and he did not look kindly on extended sermons. The Kadi spoke in sonorous tones and began, as befitted such an occasion, with a brief history of the successes achieved by the followers of the Prophet in a short space of time.

"We begin in the Name of Allah the Merciful, the Beneficent, and his

Prophet who showed us the true path. Our Sultan Yusuf Salah al-Din ibn Ayyub has brought the crescent back to this Holy City. He is the upholder of the true faith, the vanquisher of those who worship a Cross and graven images. You have revived the Empire of the Commander of the Faithful in Baghdad. Let us pray to Allah that angels may always surround your banners and preserve you for the future of our Faith. May Allah save you and your children for all time to come.

"Here it was that Omar, whose memory we revere, first planted the colours of our faith, not long after the passing away of the Prophet, may he rest in peace. Here it was then, that this great mosque was built. All of you who have fought for this day are blessed forever. You have rekindled the spirit of Badr. You have been as steadfast as Abu Bakr, fearless and generous like Omar. You remind us of the fierceness of Uthman and Ali. The first four Caliphs, watching you from heaven, are smiling today. All those who fought for this city will enter paradise.

"Soon afterwards our armies carried the Holy Koran on their swords across the deserts of Africa and to the mountains of Andalus and the lands of the Franj. It was from here that our message was taken to the lands of the fire-worshippers. The people of Persia, once we had shared our knowledge of the true path decreed by Allah, were the first to convert to our cause. As the Sultan has heard many times, one reason why Persia fell into our hands like a ripe apricot is that the poorest of the poor, those who were downtrodden and exploited by degenerate priests, were amazed at the sight of our great generals sharing food from the same vessel as the ordinary soldiers. They saw for themselves that, before the eyes of Allah, we were all equal.

"We reached the great Indian river Indus and here, too, the poor flocked behind our banners. Even as we speak our traders bear our message to the south of India, the islands of Java and onward to China. I ask you all, is it not a sign from Allah that he enabled us to reach all the corners of the world in such a short time?

"That is why it is all the more disgraceful that the Franj have been permitted to occupy our coast and this Holy City for so long without fear of punishment. Yusuf Salah al-Din ibn Ayyub, it is thanks to you and your persistence, your courage, your willingness to sacrifice your own life, which is precious to Believers everywhere, that we are praying at al-Aqsa once again. We pray to Allah to prolong your life and your rule over these lands. In one hand you carry a sharp sword. In the other a shining torch . . ."

The sermon lasted a whole hour. It was not a memorable speech in itself, but the majesty of the occasion held everyone. After he had finished, a common prayer of thanks to Allah was offered by the congregation. Then the Kadi of Aleppo stepped down and was embraced and kissed by the Sultan and soon after by the Kadi al-Fadil and Imad al-Din. Al-Fadil was in a joyous mood. When the Sultan asked him what he had thought of the sermon, the reply was poetic.

"O Commander of the Victorious, listening to the sermon the heavens wept tears of joy and the stars abandoned their positions in the firmament not to shoot on the wicked, but to celebrate together."

Imad al-Din, who later confessed that he had found the sermon tedious and uninspired in the extreme, now applauded al-Fadil and smiled warmly in the direction of the Kadi of Aleppo.

That same evening the Sultan called a council of war. Taki al-Din, Keukburi, al-Afdal, Imad al-Din, al-Fadil and myself were the only people present. The Sultan was in a generous and self-deprecatory mood.

"Let us first thank Imad al-Din, who always stressed the importance of taking this city. You were correct, as you often are, old friend. Keukburi it was who insisted that we do not lift the siege of Tyre. You too were correct. I want the army to take Tyre without further delay. Let them rest. Let them celebrate, but then we take Tyre. A letter arrived this morning from Bertrand of Toulouse. Remember him? The knight whose life we saved from the wrath of the Templars and who returned safely to his home thanks to our merchants. Imad al-Din will read the letter now. I know that we would all have preferred the presence of that beautiful Copt, who translates the Latin into our language with such grace that even those of us who do not swim on the same shores as Imad al-Din could not but admire his beauty. Alas, he is away, old teacher. It is only appropriate that you take his place."

If Imad al-Din was surprised at the Sultan's indelicacy he managed to conceal his feelings admirably. Everyone else exchanged knowing smiles. It was common knowledge that Imad al-Din was besotted with Tarik ibn Isa and had been pursuing him like a wolf on the fourteenth night of the moon. Imad al-Din read the letter from Bertrand of Toulouse to himself.

"If the Sultan and the emirs will forgive me, I will summarise its contents. Unlike the Copt I am a faltering translator. Our friend in Toulouse writes that they are preparing a massive army to retake Jerusalem. He says that their Pope has already called on the Kings of England, France and Germany to unite their armies and save the honour of the Worshippers of the Cross. He writes that of the three Kings, two have feeble heads full of imperial vapours. One alone is to be feared, for he is like an animal. He refers to Richard of England, whom he describes in the letter as a bad son, an even worse husband who cannot satisfy his wife nor any other woman but has a fondness for young men, a selfish ruler and a vicious and evil man, but not lacking in courage. He does not know when they will set sail, but thinks it could be after a year or more, since funds must be collected. He advises that we use this time to capture every port so that the ships from their lands are destroyed while still at sea. He further advises the Sultan to prepare a fleet that will give battle on water. He feels it is our weakness that we have never taken sea-war as seriously as we do the battles on the land. He signs himself the Sultan's most humble servant and follower and prays for the day when our armies will cross the water and take the Pope prisoner. He informs us that one of the knights accompanying Richard, a certain Robert of St Albans, is a secret heretic, that is, a true believer, and will be useful to our cause."

The Sultan smiled.

"I think we should ask our friend to return to our side. He is an astute thinker. This letter makes the capture of Tyre our most important objective. Are we agreed? Have you noted all this down, Ibn Yakub?"

I nodded.

The next afternoon, as I was preparing to accompany John of Jerusalem to the site of the old Temple, where others of our faith who had returned to Jerusalem were gathering to offer prayers of thanksgiving for the return of the city to the Sultan, a retainer surprised me by his insistence that Salah al-Din was awaiting my presence. I was surprised, since he had explicitly given me his blessing to participate in the ceremony. Nonetheless I followed the retainer to the royal chamber.

He was sitting on his bed, his face lined with worry. He must have been informed before everyone else. As I entered he rose from his bed and, to my amazement, embraced me and kissed my cheeks. His eyes had filled with tears. I knew that something terrible must have happened to my Rachel.

"We received a dispatch from Cairo, Ibn Yakub. The news is bad and you must be brave. A small party of Franj knights, enraged by the loss of this city and drunk on anger, rode into Cairo and raided the quarter where your people live. They burnt some houses and killed old men, before the alarm was given and our soldiers captured all of them. They were all executed the next morning. Your house, my friend, was one of them. Nobody survived. I have instructed al-Fadil to make arrangements for you to be taken to Cairo tomorrow morning. You may stay there as long as you wish."

I bowed and took my leave of him. I returned to my quarters. For over an hour I couldn't weep. I sat on the floor and stared at the wall. A calamity had been inflicted on me. Anguish dumbed me. Neither words nor tears could express the pain that had gripped all of me. I thought of Rachel and Maryam, her child clasped close to her bosom, all three sleeping peacefully as the barbarians set our house on fire.

It was as I began to pack my clothes that I found myself weeping loudly. I thought of all the things I had thought, but not said to Rachel. She had died not knowing the depths of my unspoken love for her. And my little Maryam, who I had wanted to live without misfortune and raise her children in peace with her husband.

I did not sleep, but went outside and walked on the battlements, watching the eternal movement of the stars and shedding silent tears. I felt bitter and angry. I wanted revenge. I wanted to roast Franj knights on a slow fire and laugh loudly at their death agony.

As we left early next morning I heard the oriole's mournful song and my face was wet again. I have no recollection of that journey from Jerusalem to Cairo. I know not how many times we stopped or where we slept. All I remember is the kind face of the Sultan's courier, who offered me a skin flask containing water which I drank and also used to wash the dust off my face. I remember also that at some stage during that pain-filled expedition I suddenly wanted to return to the Sultan. I felt there was no point in raking over the embers of the tragedy. I wanted to forget. I did not wish to see the charred remains of that old house with the domed room. It was too late.

Ibn Maymun was waiting for me at the ruins of the house. We embraced each other and wept. No words were spoken. Grief had melted old animosities and resentments. He took me to his house. For many months I lived in a daze. I lost all sense of time. I had no idea what was taking place in the world outside. Later I began to accompany the great physician to Cairo. He would attend to his patients in the palace. I would revisit old friends in the library, books I had read when I first became the Sultan's scribe. Sometimes the books would stir painful memories and Rachel would occupy my mind. Fresh tears would dissolve my concentration.

Ibn Maymun treated me as a friend and a very special patient. He fed me on fresh fish from the Nile, grilled on charcoal and served on a bed of brown rice. He made me drink herbal concoctions every night which soothed my shattered nerves and helped me to sleep. There were days when I did not speak a word to anyone. I used to walk to the stream near Ibn Maymun's house and sit on a stone, watching the young boys with their strings trying to catch fish. I always left when they laughed too loudly. I found their mirth disturbing.

I was lost to the world. All sense of time had disappeared. I lived from day to day, expecting nothing and giving nothing. As I write these lines I have no recollection of what I did every day apart from reading books in Ibn Maymun's large library and becoming fascinated by the treatises on medicine. I read Galen and Ibn Sina many times and always discovered hidden meanings in their work. If I failed to comprehend the meaning of what these masters had written I would consult Ibn Maymun, who would compliment me on my learning and suggest that I become a physician and help him in his work.

Many months passed. I lost touch with the world of the Sultan. I did not know what was happening on the field of war and I no longer cared.

One day Ibn Maymun informed me that a new party of Franj had landed on the coast and were determined to take back Jerusalem. His eyes filled with tears.

"They must never be allowed to take that city away from us again, Ibn Yakub. Never."

Perhaps it was the urgency in my friend's voice that revived my interest in the world. Perhaps my recovery was complete in any event. Whatever the cause, I felt myself again. The sense of loss was still present in me, but the pain had gone. I sent a letter to Imad al-Din, asking him whether I could rejoin the Sultan.

Four weeks later, as spring came to Cairo like a burst of soft laughter, a messenger arrived from Dimask. The Sultan ordered me to return to his side without further delay. I was sitting in the courtyard enjoying the sun, underneath a gnarled tree with twisted twigs. It remained the same through all the seasons and I had become greatly attached to it because it reminded me of myself. I, too, did not feel the delights of spring.

I bade Ibn Maymun farewell. It was an emotional parting. We, who had once been so close, were together again. A small slice of happiness had been recovered from the heart of the tragedy that had befallen me. We agreed never to lose contact again. I had no real desire to carry on inscribing the story of Salah al-Din's life, but Ibn Maymun was panicked by such a thought. He advised me to carry on and, "if it helps you, Ibn Yakub, write everything to me. I will keep your letters safe here, next to these notebooks with which you have entrusted me."

LETTERS TO
IBN MAYMUN

THIRTY-EIGHT

The Sultan welcomes my return;
Richard of England threatens Tyre;
Imad al-Din is sick with love

 Dear Friend,

I wish you were here so that we could speak with each other instead of relying on the courier service, which is not always reliable. As you know I was nervous at the thought of returning to Damascus, but everyone made me welcome. Some of the emirs went so far as to say that they regarded my return as an omen of good luck, for whenever I had been with the Sultan he had never lost a battle.

Everything has changed. Fortunes fluctuate like the price of diamonds in the Cairo market. When I left his side, nearly two years ago, the Sultan had conquered every pinnacle. His eyes were bright, the sun had given colour to his cheeks and his voice was relaxed and happy. Success dispels tiredness. When I saw him this morning he was clearly pleased to see me, and he rose and kissed my cheeks, but the sight of him surprised me. His eyes had shrunk, he had lost weight and he looked very pale. He observed my surprise.

" I have been ill, scribe. The war against these wretched infidels has begun to exhaust me, but I could cope with them. It is not simply the enemy that worries me. It is our own side. Ours is an emotional and impulsive faith. Victory in battle affects Believers in the same way as *banj*. They will fight without pause to repeat our success, but if, for some reason, it eludes us, if patience and skill are required rather than simple bravery, then our men begin to lose their urge. Dissensions arise and some fool of an emir thinks: 'Perhaps this Salah al-Din is not as invincible as we had thought. Perhaps I should save my own skin and that of my men', and thinking these ignoble thoughts he deserts the field of war. Or another few emirs, demoralised by our lack of success, will think to themselves that during the last six months they and their men have not enjoyed the spoils of war. They imagine that it is my brothers, sons and nephews who are benefiting and so they pick a quarrel and go back to Aleppo. It is a wearying business, Ibn Yakub.

"I have to fight on two fronts all the time. That is why I did not take Tyre all those months ago, when you were still at my side. I thought the men would not be able to sustain a long siege. It turned out that I was wrong. I overestimated the size of the Franj presence in the city, but if I had been confident of my own soldiers I would have taken the risk. The result, my friend, is a mess. The Franj kings are arriving from across the water with more soldiers and more gold. They never give up, do they? Welcome back to your home, Ibn Yakub. I have missed your presence. Al-Fadil left for Cairo this morning and Imad al-Din has not been to see me for a week. He claims he has a toothache, but my spies tell me that what aches is his heart. Remember Shadhi? He always used to refer to Imad al-Din as the swallower of a donkey's penis!"

He laughed loudly at the memory, and I joined him, pleased that my return had lightened his mood.

Later that afternoon, I did call on Imad al-Din, who received me graciously. The Sultan's informants had been correct. The great master was undergoing the pain associated with spurned love. He complained bitterly that the treasury had not paid his salary for many months and it was for that reason that he had decided not to visit the Sultan.

I was surprised, but when I pressed further he decided to confess the true reason for his state. He inflicted his troubles on me. There is nothing more tedious, Ibn Maymun, than listening to a grown man droning on about his shattered heart as if he was fifteen years old and had just discovered heartbreak. Since I had gone to see him it was difficult to bring my visit to an end.

You will, I'm sure, recall a certain Copt translator I once mentioned to you, by the name of Tarik ibn Isa. The one who caught our great scholar's lewd eye in Jerusalem, soon after we entered the city. The Sultan was pleased by the boy's abilities and, on Imad al-Din's advice, the Copt became part of Salah al-Din's retinue. That is how Tarik came to Damascus. Here Imad al-Din, desperate to vent his lust on the youth, pursued him without shame. He wrote couplets in his honour, he hired minstrels to sing quatrains outside his window on moonlit nights, he even threatened to have the boy dismissed from the Sultan's service unless he was willing to serve all the needs of Imad al-Din. Now this youth has disappeared, to the consternation of the entire court, and the great man is inconsolable.

This is not, of course, how the Sultan's most learned secretary views the emotional landscape. He tells his story differently and let your wisdom, Ibn Maymun, be the judge.

Speaking in those sonorous tones I have come to know so well, and which were pleasing to my ears solely because I had not heard them for so long, he told me:

"What I simply could not understand, Ibn Yakub, was the obstinate resistance of this shallow youth. You raise your eyebrows? I know what you're thinking. Perhaps this boy was not attracted to men. I thought so, but you would be wrong to make that assumption. I had him followed and discovered that he was in love with a man not much younger than myself, but with this important difference.

"Tarik's lover was a heretic, a blasphemer, a sceptic. He came from Aleppo, but preached his evil in this our purest of cities. He claimed to be descended from Ibn Awjal. You know our faith well, Ibn Yakub. You have heard of Ibn Awjal? No? I must say you surprise me.

"He lived in Kufa, a hundred years after the death of the Prophet. He had converted to our faith from yours, but he was desperate to be famous. He wanted to be a big man. So he published four thousand *hadith* and was regarded as a scholar, but these *hadith* were completely false. He had invented each and every one, and put blasphemous and erotic language into the mouth of our Prophet. It is said that one of his *hadith* claimed that the Prophet had stated that any woman who permitted a man to see her in a state of undress, even by accident, was obliged to give herself to that man, and if she refused the man had a right to take her against her will. May Allah burn that son-of-a-whore in hell forever. There were others of this sort, even worse. In one of them Ibn Awjal claimed prophetic lineage for the remark: 'Fornicate with your camel by all means, but never on the open road.' Another *hadith* claimed that provided the Angel Gabriel ratified the deed, a Believer could satisfy his carnal desires in any way he wished. On another occasion he wrote that the Prophet had told his son-in-law Ali to bare his arse before no person and claimed that two words were missing from the original *hadith*. These crazed imaginings could not be left unpunished. To abuse our Prophet in such a way was unacceptable. Ibn Awjal was arrested by the Kadi of Kufa. He admitted manufacturing the *hadith*. Justice was swift. He was executed immediately after the trial.

"Tarik's lover claimed descent from Ibn Awjal and began to tell his followers that many of the *hadith* published by his blaspheming forebear were genuine. When I heard this news I refused to believe my informant, who had insinuated his way into the intimate circles of this heretic. I informed the Kadi, who had all of them arrested, except Tarik. Unlike his more courageous ancestor, this pig of a sceptic denied all knowledge of what had been stated by my informant in the court. He had the audacity to claim that I had forged false evidence to put him out of the way for reasons best known to myself. The Kadi showed no mercy. The Sultan gave his approval. He was executed. That same day Tarik disappeared for ever. Nobody has sighted him, but there are rumours that he took his own life and some say his body was seen floating down the river.

"They tell me that your friend, Jamila, was enraged when she heard of the execution. She stormed into Salah al-Din's chamber and lashed him with her fiery tongue. That woman is never ambiguous or discreet, is she? She sent me a letter denouncing me as an evil fornicator and lecher and suggesting that this city would be cleaner if I were castrated. These are the real reasons for my gloom, Ibn Yakub, though it would be false if I denied to you that the Treasury seems to have forgotten my existence and this fact has caused me considerable irritation."

I was in a reflective mood as I left Imad al-Din's dwelling. I was walking back slowly to my own house and dreading the silence that would greet me as I entered the courtyard. This house is suffused with memories of Rachel, and I think I should remove my belongings from here and shift to the citadel. I was formulating a letter along these lines in my head to dispatch to the steward when I was approached by the familiar figure of the Nubian mute, who handed me a note from the Sultana Jamila demanding my presence. Nothing had changed in the city. I smiled weakly and followed the mute back to the citadel. It is strange, is it not, Ibn Maymun, how one can return to a place after a long absence and find that all the old routines are still in place? The Sultan fights his wars, Imad al-Din sulks in his house and the Sultana summons me for a conversation.

She greeted me like a valued friend. For the first time she touched me. She stroked my head and expressed her sorrow at the loss of my family. Then she whispered in my ear: "We have both lost loved ones. This draws us closer to each other. You must not leave us again. The Sultan and I both need you now."

Unsurprisingly, she had heard of my visit to Imad al-Din. Nothing escapes her. Even the most trivial conversation involving the Sultan or those close to him is reported to her. This makes her one of the best-informed people in the kingdom. Her authority is such that few deny her the information she craves.

Jamila wanted a detailed account of our conversation. I was about to speak when I realised she was not alone. Seated on a stool behind her was a young woman of striking beauty, whose face, with its sad expressive eyes, was strangely familiar. The young woman was dressed in a yellow silk gown and a matching scarf covered her head. She wore kohl to enhance the beauty of her eyes – not that anything about her needed enhancing. Surprised by the presence of this attractive stranger, I looked inquiringly at Jamila.

"This is Zainab. She is *my* scribe. She takes down my words so rapidly that my thoughts have to race to keep up with her. Her speed puts you to shame, Ibn Yakub. Now speak. What did that old charlatan tell you?"

I recounted my conversation with Imad al-Din, during the course of which the two women exchanged looks on a number of occasions. Then Jamila spoke with anger in her voice, though her language surprised me.

"Shadhi was not wrong about that swallower of a donkey's penis! Everything he has told you is a lie. He had an innocent man executed, a man whose only crime was that of being a sceptic, but then so am I, so is Imad al-Din, and even you have been known to express heretical thoughts. Only simpletons refuse to doubt anything. A world without doubt could never move forward. When Salah al-Din was young, he too was a sceptic. It surprises you? Why do you think he never made the pilgrimage to Mecca? Now he is desperate to appease his Maker, but when he had the chance he refused. Imad al-Din ordered the execution because he was jealous. An old man who could not bear the thought of being rejected and went looking for a sacrificial goat. It disgusts me, and I told your Sultan to have his secretary castrated. No boy in Damascus is safe when the sap rises in that old trunk."

She paused at this point to laugh and looked at Zainab for approval, but there were tears in the younger woman's eyes, and this made Jamila angry once again.

"Look closely at Zainab, scribe. Imagine her in a man's gown translating a letter in Latin to the Sultan."

I was stunned. Now I knew where I had seen a similar face. In Jerusalem! This must be Tarik ibn Isa's twin sister.

"Not his sister, fool. This is 'Tarik ibn Isa'. Zainab's father, an old Copt scholar, educated her as though she were a boy. They lived in Jerusalem, but prayed for deliverance. The Franj knights did not much care for the Copts, who hey regarded as bad Christians and heretics. When Salah al-Din's steward put out the call for a translator, Zainab's father dressed her as a man and sent her to he court. The rest you know. Let Imad al-Din think that he caused the death of Tarik ibn Isa. Let him suffer for the rest of his life. We are thinking of disguising Zainab as a ghost and sending her outside Imad al-Din's bedchamber. Do you think it might kill him?"

I looked at Zainab. She had recovered her composure and was pleased that her tory had astonished me. I could also see from Jamila's eyes that she had now found a replacement for the lost Halima.

Contrary to what is said, Ibn Maymun, the fickleness of a woman's heart is something we can never match.

My warmest greetings to your family.

Your old friend,

Ibn Yakub.

THIRTY-NINE

The Franj plague returns to Acre and Salah al-Din is depressed; he confides his innermost doubts to me

I envy you, dear friend Ibn Maymun. I envy your beautiful home near Cairo. I envy your peace of mind and I wish I had never left the sanctuary that you so kindly provided me in my hour of need.

I am at fault. I have not written to you for many months, but I have been moving all the time in the wake of our Sultan. How everything has changed once again. The fortunes of this war are forever fluctuating. I am writing to you from Acre, which is under siege by the Franj, whose decision to attack the city took us all by surprise. Salah al-Din was two days away, but returned with his soldiers, who were vastly outnumbered by the Franj.

Such is the power of our Sultan that the very news of his approach startled the enemy. They did not put up a fight, but instead withdrew to their camp. We sent some of our soldiers back into Acre and messengers were sent for help. Taki al-Din left his watch outside Antioch and joined us, as did Keukburi. As you know, these are the two emirs who the Sultan would trust with his life, and their arrival cheered his spirits.

The response from other quarters was limited. The in-fighting amongst the rulers of Hamadan and Sinjar and some other towns has meant that their aims no longer harmonise with those of Salah al-Din.

When the Franj finally joined battle the results were not clear. It was neither victory nor defeat for both sides. Our position grows steadily weaker and the Franj grow daily more audacious, but the final victory may belong to our side. The situation as I write is as follows. Picture the Franj trying to besiege Acre and take us by surprise. Now shut your eyes and imagine how our Salah al-Din came up quietly behind the Franj and transformed the besiegers into the besieged. In Imad al-Din's immortal words, "After being like the brow around the eye, they have now become like the eye surrounded by the eyebrow." His imagery is powerful, but I think it is designed to conceal the despair that he really feels. We began this year with the Sultan acknowledged as the supreme master of Palestine. Now, once again, we are fighting for our survival, and the Sultan sometimes wishes that he had never left Cairo.

He never pauses for a rest. He usually sleeps no more than two or three hours every night. I wish you were here so that you could advise him on how to preserve his health. Looking at him these days, he is like a candle, which still displays a piercing flame, but which is slowly burning itself out. He is over fifty years old, but he leads his soldiers into battle as if he were twenty, his sword raised and without a care in the world. And yet I know that he is extremely worried about the state of his army. It is beginning to affect his spiritual and physical health. He has not slept at all for the last three days. His face is pale, his eyes, normally alert and lively, are listless. I feel he needs someone with whom he can share all his troubled thoughts. As always I wish Shadhi was here, but even Imad al-Din or your great Kadi al-Fadil would be a useful presence. You might mention my worries to al-Fadil if this letter ever reaches you. I am not a good substitute for any of these three men, and yet I am the only one here who knows him and has been close to him for over ten years. Is it really ten years ago that you recommended me to him, Ibn Maymun? Time is cruel.

He talks to me a great deal these days, and sometimes I get the feeling that he wants me to stop being a scribe. He looks into my eyes, demanding a reply that would comfort him and ease his fears, but as you know well, I have no real knowledge of matters military and my understanding of the emirs of Damascus and their rivalries is, alas, limited. I have never realised my own shortcomings as I have on this particular trip, When Salah al-Din has needed me, I could offer him nothing.

I remember you explaining to me a long time ago that when minds are agitated, all we can offer our friends is to sit quietly and listen to their tales of woe. People in such a state rarely follow anyone's advice and can even become resentful if one says something that they do not wish to hear. You said all this in relation to love, but the emotion that is plaguing our Sultan is indecision in the face of the enemy. He thinks of two or three alternatives but cannot determine which to follow.

I sit and listen to his sad voice. Yesterday I was summoned to his tent when the full moon was at its zenith. I had been fast asleep, but as I walked to his tent the cool air refreshed my brain. These were the exact words spoken to me by the Sultan.

Hardly a night goes by, Ibn Yakub, without my feeling that Allah is beckoning me. I am not long for this life, scribe. I have spent fifty years in this world, which is a blessing from Allah. A strange thing happens to a man after he reaches fifty. He stops thinking about the future and spends more and more time thinking about the past. He smiles at the good memories and cringes all over again at the foolishnesses of which he was guilty.

These last few weeks I have been thinking a great deal of my father Ayyub. In the course of his life my noble father, may he be happy in Heaven, never had occasion to fall on his knees in order to gratify a ruler. He always held his head high. He disliked hearing his virtues praised and he was deaf to the coarse flattery that is part of everyday life in the citadel. It always gave him pleasure to oblige others.

He was a generous man. Shadhi must have told you all this, but he had a real weakness for maidservants. You look surprised, Ibn Yakub. Do I take it that this fact was kept from you by the ever-indiscreet Shadhi? Allah protect me! I'm amazed. It wasn't much of a secret. Whenever a new maidservant approached my father used to feel the sap rise in him, and he never wasted his seed. Once my mother reproached him for this and he hurled a *hadith* at her head, according to which, if it is to be believed, "the share of a man to copulate has been predestined and he will have to do it under all circumstances." My mother, who was a plain-speaking woman, after a few sentences of the choicest Kurdish abuses which I will not repeat, then asked him how it had come about that men could find a *hadith* to justify everything they did to women, but the opposite was never the case. Why am I talking about him in this fashion? I had called you in to discuss more urgent matters, but your presence always reminds me of old Shadhi, and I find myself talking with you as I used to with him, in a way I could never do with al-Fadil or Imad al-Din, and not even my own brothers.

Most of my emirs and soldiers imagine I have the solution to all our problems, but we know better. A ruler may be strong or weak, but he is always lonely. Even the last Fatimid Caliph in Cairo, surrounded by eunuchs and addicted to the *banj* which kept him remote from reality, even he once wept in my presence and confessed how the lack of even a single true friend had brought him more grief than anything else, including the loss of real power.

I have been lucky. I have had good friends and advisers, but this war has being going on for far too long. I do not deny my mistakes. We should have taken Tyre after al-Kuds. It was a grave error on my part to move down the coast, but that was not an insurmountable problem. I am beginning to think there is something that goes deep in all those amongst us who believe in Allah and his Prophet. It is almost as if this creed is so strongly rooted in us that we do not feel an obligation to believe in anything else. How else can one explain the degeneration that has taken place in Baghdad? Not even the Commander of the Faithful himself would dare compare himself to the first four Caliphs.

Our faith, which in the early days inspired us to build an empire which spanned sea and desert and existed on three continents, now appears to have descended to a grand gesture. We love extremes. When, against all odds, Allah gives us a dramatic victory, we rejoice like children who have won a game of eight-stones. For the next few months we live off our victory. Allah is praised and all is well.

After a defeat we descend low into the very heart of gloom. What we do not understand is that there are no victories without defeats. Every great conqueror in history has suffered setbacks. We are incapable of consistency. After only a few reverses our morale suffers, our spirit is weakened and our discipline disappears. Was this written in our stars? Will we never change? Has the cruelty of fate designated us to a permanent instability? How will we reply to Gabriel on the Day of Judgement when he asks: "O Followers of the great Prophet Mohammed, why, when you were needed the most, did you not help each other in the face of your enemies?"

Our emirs are easily demoralised and discouraged. Easy victories are fine, but when the will of Allah is frustrated by the infidels then our emirs panic, and when this state of mind is observed by the men who fight under their command, they too become despondent and say to each other: "Our emir is missing his wine and women. I, too, am missing my family. We haven't received any treasure for many months. Perhaps tonight, when the camp is asleep, we should return to our villages."

It is not easy to maintain the morale of a large army at a level where it is permanently in a state of readiness. The Franj have an advantage over us. Their soldiers come across the water. They cannot run away as easily as we can. All this teaches me is that men fight for a cause that is greater than their own self-interest only when they are genuinely convinced that what they are fighting for will benefit each and all.

When I was a young boy in Baalbek and the sun was shining from a clear blue sky, I would often go out with my brothers to play near the river. Suddenly large black clouds would cover the sky like a blanket, and before we could run back a ripe thunderstorm had already erupted, frightening us with flashes of lightning. t is only when my soldiers are like that thunderstorm that I can behave like lightning. That is what they do not understand and what the emirs, with a few exceptions, are incapable of teaching them. The result is what you see around you. An army in disarray. Our good friend Imad al-Din is now overcome by fear and worry. He writes to inform us that, like the plague, the Franj are out of our control. As long as the sea continues to supply them and our lands continue to give them comfort they will conquer everything. Our great scholar shows his confidence in my abilities by jumping on his horse and fleeing to the safety of Damascus and suggests that I follow him soon. I suppose he prefers to be congratulated on his safety rather than being posthumously praised for his martyrdom. Alas, this is a road specially maintained for the scholars of our realm. It is not a route along which I could travel.

I have written his words down exactly as he spoke them, and they will give you some indication as to the state of his mind. I am concerned that if his health collapses, so will our cause, and the Franj might then retake Jerusalem and burn our people as they did the first time.

I hope this letter finds you in good health and that your esteemed family have managed to survive the Cairo summer.

Your humble pupil,

Ibn Yakub.

FORTY

The fall of Acre; Imad al-Din's story of Richard the Lion-Arse; the death of Taki al-Din

 My dear and most esteemed friend,

There are many reasons why I have not written you for several months. I have been travelling a great deal from one camp to another, following the Sultan like a trusted dog and happy in my position. In the old days, before the fire that consumed my family, there were occasions when I resented being summoned to the royal presence without even a moment's notice. Now I feel he really needs me. Perhaps this is pure fantasy, but I know that I certainly need him. At his side, I am distracted from the past. My mind has to be clear to understand the events that take place every day.

There are times when writing to you reminds me of the old house in the Jewish quarter of Cairo, and then I weep. This is especially true on cold nights like tonight when I am sitting in a tent, huddled in a blanket, roasting my hands gently on a fire. Memories take over of the winter nights in Cairo all those years ago. That was one reason for the delay. There was another. I was not sure whether you had received my previous communications or not, and I had no time to make inquiries because of the calamity. We have all been in deep mourning for the loss of Acre.

I was therefore delighted to receive your message via the courier to the Sultan and am pleased that my previous letters have reached you safely. I am also touched by your concern for my health, but on that score there is no cause for worry. It is the Sultan's state of mind that bothers me. This man can ride for fifty days on horseback with only three-hour rests every night and inspire all his men, but I fear he will drop dead one day and leave us orphans to grieve on our own.

I understand your irritation regarding Imad al-Din, but you are not completely accurate in your estimate of him. As we have had occasion to discuss before, he has many bad habits. His spirit is clouded by arrogance and his body movements are sometimes offensive, especially his habit of raising his left buttock slightly when he passes wind, but this defect is counterbalanced by his many noble qualities which transcend all his weaknesses. He is a man with a romantic spirit. The timbre of his soul is gentle. Enough of him for the moment. I shall return to this subject later.

The magnitude of the disaster that befell us at Acre cannot be underestimated. Philip of France and Richard of England finally took the city. We had no ships to resist their galleys and Salah al-Din's attempts to divert their attention by a surprise attack on their encampments failed in their purpose. The large armoury in Acre contained all the arms from the coast as well as others from Damascus and Aleppo. The emirs in the citadel sent the Sultan several messages pleading for help and informing him that if they were not relieved they would have no alternative but to ask the Franj for quarter.

The sequence of events was as follows. As the situation deteriorated, three of the leading emirs fled the city under cover of darkness in a small boat. Their cowardly act became known only in the morning and caused a further decline in the morale of the soldiers. Sensing defeat, the commander Qara Kush, whom you know much better than I from his days in Cairo, asked to see the Sultans of

England and France to negotiate a surrender and the withdrawal of all our soldiers. Philip was prepared to accept the terms demanded by Qara Kush, but Richard wished to humiliate our army and refused. Salah al-Din sent a message forbidding surrender, but even though our army had received reinforcements we could not break the siege. Qara Kush surrendered without the Sultan's authority, but Richard insisted on extremely tough terms. Qara Kush felt he had no alternative but to accept the offer.

It was the greatest reverse ever suffered by Salah al-Din. He had not been defeated for fourteen years and now he wept like a child. They were tears of anger, of despair and frustration. He felt that with stronger leadership inside the city it need not have fallen. He reproached himself. He railed against the babble of futile counsel and cursed the cowardly emirs. He pledged that he would never give up the struggle to test the spirit and the faith of the Believers. He spoke of the light temporarily hidden by a cloud and he swore in the name of Allah that the stars would once again shine before the break of dawn. It was difficult not to be moved by his tears or the words that accompanied them.

Richard of England sent a messenger asking to meet the Sultan alone in the presence of an interpreter, but the Commander of the Loyal rejected the request with contempt. He told the messenger: "Tell your King we do not speak the same language."

Richard broke his word on several occasions. He had promised Salah al-Din that he would release our prisoners provided we kept to our side of the agreement of surrender. We did. We sent the first instalment of the money. The Franj leaders replied with the dishonesty that has marked them ever since they first came to these lands.

One Friday, a holy day for the followers of the Prophet Mohammed, Richard ordered the public execution of three thousand prisoners and his knights kicked their heads into the dust. As news of this crime reached our camp a loud wail rent the sky and soldiers fell on their knees and prayed for their massacred brethren. Salah al-Din swore revenge and ordered that henceforth no Franj was to be taken alive. Even he, the most magnanimous of rulers, had decided on an eye for an eye.

The Sultan did not eat for a week, till one morning after a secret deliberation, Taki al-Din, Keukburi and I knelt down before him and pleaded that he break his fast. Then he took the bowl of nourishing chicken broth from my hands and began to sip it slowly as he savoured the taste. We looked at each other, smiled and sighed with relief. After he had finished he spoke in a direct fashion to his nephew, Taki, whom he favours even more than his own sons and whom he would secretly like to succeed him as Sultan, but fears a fratricidal conflict if he were to insist on this choice.

"I will never say this in public" – Salah al-Din spoke in a weak voice – "but the three of you are amongst my closest and most trusted friends. I am sad not because of Acre. We have lost other cities in the past and a single defeat can, on its own, change little, but what distresses me is the lack of unity in the ranks of the Believers. Imad al-Din's close friends in the Caliph's court in Baghdad have informed him that, in private, the Caliph is pleased that we have lost Acre. Why do you all appear shocked? Ever since I took al-Kuds the Commander of the Faithful and his closest advisers have looked in my direction with fear-filled eyes. They think I am too powerful because the common people appreciate me more than the Caliph. Their diseased minds, wrecked by *banj*, see their victory in our defeat."

This was the first time the Sultan had directly questioned the piety and leadership of the Caliph in my presence. I was shocked, but also pleased that I was now a trusted adviser, on the same scale as Imad al-Din and your friend, the inimitable Kadi al-Fadil.

Since the fall of Acre we have suffered another big defeat at Arsluf, and the Sultan is now concentrating our minds on defending Jerusalem. There were no easy victories for the Franj. They suffered heavy losses, and some of the soldiers fresh from across the water are finding it difficult to adjust to the August heat in Palestine. Richard asked for a meeting with the Sultan. It was refused, but al-Adil did meet him and they spoke for a long time. Richard wanted us to surrender Palestine, but the audacity of the request angered al-Adil and he refused.

Over the last ninety years, even when there was a lull in the long war, we never felt these people to be anything else but usurpers — outsiders who were here against our will and because of our weaknesses. Richard was only the latest in a long line of brutal knights to have landed on these shores. On our side, the cloak of diplomacy conceals a silver dagger. The Sultan often asks himself whether this bad dream will ever end or is it our fate as the inhabitants of an area which gave birth to Moses, Jesus and Mohammed, to be always at war. Yesterday he asked me whether I thought Jehovah, God and Allah could ever live in peace. I could not supply him with an answer. Can you, dear friend?

Imad al-Din arrived from Damascus on the morning of al-Adil's contemptuous rejection of Richard's peace terms. He spent most of the day speaking with some Franj knights we had taken by surprise and who were due to be executed at sunset. Three of them converted to the faith of the Prophet and were spared, but all of them were only too eager to speak with Imad al-Din.

Next morning I was defecating at the edge of the camp when he joined me to fulfil a similar function. After we had washed ourselves and sat down to breakfast, he began to tell stories of Richard, which had not been recounted before.

"One of the Franj knights spoke of Richard as fighting with the ferocity of a lion. He said that for this reason they referred to him as Lionheart. This report was confirmed by the others, and I think that our knowledge of his warlike activities confirms this aspect of his character. He fights like an animal. He is an animal. The lion, dear friend Ibn Yakub, as we know only too well, is not the most cultured amongst Allah's creations.

"But even if we accept the appellation as an approbation, this view is not universally held amongst the Franj. Three knights I spoke with separately corroborated another view. According to them he fights ferociously only when he is surrounded by other knights. They insist that he is capable of low cunning, treachery and cowardice and has been known to desert the field of battle before any of his soldiers when he fears defeat. His execution of our prisoners at Acre was the act of a jackal, not a lion.

"We shall remember this king as Richard the Lion-Arse. I'm pleased that my prediction amuses you, Ibn Yakub, but it was meant seriously. I have chanced, on several occasions, to view the anus of a slain lion, and what has struck me every time is its gigantic size. One of the unexplained mysteries of nature.

"Richard's posterior, on the contrary, has not been enlarged by nature. Whole armies have passed through here, according to my informants, and still he is not sated. Secretly he yearns to be entered by al-Adil, the dearly beloved brother of our Sultan. Salah al-Din laughed when this was reported to him and, in my presence, remarked to his brother: 'Good brother al-Adil, in order to further the cause of Allah, I might need you to do your duty and make the ultimate sacrifice.'

"I laughed a bit too loudly at what was intended as a joke. This caused both men to become silent, look at me and then at each other. I knew what was passing through their mind. They were wondering whether I might be the person to make the ultimate sacrifice and enter the lion's arse. As you can imagine, dear friend, I did not give time for this foolish idea to mature. Pleading a call of nature, I obtained their permission to leave the Sultan's tent and did not return."

It is now three days since I wrote the above lines. Another tragedy has occurred. The Sultan's favourite nephew, the young Emir Taki al-Din, was killed in the course of an unnecessary engagement with the Franj. He had been opposed to the encounter, but was overruled by some young bloods and then compelled to lead them, when he knew they were hopelessly outnumbered. Salah al-Din took the news badly and is still sick at heart. Truly, he loved Taki al-Din more than his own sons. Taki's father had died a long time ago and the Sultan had virtually adopted him, treating him not just like a son, but, more importantly, also as a friend.

It happened like this: together with al-Adil and a few emirs from Damascus, I was summoned to the Sultan's tent. When we arrived he was weeping. They were huge sobs, and the sight of al-Adil made his anguish even louder. We were so distressed at this sight that without even knowing the cause of his sorrow, we too began to shed tears. When we found out the reason we were stunned. Taki al-Din was not simply his nephew, but one of the few trustworthy emirs who understood the meaning of this war and who, the Sultan used to hope, would see it through to the end. The courage of this emir was a source of inspiration to his men and his uncle, but the latter also knew that the timbre of his soul was gentle, and it was this quality that he loved in him. Without Taki, it became important to win as many victories as possible, in order to demoralise the Franj and send their leaders back across the water.

The next morning the Sultan handed me a piece of paper containing a tribute to his fallen nephew. In Imad al-Din's absence he wished me to cast an eye on the verse and improve it before dispatching it to his brothers and nephews. The great scholar was often brutal in dealing with the Sultan's handiwork, but I lacked the authority or the self-confidence to make any changes. Truth is, Ibn Maymun, I rather liked the verse and sent it to many parts as it was written. Do you agree?

In the desert alone, I
count the burnt-out lamps of our youths.
How many have been claimed by these execution-grounds?
How many more will die?
We can never call them back with the sound of the flute or the songs we write,
But every morning at sunrise
I will remember them all in my prayers.
Death's cruel arrow has claimed Taki al-Din and
the harsh walls of this world have closed in around me.
Darkness rules.

Desolation reigns.
Can we illuminate the path again?

Your friend,
Ibn Yakub
(Personal Scribe to the Sultan Salah al-Din ibn Ayyub)

FORTY-ONE

The Lion-Arse returns to England and the Sultan retires to Damascus

 Good friend, Ibn Maymun,

We were in a state of great perplexity. There was so much dissension amongst the emirs that had Richard laid siege to Jerusalem, who can say that he would not have succeeded? There were times when the Sultan used to go to al-Aqsa and moisten the prayer mats with his tears. He, too, was not confident that his emirs and soldiers would be able to resist the onslaught.

At one council of war, an emir addressed Salah al-Din in harsh language and insisted: "The fall of Jerusalem would not damage the faith. After all we have survived many years without Jerusalem. It is only a city and there is no shortage of stones in our world." I had never before seen the Sultan so angry in public. He rose and we all rose with him. Then he walked up to the emir who had spoken thus and looked him straight in the eyes. The emir averted his gaze and fell on his knees. The Sultan did not speak a single word. He returned to his place and said in a soft voice that Jerusalem would be defended to the last man and that if it fell he would fall with it, so that in times to come their children would remember and understand that this was no ordinary city of stone, but a place where the future of our faith was decided. Then he left the chamber. No one spoke. Slowly, the room emptied.

Left on my own I sat there and reflected on the tumultuous events of the last few years. We had grown too confident after our victory in Jerusalem. I loved the Sultan as I would my own father, but there was a flaw in his character. At times when he needed to be decisive, to make unpopular choices, to be alone in the knowledge that his instincts were correct, at such a time he weakened and allowed himself to be swayed by lesser men than he. Often I wanted to transcend my position and speak to him as a friend, just as you have so often spoken to me. Are you wondering what I would say? I'm not sure myself.

Perhaps I would whisper in his ear: "Don't lose your courage if some emir deserts you now, or if the peasants disregard your instructions and supply the Franj with grain. Your instincts are good. You are usually right, but the guarantee of our final victory lies in nothing but an extreme unwillingness to yield, the strictest straightforwardness when speaking to our soldiers and the rejection of all compromises with vacillators in our own ranks. It was in this directness, this quality as of a javelin in flight, that lay the secret of your uncle Shirkuh's victories."

Fortunately for us, Richard too was frightened of defeat. He feared the sun. He feared the poisoned wells. He feared our wrath, but above all, he feared the Sultan. He was also anxious to return home. One of the few occasions when I have heard the Sultan laugh was when one of our spies reported serious dissensions within the enemy camp. Richard and the French King did not agree on any single issue. Their hatred for each other grew so fierce that it began to outweigh their desire to defeat us.

"Allah be praised," the Sultan had laughed, "it is not only our side that is divided by petty conflicts and rival ambitions."

He thought this was a good time to conclude a peace. The Franj could keep their coastal towns. Let them have Tyre, Jaffa, Ascalon and Acre. These are nothing compared to what we now control, and though we have not driven them into the sea, time is on our side. That is how the Sultan reasoned, and in this he was correct.

Richard has left our shores. He stayed for two years, but failed to take the Holy City. His expedition came to naught. He may have taken pleasure in executing helpless prisoners, but his crusade failed and therein lies our victory.

Our Sultan remains the only sovereign ruler of this area. I know you will not be surprised to hear that no sooner had Richard bade farewell to our shores than we began to receive deputations of Franj nobles, desperate to seek the protection of the Sultan against each other. They wish to buy their security by agreeing to become his vassals.

And this is how we returned to the citadel in Damascus, from where I am writing these lines. I now have three large rooms at my disposal and am treated as a guest rather than a servant. The chamberlain visits me regularly to ensure that my needs are not ignored. He does so on the express instructions of his master. It is as if Salah al-Din has decided to reward my diligence over the years by ensuring that my last years are pleasurable and not lacking in comfort.

I see the Sultan every day. He talks often of his father and uncle, but the person he misses the most is our old friend, Shadhi, the Kurdish warrior who was also his uncle by blood and who never hesitated to speak the truth. Yesterday he reminded me of "Shadhi's capacity to turn rhetoric into logic" and we both laughed, not as ruler and servant, but as two friends mourning the loss of something precious.

I worry about him a great deal, Ibn Maymun, and sincerely wish you could travel to this city and be his physician. He needs care. His face is lined and shows signs of real weariness. White hairs dominate his beard. Exertions tire him and he finds it difficult to sleep through the night. Could you recommend some herbal infusions?

Yesterday, after his afternoon rest and on a pure whim, he sent for Imad al-Din. The great man did not arrive till much later, long after we had finished our evening meal. He apologised for this, claiming that he had only been informed of the Sultan's message half-an-hour ago. Salah al-Din smiled and did not challenge the falsehood. It is known everywhere that Imad al-Din avoids eating with the Sultan, because of the latter's frugal taste in food.

"What did you eat tonight, Imad al-Din, and where?" asked the Sultan without a smile.

The secretary was shaken by this unexpected question. His drooping eyelids lifted and his entire posture became alert.

"It was a modest repast, O Commander of the Brave. A little grilled lamb, followed by one of my own recipes, quails cooked in curds from sheep's milk and flavoured with salt and garlic. That's all."

We laughed, and he joined in. Then after an exchange of pleasantries the Sultan announced his wish to make the pilgrimage to Mecca and asked Imad al-Din to make the necessary plans. The secretary frowned.

"I would not recommend it at the moment. The Caliph is already envious of you. He knows the people love you. He will regard your visit to Mecca as an indirect challenge to his authority in Baghdad."

"That is the talk of the insane, Imad al-Din," the Sultan interrupted his chief adviser on protocol. "It is the duty of a Believer to visit Mecca once a year."

"I am aware of this, Sultan," replied the secretary, "but the Caliph might inquire why you have chosen this time for your first visit. He might even listen to evil tongues which gossip that you were once a sceptic and, as such, attached little importance to the rituals of our faith."

"Do as I say, Imad al-Din," came the stern reply. " I will visit Mecca before this year is out. Inform the Caliph of our intention and inquire politely whether we should stop and pay our respects to him on our way."

Once this question was settled, Imad al-Din made as if to take his leave, but the Sultan indicated that he should stay.

"It is not often we have the pleasure of your presence these days, Imad al-Din. Tell me, have you found a new lover?"

It was not like Salah al-Din to be so intimate, and the secretary was surprised and a little flattered by the familiarity shown by his sovereign. He parried the question with a joke which amused neither the Sultan nor me. Frustrated by Imad al-Din's excessive desire for secrecy, Salah al-Din became serious.

"I know you have studied the Christian faith closely, Imad al-Din. Is it not the case that the early Christians from whom the Copts claim their descent viewed icons and images with the same repugnance as ourselves? Here I include Ibn Yakub and the followers of Musa, whose faith, like ours, is built on a rejection of image-worship. How did it happen that the later Christians abandoned their early beliefs and began to worship icons? If it happened to them, could it not happen to us?"

For a moment Imad al-Din was buried deep in his own thoughts as he stroked his beard. Once he had composed a reply in his head, he began to speak slowly as if he were instructing a pupil.

"The early Christians were indeed deeply offended by the worship of images. They were, in the main, descended from the people of Musa and, as such, they carried within them many of the old Jewish precepts. They were also hostile to the Greeks. In fact some of the early Christians used to mock the pagans by arguing that if statues and images were capable of thought and feeling the only person they would love would be he who had created them.

"The change came three hundred years later when the pagans had been decisively defeated. The luminaries of the Church thought that images of Isa and the saints and relics such as the Cross could act as a bridge between them and a sceptical multitude which recalled the past with affection and whose memory was still infused with the more delightful aspects of pagan rituals. If the followers of Pythagoras could only be won over by images of Isa nailed to the cross, then the bishops were prepared to tolerate this departure from their own past.

"Reminded by newly converted pagans that their faith lacked an Athena, a Diana, a Venus, they set the minds of their new flock to rest by elevating Isa's mother, Mary, into one of the most popular images of their religion. The figure of a mother was necessary for them, as they ruled over countries where goddesses had been worshipped for centuries. Our Prophet, may he rest in peace, was aware of this problem, but resisted the lures of Satan in this regard.

"The Sultan asks if we will go the same way. I think not. The purity of our faith is so closely tied to the worship of Allah and Allah alone, that to worship the image of anyone would not simply be profane, it would seriously challenge the authority of the Commander of the Faithful. After all, if power resided in a relic or an image, why bother to accept the power of a human being? I know what you're thinking, O Commander of the Intelligent. The Pope in Rome? I thought as much, but as the years pass their faith will witness schisms and a challenge to the Pope's authority. That is the logic of worshipping images.

"If *we* were to go in that direction our faith, unlike that of the Christians, would not be able to withstand the strain. It would collapse."

The Sultan stroked his beard thoughtfully, but was unconvinced by Imad al-Din's logic.

"The power of their Pope or our Caliph may well be challenged, Imad al-Din. That much I grant you, but where I disagree is your assumption that all this flows from the worship of images and icons. You have not proved your case, but the subject interests me nonetheless. Speak with the chamberlain and let us have a conference of scholars next week to discuss this matter further. I will detain you no longer. I am sure that somewhere in the heart of Damascus a beautiful young creature is waiting patiently for you to enter his bed."

The secretary did not reply, but permitted himself a smile and kissed the Sultan's cloak before he departed. It was not late, but Salah al-Din was tired. Two attendants, laden with sheets, soaps and oils, came to accompany him to the bath. He looked at me with a weak smile.

"Jamila will be angry I have kept you so long today. She is desperate to speak with you. Like me she has grown to value your friendship. Your presence reassures her. Better spend the day with her tomorrow."

I bowed as he left, resting his arms on the shoulders of the attendants. Both of them were holding lamps in their right hands and as he walked out positioned delicately between them, the soft light shone on his face. For a moment it appeared as a light from another world. From paradise. He talks sometimes of the unexpected gifts bestowed on him by kind Fate and speaks of himself as a mere instrument of Allah. He is only too well aware of his mortality. He is not well, Ibn Maymun, and this makes me sad.

The next day I followed the Sultan's instructions and went to pay my respects to the Sultana Jamila. She received me alone and bade me welcome in the most affectionate fashion. She handed me a manuscript, and as I leafed through its pages I began to tremble for her and for myself. Both of us could be beheaded: she for writing the offending pages and I for reading them dispassionately and not reporting her to the Kadi. Her work contained blasphemies so flagrant that even the Sultan would have found it difficult to protect her from the wrath of the sheikhs. I will discuss these with you when we meet again, Ibn Maymun. I am fearful of confiding them in a letter which will be carried by a messenger. It is perfectly possibly that our letters are opened, read by prying eyes, their contents reported to al-Fadil and Imad al-Din and then resealed and dispatched.

I pleaded with Jamila to burn the manuscript.

"The paper might burn, scribe," she retorted with fire in her eyes, "but my thoughts will never leave me. What you do not understand is that something terrible has happened to me and I want to go south forever. I can no longer smile. The wind has burnt my lips. I wish to die where I was born. Till that day arrive I will continue to transfer my thoughts to paper. I have no intention of destroying this manuscript. It will be left in a safe place, and it will be read by those who understand my quest for truth."

Even though I could read the answer in her eyes, I asked the nature of the calamity that had befallen her. She had grown tired of the beautiful Copt girl. Her surfeited heart had felt sudden disgust. She offered no reason and I asked for none. She was searching for Halima and had not found her in the Copt. Would the search continue when she returned south, or had she resigned herself to a life of scholarship? I was about to ask her, when she startled me with an unexpected offer.

"Your life too, Ibn Yakub, has been affected by misfortune. You have won respect and praise from everyone, but you and I are like beggars. We have nothing. It is true I have two strong sons, but they are far away and they will die fighting, defending some citadel in this cursed war. I doubt that they will even provide me with grandchildren to help my old age. I foresee an empty life after the Sultan goes, and so do you. Why not accompany me to the South? The library in my father's palace has many rare manuscripts, including some from Andalusian sceptics. You will never be short of reading matter. What do you say, scribe? You need time to think?"

I nodded, while expressing my gratitude to her for thinking of me so kindly. The truth is, Ibn Maymun, that I would much rather return to Cairo, find a small room somewhere and be close to you.

Your loyal friend,
Ibn Yakub.

FORTY-TWO

Farewell to the Sultan

 Dear friend,

There is a winter mist over the citadel as I write these lines, but it is as nothing compared with the dark clouds that have covered our hearts for the last seven days. He, who was accustomed to war, now rests in peace, in the shadow of the Great Mosque.

My own future is uncertain. The Sultan's son, al-Afdal, has succeeded him and wants me to stay here as his scribe. Jamila is preparing to depart for the South and wishes me to accompany her. I think I will plead ill-health and return to Cairo to recover my thoughts and reflect for some time on the life of this man, whose departure has left us all in darkness.

His health, as I wrote you before, had not been good. During our last weeks in Jerusalem he would sigh and complain of lack of sleep, but insist on fasting, which his physicians warned him was unnecessary. The fast would weaken him further and I would often see him, his head hanging wearily as he stared at the ground.

But the return to Damascus had revived him, and his death was all the worse 'r being so unexpected. For the last month he had spent much time with his 'other al-Adil and his sons. His health appeared to have recovered. He ate well d there was colour in his cheeks again. Much laughter was heard as they rode it of the city to enjoy the hunt.

Once we were sitting in the garden and his oldest boy, al-Afdal, came to pay 's respects. The Sultan, who had been talking to me of his love for his dead :phew, Taki al-Din, fell silent as al-Afdal came and kissed his father's hands. he Sultan looked at him sternly.

"I am leaving all of you an empire that stretches from the Tigris to the Nile. :ever forget that our successes were based on the support we received from our :ople. If you become isolated from them, you won't last long."

On another occasion I heard him plead with al-Adil to safeguard the interests ' his sons. He knew, as did his brother, that amongst the mountain clans there no particular regard for heredity. The clan chooses the strongest from within ranks to lead it and defend its interests. The Sultan's younger brother, al-Adil, 're a strong resemblance to their uncle Shirkuh and his character and appetites, o, were not unlike his uncle's. Salah al-Din knew, as did his brother, that if his tainers and soldiers were given the choice they would choose al-Adil to be eir Sultan. He pleaded with al-Adil to protect Afdal, Aziz and Zahir against all nspiracies. The younger brother bent and kissed the Sultan's cheeks, mutter- g: "Why are you in such low spirits? Allah will take me away long before you. e needs you to clear the infidels off our shores."

When al-Adil spoke those words I agreed with him. The Sultan was in high irits and reminded me of those early days in Cairo when he was learning the : of statecraft. But the Sultan must have had a foreboding.

Early one morning he ordered me to be woken up and join him. Having led to visit Mecca he wanted to go and greet the returning pilgrims outside the y walls. I think he truly regretted his own inability to make the pilgrimage. iring his youth it had been an act of defiance, but as he grew older he felt it as a loss. However, the war against the Franj had occupied him for two score years and of late he was simply too exhausted to make the journey. Imad al-Din had prevented him by utilising the Caliph's rivalry as a motive, but in reality the secretary had confessed to me that he feared the Sultan would not survive the journey. His physicians confirmed that this was indeed the reason why they had forbidden the exertion. He accepted all this with bad grace, and his desire to greet the returning pilgrims was by way of making up for his own failure.

As we rode it began to rain. The downpour had struck without warning and it was cold winter rain, which froze our faces. I saw him shiver and realised that he had come without his quilted jacket. I took my cloak and attempted to put round his shoulders, but he laughed and threw it back at me. It amused him that I, who he regarded as a weakling, was trying to shield him from the weather.

The rain fell with such force that the road became divided by wild streams and virtually impassable. The horses began to slither in the mud, but he continued to ride and we continued to follow him. I can see him now, his clothes and his beard splattered with mud as he caught sight of the rain-soaked pilgrims and greeted them.

When we returned the rain had stopped and the sky had cleared. The people of Damascus, in all their finery, came out on to the streets to cheer the Sultan and welcome the caravan from Mecca. We avoided the crowds and took a small path back to the drawbridge.

Late that night he was possessed by a raging fever. I doubt whether a physician even of your skill would have been able to save him, Ibn Maymun. The fever grew worse and the Sultan was barely conscious. He saw his sons and al-Adil every day. I never left his side, thinking he might recover to dictate his last testament, but on the tenth day he fell asleep and never woke again. He had just passed his fifty-fifth birthday.

The city wept for three whole days. No instructions had been sent, but the shutters remained drawn over the shops and the streets were deserted. I have never seen such mass grief so openly displayed. The whole city was present as we accompanied his body to its last resting place, walking in absolute silence. His physician Abd al-Latif, himself an old man, whispered in my ear that he could recall no other instance where the death of a Sultan had so genuinely tormented the hearts of the people.

Imad al-Din, his face disfigured by pain and tears pouring down his cheeks, prayed aloud: "Ya Allah, accept this soul and open to him the gates of Paradise, and thus give him his last victory for which he always hoped."

When we returned to the citadel all was silent. It seemed as if emirs and retainers alike could not even bear to listen to the sound of their own voices. The Sultan's son, al-Afdal, came and embraced me, but no words were exchanged.

That same evening I suffered an attack of nausea and was sick. I was shivering. My body seemed to be on fire. I consumed three flasks of water and then I fell asleep.

When I woke the next morning, the sickness had gone, but I felt weak and overcome by a foreboding of disaster. I sat up in my bed and realised that the disaster had already occurred. The Sultan was dead.

My task is complete. There is nothing more to write.

Peace be upon you, till we meet,

Your loyal friend,

Ibn Yakub

(Scribe to the late Sultan Salah al-Din ibn Ayyub)